Of A Different Stamp

Of A Different Stamp

Finnegan Gilhooley
Book 2

R.F. Ryan

Of A Different Stamp
Paperback Edition

Wolfpack Publishing
1707 E. Diana Street
Tampa, Florida 33610

www.wolfpackpublishing.com

Paperback ISBN 979-8-89567-259-4
eBook ISBN 979-8-89567-258-7

"The "bad men" or professional fighters and man-killers, are of a different stamp, quite a number of them being, according to their light, perfectly honest. These are the men who do most of the killing in frontier communities; yet it is a noteworthy fact that the men who are killed generally deserve their fate. These men are, of course, used to brawling, and are not only sure shots, but, what is equally important, able to "draw" their weapons with marvelous quickness. They think nothing whatsoever of murder and are the dread and terror of their associates; yet they are very chary of taking the life of a man of good standing, and will often weaken and back down at once if confronted fearlessly."

—Theodore Roosevelt
Ranch Life and the Hunting Trail

I believe in hanging. Just so long as I'm not the one being hanged.

—Richard Eugene Hickock
Statement Prior to his Execution

Of A Different Stamp

Chapter 1

INDEPENDENCE, MISSOURI

October 20th, 1882

THE OUTSIDE OF THE JACKSON COUNTY JAIL, OFTEN referred to as the Marshal's House, closely resembled a simple brick house. Finnegan had gone straight from the train depot to the jail. He had no interest in diversions or even a meal or sleep. What he required were answers to his questions. Just inside the door of the building, he found a sturdy fellow wearing the badge of a deputy U.S. Marshal. Finnegan squared up in front of the table the man was using as a desk.

"I wish to speak to a prisoner." He produced the small badge the Pinkertons used as identification.

The deputy marshal slowly nodded. "I see. I would assume there is little purpose in asking which prisoner you wish to have words with."

"That is correct, sir."

"Very well. He is not currently engaged. You must remove your guns..." The marshal looked Finnegan up and down. "And any other weapons you may be carrying." He pushed a ledger book across the table. "You must sign in and state your business briefly for the record." The marshal held up one finger as Finnegan reached for the book. "Sir, if your intention is to agitate the prisoner, you may as well leave now. I must also inform you that if the prisoner asks for you to leave, you must leave or be removed."

"Removed?" Finnegan nodded slowly and took up the book. "It is good to know you keep your prisoners in such comfort, sir. I have stayed in many a hotel that does not take the well-being of a guest so seriously." He pushed the book back, having scribbled in the various columns.

The deputy marshal sighed. "Mister..." He stared down at the book. "Gilhooley, ah, that explains much. Mr. Gilhooley, you may be able to flit in and out of this jail as you please, but I must stay here and see to this man for however long a veritable herd of judges and lawyers see fit to torture me with this duty. I have not put these rules in place for the prisoner's comfort, but for mine. Given your profession, I am sure you can appreciate the difficulties of my position."

Finnegan nodded and began to unstrap his guns. He laid the gun belt that held his 1875 Remington on the desk and withdrew the Cloverleaf Colt he kept in the small of his back. Finnegan set the small Colt on the table and tapped it with one finger. "Your allowing me to keep this, combined with a smart remark from the prisoner, could shorten your length of duty here considerably, Deputy."

"Yes." The deputy marshal sipped his coffee. "That is why I am relieving you of it." The deputy took hold of the carpet bag Finnegan had set on the table, which contained his travel kit. He opened the bag and carefully set the guns inside. "I will keep a close eye on all your property, Mr. Gilhooley."

Fully disarmed, and patted down to ensure his honorable behavior, Finnegan was allowed into the rear portion of the jail and sent up a flight of stairs to the building's second story.

At the top of the stairs, he found yet another deputy marshal who was busily engaged in sitting in a chair, smoking a pipe, and reading a dime novel. He glanced up at Finnegan. "You wish to see the prisoner?"

"I do."

"If he does not wish to speak with you, you must leave."

"I have been made aware of the jail rules of etiquette. Perhaps it is time we inquired of His Highness if he will lower himself to being disturbed by the likes of me?"

The deputy leaned back in his chair so that he might yell down the line of cells. "Hey, you feel like conversing with an Irishman this morning?"

A voice drifted up from the iron bars. "I might consider it. Send him back."

Finnegan walked over the ill-fit planks that led to the rear of the small cell block. At the end, he discovered that several of the bars between cells had been removed to form one large enclosure. The prisoner had a proper desk, complete with an oil lamp and a chair for reading set up against the far wall. With an affable smile, the man swiveled in the desk chair to face Finnegan as he approached. It was the first time Finnegan, or any Pinkerton for that matter, had obtained a good look at Alexander Franklin James.

James set his book down on the desktop and continued to smile with a tired, well-lined face. "Ah, the Irishman who is not a Yankee. We were never well acquainted, but I remember you well."

Finnegan stood with his hands behind his back. "And I remember you."

James scratched the back of his head. "Did you pass my message along to Allan Pinkerton?"

"I did, indeed."

"Did he have a response to offer?"

"As I recall, he merely stated that a man in your position should be more concerned with matters pertaining to this world, instead of the next."

James nodded and swiveled back and forth in the chair a bit. "Your employer is a very practical man, in some instances."

Finnegan leaned slightly toward the bars. "Yes, in some instances." He scowled at the prisoner. "You will explain yourself, sir."

"Explain myself...to you?"

"I can think of no one else who could be owed an explanation. Of all the men who walk this earth, I have certainly earned it."

"Earned?"

"Sir, I have chased and harried you over what feels to be most of the nation. I cannot, just now, tell you how many of your friends, confederates, and damned cousins I have shot in search of you..."

"A great many, by my count."

"Precisely, sir." Finnegan got himself under control and leaned back from the bars. He twisted his head and made an attempt at regaining his composure. "It is for that reason, Mr. James, that I feel I am owed by you. You will give me an accounting of your actions."

James rubbed one side of his unshaven face. "You wish to hear a confession?"

"What? Damn you, sir. What the hell could I possibly want with such a declaration? I know your crimes, all too well. I have even witnessed some. I have no need of your confession. I know you are doomed to perdition. All I wish you know is how you could have possibly chosen such an inexcusable path to it."

James slowly raised himself from the chair and took a

small step toward the bars. "My apologies, Irishman; I do not follow you."

Finnegan's lip quivered and his hand clutched for the gun he had been relieved of. "You do not follow me? Sir, of all your abominable, cowardly, unconscionable acts of villainy, this most recent act is truly beyond the pale, and you have the damnable nerve to claim you cannot follow?"

"You consider the robbing of a Corps of Engineers payroll my most vile act?"

"What?"

"That is the most recent...most recent crime I stand accused of."

"Surrendering, you insufferable jackass!" Finnegan made a small move forward with the intention of reaching through the bars, but caught himself. He slowly turned to smile at the deputy who remained perched at the end of the hall. Finnegan offered a small wave to the man to show he was not too far outside the jail's policies. With the deputy placated, he turned back to James. "Your surrender -- I wish for you to make an accounting of your actions. For you to simply waltz into some damned governor's office and throw your hands in the air...damn you, Alexander, I would not have thought even you capable of such dastardly behavior."

James took another step forward. "I am confused, Pinkerton man; you have spent all this time pursuing me and killed so very many of my kin, was that not all in an attempt to bring me into the hands of justice? Is that not precisely where you find me?"

"Do not play coy with me, Mr. James. You were made aware of my stated goal the night we met in the Blue Earth Woods, and you damn well know it has not changed. You were never meant to be delivered into the hands of justice, you are meant to be dead, by my hand, and none other."

"Dead, as my brother lies dead?"

"You bloody well know that was none of my doing." Finnegan spit down onto the plank floor. "That was a cowardly act perpetrated by a cowardly dog. I would have given you or your brother a fair fight, and you damn well know it. It has been there for the asking since the day I took up your trail. And I ask you, Alexander, would it not have been preferable to this...this pathetic imitation of justice? At least I can take some comfort in knowing I harried you to the point you could no longer run, knowing you gave up the ghost and turned yourself over to the gallows in search of succor. Still, it is a damned unbecoming end, sir."

James smiled and slowly returned to his chair. "You naturally assume the scaffold awaits me?"

Finnegan chuckled. "How can it not? I do not wish to swell your head any more than has already been done, but you are, by your own admission, Alexander Franklin James. Only your brother exceeded you in a reputation for vile wickedness. Your own fame must, of necessity, hang you, sir."

James leaned back in the chair. "You truly believe that Missouri would hang one of its own heroes? Hang a man who fought bravely for southern rights in the war of northern aggression?"

"Perhaps not, but Minnesota would, quite happily."

"Ah, but I am not headed to Minnesota."

"Is that what you have been told?" Finnegan chuckled again. "Mr. James, do you honestly believe that any authority would get hold of a man such as yourself and then turn him loose again? That would be as foolish as catching Lucifer in a bottle and then pulling the cork simply because you miss his company. No, you will hang, sir. If the Missourians do not come to their senses and see to it, the Minnesotans will surely take hold of you. If all else fails, perhaps the Army will shoot you for that payroll you so blithely mentioned. Now that I take a moment to consider it, that may be best. It would be poetic for the Blue Coats to be the ones to finally put you down."

James shook his head. "That is sourness talking, Irishman." He grinned. "I do not think you are truly angered by my choice to surrender, or my chances of acquittal. I believe what sticks in your craw is the simple fact that the chase is over. Whether I hang or not, you must find something to do with yourself, Mr. Gilhooley. You can no longer while away your days shooting my cousins or former school companions. What will you do to earn your living now?"

"I'm sure I will find something to pass the time. Do not concern yourself with it, Alexander."

James stroked his chin. "After you shot it out with us on the road in Northfield, you were famous yourself, Finnegan. I can recall seeing your name in more than a few periodicals of note." He shook his head. "How does it feel to no longer be the man who shot Jesse James?"

Finnegan sighed. "I have never given a damn what newspapers print."

"Even so, I believe Jesse would have found your loss damned amusing."

"Your brother found amusement in many things I never understood, Alexander." Finnegan eyed the prisoner carefully. "Do you honestly believe you will slip the noose?"

"Mr. Gilhooley, I never had a doubt in my mind that I would survive the war. I never doubted I would ride out of Minnesota. I do not doubt for a moment I will die a free man."

Finnegan reached in his pocket and produced two cigars. "Smoke?"

James stood and walked to the bars. "Don't mind if I do."

Finnegan struck a match and lit both cigars. "Of course, you realize that if the rebel scum of this sad state, or those damn Yankees up north do not see to your demise, I will feel honor bound to see to it myself."

"That is a very unprofessional thing to say, Mr. Gilhooley." He grinned around the cigar. "Perhaps we will have that fair fight yet."

"Perhaps. Good day to you, Mr. James."

"Good day, Mr. Gilhooley."

Chapter 2

CHICAGO, ILLINOIS

January 25th, 1884

AT FIRST, FINNEGAN HAD NOT HALF MINDED RETURNING to what every Pinkerton thought of as the home office. When he initially returned, it had been good to leave behind the mosquitos of Missouri and the various bed bugs of Texas. The Chicago boarding house he had taken residence in was only a few mere blocks from Mr. Pinkerton's home, where Finnegan was a steady fixture for Sunday dinners. Allan Pinkerton had always treated Finnegan as a member of the family and his status remained unchanged.

To a certain extent, Finnegan had begun to think of the sprawling city of Chicago as home. Of course, Finnegan was a man who rather prided himself on the number of times he had left one home for another. It was undeniable that the day-to-day drudgery of his work for the agency often gave way to fits of boredom. Since the elder James brother had shown the audacity to turn himself over to the law, Finnegan had been forced to make himself useful to his employer in more mundane ways. Often, he missed following the trail of the great Frank James. Ferreting out counterfeiter rings or tempting the virtue of railroad mail clerks lacked the excitement of Finnegan's previous commission. Most weeks, Finnegan's greatest entertainment was a visit to a shooting range that featured moving metal targets. It was not much, but it was something.

It had been more than a year since Finnegan had visited Frank James in his cell. In that time, Finnegan had begun to feel slightly trapped, both by Chicago and by his work. On the one hand, he wished to leave and seek adventure in the greater world once again. On the other, he lacked the funds to begin any sort of endeavor requiring much initial financing and his work for the Pinkerton Agency paid far better than any other labor he could hope to procure. He had some money saved, but it never felt substantial enough to pull up stakes and begin again somewhere new. As the months flowed past, he miserly husbanded his wages and bided his time. His intention, though never openly stated, was to build enough of a grubstake to enter into some sort of venture of his own. In past years, he would never have considered leaving Mr. Pinkerton's employ, but as the first month of 1884 slipped away, it had begun to seem as if Finnegan's nearly lifelong patron had little need of him any longer.

The sense that he served a dwindling purpose was what made Finnegan's summoning to the old man's office such a request of note. Upon hearing that his presence was required, Finnegan, not bothering to hide his elation, had fled from the post office he had been observing for three days straight and rushed to the main Pinkerton offices. Allan Pinkerton's secretary only waved one hand to the well-known Irishman and pointed to her employer's door. Finnegan nodded and stepped inside.

The world's most famous detective looked away from the man he was already entertaining and smiled at his favorite blunt tool. "Finnegan, my boy. I am very pleased that you have arrived. This gentleman was just regaling me with a tale of jungle intrigue I am certain you would enjoy." Pinkerton pointed to the man who stood across from him, sipping a drink. "Finnegan Xavier Gilhooley, allow me to introduce one of your fellow countrymen, Ephraim Haig Kilkenny." Pinkerton grinned broadly. "Mr. Kilkenny, this is Finnegan Gilhooley, formerly the man who shot Jesse James."

Kilkenny took a step forward and extended his hand. "A pleasure to meet you, Mr. Gilhooley. Let me say, I believe the coward Robert Ford to be a poor replacement for you."

Finnegan shook the hand of his fellow Irishman. "Oh, he is welcome to that particular accolade. In truth, I never much coveted it. A pleasure to meet you, as well, sir." Finnegan grinned. "I dare say there is not a proper Irishman on the face of the earth who is not familiar with your family name."

Kilkenny held up his glass. "Some would say my family's vocation is the sole reason the Irish will never rule the world."

Finnegan shook his head. "If that is the case, sir, your family has saved the world from a terrible fate."

All three men laughed. Pinkerton motioned to a pair of leather clad chairs and took a seat on his desk for himself. "Ah, somehow I knew the two of you would take a liking to each other." The old detective pointed to their guest. "Finnegan, as you say, you are fully familiar with the dynasty built by Mr. Kilkenny's predecessors. The commendable business of providing the world with whiskey is not the path this fine young man wishes to walk, however. This Mr. Kilkenny wishes to expand mankind's understanding of the sciences. A commendable aim, and one I always longed to have more time to commit to."

Kilkenny's brow furrowed. "You do not consider the detection of criminals a science, sir?"

"Oh, yes, I would surely claim it as one of the finer sciences. Unfortunately, the last several decades, of necessity, have mostly been spent in the drudgery of business management and the glad-handing of railroad barons. It is a vexing bit of labor, I assure you, and an intolerable distraction."

Kilkenny smiled. "I am sure you greatly prefer the glad-handing of whiskey barons."

Pinkerton threw his hands in the air. "Most assuredly. Your kind is simply a better sort. Most noticeably, your customers adore you and that gives you a pleasant countenance. All the world hates a railroad baron."

All three men chuckled yet again, and Finnegan produced several cigars from his pocket. He offered one to Kilkenny, who readily accepted. "What disciplines of science interest you, Mr. Kilkenny?"

"Ah, botany, zoology. I am simply enthralled with Mr. Darwin's theories. The last three generations of my family have been endlessly intrigued by the refinement of the whiskey still, but it never held a jot of interest for me. I am most at home in some nice patch of wild country playing the naturalist."

Finnegan nodded and handed a cigar to Mr. Pinkerton. "Yes, the animal kingdom is a source of endless wonder."

Pinkerton inspected the gifted cigar. "It is the expansion of man's knowledge regarding the animal world that brings us together today, Finnegan. Mr. Kilkenny is planning an expedition to the territories of the northwest. He has been informed that there is no better security for both body and property than the employment of a Pinkerton agent." Pinkerton struck a match and lit his cigar. "How did you put it, Mr. Kilkenny?"

"Oh, well, I was informed some years ago that this agency was not only the foremost provider of detectives, but an unrivaled source of gunmen and shootists, if such are required."

Finnegan found a match for himself. "That would be a rather sufficient way to sum up our services. Who is it that has been bragging to you about us?"

"A gentleman formerly of my acquaintance first mentioned your agency. A fellow involved in the railroad industry. I believe for a time he might have qualified as one of the barons Mr. Pinkerton mentioned. Scottish chap by the name of Enoch McLeod." Kilkenny leaned forward and Finnegan lit his cigar.

Pinkerton cleared his throat. "Ah, yes. I remember the man well. His passing was a great pity."

"A great pity." Finnegan shifted a bit in his leather chair.

"Mr. Pinkerton has informed me, Mr. Gilhooley, that you have often expressed an interest in traveling to the western portions of this continent."

Finnegan nodded. "Some portions, certainly. I have a current interest in the territory of Montana."

Kilkenny blew out a cloud of smoke. "That, sir, is precisely the destination I have in mind. My intention is to travel to one of the territory's larger outposts, a place known as Helena -- strange what grand names they give to grubby little camps, is it not? Once there, I intend to be guided by one of the territory's original settlers, a man by the name of Granville Stuart. Are you familiar with him?"

"No, sir."

"Well, at any rate, he is apparently rather well known in the western wilderness, at least he would have me believe so from his letters. The fellow has offered to guide me into some of the more wild country, most of it between the great metropolis of Helena..." Kilkenny paused to grin at both members of his audience. "And a cattle concern he is superintendent of. From there, I hope to make a rather languorous passage through the area referred to as the Dakotas, collecting specimens all along the way, of course. My stated goal is to procure at least one example of the more noteworthy forms of large animals and some of the more intriguing small game as chance may present them."

Finnegan puffed his cigar. "That is an ambitious journey, sir."

"It is, and I would assume I will encounter more than a few perils and dangers along the way. That is why I have come here to Mr. Pinkerton. I have told him that I wish to obtain the services of his finest gunman, assuming that the man is willing and appears to be a somewhat tolerable traveling companion." Kilkenny took a small drag on the cigar. "I have heard many tales involving the ruffians and highwaymen of the far west. I believe it would be best to travel there in the company of a man experienced in dealing with such rascals."

Finnegan rolled his cigar in his fingers, considering the matter. "I have spent a great deal of time reading of the far west in the last year, sir. Ruffians and colorful villains are a danger, but nothing I have not handily dealt with in the past. A danger of greater concern to me would be the bears, sir."

"Bears?"

"I have read several quite disturbing accounts of them, Mr. Kilkenny. One in particular, describing the experiences of a man named Glass." Finnegan shook his head. "If I was to consider accompanying you, sir, I would have to insist on being well equipped and well-armed. The arsenal I usually carry is more than sufficient for men; the great bears would require something more."

Kilkenny's face turned into a smile that made him appear a bit like a Jack-o-lantern. "Mr. Gilhooley, it is my intention to collect at least one specimen of all the species of great bear in the far west. Naturally, I will be properly equipped for that task. If you are to accompany me, it is not unreasonable for you to expect to be so equipped, as well. I would have it no other way."

Finnegan rubbed his chin for a moment and then

extended his hand to Kilkenny. "Sir, your proposal interests me. I would be pleased to be of service."

Kilkenny took Finnegan's hand and gave it a shake. "Very well then, Mr. Gilhooley. I believe you would make a fine companion for this particular adventure."

"Brilliant, gentleman." Pinkerton threw his hands in the air once more. "There is nothing that gives me more pleasure than facilitating arrangements that please all parties." He shook one finger at Kilkenny. "Just be certain to return my friend in good condition. From time to time the man proves himself absolutely indispensable."

"As I am certain he will during our travels." Kilkenny knocked the ash from his cigar. "We will be on our way as soon as the remainder of my kit arrives and this damnable climate allows for travel along the northern railroad those New York scoundrels have been stringing together." Kilkenny chuckled. "It is my understanding that the trains and tracks suffer such frequent failures that a man generally ends up riding in a wagon and he begins to consider himself a legitimate bullwhacker, like one of those chaps so famous in the southern desert." Kilkenny took a few puffs of his cigar. "Of course, the railroad does offer transport as far as the Pacific, it has just been my experience that what railroads offer and what is actually provided are seldom the same thing. I believe if we are to be marooned in the vast prairies it would be best to have it occur while enjoying good weather. It would be a pity to be forced to eat the other passengers, like those poor devils in California some years ago did." Kilkenny grinned at his humor.

"The delay is for the best, sir. It will give us time to make certain everything is in place and offer us plenty of time for target practice. I detest going into the field with an unproved weapon."

"There should be more than enough time for that, Mr.

Gilhooley. The bulk of my equipment, including guns and ammunition is slated to arrive within the week. A fascinating chap by the name of Bannerman in New York has seen to collecting most of it for me. The man is a marvel."

Finnegan nodded. "Just so long as we have armament sufficient for the bears."

Chapter 3

CHICAGO, ILLINOIS

March 28th, 1884

THERE WAS PLENTY OF OPEN GROUND IN THE VICINITY of Lake Calumet and the Michigan Central line. The ground was often swampy. Even those few brave souls who still kept livestock in Chicago did not let their animals venture into what had once been a quagmire. While most of the populace had little use for the area, Finnegan and a certain Irish whiskey baron had found great utility in the fen as a target range. They had been meeting at the designated spot once or twice a week since their first introduction at Pinkerton's office. So far, Finnegan had been more than impressed with Kilkenny's choice of weaponry.

Finnegan came slopping back to the dry ground they fired from. He had lost the coin toss, so the duty of placing whiskey bottles on the wooden rack roughly a hundred yards out had fallen to him. He did his best to fling the excess mud from his boots before leaving the swamp behind. "Do you have your relatives shipping those to you so that we do not want for targets?"

Kilkenny laughed. "I am sad to report that I create most

of them through my own predations." He sighed and withdrew a rifle from a leather case that sat across a pair of sawbucks. "I find this city terribly dull, Finnegan. I have no idea how you tolerate living here."

Finnegan nodded and opened up a second rifle case. "This town does possess several attributes I could do without. There are too many people within its confines and their presence creates a godawful stench. I suppose much of the less-than-inviting portions of the place could also be blamed on the slaughterhouses and tanneries. I find the one creek that continually bubbles to be quite disturbing."

Kilkenny nodded. "Yes, in terms of the general aesthetic, this place is dreadfully dreary, but I also find the societal constraints vexing."

"Constraints? I do not follow you Ephraim."

"Well, how shall I put it? During my travels through the Solomon Islands, we would frequently encounter natives and become fairly immersed in their culture for a time. Those people were in no way tethered by anything you or I might consider to be...constraints. They suffered no knowledge of ethics or responsibility, much less an idea of Christian guilt, or Hebrew commandments. Life among them was quite pleasing. A bit off-putting in some respects at first, but quite pleasing."

Finnegan chuckled. "Ephraim, if the breaking of commandments interests you, I am certain the city of Chicago contains no end of willing confederates eager to assist in your revelry."

Kilkenny sighed again. "Yes, certainly. And do not believe for a moment that I have not sampled some of what this mediocre Sodom has to offer. Sadly, it simply does not measure up to what I have previously been privy to. It is one thing to go on a bit of a binge with some likeminded deviants, but it is quite another to indulge in such revelry with those who have no idea of the concept of deviancy. Does that make any sort of sense, Finnegan?"

"I suppose if a thing is worth doing it is best to do it correctly."

"You may have put your finger on it there, my friend." Kilkenny began unrolling the rifle he held from the oily cloth that it had been shipped in. "These just arrived this week. I took the liberty of procuring one for each of us, along with an ample supply of ammunition, of course."

Finnegan cast a skeptical eye on the rifles. "They resemble the old Kennedy."

"They are, in fact, Marlin rifles, built by a fellow formerly associated with the Ballard firm. Have you any experience with the Ballard rifles? They are grand things, Finnegan. I dare say they offer the most superior accuracy I have encountered. I am hoping these repeaters from Marlin will offer the same consistent accuracy, with the added benefit of extra rounds to aid us, should the man behind the gun momentarily falter." Kilkenny smiled and removed a small silver flask from his pocket. He took a sip and placed the flask back in his vest. "To steady my hand, of course."

"Of course." Finnegan shook his head. "The Ballard is a fine target arm, Ephraim. If these rifles shoot as well, what do you intend to use them for?"

"Ah, well, I have it on good account that the pronghorn antelope of the western badlands requires no small amount of skill to obtain. That is the beast I had foremost in mind when I ordered these. They are chambered for a rather ingenious cartridge offered exclusively by the Marlin firm. It makes use of a .45 caliber bullet weighing a svelte 285 grains. The charge is 85 grains of powder. This greatly increases the rate of speed the bullet travels at, thus allowing for a flatter trajectory of the ball."

Finnegan took hold of the rifle and hefted it. "If you wish

to shoot some sort of antelope with these, I will not object." He withdrew a cartridge from the box that lay in the gun case. "They might also be of some use fighting road agents. I have certainly had luck knocking over men with smaller cartridges. If these rifles prove reliable and accurate, I have no objection to your using them on small game. When we enter the country inhabited by the great bears, I must insist on carrying one of the express guns. You may do as you please, Ephraim. I will do the same."

The naturalist whiskey baron laughed out loud. "Finnegan, somewhere your father rolls in his grave. You honestly mean to tell me that you would disregard the use of a rifle made in your own adopted country for one made by the damned British? That is an act unacceptable for an Irishman. You betray all a man such as yourself should show loyalty to."

Finnegan set the 1881 Marlin back in its case and withdrew a cigar from his pocket. "Mr. Kilkenny, as you well know, I will damn the bloody English until my dying day, and with my final breath, but I must admit: they make a damned fine weapon." He struck a match and got the cigar going. "I have never seen rifles as fine as those made by Purdey."

"They say Queen Vic herself has purchased one for hunting in Africa."

Finnegan nodded and puffed his cigar. "I hope it is not damaged when, God-willing, the bitch is eaten."

"Vic has not been half as rotten to our home island as some who came before her."

Finnegan waggled one finger at his friend and current employer. "Still, it is my policy that all English monarchs should be shot on sight."

"I suppose that is the only way to be assured of their eradication. Shall we see if these American rifles toe the mark?" Kilkenny picked up a handful of cartridges.

"Certainly." Finnegan removed a second rifle from the case and began unwrapping it. "Where, precisely, are the Solomon Islands, Ephraim? I never happen to have a globe handy when you reference these places."

"If you consult an atlas, you will find them up and to the right of Australia. While I was there, I discovered a new species of vulture. I dare say it ranks as one of my greater achievements."

"In truth, your own species of vulture? Did you get to name it?"

The whiskey baron blushed a bit and looked down at his rifle. "I did, although if I had a second opportunity, I would have assigned it a different moniker."

"Why? The Kilkenny vulture has a fine ring to it. I would think it would appear quite dashing on the label of your family's bottles."

Ephraim raised his eyebrows, clearly the idea had never occurred to him. "That would have been fine, yes. Unfortunately, I did not give the vulture my family name."

"Whose name does it bear?"

"I named it the Vivian's Vulture, after a very fine lass who was in firm possession of my heart at the time. I sent specimens ahead for the Royal Academy to review, complete with the name I had allocated."

Finnegan thoughtfully knocked ash from his cigar. "Sent them ahead of you, so that they arrived home before you?"

"Indeed. Upon my arrival, I discovered my one true love had married another, and a damned Englishman, at that."

"That is unfortunate, Ephraim." Finnegan pondered for a moment. "What do you think the chances that you would discover an animal whose name offered alliteration with your intended?"

"Oh, roughly the same as her being eaten along with

Queen Vic." Kilkenny shrugged. "If that is the case, that is what she deserves for marrying an Englishman."

"I could not agree more." Finnegan decided to change the subject to something less depressing. "What sort of fellows were the natives in the Solomon chain?"

"Oh, like all people, some were quite friendly and hospitable, others, not as much. You might find their culture to your liking."

"How so?"

"They have an odd sort of martial tradition. When they go to make war on the other tribes, they cut the heads off of the chaps they kill in battle. They drag the heads home and believe that the souls of the poor blokes belong to them for evermore. Slaves in this life and the next. In their world, the man with the most heads on his mantle has the most wealth."

"Intriguing"

"Yes, I thought you might like that. In the Solomons, you would be quite the skull baron, Finnegan."

"I must confess to harboring an interest in becoming some sort of baron." Finnegan contemplated his cigar. "I am very interested to look over the cattle ventures in Montana, and the mining opportunities, as well."

Kilkenny shook his head. "Many a king's ransom has been frittered away on such foolishness, Finnegan. I have always believed that if a man is to make his fortune, he will do it by utilizing his God-given talents."

"I am told the cattle business requires little capital to start."

"I am told someday the savior will return, but I have not seen it yet."

Finnegan grinned. "Then we had best have a look around, eh, Ephraim?"

"The thaw is coming along wonderfully. It may be proper for us to load the guns on the train and begin this adventure we have been threatening for so long. I must confess, I will not miss Chicago."

Finnegan tossed his cigar down into the morass. "You should wait to see how well you like the place you are going before deciding whether or not to miss the place you left."

AFTER TARGET PRACTICE, Finnegan left Kilkenny, who was to see to travel arrangements. The man had apparently traversed most of the earth; Finnegan assumed the whiskey baron could obtain two tickets on the Northern Pacific.

There was much to do before leaving Chicago. The first item on Finnegan's list was to bid goodbye to the few people he had come to consider family during his time in the city. Instead of accompanying Kilkenny to the train agent, Finnegan made his way down into the depths of the slaughterhouses that seemingly grew in number every day. He did his best to ignore the smell of the offal and the cries from the animals that had not yet fallen under the knife or saw. There were times when Finnegan disliked being a Pinkerton agent, but the occasional visit to some sort of industrial district always reminded him that there were far worse professions to follow. While he did not have an exact location for the young man he was searching out, he had only to survey the denizens of several saloons before noticing the fellow sitting at a bench in the rear of the canvas-covered building. After spying the young man he was after, he moved around to the rear of the place and entered through the back door. He sat down on the bench next to the youngster and slapped him on the shoulder. "Why do you stare so at that man up there at the bar? Do you intend to steal his watch?"

Abijah Smith shook his head. "Good day, Finnegan. I see

you have finished your toilsome labors with the whiskey baron early today. How many ducks did you kill?"

"Oh, there was no sport shooting today. We sighted several of his shiny new acquisitions and knocked off early so that preparations for travel could be made." Finnegan felt an odd sense of pride every time he noticed how well the young man had grown up. He had known the boy since he was twelve and now that he was in his majority Finnegan could not help but feel as though he had raised the boy in some manner.

"So, you are leaving for the wilds of Montana?"

"Indeed." Finnegan pointed toward the bar. "The fellow in the red shirt is your object of interest?"

Abijah nodded slightly. "He is, indeed. The man is a well-known anarchist and union agitator. I am charged with keeping track of him. Mr. Pinkerton feels it is of the utmost importance."

Finnegan shrugged. "Well, a client feels it of the utmost importance."

"And what of your object of interest, Finnegan? You have discovered her whereabouts?"

"I have it on good authority that the young lady resides in the city of Helena. As it happens, I am in route to that very town."

Abijah chuckled and shook his head. "My oldest friend, how long has it been since you have laid eyes on this woman?"

"Some seven or eight years, by now."

"Finnegan, is not chasing after this woman a bit of foolishness?"

"Chasing any woman is foolish, young Abijah. I console myself with the knowledge that I have only elected to ever chase one. Some men fritter away the better part of their lives on the practice."

"You may fritter away what remains of yours, my friend. I have read some terrible things regarding the western territories. Wild Indians still run rampant in many areas. That is to say nothing of the beasts that may eat you up. I have never seen a wolf, but they seem a fearsome sort of villain."

Finnegan smiled. "I will simply have to do my best to avoid the wild men and the snarling wolves. In truth, neither of them gives me much pause. If I had to name my primary concern, I would say the idea of encountering a bear is much more troubling, or would be, if Mr. Kilkenny had not fit us out with such fine rifles."

"I suppose as long as you have a rifle handy, you have little to worry over. Still, I will miss your company."

"Abijah, in all likelihood I will return before you hardly have a chance to notice my absence. I talk a great deal of guff regarding my future plans, but in all honesty, I have always felt I will remain at my present station until I am too old to perform my duties."

The young man shook his head. "You have the luck of the Irish, Finnegan. If any man can trip and fall into a Montana gold mine, I should say you have the best chance."

"Well, if I do, I shall send for you promptly. I will be needing a good foreman to see to it that things are kept in order."

"You would leave me to sweat in a mine while you run off with your paramour to enjoy your millions?"

"Only until the ore runs out." Finnegan nodded toward the bar again. "Do you believe you will have cause to shoot that man?"

"I doubt it. I have been following like his shadow for a week and have never seen him in possession of a firearm. I do not believe he has ever possessed the funds to purchase one, or had a proper opportunity to steal one."

"Such a man hardly seems worth following."

"He is thought to be one of the communists Mr. Pinkerton is so concerned about recently."

Finnegan raised his eyebrows. "Well, our employer is always concerned about someone, I suppose that is his lot in life. Are you still certain you would not prefer to accompany me to the wilds of the western frontier? It should not be difficult for our employer to find another man who can handle the heady business of tracking this penniless agitator."

Abijah shifted around in his seat a bit. He appeared to have something to admit that he was not quite comfortable with. "Finnegan, I know that you have never been assigned to the infiltration work the agency engages in, so you may not appreciate the opportunities for advancement it offers." It looked as if it pained the young man to explain certain facts to his much older mentor.

"No, Abijah, I do not suppose I would." He shrugged. "No need to feel apprehensive bringing it to my attention. Does it not make sense that a man would not understand the fine points of something he has no experience with?"

"Very well. Finnegan, it has been explained to me by Mr. Pinkerton's son William that if I continue to produce results as I have been, there is a good chance I will be advanced to a position just under the man in charge in St. Louis. After some time in that position, I may be placed in charge of a branch office of my own, sir."

Finnegan smiled and patted his young friend on the back. "That is wonderful news, Abijah. William knows a good man when he sees him." He gave Abijah a quizzical look. "Why were you hesitant to tell me that news? I am more pleased than you can imagine to hear it. I was, after all, the man who introduced you to this vocation. Why should I not be proud to hear you have taken to it so well?"

"Well, Finnegan, it is only that I have so often heard you mention that you do not believe you will ever be elevated above your current position in the agency. I thought... perhaps..."

"Perhaps I would not be happy to hear good news from a friend? You know better than that." Finnegan shook his head. "Abijah, it may be that you fail to understand something that I have always understood very well. I do not doubt for a moment that, if pressed, Mr. Pinkerton would be willing to leave the direction of a branch office to me. I have been in his employ a long time and he is a man who holds loyalty in high regard. My not occupying a desk in some office somewhere is merely due to a mutual agreement between myself and our employer. We both understand that I would not prefer it, and I would probably not be very well fitted to it."

"You feel no bitterness about it, then?"

"No, Abijah." He patted his young friend on the back once more. "Besides, what use would I have for a promotion? I am off to Montana to locate a gold mine."

"I wish you nothing but success."

"No need. You have never met a man with more consistent luck."

FINNEGAN'S next stop was the downtown main office of the Pinkertons. It would simply not do to leave town without saying goodbye to the man who had become almost a father to Finnegan since his own father had perished in the war. Finnegan was admitted to the old detective's office, and he took a chair before his employer's desk.

"Sir, Mr. Kilkenny has informed me that we will be departing in due haste for the western territories."

"Ah, very good, Finnegan." Pinkerton opened a box from his desk and Finnegan selected a cigar from it. "It should be a fine outing. I must admit, I am a bit jealous of you for having the opportunity to take it. If I were a younger man -- well, I suppose if that were the case there are more than a few things I would change."

"All men probably would, sir." Finnegan lit his cigar and smiled. "I have come for my orders, sir. Do you wish for me to make regular reports, as usual?"

Pinkerton shook his head. "That will not be necessary, Finnegan. Send a telegram now and then so that I may know you have not been laid low by Indians or swallowed by some ghastly beast. That will be sufficient. I do not need to be privy to the wanderings of a whiskey baron who lacks the good sense to stay home."

"No, I suppose not, sir."

Pinkerton eyed the man he had seen grow up before him. "Kilkenny tells me that you have asked him to make inquiries regarding the whereabouts of a woman in Montana."

"Um, yes, sir."

The old man grinned knowingly. "And were these inquiries made in a professional or personal capacity, my friend?"

"They are of a personal nature, sir."

"Excellent. You should see to that expeditiously when you arrive. If I were in your place, I would not hesitate to take the opportunity to investigate the other opportunities fortune may present. The west is a wide-open expanse, Finnegan. Many a man has gone west a pauper and ended as a prince."

"You yourself are a good example, sir."

"Indeed I am." Pinkerton lit his cigar. "Ah, if you do find a silver mine out there, I do not know how I will replace you. I have never met a man who can so unflinchingly face the hazard as you do, Finnegan."

"I would suggest young Abijah Smith. Unfortunately, he seems more interested in the... shall we call them the less aggressive aspects of our work?"

"That might be a fitting way to bifurcate the two sides of it. He is an outstanding young fellow, Finnegan. I cannot thank you enough for bringing him into my employ. He has a real head for this business."

"He does indeed." Finnegan knocked ash from his cigar. "I made my farewells to him earlier. He was doing a fine job of following some ruffian you have attached him to."

"That is no simple ruffian Abijah is charged with observing. That man is a cog in a large and insidious apparatus. That man is a communist, and I suspect he has been dispatched here by his confederates in either Germany or France. He was sent here to eat away at the soft underbelly of our society. I would have been well within the bounds of morality to place him under your purvicw instead of assigning Abijah to him. Sadly, I must gain a knowledge of his machinations before doing this nation a service and having him gunned down."

Finnegan thoughtfully rolled his cigar between his fingers. "Sir, pardon my curiosity, I know it is not my place to question such things, but I have always wondered something about these communists you have taken to chasing."

"Ask, Finnegan. There is no man I would sooner educate as to the danger they pose."

"Sir, did you not, some years ago, explain to me that widespread criminal conspiracies were fallacies produced to sell newspapers? You have always said that the basic selfish nature of criminals prevents them from forming into large, organized groups. Have you changed in your opinions, sir?"

Pinkerton puffed his cigar and frowned. "Ah, yes, I can see how you may find yourself confused by that. What must be understood regarding these communists, Finnegan, is that these men are not criminals in the traditional mold." He rubbed his chin. "How to put it?" He gave the cigar several thoughtful puffs. "A criminal of the type you and I have dealt with these many years, a rogue such as that which wishes to steal your watch is different from a communist. A communist wishes to steal your good sense. Communists would twist the world until you lose sight of the fact that your watch is your property. They would have you believe that it is not yours because your possession of it is a crime against your fellow man." Pinkerton arched one eyebrow. "Never mind that their end goal is to gain possession of the watch; they would have you be thankful to be relieved of it."

"I do not think I understand, sir."

Pinkerton mused for a moment and then brightened, feeling he had stumbled across the proper metaphor. "Mull this over, Finnegan. Do not think of these communists as traditional criminals. Envision them more as a religion, a religion along the line of the Catholics. I am sure you are aware that while the dictates of your Pope do not warrant much attention these days, there was a time when his word was beyond contestation and could cause all of Europe to leap to their feet in unison from fear of perdition." Finnegan nodded. "Are you at all familiar with the crusades, dear boy?"

"The church's war against the Saracens. Yes, sir."

"Yes, those wars were the sole product of central direction from the Pope. That one man had operatives all across the known world, rushing to do his bidding less they suffer eternal hellfire. These communists I am currently attempting to ferret out have an organization much the same as the Catholic Church, without the religious claptrap, of course. These men have operatives in every nation, Finnegan. Anywhere mankind tries to better himself through honest labor and industrialization, these men have insinuated themselves into the working classes."

Finnegan knocked more ash into the tray, looking slightly skeptical. "To what end, sir?"

"The dissolution of private property, Finnegan. These

villains would have all property rest in the hands of the government."

Finnegan shrugged. "Pardon me for saying so, sir, but that seems like a poor criminal enterprise. Why bother with stealing property, only to have it end up in the hands of someone else?"

Pinkerton smiled. "Ah, yes, but that is assuming these villains will not someday constitute the government. Finnegan, if all the land in Chicago was somehow or other seized by the U.S. Congress, who would it belong to?"

Finnegan pondered for a moment. "The Congress, I should think."

"Yes, but the Congress is composed of ordinary men, most less than ordinary from what I have seen of them. In effect, if the land belonged to Congress, in practice it belongs to the men who sit in the Congress. These communists claim their goal is to rob from the rich and give to the poor. My theory is that their true motives, as it is with every common sneak thief, is to rob from the rich and give to themselves. They wish to do this on a grand scale, Finnegan, using the working classes of this country as their ignorant, duped dragoons." Pinkerton straightened up in his chair. "I and a few of the more foresighted men of this country are not going to allow that to happen."

Finnegan smiled. "You have always had great ability to see what lies over the horizon, sir. I wish you luck. Of course, upon my return I will do everything I can to assist you."

"Oh, it may very well be required." Pinkerton stared out his office window for a moment. "This nation is rapidly approaching greatness, Finnegan. Soon, I do not doubt, we will be the richest nation in the world. Where there are great sums of money, there will always be great treachery. You and I are the type of men fate has tasked with fighting such treachery."

"I have always believed so, sir."

Pinkerton sighed. "Unless, of course, you locate a proper gold mine or discover a method for making millions in the cattle trade. If that is the case, contact me immediately and I will happily leave this wretched city forever."

Finnegan laughed. "Keep a wary eye out for the telegram, sir."

Chapter 4

DAKOTA BADLANDS, DAKOTA TERRITORY

April 20th, 1884

From St. Paul to the Missouri at Mandan, everything had run quite smoothly. The trains and track had been in good condition. The journey into the wilderness of the west seemed no more of an inconvenience than journeying from Chicago to St. Louis. Both Finnegan and Kilkenny had spent many hours watching the scenery change from the swamps of Minnesota to the black earth rolling hills of the Dakota Territory.

It was after steaming for several hours into what appeared to be a vast, endless nothingness of coulees and gullies that the engine of the train had emitted a tremendous howl and had ceased to operate. The entire grand machine had come to a screeching halt and had not budged for the two days since. Finnegan and Kilkenny had been attempting to make the most of their time, but they did not have many options. The train carried no horses or wagons, so their only choice would have been to try and move further along the rail line on foot. The train crew assured them that walking to the next town was not practical. With nothing better to do, and an interest in obtaining some fresh meat, the two interlopers had dragged some of their equipment out of the baggage car and had marched out into the prairie to obtain some specimens. Finnegan had been tentative at first; he did not particularly trust the train crew enough to count on them not to leave while Kilkenny wandered about. Eventually, boredom trumped his misgivings. Even if the train did depart without them, they would not be in noticeably worse straits. They would only need to wait for the next train and the only lost time would be that spent locating the original train crew so Finnegan could give them a proper drubbing.

After their second long trek away from the train, Finnegan was not surprised when they topped a ridge and stared down to see that their one and only form of transportation remained inert. "This damned northern railroad was said to be a miracle of the modern world when it was under construction. Now that it is finished, they do not seem to use it for much. Is that rotten heap we see below the only train owned by this railroad?" He rolled the pack board he was carrying off his shoulders and placed it on the ground. The board contained the four quarters, head, and partial hide of a pronghorn antelope Kilkenny had shot. It was the second specimen they had collected so far. Finnegan rubbed his shoulders. "For a small animal, these antelope are heavy."

Kilkenny pulled his hat from his head and wiped his brow. "The going would be easier if you did not insist on carrying that Purdey, Finnegan. There is no reason to lug that thing about. There are no buffalo to be seen, and I hardly think we need two rifles to kill one antelope."

Finnegan hefted the rifle and leaned on the pack board. "I do not intend to let this rifle out of my sight until we return to civilization proper. That Marlin is a fine shooting rifle, but I feel it is a bit small for bear."

"Bear?" Kilkenny motioned to the surrounding country. "Finnegan, this place is a barren waste marginally fit for skinny antelope. It is hardly the type of place I would expect to encounter a bear."

"It was in the general vicinity of this place that Hugh Glass was attached by a large bear. I have read an account of the incident. It chills the blood, Ephraim."

"Finnegan, in a wilderness such as this, one man here and there is bound to perish. What makes this man Glass so special?"

"He was badly mauled by the bear that attacked him, then abandoned by his traveling companions. They left him to die in this empty place. The man crawled to settlements to the west of here. He survived by eating these prairie dogs and other varmints that seem to abound in this desert. It is hard to imagine the suffering the poor man must have endured."

Kilkenny chuckled. "And you honestly fear the same may happen to you?"

"Worse -- I lack that man's fine sense of direction. I dare say if I am unable to stand and get my bearings, I might spend what remained of my life crawling in a large circle making no progress whatsoever."

"You do select the oddest things to worry over, Finnegan."

"You do not find the prospect of being chewed, spit out, and left to die in this barren place worthy of some worry?"

"Of course I do. What puzzles me is that a man such as yourself should contemplate it much. How many times have men tried to gun you down, Finnegan?"

He shrugged. "I have honestly lost count."

"And the prospect of facing such an encounter again someday does not cause you to worry?"

"That is my work, Ephraim. I count on my superior skill and unrivaled Irish luck to carry me through."

"All right, then, what of other matters? You have told me that you have not laid eyes on this woman you seek in Helena in many years. She has not answered any of your letters since she left Minnesota. Do you not worry that you may find her married and chasing her many children about in the yard?"

Finnegan thought on it for a moment. "It might come as something of a relief, in truth. It would surely simplify my future plans, at least to some degree."

"Ah, well, then, we have arrived at a solution." Kilkenny removed a flask from his vest and took a short sip from it. "Do not dwell on the hideous end you may meet under the claws of a bear. Instead, view your possible dismemberment as a most drastic simplification. Before the bear has at you, you will be weighed down with all your normal concerns and difficulties. After the mauling, you need only worry over crawling in the proper direction and obtaining prairie dogs. You may even find it soothing after the first few weeks."

"Perhaps we will be lucky enough to be mauled at the same time, so that we may both revel in paradise together." Finnegan pointed down toward the locomotive. "How is it possible another train has not come along in all this time? Is that the only engine this railroad has seen fit to purchase?"

Kilkenny took a longer sip and put his flask away. "It is my understanding the company is in financial straits, but what railroad is not? I am often approached to invest in such ventures. I have yet to hear tell of a railroad that is not flat broke, yet continues spinning off a dividend and paying its bills to the construction company owned by the assembled cousins of the board members. If you truly had a mind to shoot scoundrels, Finnegan, you should have forgotten the kinfolk of the James Brothers and taken to killing railroad barons."

"Ephraim, even I know enough regarding business to know that if one wishes to be a mercenary, he must work for those you have sufficient funds to hire him."

"Ah, well, you have me there. I do not possess even such a rudimentary knowledge of business matters as you."

"We are quite the pair in that respect." Finnegan pulled a cigar from his pocket and took a seat of sorts on the pack board. "What is your impression of this man we are going to meet in Helena, this Stuart fellow?"

Kilkenny found a dry patch of ground and flopped down to sit on it. "It is hard to judge a man from letters alone. He seems to be swung about by his passions a great deal. In one bit of correspondence, he claims to be hanging on by a thread, in others, a man could be led to believe Mr. Stuart will soon own most of the territory and be elected to the ridiculous Parliament these Americans have assembled." Kilkenny withdrew the flask yet again. "Have you ever met that rare breed known as a Congressman, Finnegan?"

"No, and I am told I am fortunate in that regard."

"I had the opportunity to observe several of them in their native habitat, that gaudy awful capital in a swamp on the eastern coast. A more vigorous pack of drunks and whoremongers you are unlikely to ever encounter. Even by my standards, they are debauched."

"That alone is astonishing, Ephraim." Finnegan chuckled. "I cannot say that I have much care as to whether or not Mr. Stuart lacks moral fiber. If the man chooses to be hell bound, that is his prerogative. I was only wondering if he might be of use suggesting some venture I could engage in." Finnegan motioned out around them. "I have to admit that it is vexing to be marooned here waiting for the next rickety locomotive to present itself, but it is far preferable to Chicago." He chuckled again. "If this place were filled with bears, it would still be preferable to Chicago."

Kilkenny found his flask once again for more of his family brand. "I got the sense you were not happy with your posting there, Finnegan."

"I have never much cared for Chicago. The town has a vile odor to it, even with the damned wind. I was considerably more content in Missouri or Texas. I can offer few compliments to Alexander Franklin James, but I will say he always had the good sense to avoid large cities. I did appreciate that kindness while I was chasing him."

"I cannot claim to care for cities, either." Kilkenny tipped his hat to the rolling hills before them. "I greatly prefer a place such as this."

Finnegan shrugged. "As a gunman, I require a certain number of people around to shoot if I am to make my living. Still, Chicago features a gross overabundance. I am not so greedy as to wish to become a millionaire by shooting them for a dollar apiece."

Kilkenny laughed. "Yes, surely no reason to make a pig of yourself."

Finnegan motioned to the pack board. "If we are stuck here another day, would you mind terribly if I shot the next antelope?"

"Certainly. I take it you have never shot one?"

"No, nor even a deer. I have not shot all that many animals." Finnegan lit his cigar and thought back on the topic. "A few horses, as circumstances required, of course. I shot a milk cow one dark night during the war. We were terribly desperate for food. Normally, I would never shoot such a beast, but at that moment my stomach would accept nothing less. I still feel fortunate that it was a type of animal I could eat without some sort of regrets after the meal. That night I would not have cared if it was a house cat or General Hooker. I would have ingested either with equal vigor."

"It is always interesting to play a part in procuring the food you eat." Kilkenny smiled. "I have been shooting and collecting specimens since I was a boy. It might be fair to say that my experience has been the opposite of yours. I have shot hundreds of animals, but never a man."

Finnegan arched one eyebrow. "Truly? Never?"

"Never. I have never even so much as seen a man shot. I have seen men die in a variety of other ways, but have never witnessed one of the pistol matches these Americans so revel in. I had rather been hoping to get a look at one during my travels."

"If that is the entertainment you seek, we should have lingered in Chicago a bit longer. It would have only been a matter of time before Mr. Pinkerton would have found someone for me to shoot." Finnegan turned to the east. "Ephraim, do my ears deceive me, or is that the sound of a locomotive?"

"Aye, I believe it is. Comes as something of a shock, does it not? I had begun to think they had abandoned this particular railroad."

Chapter 5

COULSON, MONTANA TERRITORY

April 27th, 1884

"I will grant you, Ephraim, we are moving along more quickly than we could hope to on our own, but our progress seems slow, nonetheless." Finnegan leaned back in the café chair and pushed his plate away from him. It had been a fine meal of what was claimed to be beef steak, but could have been almost anything that had run afoul of the café owner.

The whiskey baron pushed his own plate aside. "Oh, it only seems that way because you have been hopelessly spoiled by the system of rail in the eastern portion of this country. There, if the tracks are washed away, a gang of men sees to their repair that very day. If the locomotive is disabled, another is produced as if by magic. Not even England can match the railroads of the east for constant motion. I had a suspicion that would not be the case as we made our way into the unsettled colonies." Kilkenny pointed to Finnegan's jacket pocket. "Might you have an extra cigar on you, old boy?"

"Certainly." Finnegan pulled two from his pocket and passed one across the table. "This is lovely country, and I have enjoyed lingering here, but tomorrow will mark our third day in this tiny settlement. This railroad crew begins to vex me."

Kilkenny lit his cigar. "I am simply pleased that you have not felt the need to carry the Purdey with you while we loll in this town. I had begun to think it would be your constant companion on this trip."

Finnegan shook his head. "There is no need for the rifle here. One of the so-called grizzly bears that inhabit these parts would never attempt to kill and eat more than one man at a time. I feel confident that I should be able to outrun the majority of this town's citizens, should it come to that."

"A well thought out plan, Finnegan." Kilkenny stared quizzically. "What is it precisely about the bears here in the western wilderness that you find so troubling?"

"Troubling?" Finnegan lit his own cigar. "I assume you have perused the account of captains Lewis and Clark, the initial explorers of this region?"

"Oh, yes. Fascinating."

"Then you are aware that the bears of these western regions can be shot many times, in the lungs, in the heart, in the head, before expiring? You are aware that they often continue to attack men after receiving wounds that would cause any other beast to promptly perish?"

"I have read those portions of the captains' journals, yes." Kilkenny puffed his cigar. "Still, Finnegan, you of all men must be aware of the exaggeration that takes place when an exploit is first related and then related again and again. The first telling is of a country preacher helping an old woman down the road and it eventually expands into Moses leading his people from bondage. We have not even seen one of these bears, as yet. We have no way of knowing what is fact and what is fancy in those accounts."

Finnegan thought on it for a moment. "I may not have

seen one of these great western bears, but I have seen a whale. I have seen several of those leviathans brought in by sailors for their oil. I have seen them in Boston and other ports."

Kilkenny nodded slowly. "The whale, in its various species, is an awesome creature. What does that have to do with our discussion of bears?"

Finnegan pointed his cigar accusatorily toward Kilkenny. "In 1602, a Spanish ship off the coast of California, at a place known as Monterey Bay, observed several large bears dining on the flesh of a dead whale." Finnegan puffed his cigar. "Now, I will grant you, there were several of them, but to do such a thing to a creature as grand as a whale is no small feat, Ephraim."

The whiskey baron chuckled. "Finnegan, those bears did not kill that whale, they were merely feeding on it."

Finnegan's eyes narrowed. "If the bears did not kill it, how did it end up dead?"

"Do you believe they swam out into the ocean and slew the great beast?" Kilkenny grinned.

"I have read that bears are ample swimmers, why not swim out and kill a whale if the opportunity presents itself?"

Kilkenny shook his head. "Finnegan, in all likelihood, no creature killed the whale. I would say there is an excellent chance that it was the agent of its own demise. Whales are given to such behavior. They fling themselves upon the shoreline and find it impossible to reclaim the water. They lie on the sand and perish, cut off from the sea."

Finnegan raised his eyebrows. "Fling themselves upon the shore, Ephraim? I should say I am not the only one at this table to be taken in by fanciful tales."

Kilkenny shrugged. "It is the gospel truth."

"Ephraim, honestly, if whales made a habit of flinging themselves onto shores, why would sailors go out for years, to the most perilous waters, to harvest them? Would it not be far simpler to drive a team of oxen up to the dead whale and collect whatever one pleased? I have yet to see an oxcart that is not a more reliable vessel than a sailing ship."

"I, uh, well...you make a point there, Finnegan."

"So, then we are in agreement?"

"Yes, you have convinced me. Bears frequently kill whales and may kill us at any moment."

"It is good you have come around to my way of thinking." Finnegan pulled his watch from his vest pocket. "It grows late, my friend." He replaced the watch. "I have been considering your vulture, Ephraim."

"My vulture?"

"Yes, it must be quite...satisfying to know that you have achieved a certain level of immortality with such a discovery. There are few men who could make a similar boast."

Kilkenny laughed again and produced his flask. "I should think that there are far better methods for obtaining fame than discovering a vulture. Outside the Royal Society, I am almost certain hardly a man knows my name." He knocked ash from his cigar. "In truth, you have gained a far greater level of notoriety than I could ever hope to. You are the man who shot Jesse James."

Finnegan waved one hand absently. "A mere flash in the pan. A hundred years from now school children will be reading about you and your vulture. Five years from now no one will even recall who Jesse James was or who bothered to shoot him. At any rate, I have difficulty taking much pride in the matter. To my way of thinking, I am merely the man who failed to shoot Jesse James' brother."

Kilkenny tapped away more ash. "What is to become of the brother? It is my understanding they hold him in custody."

Finnegan grimaced. "Yes, the bastard had the nerve to

turn himself over to the law. He has managed to forge some sort of devil's bargain with the corrupt swine governor of Missouri. He was acquitted of his crimes at the sham of a trial they had there." Finnegan shrugged. "He was also tried in Alabama, but failed to receive his right and proper. It remains to be seen if one of the more northern states he committed villainies in will take him to task."

Kilkenny took another sip from his flask. "This country has such a strange affinity for criminals."

Finnegan waved one hand. "In this case, the issue revolves around the politics of the civil war they fought here. The country was divided with their southern states on one side of the conflict and their northern states on the other. Frank James, as he is best known, fought for the southern contingent. The people of those states hold their veterans in high esteem, even if they failed to win the war. Frank James will most likely make use of that esteem and manage to remain in sanctuary."

Kilkenny leaned back in his chair. "And what if he does, dear friend? Will you see to the conclusion of your vendetta, even though he has been declared a free man by the courts?"

Finnegan shrugged. "I suppose I will look into the matter when this journey is concluded. I have told the man as much. It does not do for a man such as myself to become lax in his vendettas."

"So, then, you will simply locate him and..." Kilkenny snapped his fingers. "Find him and shoot him down in the street. Like the hero in one of those tawdry books."

"There may be more subtly to it than that, but, yes, essentially."

"Ah, now, that is an aspect of this country that truly fascinates me. The way Americans go around shooting each other, with little structure, over these petty slights and insults is incredible to me."

"I tracked the James brothers for many years, Ephraim. My vendetta against the elder brother is based on far more than some petty slight."

"Oh, of course, but you know what I mean. Such behavior is simply not seen in other civilized countries. It is also quite fascinating to me that you have so readily embraced their culture."

Finnegan chuckled. "I was not given much choice in the matter, Ephraim. You may recall I told you of how I was pressganged into the army of this country when I stepped off the ship that brought us here?"

"Yes, well, I suppose that does rather settle the subject all at once." Kilkenny stretched out his arms. "Ah, I shall sleep well tonight, Finnegan. I believe I will make my way back to our train car and turn in." Coulson's one and only boarding house had no room for the weary travelers, so they had made do by converting a boxcar to their needs. "Will you be accompanying me? Perhaps we can have a few hands of cards to top the evening off."

Finnegan slowly got up from the table and pushed in his chair. "I will join you presently, Ephraim. Before returning to the train, I think it might be best for me to inspect the tavern just down the way. I noticed our engineer wandering in there as we came in for dinner. I have come to suspect that man's progress in repairing the locomotive may be slowed by his love of that damn whiskey den. I intend to collect him and cut his evening short."

Kilkenny shook one finger at Finnegan. "Do not speak ill of whiskey dens, old boy. That is what paid for your dinner."

"You make an excellent point. I will confine my comments to the engineer's character and touch on no other subject." Finnegan straightened his coat. "I will be along presently."

The two men left the café. Kilkenny turned left and began

sloughing through the mud toward the town's makeshift train depot. Finnegan turned right and made his way toward a wood frame and canvas structure on the far end of the town. As he approached, he could hear the sound of a piano being abused and the laugher of various revelers. Finnegan was not fond of taverns, or the men that inhabited them, but he had honestly come to believe the engineer's enjoyment of Coulson's prosperous gin joint had halted their progress toward Helena considerably more than any mechanical issues.

He had glanced back after leaving the café and had seen a man in a bright red shirt exit. He had also noticed that the man had turned to follow, but Finnegan took little note. There were few places in Coulson to visit that time of the evening, so it was not strange that another man should take the same path as Finnegan toward the saloon. By the way the fellow staggered, it appeared as though he had already spent some time at the bar previously.

Entering the tavern, it only took a moment for Finnegan to spot the engineer sitting at a table with one of the local lewd women perched on his knee. Finnegan ran a hand over his face and sighed before approaching the wayward railroad worker. He stepped to the man's table and slid the whiskey bottle out of reach just as the engineer extended his hand toward it. "Mr. O'Neil, it is time for you to return to the train. It is imperative that you begin early so that we may be on our way in the morning."

The engineer gave Finnegan a hard stare with his bleary eyes. "You are not my mother, so I have no idea why you might presume to tell me when my bedtime is nearing. I will return to that damned train when it pleases me." He shifted the woman a bit and attempted to reach his bottle. Finnegan removed the bottle from reach once again.

"Mr. O'Neil, I realize that it is not my occupation to

order you to work and I assure you that under other circumstances I could not give a tinker's damn how late you stay here to cavort with these tarts. My only reason for seeing you out of this place is to insure a prompt departure in the morning. After that, you are welcome to destroy your health and virtue in whatever manner you see fit."

"Well, you are an uppity one, aren't you? Be gone, or I shall take it upon myself to teach you to keep your nose out of other men's affairs."

Finnegan sighed again. "Mr. O'Neil, if you do not depart this place with me of your own volition, I will be forced to slap the teeth out of your mouth, so that you resemble the harpy in your lap. Then, I will drag you to that damned train. Please, keep in mind that the only purpose you can possibly serve to me is in the capacity of a train engineer. If you refuse to act in that capacity, there is little cause for me to not turn you into one of the many carcasses that litter the alleys of this town."

"You dare threaten me?" The engineer looked as if he intended to elaborate, but a booming voice from the other side of the saloon stole his attention.

"Robert Ford, your last day has come!"

The declaration was so loud that it caused the din of the tavern to cease. Finnegan slowly turned to see who had yelled out. The man in the red shirt who had followed him from the café stood at one end of the bar with a few other rough-looking characters gathered about him. Dismissing the fellow as a drunken fool, Finnegan turned back to the engineer. "Mr. O'Neil, as I said, you will..."

"Do not turn your back on me, Ford. You have lived as a damned coward; you may as well die like a man."

Finnegan rubbed his face and turned back once more. "Are you speaking to me, you damned drunken sot?"

"I am speaking to you, Robert Ford. You killed a great man, and you will pay for it this night."

Finnegan sighed. "Fool, I would rather not waste my time arguing idiocy with you. In the interest of brevity, I will simply assure you that I am not Robert Ford. That man is a sawed-off imp easily ten years my junior. Be on your way, sir."

The man scowled and squinted. "You yourself claimed to be Robert Ford not ten minutes earlier. I was in the café when you made the damnable claim."

"I did not claim to be Robert Ford, fool. I have never claimed to be Robert Ford, and would never claim such a thing. Robert Ford is a worthless cur. I once nearly had opportunity to kill him outside Blue Cut, Missouri and do truly regret that it did not come to fruition." Finnegan took a deep breath. "Now, then, for the last time, I am not Robert Ford. Be on your way, sir."

"I will not stand here and be lied to by the man that killed the hero Jesse James. You cowardly back-shooting son of a..." The man pulled on the Colt slung at his side, but had failed to remove the leather thong from the weapon's hammer. The gun would not budge. Finnegan's gun was not nearly so hampered. Before the fellow had even realized his mistake, Finnegan placed the front sight of his Remington on the man's chest and fired. The red shirted aggressor stumbled toward the bar while one of the men behind him reached to his holster. Finnegan was in no mood to wait and see if the blowhard's confederate wished to engage in battle or was merely bluffing. He fired at the man twice and pulled his Cloverleaf Colt with his left hand. The man stumbled, so Finnegan fired at him twice more with the Cloverleaf. That sent the fellow to the saloon's filthy floor. Off to the side, the blowhard in the red shirt had one arm draped over the bar for support and was still fighting with his holster with his right hand. Finnegan paused for a split-second, debating whether or not to shoot again.

"Let it pass, fool. You may still live."

With what might have been his last full measure, the man tore the gun free from the holster and fired a round toward Finnegan. The bullet did not come overly close, but Finnegan fired twice more into the man and only stopped when a dull click emanated from the Remington. The blowhard fell to the floor next to his dead friend. Finnegan covered him with the Cloverleaf while scanning the other men in the saloon to see if any of them wished to enter the fray. None of them seemed overly interested, which was a mercy to Finnegan. His guns were very nearly empty.

Since no one appeared to be an immediate threat, and Finnegan always liked to make use of an opportunity, he slipped the Cloverleaf into the front pocket of his vest and began removing the spent brass from his Remington while slipping fresh rounds into the cylinder. Most of the saloon patrons, those who had not fled out the door, were staring down at the corpses. With his gun reloaded, Finnegan turned back to the engineer behind him. "Well, after such a donnybrook, I should think you would be more willing to leave this sordid pit and..." He paused to stare at the newly-formed hole between the eyes of the engineer. "Ah, bloody hell." Finnegan hung his head and only brought it up when he heard boots approaching behind him. He turned and looked up to see a large man, roughly the same build as himself, with a worn tin star hanging from the lapel of his coat. The lawman's face betrayed no emotion one way or the other beneath his thick black beard. "Ah, constable, it is good you are here."

The lawman brought up the Sharps rifle he held and planted the brass butt plate of the weapon directly on Finnegan's forehead. As Finnegan drifted into unconsciousness, he could just barely hear the lawman ask the saloon crowd a question. "Is he the one that done the shootin'?"

Finnegan had briefly regained consciousness as the large thumper was dragging him down the muddy street. Another whack on the head from the buffalo gun had placed the Pinkerton back into oblivion and Finnegan had barely noticed when he was tossed onto a filthy cot and the wrought iron door of the cell had been shut. Unaware of the lousy nature of the bed he found himself on, he had allowed himself to drift off. His pride might have wished to rouse him, but his body won out and elected to remain somewhere soft while circumstances allowed it.

When he finally came back to the waking world, he was confused. He was fairly certain he had been dry-gulched in a saloon and flung into a jail cell, but he could hear the voice of Ephraim Kilkenny, which should have meant a return to the boxcar. Eventually, the incongruity of the situation annoyed him to the point that he opened his eyes and sat up on the cot. Before him, he viewed an unlikely scene. The large man who had bashed him over the head sat sipping coffee on one side of a woodstove. On the other side of the stove, Ephraim lounged with his feet up on a small table and his flask clutched in one hand. The two were swapping yarns and laughing as though they were old friends. Finnegan took a moment to feel about on the two sore portions of his head, both front and back, before clearing his throat to get the mens' attention.

Ephraim turned, grinning. "Ah, Finnegan, good to see you have come out of your nap. I had begun to think you meant to lay there all night."

Finnegan gently pressed the center of his forehead and

quickly drew his hand away. "My intentions seem to hold little sway determining the events of this night."

Ephraim shook a finger at the cell. "I cannot believe you were so rude as to shoot men in that tavern without inquiring whether or not I wished to observe. You know I find this American gunfighting a fascinating practice. You could have at least invited me along."

Finnegan spit a small bit of blood onto the cell's floorboards. Apparently, he had bit his lip at some point. "I apologize, Ephraim. I was unaware a fight was impending. If I had been, I assure you, I would have left that damn engineer to his own inclinations."

"Oh, posh." Ephraim waved one hand. "Regret does not become you. At any rate, this fellow tells me that you performed quite well. Two men dead, and the rest terrified to trifle with you further. Very impressive, Finnegan."

"Yes, it was my finest hour. I suppose you have heard the engineer is dead."

"A minor matter." Ephraim took a drink and smiled. "I imagine there are plenty of train men to replace him, and it is my understanding that he will not be much missed." The whiskey baron pointed to the large lawman to his left. "More importantly, I have already discovered the silver lining in this particular cloud. Your barroom fracas has afforded me the opportunity of meeting this gentleman, who is, by his own admission, that rarely encountered breed of American cannibal."

"Cannibal?" Finnegan looked the man over. "I might call him bastard for clouting me, but I do not recall him attempting to eat me."

The lawman laughed and leaned back in his chair. "No, no, Ephraim. Now don't go spreading tales. My reputation can hardly afford any more of that. What I was attempting to explain to you, just before your friend here woke up, is that I ain't no cannibal."

Ephraim motioned to the man with his flask, slopping a bit of whiskey to the floor. "Oh, yes, Finnegan, you must hear this. The people of this settlement, they refer to this chap as Liver-eating-Johnson. Isn't that simply wonderful? He stands accused of killing more than three hundred Indians and feasting on them like so much mutton."

"Damn it, Ephraim, there you go again. Just like every other fella in this town you are intent on sullying my good name. Do you want to hear the story about how I got that name, or not?"

"Oh, please tell it." Kilkenny took a short sip. "I would like nothing better."

"All right. Now, after you all hear this explained, you'll understand that all that liver eatin' business is just folks talkin' to hear themselves spit. Now, it was back about...hell, maybe '69, I knowed it was after the war. Anyway, I was working as a woodhawk. Them steamboats on the Missouri will burn thirty cord a day if they're really pushing, so there was good money in woodhawkin'. I was working with old Moses Maloney and a young fella by the name of Ross. Anyhow, the riverboat was coming great guns up toward us one day. I believe it was the *Huntsville*, pouring steam, and this damned band of Crow, or Sioux, or some damned digger Indian heathens fell upon us." He paused to sip his coffee.

"You were unable to identify the tribal affiliation of the savages?" Ephraim sat with rapt attention.

The lawman shrugged. "I always did have trouble tellin' one from another. I think most folks got the same trouble, no matter what they claim. Most injuns will get around to tellin' you what tribe they are or some such thing. That day on the river...ah hell, maybe they was Flatheads."

"Mr. Johnson, I am not one to tell a man his own business in his own office, but would you mind terribly either getting on with the tale or shutting the hell up?" Finnegan offered a hard stare.

Johnson ran one paw over his bearded face. "Grumpy when he first wakes up, eh?"

"It is something of a constant condition." Ephraim smiled. "Please continue, sir."

"Oh, yes, well, we was on the river there and five or six of them fell upon us. We took to butcherin' them with whatever was handy. Musket, axe, knife, whatever was in reach when the devils were in reach. Ever done any Indian fightin', Ephraim?"

"No, it sounds terribly vigorous."

Johnson laughed. "Yeah, that'd be one way of puttin' it. So, we lit into them and when the frolic was over, I looked down and there was a hunk of liver hanging off my old bear skinnin' knife. Just a purple hunk a hangin' there. I don't know why I thought it would be funny, but a strange lark came into my head. I looked to that young pup Ross and asked him if he knew there was nothing more nutritious than raw Indian liver. Told him nibblin' a bit would make it so the boy could finally start shavin'. I held up that chunk of liver for the boy to see and made like I gobbled it, you know, like such." Johnson pantomimed moving something past his mouth. "At the time I couldn't have known the trouble it would brew." He shook his shaggy head. "That pup, well, he fairly lost his composure when I made the jest. That steamboat moored on the shore and that boy ran to it and hid out inside, wouldn't come out when the captain cussed or cursed. They hauled the boy off to Fort Benton and he must have told every soul he met the rest of his days how old John Johnson ate Indian liver." He shook his head again. "I know it's my own damn fault every time some cur flouts it again, but..." He shrugged. "It ain't as if I can explain myself to every man I meet."

Finnegan groaned and rubbed his head. "That is a singularly disgusting tale, Mr. Johnson. Thank you ever so much for sharing it with us."

"Well, there ain't too many who will take the time to listen. I appreciate it, men, I truly do."

Finnegan slowly rubbed his eyes. "It has been my honor. Now, would you mind terribly opening this damn cell door and allowing me to be on my way? Though, I cannot say I will go far. Locating another engineer may prove difficult."

Johnson shook his head and frowned. "I apologize, friend, but I cannot do it."

Finnegan spit out another bit of blood. "Sir, you may take me at my word when I tell you that I know the difficulties involved in performing one's duty, but this seems beyond any commission you may have had lain upon you. If you had ever made the acquaintance of the men shot in the tavern you must know they were of poor character, and you have a man sitting before you who can stipulate to my good character. What more could possibly be required for you to make a determination as to the justness of the previous incident?"

"Sheriff says any man caught in a shootin' scrap has got to stay in this here hoosegow until he says they can go." Johnson reached over to the stove and refilled his coffee cup.

Kilkenny rose from his chair and walked to the cell. "Would you have a cigar, Finnegan?"

The Pinkerton sighed. "I would think a man of your means would keep himself better supplied with tobacco." He felt in his pocket and managed to withdraw a cigar that had not been damaged during his beating and dragging.

"Ah, thank you." Kilkenny returned to his chair. "What precisely was the cause of the scuffle, Finnegan? Where the men confederates of the engineer?"

"Though it may seem strange, you were the cause of the scuffle, Ephraim."

"Me? How could that be?"

"One of them, a damned fool who patently refused to listen to reason, overheard you refer to me as the man who shot Jesse James."

Johnson's bushy eyebrows elevated. "You are Robert Ford? Sir, you are a damned sight more famous than I. I do not suppose you would consider remaining in this town? If you chose to live here these people would soon forget to pester me about the Crow I killed."

"If I agree to make this place my home, will you open the damn cell?"

"Oh, I don't know if that would be proper."

"Then to hell with you. I hope these people run you out on a rail at their earliest convenience."

"Gentlemen, please." Kilkenny paused to light his cigar. "This prattle will get us nowhere. Mr. Johnson, this man is not Robert Ford. He is Finnegan Gilhooley, the first man to shoot Jesse James."

Johnson rubbed his chin. "I was not aware the man was shot twice, from what I was told he got shot once in the back of the head and that was the end of it."

"No, Mr. Johnson." Ephraim blew out smoke. "That was when he was killed by Robert Ford."

"Well, now how the hell can a man be killed twice?"

Finnegan let out a low groan. "Would it be too much to ask that I could be hung for my crimes this very evening? I would prefer to not have to listen to this."

"Oh, now, Finnegan, always such a dreary outlook." Kilkenny sampled his flask again and turned to Johnson. "My good constable, when is it the Sheriff is to return?"

"Oh, he comes through at least once a month. By my reckoning, it seems like once a month, anyway."

"Ah, I see, and when is he due to pass through this hamlet next?"

"Uh, well." Johnson scratched his beard. "I can't say as I exactly recall the date he last departed." His eyes narrowed. "By the by, what month is this?"

"Ephraim, I do not care to listen to this any longer." Finnegan pointed to his guns which lay on the table by Kilkenny's feet. "Would you mind passing me one of those so that we might be on our way?"

"Finnegan, honestly, it simply will not do to go around shooting constables."

"In fact, I am a deputy." Johnson seemed quite concerned with the distinction.

"My apologies, sir." Ephraim smiled at their host. "Mr. Johnson, you are a reasonable man, and I am certain we can come to some sort of accommodation."

"Mr. Ephraim, I hope you ain't offering me no kind of bribe."

"Certainly not."

"That's good, because I can't accept 'em. Sheriff left specific instructions that all bribes has got to come through him direct. He will tolerate no devious behavior in his jurisdiction."

Kilkenny nodded. "Nor should he. No, Mr. Johnson, I would never suggest that a man of your character would accept something as tawdry as a few coins in exchange for your honor."

"Well, it's just that the Sheriff was quite specific, you understand."

"I am sure he was, Mr. Johnson." Kilkenny grinned at Finnegan. He seemed to be enjoying the farce a great deal. "No, sir, you seem to be performing your duties quite admirably, and I can take no umbrage with your actions so far."

"I damn well can." Finnegan scowled from his cell.

"And that is a very natural reaction, as well." Kilkenny laughed. "Mr. Johnson, I cannot suggest any malfeasance in the commission of your duties. All I might question, in all earnestness, might be if you are properly interpreting the orders left for you by your good sheriff."

Johnson smoothed his beard once again. "Uh, how so, Ephraim?"

"Well, as I see it -- and it may very well be that I am confused as to the nature of such things, due to my lack of experience in such matters -- but as I see it, the orders regarding the keeping of men involved in shooting scraps, as you call it, those orders certainly do not apply to you yourself."

"To... myself?"

"To yourself, when acting in your capacity as a constable, or deputy, rather. Obviously, if you were to shoot some miscreant in the course of your duties, you would not lock yourself in that cell until the sheriff returned to assess the propriety of your actions."

"Uh, well, no." Johnson gave his beard a good scratching. "As the deputy, I suppose I may shoot who I please without direct orders from the sheriff."

"Ah, very well. Then you will be quite pleased to hear that Mr. Gilhooley here is no less that an agent of the famed Pinkerton Detective Agency and works in the great city of Chicago in a capacity very similar to the one you serve in here in this lovely glen."

"He is an officer of the law?"

"He is, indeed." Kilkenny assumed a very serious demeanor. "Now, then, as we happen to find ourselves in a country where all men are created equal, as your own Thomas Jefferson was so fond of pointing out, then I can only assume that all officers of the law are to be considered equal, as well. Would you not say the same, Mr. Johnson?"

"I suppose I might, yes."

"Grand. Since we have already established that you would not require jailing after a shooting incident, and that one officer is as good as the next, we are left with no other reasonable option than releasing Mr. Gilhooley from confinement."

"By God, I would say you are correct, sir." Johnson stood and fished a key from his pocket. "Uh, I suppose there ain't nothin' wrong with releasing you from custody, since old Ephraim here took the time to explain it so pretty. I will have to insist that you come back to town when the sheriff is here so that he can make a determination of his own." Johnson let the door creak open.

Finnegan slowly stood and stepped out of the cell. His first movement was to the table, where he began strapping his guns back on. "Oh, be assured, Mr. Johnson, I have every intention of returning to this town someday to pay you a visit."

"Damn decent of you." Johnson refilled his coffee before sitting back down. "Ephraim, you sure got a fine way of layin' things out straight. We got a town meetin' here about twice a year, you think you could come down and explain to everyone about my liver eatin'? Explain it like you did with your partner in the cell. If you did, I sure would be obliged."

"Oh, I would not mind a bit, Mr. Johnson. Although it might strain my oratorical abilities to their very limits."

Chapter 6

HELENA, MONTANA TERRITORY

June 2nd, 1884

THE COSMOPOLITAN HOTEL DID NOT COMPARE favorably to some of the better Chicago hotels, but Finnegan was quite pleased to be ensconced within its walls. A proper bathtub, sink, and other indoor plumbing were only a few of the minor amenities he had been missing in the boxcar. Finnegan had spent a good deal of his life roughing it. During the war he had slept out nearly every night, rain or shine or snow. During his pursuance of the James contingent, he had slept in more than a few musty old barns, when not simply sleeping in the saddle and trusting to his horse's navigation skills. Finnegan was no stranger to the outdoor life, but that only meant his interest in it had well-developed limits. In truth, the portion of Kilkenny's adventure that would largely feature living out of tents was the portion he was least looking forward to. If he had his druthers, they would stay at the Cosmopolitan, and the whiskey baron could use that relatively soft and safe place as a base of operations.

It had taken two days to locate a replacement for the dead engineer. When that fellow had arrived, he showed no interest in the environs of Coulson and only wished to move farther down the line with all rapidity. He definitely gave the impression he was fleeing something behind him. Finnegan developed an instant liking for the man as he himself wished to flee with some rapidity. The longer he remained in Coulson, as Finnegan saw it, the greater the chances that either Johnson would wish to arrest him once again, or Finnegan's stewing anger would spill over, and he would shoot down Johnson. Unpretentious flight seemed the best action for all parties concerned.

Kilkenny had procured one of the two large suites the hotel offered on its third floor and Finnegan was greatly enjoying living like a human again, with his own room, bed, and privacy. Sadly, all things come to an end, and their second day in the suite was the time scheduled for a meeting with the Montana pioneer Kilkenny had been corresponding with for such a long time. Finnegan's presence was required in the drawing room the two bedrooms of the suite shared. The gunman had been informed to dress up a bit as the pioneer was not coming alone. Stuart wished to bring what was known as the Helena Board of Trade with him along with a few others who wished to meet a descendant of Irish liquor royalty. Altogether, the guests supposedly formed the Montana Stock Grower's Association. It had always amused Finnegan to observe that men so dearly love to give themselves titles.

As ordered, Finnegan had brushed down his frock coat, polished the leather of his holsters, and cleaned his guns so they would not appear slovenly in front of company. Beyond that, Finnegan had little conception of what it meant to dress up. He strolled into the drawing room after the other guests had arrived, having suffered difficulties in locating his better vest. Kilkenny was already holding court with a glass in one hand and a smile playing across his face.

"Ah, gentlemen, now the final guest. Please allow me to

introduce Finnegan Gilhooley, famed Pinkerton detective and dispatcher of riffraff, seemingly wherever he travels." Kilkenny motioned for Finnegan to move toward the assembled men. "Finnegan, this first fellow is the esteemed Granville Stuart, whom I have been penning missives to for some time." A tall, thin man with a chest length graying beard came forward a half-step. His face betrayed a long, hard life in a tough climate.

Finnegan put out his hand. "Mr. Stuart, I have heard a great deal about you, and it is a pleasure to meet you in person."

Stuart looked the gunman over. "It is fine to meet you, as well, Mr. Gilhooley. Ephraim has mentioned you to me on several occasions, and I am glad to have a face to put with the exploits." Stuart glanced down at Finnegan's weaponry. "I hope you are not planning on expanding your fame this evening."

Finnegan smiled and shook his head. "No, sir. No intentions, whatsoever. It is only that Ephraim has informed me that the latter part of the evening may be spent at dinner downstairs, and I have already encountered some difficulties in a saloon in this territory."

Stuart nodded. "Best to be prepared."

"My thought exactly." Finnegan moved one step down the line with his hand extended.

Kilkenny motioned to a much shorter man with a mane of grey hair. "This gentleman is Andrew J. Davis. He is very active in the civic life of this settlement, as well as with one of the settlements to the south known as Butte."

Finnegan smiled and shook the man's hand. "Very nice to meet you."

The Butte banker looked Finnegan over. "I have occasionally read about you in periodicals, Mr. Gilhooley. I must say, you fit the image in my mind rather well."

"I suppose I will take that as a compliment, sir." Finnegan grinned and moved to the next man who was even shorter yet again, but still had a black head of hair and a neatly clipped beard. "Hello, sir."

The man put out his hand. "Samuel T. Hauser. Pleased to make your acquaintance."

Kilkenny slapped Finnegan affably on the shoulder. "Mr. Hauser lays claim to the auspicious accomplishment of founding the first bank in this territory, Finnegan." He motioned down the line. "With the assistance of Mr. Davis and Mr. Stuart, of course."

"Well done." Finnegan nodded approvingly.

"Banks are far easier to begin than operate, I assure you." Hauser let out a small laugh and Finnegan moved down yet again.

Kilkenny felt the need to introduce the next fellow who stood ramrod straight. He was a well-built man, roughly the same height as Finnegan, and sported a waxed mustache that stuck up at the tips. He wore an elegant traveling suit and his hair glistened from some sort of balm. "Yes, Finnegan, I imagine as a boy you never thought you would find yourself in the same room with the French aristocracy, but here you are. Allow me to introduce the Marquis de Mores, though his friends call him Antoine."

"Sir." Finnegan shook the man's hand.

The descendant of several severed heads shook Finnegan's hand. "A pleasure to meet you, Mr. Gilhooley. Ephraim and I knew each other when we were children. I hope he has not told you too many lies regarding my conduct."

Kilkenny patted the Marquis on the arm. "I never mention you at all, Antoine. It is simply not safe to speak of you." Kilkenny nudged Finnegan. "Antoine is far too fond of challenging those who offend him to duels for my taste. Although, you two should get along quite well."

Finnegan shook his head. "I know nothing of dueling, sir. I have always loathed giving notice."

The Marquis laughed. "A fine policy, to be sure."

Finnegan turned to the last and youngest man at the meeting. The fellow wore a set of tweeds that had obviously been rolled up in a blanket previous to the evening. He kept flashing a grin with his oversized teeth and had a pair of spectacles perched in front of his bright eyes. Kilkenny could not conceal his amusement at the man's exuberance. "Last, but hardly least, Finnegan, we find Mr. Theodore Roosevelt. Mr. Roosevelt is involved in a rather successful cattle venture in the Dakotas and is something of a bounder in the politics of his homeland." Kilkenny laughed. "Mr. Roosevelt has the stated – and, may I say, audacious -- goal of expelling all the corrupt politicians from the city of New York."

Finnegan leaned forward and took the man's hand. "Will it not be lonely living in New York all by yourself, sir?"

"Ha, yes, I should say so!" Roosevelt gripped Finnegan's hand and shook it with an unexpected vigor. "Very droll, sir. Excellent." He released the gunman. "Sir, may I say, I have somewhat followed your career in the *Police Gazette* over the years. As well as a man can when attempting to separate the fact from the fiction and the wheat from the chaff, as it were. Very impressive, sir. Splendid. I might add that I believe the state of Missouri would be far better off today if your bullet had found a vital organ years ago in Minnesota when you encountered the James brothers."

"Thank you, sir. I would wholly agree."

Roosevelt pointed to the pistol butt protruding from underneath Finnegan's coat. "Is that the Frontier Model of the Colt revolver?"

"It is, sir." Finnegan pulled the weapon from the low-slung shoulder holster it rode in. He had very nearly run out of ammunition in Coulson and had no intention of allowing it to happen in Helena. There were now three revolvers on his person when he traveled about town. "This one has had the hammer spur removed to aid in its concealment." He handed the foreshortened revolver to Roosevelt. "I relieved a fellow of it in Chicago and felt it to be quite a practical addition to my collection."

"Oh, yes, very fine." Roosevelt ogled the gun. "Very effective close-in, I would imagine."

"I have yet to test it in the field, but that is my assumption, yes. Although the mechanism is a bit delicate for my taste, if I had to lodge a complaint."

"You worry over its dependability?"

"Theodore." The Marquis twisted one moustache tip. "If you begin discussing those damned revolvers with that man, we will talk of nothing else tonight. For brevity's sake, please."

Roosevelt handed the gun back to Finnegan. "For a confessed member of the aristocracy, my French friend has a very poor appreciation of the finer things in life. Thank you for showing it to me."

"Perhaps we can find the time for some target practice while we are both here in Helena?" Finnegan shoved the revolver back in its holster and concealed it beneath his coat once more.

"I would enjoy that greatly." Roosevelt grinned as Kilkenny began ushering the assemblage toward chairs laid out in a sort of semi-circle in the drawing room.

When everyone had found a seat, Kilkenny produced a bottle of his family brand and made the rounds handing it out to all those who cared for some. When that was accomplished, he produced a piping hot coffee pot and poured Finnegan a cup of his preferred beverage. Finnegan sipped the thick brew. "Ah, that is fine, Ephraim. I had no idea you had taken up a new career as a café waiter."

"The whiskey business may fail someday; all men need plan for their future." With the coffee seen to, Kilkenny flopped down into a chair of his own. "Before you came in, Finnegan, these men were discussing a problem of sorts they suffer from that might have something of an effect on your future."

Finnegan sipped his coffee. "My future?"

Hauser leaned forward. "Ephraim tells us that you are interested in possibly investing in either cattle or mining concerns while you are here, Mr. Gilhooley?"

"I have given the matter some thought, yes. I am not certain if I have the funds to enter into business for myself, so entering into some sort of partnership may prove to be the best option." Finnegan let his eyes roll over the other men. For some reason he could not discern, they seemed deeply interested in his financial plans. As far as he could recall, they were the first men to show any curiosity regarding the topic. "I had hoped to receive some advice regarding the different possibilities from men such as yourselves while I am visiting here."

Davis nodded. "For a man who is willing to do his part in a given venture, there is almost limitless opportunity in this territory, Mr. Gilhooley."

"That is pleasing to hear."

The Marquis leaned forward. "Mr. Gilhooley, if you would not consider it rude, might I enquire as to the amount of capital you wish to invest? I am ignorant of the pay received by a detective, and the amount of available capital often influences the investments a man should make."

"Ha, yes, it certainly does." Roosevelt slapped one hand across his leg. "As an example, I have robbed and borrowed from Peter, Paul, Luke, Judas, and any other fool I could find on Wall Street to form up my rather modest ranching concern, while my friend Antoine has purchased nearly every cow in Christendom and built his own slaughterhouse without yet seeking credit. Although, I must say that I enjoy the ranching life greatly. It is not the future financial inducements that makes me gravitate toward it, but a sense of freedom and purpose that simply cannot be obtained..."

"Theodore." The Marquis shook his head. "Mr. Gilhooley wishes to speak of investments. He does not ask to be bothered with your libertine philosophies."

"Libertine! Hardly. You aristocrats claim such things every time a man dares to espouse some system that does not involve bowing and scraping to you. I dare say you would call any man interested in bettering his lot in life a communist, and accuse him of helping with the barricades in Paris."

"Theodore, really, must you take everything so seriously?" The Marquis laughed.

Finnegan's ears perked up at the mention of some topic he had a blushing familiarity with, but decided that a change of subject might be better for everyone. "In answer to your question, sir, I have somewhat over seven thousand dollars that I could place in an investment, hoping to see it grow, of course."

Stuart slowly sipped his cup of coffee; he was the only other member of the group who had elected to have some. "Seven thousand...Being a detective pays better than I would have thought."

Finnegan shrugged. "Some of it is from saved wages, some profit from other endeavors." He chuckled. "The sum might be greater if it had been placed in the hands of a wiser man. I have experienced gains and losses playing my hand with stocks and those damnable railroad bonds." A round of laughter circled the room as each man was forced to think back on his own follies. "Yes, well, it is comforting to know I am in good company in that regard." Finnegan pulled a cigar from his coat. "Naturally, I would be in much better straights if I were given advanced notice of bank failures, but I suppose all men must run that hazard."

"Even bank presidents." Hauser grinned.

"I suppose so, sir." Finnegan smiled at Kilkenny and tossed the cigar to him. "Gentlemen, if you smoke, you should steer clear of that particular scoundrel." They all laughed again, and Finnegan found a second cigar. "So, then, gentlemen: given my financial status, and keeping in mind my dislike for an overabundance of manual labor..." He smiled to the group. "How would you recommend I make my fortune?"

Hauser took a sip of his whiskey and sat forward on the edge of his chair. "Mr. Gilhooley, I believe I speak for every man present when I say that there could be no better or safer home for your moneys than in cattle. As you have pointed out, banks fail. Railroads go bankrupt. Gold mines, oh if only I had back all I have squandered on gold mines, I could melt it down, seed some hole, and rival the Drumlummon Lode. Just having back what I have frittered away would make me richer than old Tommy Cruse." The man stopped and sipped again. "Cattle are a far safer and lower cost method to increase your riches, Mr. Gilhooley. To my way of thinking, cattle are a wonderful commodity. They are the only investment where you gain interest not from the machinations of some accountant, but by a law of nature. Every spring a man with cattle can ride out onto the range and discover that his herd has increased simply because that is what God intended when he placed cows upon the earth."

Finnegan nodded and rolled his cigar between his fingers. "It is quite consistent?"

Davis snorted. "You can set you watch by it, Mr. Gilhooley. That perfect consistency is why myself, Mr. Hauser, and

Mr. Stuart have established the DHS Ranch. I would assume the steady growth of the market and the infallible increase of the herds is what has brought Mr. Roosevelt and the Marquis into the business, as well." Davis sampled his drink. "Are you familiar with the system of open range grazing that is utilized in this territory and the Dakotas, Mr. Gilhooley?"

Finnegan nodded. "Ephraim attempted to explain it to me before we embarked from Chicago, but I confess, I could not fully understand it until I had seen this country for myself. Before appreciating the size of this land, I would have been tempted to call him a liar."

"Each man using a portion of the range for their own purposes, while it remains open to all." Roosevelt pulled his glasses off and vigorously cleansed them. "It is a wonderful, cooperative effort, so long as all parties agree to properly husband the resources available."

"Cooperative effort." The Marquis sneered. "I was right, you are a damned communist."

"A splendid jest, Antoine." Roosevelt replaced his spectacles.

"And the opportunities expand yearly, Mr. Gilhooley." Hauser had finished his whiskey and had the glass extended toward Kilkenny. "As it stands, we are on the verge of wrestling back some of the most prime grazing lands from the savages that currently infest them. Nothing is more appalling to a man of enterprise than waste, and we are slowly bringing the dull members of our national assemblies around to understand what a startling waste an Indian reservation is. That is to say nothing of the position all enterprising members of the Stock Growers Association will find themselves in when the age of the open range does eventually come to an end."

"An end, gentlemen?" Finnegan arched one eyebrow.

Hauser fielded the question since he had broached the topic.

"Nothing continues forever, Mr. Gilhooley. Someday, after a certain level of settlement has been achieved, the land that currently constitutes the open range, both here and in the Dakotas, will be transferred to private ownership." He looked to the other members of the group. No one appeared in disagreement. "When that day arrives it is the ranchers, those currently in the vicinity of the open range, who will have both the financial ability and the tangible intelligence to purchase the land in ways that will maximize its utility for grazing and other purposes."

Finnegan nodded slowly. "I see. An excellent point." He rolled his cigar once again. "Would you gentlemen have any advice regarding which area to begin such an enterprise? This territory is vast."

Davis smiled. "That is a matter that deserves long and careful contemplation, Mr. Gilhooley. Mr. Stuart spent the better part of a year traveling and assessing locations before settling on the site our cattle venture currently occupies. There are a great deal of factors to take into account. Weather, elevation, access to the railroad or future railroads. Of course, it is also important to take the condition and proximity of the savages into account. Our outfit lies close to Fort Maginnis, isn't that right, Granville?"

Stuart nodded, looking sullen. "Yes, the Fort being hard by the ranch is quite useful. My daughters never want for suiters and those damned galvanized Yankees never fail to watch in awe as the tribes pass by to steal our stock."

"Oh, now, it is not as bad as all that." Hauser smoothed his moustache. "My friend often becomes despondent waiting for spring to come into full bloom, you will have to excuse him." Hauser cleared his throat. "Ephraim tells me you will be passing through a great deal of the territories during your current adventure. I should think that you could make a rather complete survey in the time allotted. A very thorough survey if you are inclined to accept our offer, as well."

Finnegan lit his cigar and shook out the match. "My apologies, sir. I was not aware you had made me an offer."

Davis laughed. "Ah, that is usually the way of it with Sam. He is always getting ahead of himself. I still recall how he had all the bank's money loaned out before the depositors materialized." He shook his silver head. "Mr. Gilhooley, please allow me to fill you in as to the details of what my friend has alluded to. Mr. Kilkenny has been in correspondence with Mr. Stuart for some time. When it was mentioned that Ephraim would be accompanied by the likes of Finnegan Gilhooley, Granville mentioned it to us in our various turns and we began to formulate a plan for your visit."

Finnegan could not help but chuckle at the way the man beat around the bush. "A plan, sir?"

Davis smiled and nodded. "Mr. Gilhooley, as we have been telling you, the environs of the Montana territory and the Dakotas are nothing short of a cattleman's paradise. Given the proper circumstances there is no reason we should not all become quite rich in short order." Davis grinned to the other men present. "There is, however, one nagging problem that continually bedevils us and affects our profits. It boils down to the sad fact that there is not recognized legal authority in these territories."

Finnegan stared at the man for a moment. "Sir, I beg to differ. On my way here I was unfortunate enough to make the acquaintance of a legal authority. Aside from the man claiming to be a reformed cannibal, there was little to note about the fellow."

Stuart let out a chuckle. "Cannibal, eh? You met old Johnson? That would explain your head. Is he still bashing men with that buffalo gun?"

Finnegan nodded. "He is, although I may take it upon myself to put an end to his habit before my trip is through."

Stuart chuckled a bit more. "That man is a pip."

Davis shook one finger at Stuart. "That attitude is precisely what I speak of, gentlemen. Some ruffian like that is not the type to bring order to this place. As I said, we lack a recognized legal authority. Mr. Gilhooley, we believe that you could fill that particular role."

Finnegan narrowed his eyes. "I am sorry, my friends, but I did not come here to become a constable. If I wished that fate for myself, it could have been easily accomplished in dreary old Chicago."

"No, no. That is not what we have in mind at all, sir." Hauser took a long sip of whiskey. "What we require is a man who can do more than a simple policeman. As you pointed out, Mr. Gilhooley, this territory is vast. No one man could hope to monitor the criminal activity across its breadth. What we require is a man who can bend the criminal element to his will, through sheer force of will, much in the same manner as you did with the James contingent."

Finnegan tapped the ash from his cigar. "I am not certain what you are referencing, sir."

Hauser's small frame shook with enthusiasm. "Is it not true that the James brothers' criminal careers were essentially brought to an end when you caught up to them in Minnesota? After encountering you, they were forced to spend their final days running and hiding, reduced to the status of the petty criminals they truly were."

"Ah, well." Finnegan shrugged. "I suppose it could be looked at in that manner, but I would hesitate to claim responsibility entirely."

"Regardless." Hauser took a breath and steadied himself. "We require a man whose very name will strike fear into those rascals that plague us. A man whose reputation will proceed him and hopefully winnow the ranks of the territory's villains without ever meeting the majority of them."

"Um, well..." Finnegan scratched the back of his head. "From what I have seen, gentlemen, this territory does not lack for men of low character. Is there a particular breed of villain you have in mind for extermination?"

"Horse thieves." Stuart spit out the words with great disdain. "We wish to rid ourselves of horse thieves, Mr. Gilhooley."

"Horse thieves." Finnegan nodded. "Are you gentlemen certain you would not wish for me to shoot a few people guilty of selling apples without a license or some such similar crimes while I am about my work?" He smiled, but the other men did not seem to appreciate the jest. "Perhaps there are extenuating circumstances to this horse theft I am ignorant of? Normally, I chase killers, bank robbers, train robbers, and anarchists, of late. It has been quite some time since I have been called on to investigate the theft of a horse. Even then, as I recall, the case was solved when it was revealed that General Meade was deep in his cups and had simply misplaced the animal." That jest coaxed a laugh from everyone but Stuart.

The elder gentleman sipped his coffee and stared at Finnegan. "Mr. Gilhooley, we find ourselves dealing with no common horse thieves here in the territories. These men do not intend to make off with my plow horse. They are making off with scores of our cattle ponies every season. A cowboy is only as useful as the mount he rides. Without sufficient numbers of horses, a ranchman may as well move back to the settlements and go into the mercantile business. That is to say nothing of the fact that the bastards live off our herds while they are about their chicanery. The beef they put in their bellies, the hides are sold to the Indians. The horses go to the British." He spit out a hunk of coffee grounds onto the hotel floor. "They are kind enough to offer to sell our horses back to us every spring when we discover how desperate we are for horseflesh. Very practical men, the British."

Finnegan gave his cigar a puff. "How many of these horse thieves do you estimate to be dealing with, Mr. Stuart?"

"I should think there cannot be more than a hundred of them between here and the Dakotas. Although, as I have explained to my associates several times, there is little purpose in speaking of extermination. They are too spread out and disappear like smoke when pursued."

Finnegan nodded. "Yes, I have dealt with that sort before. Bluster, followed by prompt departure." He contemplated the problem for a moment. "My advice would be to locate some party of these men, preferably one of the larger parties, and make a proper example of them. Let word spread of the consequences of theft, and you will find it far more efficient than bullets."

"Most assuredly." Roosevelt poked his stubby finger toward the sky. "Now we are getting somewhere, gentlemen. All this talk of extermination is foolishness. What we require is a thorough housecleaning, as it were, in one of the areas most affected. Round them up, turn them over to the law, let the exposition of their trials and sentences be broadcast through every periodical. Whether they serve their years in the penitentiary or face the scaffold, it will speak sternly as to our dedication and resolve."

Stuart squinted one eye down and leaned toward Roosevelt. "Sir, are you not imbibing liquor presently because you had your fill earlier?"

"What? No. Certainly not." He pulled his spectacles down once again and began cleansing them once more. "You would take umbrage with my statement, Mr. Stuart?"

"I damn well would. I, for one, have no intention of traipsing all over this damned country in pursuit of these worthless whore's sons that continue to rob us with impunity, only to spend a month in search of some sucker-faced sheriff, in the event we are somehow lucky enough to capture some. Pity's sake, Roosevelt. Turning a horse thief over to a sheriff would be as idiotic as casting a nugget back into the creek to see if fortune wishes to bless you a second time." Stuart pointed to Finnegan. "I like the Irishman's plan better. Let us corral them, shoot them, and spread the word with all due haste that we intend to do the same to any other man who would dare steal our property."

Roosevelt stood. "Gentlemen, I did not join this Stockgrowers's Association to sit here and form a vigilante committee. The whole purpose of organizations such as this is to bring order and law to this country, not propagate the kind of barbarous behavior practiced by saloon fighters."

Stuart waved one hand at the young rancher. "Well, if you don't like it, feel free to cease paying your dues, Theodore."

"I very well may, sir."

"Gentlemen, please." Kilkenny stood and brought the whiskey bottle from man to man and approached Roosevelt last. "Coffee or something stronger, Mr. Roosevelt?"

"Still nothing. Thank you, Mr. Kilkenny."

"Mr. Roosevelt, you will have to excuse the exuberance of these western types. It takes them a terrible short period of time to get around to the suggestion of shooting someone. I can assure you, cooler heads frequently prevail, and I have certainly never known Mr. Gilhooley to make use of a firearm when it is not absolutely required."

Roosevelt glanced to Stuart and resumed his seat. "Very well, Mr. Kilkenny, please excuse my outburst. It is poor form to do such a thing in another man's lodgings."

"Think nothing of it, Mr. Roosevelt. It is rather refreshing to meet a politician who can become adamant about a matter other than his bank book." All the men laughed, some took more whiskey, and Kilkenny returned to his seat.

Davis sipped his drink and leaned forward. "Mr. Gilhooley, I would assume you have, in the past, delivered more than a few men to the courts."

Finnegan nodded. "My fair share." He turned toward Roosevelt. "You gentlemen may discover, as this endeavor progresses, that these horse thieves themselves will do most of the work when it comes to setting an example and warning off their compatriots. Alexander Franklin James is fond of telling newspaper men that I have killed more than a score of his kinfolk over the years, when in fact, I doubt if I have shot more than six or ten altogether. All bad men tend to exaggerate, whether in relation to their own deeds or those of other men." Finnegan smiled at the politician. "Locating a goodly number of these men, perhaps wounding a few, and then delivering them to the law should provide a sufficient foundation for the legend to quickly grow into a massacre coupled with a bible story."

Stuart chuckled. "You truly believe these men can be made to surrender to you?"

Finnegan shrugged. "Did any of you men have the misfortune to serve in the war between the states?" They all slowly shook their heads. "Well, in that conflict, and in several instances since then, I have taken notice of the fact that most men, given the opportunity, would much prefer surrender to dying. There are simply not that many causes men will lay down for, or fates they would not prefer to perdition. I cannot claim that this venture can be accomplished without bloodshed of any type, but there is not reason to assume gratuitous violence should be required." He puffed a bit more on his cigar. "As for the wasted time locating sheriffs, I cannot speak to the duration from experience, but I can say that the larger number of men made privy to a large group of thieves being marched about will only aid us in the building of this territory's reputation for intolerance toward horse thieves."

Davis nodded with great approval. "Well, then, there you have it, Roosevelt, from a man with experience in such matter as perhaps no other can claim." The grey-haired gentleman smiled. "Now, then, Mr. Gilhooley, you will have to excuse me an eccentricity, but as a banker, I must ask that we take a moment to discuss your pay. Such things are generally on the forefront of my mind."

Finnegan laughed and knocked some ash. "Gentlemen, if you please, I do not believe there is need for any such discussion. What we have been speaking of is, as they say, hypothetical. I will be occupied the entire summer following Ephraim about while he collects rabbits and tigers and whatever else may live in these mountains. It is very fine of you gentlemen to offer so much advice to me, along with the opportunity for employment, but I cannot simply abandon one commission for another whenever the fancy strikes me."

"Think nothing of it, Finnegan." Kilkenny lit his purloined cigar. "These gentlemen informed me of their offer to you previously and after giving it some thought, I have come to the conclusion that we should be able to see to both our goals in the course of our journey. As I see it, there should be no trouble traveling with Mr. Stuart to his ranch. Along the way we can collect as many specimens as luck affords us. Once we reach the environs of the DHS Ranch, I will continue to gather my heads while you gather yours." Kilkenny turned toward Roosevelt. "Metaphorically speaking, of course."

The young statesman nodded approvingly. "I only wish I had the time to accompany you, sir. I have always longed to collect one of the rare white goats that inhabit this area. Do you think you will be able to obtain one?"

"Oh, possibly. Although, as you well know, Mr. Roosevelt, luck is the deciding factor."

"You may say that again, sir. I recall once while hunting buffalo..."

Davis broke into the revelry to divert the group back on task. "Mr. Gilhooley, as I said, in reference to your pay." He cast a rather chiding glance toward Roosevelt. "From what you have told us, I believe it could be said that you possess sufficient funds to purchase a small ranch or homestead in this territory and enter into the cattle business. The fact that the base of any given operation is quite affordable is part of what makes the business so attractive to those looking to expand their fortunes." Davis paused and adjusted his suit coat. "What you would lack would be the capital to purchase a sufficient number of cattle to begin building a herd. As I said, nature sees to this quite well, but for a man to see proper returns before he becomes pauperized by expense, it is necessary to start things off with a respectable number of cows."

Finnegan contemplated his cigar for a moment. "Sir, am I to understand that you are offering to pay me for my services in cattle?"

Hauser slapped one leg and sat forward. "No finer coin of the realm can be traded currently, young man. I would damn well trust beef on the hoof over the U.S. dollar as I lay awake at night. What is more, if you wish to enter into the cattle business, you may find cattle difficult to obtain at any price very soon. Or, more to the point, cattle not infested with that damn Texas fever or some other such malady. What we can offer you as payment is something that cannot currently be found elsewhere. We are offering to pay you with the promised calves of the coming year. This association can offer you healthy, northern range-bred cattle. We have all agreed to take a portion of the increase in our respective herds and donate it to your burgeoning enterprise. We have all agreed to keep your percentages on our books until you decide on a proper location for your outfit." He turned to the other cattlemen. "Naturally, if you need some operating capital in the meantime, as so often happens..." They all had a small laugh. "You may receive funds from your portion of any given increase when the cattle are sold to market."

Finnegan could not conceal his surprise. "That is a fine offer, gentlemen. This percentage I would receive, it would surely be sufficient to build a legitimate cattle herd here?"

Davis nodded vigorously. "Most assuredly. We have seen to that for certain, Mr. Gilhooley. That is the beauty of an organization such as this Stock Grower's Association. When all men with a concern in an industry work together, there is little that cannot be accomplished."

"Well, then." Finnegan shrugged and looked to Roosevelt. "If all members of the association are in agreement?" They nodded. "And Mr. Kilkenny raises no objection?" Kilkenny shook his head. "Well, then, gentlemen, I believe you have just hired yourselves a horse constable." He smiled.

Stuart laughed and shook his head. "We have been making use of the term 'stock detective', Mr. Gilhooley."

"Ah, well..." Finnegan grinned at Kilkenny. "I have been most every other kind of detective, why not try my hand at this?"

After adjourning the meeting, the assembly all retired to the confines of the saloon and café that was operated on the ground floor of the Cosmopolitan. After much food, drink, and cigars, the group went their separate ways. The Marquis seemed a bit miffed that he had been unable to find a vacancy at the Cosmopolitan, but otherwise the evening was a thorough success. Since Stuart, Roosevelt and Finnegan were the only three of the group to abstain from liquor, they found themselves as the last three men gathered around the table when the clock neared midnight.

"It is patently absurd, Mr. Gilhooley. I will grant you, my rifle was a Webley, not the Purdey, but the Winchester and its cartridges are the far superior choice for hunting." Roosevelt grinned at his new kindred spirit. "I am certain our friend Granville would agree."

Stuart took a short sip of coffee and nodded. "I have never had opportunity to try one of the English doubles, but I can boast of having fussed with some English single shot rifles, the Sharps, many that fire those old, long rounds with a bullet the size of a billiard ball." He chuckled. "For most purposes, I would have to agree with Theodore. The repeater is preferable. I have grown truly sweet on my '76 Express. It is a fifty, but the ball is lighter than the old Sharps or Ballard. It is a good killer, generally speaking."

Finnegan nodded and sipped coffee. "I have looked over the '76 in the calibers offered. I must say they seem a fine weapon, but I feel something more is required when dealing with a large bear."

Stuart lowered his eyebrows. "You have hunted bear?"

Finnegan shook his head. "No, never. I have read many accounts of the great beasts, though, and they sound quite formidable."

"That would be one name to level on them." Stuart motioned behind him in the general direction of west. "Over in the Deer Lodge Valley, when I first came here, there was a bear they said had picked off forty prospectors and who knows how many injuns. Called him Old Moses, although they are fond of calling every bear that has ever tasted of man by that same name. That habit may be the reason some of these bears amass such a record."

Roosevelt shook his head. "I should think that most of the animal's reputation could be attributed to yarning."

Finnegan shrugged. "I have read that the bears of India are to be more feared than the tigers. Those animals are of considerably smaller size than the grizzly variety of bear found here."

Stuart smoothed his beard and sipped his coffee. "I had fairly well forgotten about Old Moses and his ilk until you brought him up." He grinned. "Perhaps I should ask Kilkenny if he has another of those Purdey rifles on hand."

The three men laughed, and Roosevelt slowly got up from the table. "Ah, gentlemen, I have greatly enjoyed discussing the sporting life with you, but I am afraid I must retire. It has been a long day and, I must confess, I am eager to see how the Marquis has settled into our quarters down the street." He grinned broadly. "The structure is a converted stable. It makes me proud to be an American knowing that, not far from here, a nobleman sleeps in what was recently a horse stall. A wonderful statement on the equality of our society, don't you think?"

Finnegan raised his coffee cup. "May God bless the Republic."

Stuart chuckled. "I cannot claim a perfect understanding of either equality or society, but I do know a great deal about sleeping in horse stalls. You should counsel the man to be content; it can always get worse."

"I shall see if that line of reasoning comforts him." Roosevelt put out his hand and the two men shook in turns. "Good night, Mr. Stuart. Good night, Mr. Gilhooley. It has been a pleasure."

Finnegan found a cigar in his pocket. "I have enjoyed the evening, sir. I shall have to remember to vote for you the next time I find myself in New York."

Roosevelt gave him a quizzical look. "You must be a resident of the city to vote in its elections, Mr. Gilhooley."

Finnegan waved one hand dismissively. "I have it on good authority all that is required is to be Irish and available."

Roosevelt shook one finger at his new friend. "Ah, there is the root of the misunderstanding. That is all that is required to vote for the Democrat ticket. If you wish to vote for me, you must be a resident. Good night, gentlemen."

The two men watched Roosevelt leave. After a few moments, Finnegan turned to Stuart. There was a topic he had been waiting to discuss the entire evening, but had waited until the two men could have some privacy. Before he could begin, Stuart spoke once more. "If you do not consider the question too intrusive, Mr. Gilhooley, I cannot help but notice that you do not imbibe liquor, or at least have abstained this evening."

"I am not certain what you are asking, sir."

Stuart chuckled. "Well, it is only that you are the first Irishman I have met who behaves in such a manner."

Finnegan gave a nod. "It is a rarity amongst my race. Although, it would seem to be a rarity among you frontiersmen, as well."

Stuart contemplated his coffee cup. "It has not always been the case. As a younger man I was given to exuberance as much as any. As I have aged, I have found it is best to keep one's wits about him." He gave Finnegan a hard stare. "I must say, being an Irishman, a veteran of the past war, and a gunman is not what I would assess to be a combination for a teetotaler."

Finnegan shrugged. "I have always posited that the majority of gunmen drink to soothe what little conscience God has bestowed on them."

"You do not?"

"Unlike most gunmen, I do not revel in my work. I am

also careful to avoid action that may burden a clear conscience." He shrugged again. "As such, I have no regrets that require drowning. I would also point out that most men in my profession find the end of their career in a saloon when they do not have their wits about them. I avoid such things and have lived much longer than most."

"I could probably trace my abstemiousness to the same line of reasoning. Many a man in the mining camps saw his end by ball, knife, or rope, all because of whiskey." Stuart pointed upward. "Your employer, Ephraim, is a very affable fellow, but he has killed far more men than you or I could ever aspire to."

Finnegan shook a finger at Stuart. "That would be his family, sir. Do not level the sins of the father upon the son. Poor Ephraim is only an innocent bystander."

Stuart laughed. "I would have an easier time believing in his innocence if he truly were poor."

"Perhaps such things do need to be taken into consideration while leveling guilt." Finnegan smiled and shook his head at the old man's humor. "Mr. Stuart, it is my understanding that Ephraim has asked you to make a few enquiries regarding a lady of my acquaintance that I wish to locate while I am visiting."

"Ah, yes." Stuart took up the coffeepot on the table and poured himself another cup. "I did make a few inquiries regarding the young woman. It was a small matter to find her here teaching school." He sipped his coffee and smoothed his beard. "Although, I cannot help but wonder why it is, Mr. Gilhooley, that you did not locate the woman yourself. As you say, you are a former acquaintance of hers." He grinned. "From the look of the lady, I would find it difficult to believe she was one of the counterfeiters or train robbers you Pinkerton men are always chasing. If you knew what town she resided in, why not simply send post? This place is not so large that the letter carrier would not promptly deliver it."

"There is no perfidy at work, sir, I assure you." Finnegan puffed his cigar. "It is only that I felt it might be preferable for me to surprise the young lady. I have not seen her in quite some time and have not been as consistent in my correspondence as I probably should have been."

Stuart let out a laugh, looking truly shocked. "Mr. Gilhooley, you have come all this way with the intention of seeing this woman in person? There must have been quite a shift in the population since I last toured the settlements. Are there not still a fair number of women in the eastern states?"

"There are." Finnegan knocked ash to the floor. "I simply prefer the company of Miss Malinda Meagher to those other ladies. Now, then, whereabout this town might I find the young woman? Where is her school located?"

"Oh, well..." Stuart sipped his coffee once more. "She was formerly teaching the Catholic children, that being her persuasion."

"Formerly?" Finnegan sat forward a bit.

"Well, sir, I had no way of knowing what your intentions toward the woman were and Ephraim's inquiring about her placed the lady in the forefront of my mind when the schoolmarm in Maiden took ill. At the time, all I thought of was finding a replacement and somehow convincing the citizens that there was no need to burn the school to guard against transmission of whatever it was that killed the schoolmarm."

"Sir, what precisely are you saying?"

"Your friend, Miss Meagher, no longer resides in Helena. I hired her away from the Catholics to serve as the teacher in the town of Maiden."

Finnegan sat up straight in his chair. "What the hell for?"

Stuart shrugged. "I am the superintendent of the school district in Maiden. Such things are my duty."

"What? No. I do not care what petty office you hold. Why is it you have chosen my teacher, of all the teachers in this village, to transport elsewhere?"

"As I said, I had the lady in mind from Ephraim's inquiry. When I went to speak with her, she expressed great interest in moving to a more unsettled area. Most women in this territory long for more settled living. Given her qualifications and inclinations, I could conceive of no finer accommodation."

Finnegan rubbed the bridge of his nose. "And where the hell is Maiden?"

"Some twenty miles east of my place in the Judith Mountains. It is a mining town, and the school serves for most of the families in the area."

"East of...of your ranch?"

"Yes."

"You sent my Molly out into the middle of the wilderness to teach some brats arithmetic? By God, sir, if anything has happened to her..."

Stuart looked a bit confused. "Happened to her? Mr. Gilhooley, I would dare say to a certainty that there is nothing that can happen to the woman in Maiden that could not happen to her here. If anything, she was in far greater danger here. This place is a pit of crime, infested with drunken louts who can commit crimes with anonymity, thanks to the larger numbers of them. At least in Maiden, all the malefactors are known."

Finnegan calmed some. "Yes, yes, of course. My apologies, Mr. Stuart, I was looking at it in the wrong light and...I am well familiar with the young woman's sense of what she terms adventure. I am just lucky she did not take some damn position in an African jungle or some such place."

Stuart nodded. "At any rate, she can be easily located once we reach the Judith country, if that is your aim. I am sorry, but it did not occur to me that you would care where the young lady had a position, so long as you knew where she could be found. Of course, I did not have much choice in the matter. It is not so easy to find women who are single and willing to take up employment in a place such as Maiden, but your Malinda fairly jumped at the chance."

"Oh, I am certain she did. Just as I am certain this town of Maiden is most likely in the neighborhood of some damned Indian tribe."

"It is somewhat close to both the Fort Belknap and Crow reservations." Stuart smiled. "The lady has an interest in Indians?"

Finnegan shook his head. "Has since childhood, as far as I know. The woman will not be happy until she loses her hair like one of those sooner women in a dime novel, torn from a wagon and scalped on the plains."

Stuart chuckled. "She sounds like a handful, Mr. Gilhooley. I cannot say as I have had the opportunity to get to know the young woman personally. I would have thought that if she had an interest in Indians, she would have spent more time with my wife when they met."

Finnegan gave his cigar a few puffs. "You are married to an Indian?"

"Well..." Stuart sat back in his chair with his coffee cup. "As married as a white man might be to a squaw. Years past, things were different here. When we first came up into this country, through the Beaverhead and into the Deer Lodge Valley, there weren't any white women to be had. Naturally, we took up with the Indian gals. There were no ceremonies with flowers or some damned priest, mind you. No, these Indians practice a more efficient, and I might say, damned more civilized type of union." He sipped his coffee. "One day the woman brings her traps over to your teepee, or in my case, a shack, and she stays for as long as it suits her. There is none of this ridiculous 'till death do us part nonsense. If the buck becomes a nuisance, she goes back to her father's camp. If the squaw proves untenable to live with, you pile her traps outside and cast her back where you found her."

Finnegan stubbed out his cigar. "It does sound rather more simplistic than the Catholic version."

"Oh, I should say so. I ask you, Mr. Gilhooley, is it not preferable to simply part ways instead of chopping heads and starting wars in the tradition of fools like Henry the Eighth? Of all the foolishness mankind indulges in, I have always held religion to be the greatest fool's errand. Do you keep with the religion your parents foisted upon you, sir?"

Finnegan abandoned his cigar and took up his coffee cup once more. "If you are asking if I made it to mass this last Sunday, I must admit to being elsewhere. Now that I think on it, many years have passed since my last confession. I must admit to finding many aspects of it silly as I passed into manhood." He smiled and sipped his coffee. "I suppose it occurred to me that God must have already seen what I had gotten up to, so there could be little sense in retelling it to a priest. Aside from taking the opportunity to adjust the tale in my favor, of course."

"A trait I would imagine is quite common among those who confess." Stuart slugged down the last of his coffee. "I am sorry if my hiring the schoolteacher has caused a difficulty for you, Mr. Gilhooley."

"It is not the first difficulty I have encountered with Miss Meagher, and I doubt it will be the last. Think nothing of it."

"Very well, then." Stuart rose from the table and slipped a heavy fur coat over his shoulders. "I have but a short walk to Hauser's place. Good evening, Mr. Gilhooley."

Finnegan got up from his seat and extended his hand to

Stuart. "Thank you for the conversation, sir. It has been... informative."

"That is one of the kinder ways my conversation has been described. Thank you, sir." He shook the gunman's hand and left the café.

Chapter 7

DEEP CREEK CANYON, MONTANA TERRITORY

June 4th, 1884

As it worked out, there was no time for target practice. Stuart had received word that some band of Indians or white horse thieves had engaged in further predations of his stock. The news put the man in a regular dither, and he had announced that a speedy departure was required. Unfortunately for Stuart's temperament, the departure had been quick, but the trip was proving rather sluggish. Kilkenny required an entire Conestoga wagon for his traps. Stuart was disappointed once again when he discovered that his men had purchased enough supplies and other claptrap that they would require two wagons for transport.

The first day out of Helena, Stuart and the men in his employ had been grumpy enough that Finnegan and Kilkenny had opted to ride horseback, rather than take a seat in a wagon with any of them. By the second day, Kilkenny had grown weary of the saddle and had opted to ride in the back of a wagon piloted by a man named Reece Anderson, who had apparently been partnered up with Stuart almost since the day the man had come to Montana, at least to hear them tell it. Kilkenny had lounged in the wagon most of the day, sipping on his flask, reading, and gazing out at the scenery. Finnegan had opted to remain on his horse and keep his own company for most of the day. As the sun began to sink, he adjudged that Stuart might have calmed enough to try for a bit of conversation, even if it was simply an inquiry as to how long their trip might take.

Finnegan rode up next to the giant creaking Conestoga that had Stuart perched on its bench seat. The gunman pulled a cigar from his pocket and worked at lighting it while the pioneer bumped and jiggled above. "You appear to have extensive knowledge of mule teams, sir." Finnegan struck a match on his belt buckle and got his cigar going.

Stuart shook his head. "If only I could say I did not, that would be a grand thing." He snapped the heavy leather reins. "For my dollar, I would take oxen any day. They pull better, keep serene, and certainly eat better if a fellow finds himself lacking for victuals."

Finnegan cast his match away. "Is this the quickest route to your farm, Mr. Stuart? You appeared in rather a hurry when we left."

Stuart shrugged. "It would most likely be quicker to take the Mullen Road over, but I do not have the luxury of picking the route. I have both men and supplies to gather in the vicinity of the Sulphur Springs, and more yet again to collect in the Judith Basin. We take this route out of necessity, not by my choosing."

"I see."

"Worried that we will take too long in our travels and you will arrive to discover your schoolteacher has married a miner?"

Finnegan stared at the man for a moment to determine if the fellow was only having a jest or truly attempting to get a rise out of him. The grin on Stuart's face gave him the answer. "I am not particularly worried with regards to Miss

Meagher's matrimonial status. She has gone unwed this long; I suppose she will keep a bit longer."

The older man nodded. "Miss Meagher has a certain way about her that I must admit is rather fetching. She seems to have something rather restless in her. I can understand how a man such as yourself might find her well worth pursuing. Might I inquire as to where you first made her acquaintance?"

"Not far from her family home in Minnesota."

"It is my understanding the state of Minnesota is some distance from here."

"It is, sir." Finnegan guided his horse away from the wagon to avoid a pine tree and then returned to the side of the rig.

"You made mention of the fact that your Miss Meagher is interested in Indians."

"She is, yes."

"In what way?"

Finnegan took a moment to decide how best to answer. In truth, he had never been wholly certain how to describe the lady's interest, as he had never fully understood it. "She is interested in how the government plans to...settle them, or disperse them, or deal with them, in general. In times past, she has spoken to me of the issue at great length, but, honestly, I only pretended to follow her, as good manners dictated."

Stuart laughed. "Yes, well. It simply won't do to let a young lady know you don't know what the hell she's talking about." He pulled a piece of jerky from the burlap sack he kept beside him on the seat. "I might suggest you would find better romantic prospects among the Indians, sir. My wife and I rarely know what the other is talking about and it has become such a commonality that we barely notice anymore."

He bit off a hunk of jerky. "Have you spent any time amongst the Indians?"

"The majority of red men I ever saw were at various rail stops traveling here. They were all dressed like farmers. I must say, it was a bit disappointing. They bore little resemblance to the pictures in the newspapers and nickel books."

"Well, thankfully, most of them no longer resemble the old woodcuttings anymore. With luck, none of them will, someday."

"You would say they are no longer a danger to the settlers in this area?"

Stuart laughed again. "That would depend on what you mean by dangerous." He shook his head. "I don't believe anyone much worries over them razing a town anymore or massacring the soldiers in the forts. The real danger that they still pose is of a more subtle nature. The simple fact of the matter is that until the Indians themselves let go of the ridiculous notion that they can run off somewhere and find a part of their old world that remains unchanged, or live on the edge of the white man's world and move back and forth as though the two were not interwoven, they will continue to pose a problem." He gobbled more jerky. "It is an absurdity."

"You do not believe the Indians should have their own lands?"

"I believe they should have their own lands in the same way I have my own land. These ridiculous reservations will only serve to allow the Indian to remain segregated from the greater part of society. Currently, they use their reservations to serve as an origin point for all manner of nefarious deeds. They come into the settlers' lands, steal, kill, ravage, and return to the safety of their reservation when they have had their fill. Such a situation cannot continue forever, that much should even be obvious to those fools in Washington. While the reservations do exist, they are certainly not helpful to the character of the Indian."

Finnegan adjusted his slouch hat and puffed his cigar. "Sir, you must excuse me if I stray into rudeness, but I am new here and have always been curious by nature."

Stuart finished his jerky. "Ask your questions, Mr. Gilhooley. You will find that there is little I take offense to."

Finnegan nodded. "That is an admirable trait."

"I find it eases my path through life. What would you like to know?"

"You have children with your wife, sir?"

"Well, of course." Stuart grinned. "I have many progeny, and the herd seems to have increased every time I return."

Finnegan chuckled. "Yes, well, I suppose it is pleasing in some respects to have a large family. I am wondering, sir, if it would not be too impertinent to ask, but I am curious as to what position your children occupy in this frontier society of the territories."

"I would say that is a reasonable curiosity to have." Stuart spit down into the sagebrush and took a drink from his water jug. "The position of my children has much to do with where they find themselves standing. Amongst their mother's people they would be utter outcasts, the product of a woman keeping company with one of the evil devils that have so harried them over the years. Amongst my associates in civilized society..." He motioned in the rough direction of Helena. "The subject is never discussed. To a certainty, I can tell you that neither Davis nor Hauser would let my children through the front door of their house. Perhaps they would be allowed to pass through the back door and might receive a small meal in the kitchen, if carefully hidden." Stuart spit down again. "If I rise in polite society, the existence of my children will never be discussed."

"That must be a rather difficult way for the poor young things to go through life."

Stuart shook his head, looking rather sad. "No, Mr. Gilhooley, through careful planning and more than a bit of guile, I have seen to it that they are, largely, ignorant of the conditions I have explained to you. When our first child arrived, I had a small store in the Deer Lodge Valley. Then, every white man who had not brought a woman with him kept a squaw. The few white women in the valley soon folded the squaws into their sewing circle and we all lived together very well. Later, at Virginia City, there were a few bible thumpers and Easterners who made a stink, but they were hollered down easily enough, and people were allowed to live as they pleased. Now, it is more difficult, but I have managed."

"Your children enjoy life on the open range, sir?"

"Of course. To the cowboys, my oldest daughters are swans. The sole source of feminine beauty for many miles. My sons are a rare source of youthful exuberance for the soldiers of the fort to marvel at. Naturally, all of the children are given the respect that is due to the offspring of the foreman." He smoothed his long beard. "I once knew a man named Grant. He kept four wives in a house he'd built near our first strike at Gold Creek."

"Four wives? Was he one of these Mormons I have heard tell of?"

Stuart laughed. "No. If old Johnny Grant had religion, I never heard him speak of it. As I recall, his situation rather developed over time as one squaw in the area would lose a buck and would come to stay in the house with the first wife. Later, another was added and so on and so forth. Indians are quite fond of their relatives and it ain't uncommon for the squaw to drag along a few in-laws and cousins and such when she takes up residency. By the time Johnny Grant had wife number four, the man could nearly lay claim to a tribe all his own."

Finnegan chuckled. "I suppose such a thing could sneak up on a man, if it occurred over time. What became of the fellow?"

"What became of him is my purpose for mentioning the man. By the time Deer Lodge became a real town, there was no place for those of us who had settled the valley, people who wished to live as they pleased. Johnny Grant saw no choice for himself and his rather large brood. He packed them up like a wagon train of old and took them all with him to Quebec. Grant was reared there and often spoke of how there was no distinction between the white man and the red man there. I can only assume it played out as he had hoped. I never saw him coming back the other way with his fifty kinfolk, so perhaps all is well."

"Mr. Grant took his family to Quebec, and you have taken yours to the wilds of the cattle range."

"It seemed to be the best possible solution. With a great deal of determination, and a good supplement of luck, I hope to find the fortune that has so long alluded me on the lands around the DHS Ranch. If all goes as planned, I will become a well-to-do man and my family will find what happiness there is to find in this harsh life."

"It would seem to be a fine compromise, sir." Finnegan puffed his cigar.

"Hopefully so." Stuart stared down at the Pinkerton for a long moment. "Mr. Gilhooley, if I stray into rudeness you will have to excuse me, as well, but if you don't mind me saying so, you are a bit more of a free thinker than the average bogtrotter I have bumped into."

Finnegan laughed. "Bogtrotter! I dare say I have not heard that since the war." He coughed a bit, unused to truly guffawing. "Very glib, sir. You have found the Irish to be rather stuck in their ways?"

"Oh, most assuredly. I theorize that it is a combination of Catholicism, penury, and feudalism that makes them so damned pigheaded. As though the English king and the Pope might arrive to scold them at any given moment of their lives."

"That may be the cause of their morose nature." Finnegan avoided yet another tree. "Perhaps I appear different because I have had little training in becoming a proper Irishman. I left the old country when I was but a boy, and I did not find myself in one of the Irish brigades during the war. I have spent more time in this country than the one of my birth." Finnegan guided his horse toward a puddle in the wagon road and tossed his cigar down into it. "When a man has no set of ideas handed to him, he has little choice but to contemplate the ideas he stumbles across."

"That is most likely a fine way to look at the world, Mr. Gilhooley." Stuart took a long drink of water. "What the hell was it you asked me about when we first began yapping?"

"I inquired as to the quickness of our route."

"Ah, yes. Call it a week, barring any serious trouble."

"And what might constitute serious trouble?"

"Indian bandits, white bandits, a freak snowstorm, one of your giant bears eating all the mules. Anything is possible in this territory, sir. Even a sober Irishman."

They made camp that night on a broad plateau near a spring and a copse of willow brush. The mules drank their fill and were turned loose, hobbled, to graze. The men made their camp as best they could and settled in to get some rest and relaxation. After dinner, everyone gathered around a large fire and sipped coffee. Some elected to spruce theirs up with some of Kilkenny's seemingly endless supply of his family label.

Reece Anderson, Stuart's right-hand man, had developed quite a rapport with Kilkenny over the course of the day and the two continued to chat in camp. "How long were you in California, Mr. Anderson?"

"Oh, I would say about two years. Trouble was, they was the wrong two years. By the time I arrived there wasn't a dime left to squeeze out of the place that didn't have to be begged from them that got there first. Time I got there, men was buying water from them that had land claims up high. Had to buy water to pan anything you laid claim to that was below the ridgeline of the whole damn Sierras. Newspaper I read back east said California was an unsettled wilderness of boundless opportunity. Now I ask you, what the hell kind of unsettled wilderness is it if a man can't get a damn bucket of water without first paying the freight on it?"

Kilkenny laughed. "I can see how that might be vexing. Although I, personally, do not care for water much, many men do." He took a sip from his flask.

Reece flopped down on a log opposite the fire from Kilkenny. "By the time them bastards was done tight-fisting that water, it might have been cheaper to pan with whiskey. A damn site more entertaining, for sure." Anderson leaned forward and Kilkenny handed him the flask, which he used to spice his coffee. "Thank you much." He took a small sip and grinned. "When I found out a man needed a gold mine to use as collateral just to buy water, well, that was around the time I met up with Granville and his brother. His brother was going broke, same as me. He was still working the claim they'd gotten with their daddy." Reece turned to Stuart. "I still can't help but wonder if maybe your daddy was the only smart one out of all of us."

Stuart nodded. "Perhaps."

"Your father found gold in California?" Kilkenny seemed truly intrigued by the family history.

"No, sir." Stuart grinned. "My father went back east where he come from."

"Like I says," Anderson chuckled. "He was the smart one." The small, furry man sipped his spiked coffee. "So, their daddy had turned a go-back, and James was working for wages when the water proved too expensive. Granville here, he'd turned to meat hunting for the camps, and he was making a living."

"You were supplying the miners with food, sir?" Finnegan sat forward a bit, interested to hear of yet another way a man could turn a profit with a gun.

"Oh, very much so, Mr. Gilhooley." Stuart filled his coffee cup. "In them days, I would get upwards of four dollars for a deer." The aging man stared down into the fire embers. "Reece ain't lying. There was good money to be had back then if you were a good hunter. Put every nickel of it into that damn hole James and me were digging in." Stuart pointed across the fire. "Reece and me, we did pretty well deer hunting for a spell. Then, Reece got sick with some damn malady, never did know what precisely. Took weeks to nurse him back to health and then James and me couldn't find wage work and, well, I took what little we had left and made it down to Klamath Lake. That was where the road to Oregon came through and I was able to trade for some cows them Yankees had brought with them. They was not much more than hide and bones, but I fattened them up over about a month and then pushed them nice and slow to Dogtown. Got them sold off and that made for enough of a grubstake that I figured it was time to lit out for a new territory."

Reece Anderson laughed once more. "I still remember the mighty bit of intellect we devoted to that choice, as well.

We all knew California was played out. We'd never heard of gold in Oregon. Utah was Mormon country, and they could damn well keep it from what we had seen of the place. There was word that men were finding color in Montana, so we went in that general direction and didn't stop to check a creek until we found a half-mad old trapper who claimed we was in Montana. That fool assured us we was in a new territory and we begat to panning again. You got more gold in your pocket watch than all we ever found in the Beaverhead. That was when we started following news of other strikes. Sucking hind tit all over again."

"We hit the first strike at Gold Crick." Stuart spoke the words with a fair amount of pride.

"We did." Anderson scanned the assembled men. "That vein had to be at least as long as the chain on Mr. Kilkenny's watch."

"Yes, well, not every man can expect to find a gold mine." Stuart chuckled in a sorrowful sort of way. "In our case, it was not from lack of trying, I assure you."

"We looked under every rock between here and the British." Anderson nodded and slipped down to use the log as a backrest instead of a seat. "It took us a good long while to get that damn gold fever out of us. The day finally come when we got to ruminating on the problem and came to the conclusion that we couldn't compete with them other fellas in terms of luck, so we'd best figure a way to put their gold in our pockets. Mercantilism, is what James always called it."

"My brother James was always a great one for business, at least in theory. His next idea was always going to make us rich. Poor bastard died attempting one of his varied schemes. Caught ill amongst the Blackfeet at Fort Browning while he was trying to barter in buffalo hides." Stuart shook his head. "Might have saved him from a worse fate. In his boredom he had taken up with several squaws and it may have only been a matter of time before some buck or squaw's daddy came looking for payment or vengeance." He tossed a hunk of juniper onto the fire. "Pity, really. In time we may have come off quite well in the mercantile business."

Anderson took up the narrative. "Trouble was, every time we'd get a few pennies to rub together, along would come another mining venture that seemed a sure bet. You boys should have seen what we had going down in the Beaverhead around Monida. Had a processing mill and the whole shebang. Were even pulling silver out of the hill at a respectable rate, but..." He spit down into the fire and it sizzled. "Shipping costs killed it. No way to make silver pay without a railhead close at hand." He looked over to Stuart. "Bet you anything that damn big mill is still sitting there, just waiting on a railroad."

"Probably be there waiting long after we have all turned to dust." Stuart reached into a burlap sack and produced a can of peaches he intended for his dessert. "It has taken a good long while, and cost me much, but I have finally come full circle and am attempting to make my fortune much in the manner of the last truly profitable venture I can recall."

Finnegan found a cigar and smiled. "You would compare the cattle business to the deer hunting business?"

Stuart nodded. "If fate will not provide me with a gold mine, or gold miners wealthy enough to make me a rich merchant, I will default to that most basic of all human needs. All men must eat. There are no longer enough deer to feed the miners. There are not nearly enough buffalo left to feed the Indians. The time will come when the only square meal to be had is beefsteak. When that day arrives, I will finally find that damn fortune." He shrugged and found a can opener. "I merely need to stay alive long enough and find some remedy for these damn horse thieves. Given those two minor bits of luck, I should do quite well for myself and rise who knows how high." He popped open the can and fished out a peach.

Anderson pointed across the fire. "Granville wishes to be sent to Congress, when this territory becomes a state. Thinks Washington will suit him."

Stuart shook his head with his beard chasing to catch up. "My friend Reece misunderstands. What I said, is that I would like to have congress with every woman in Washington Territory, before it becomes a state." There was a round of laughter. "I suppose I have always suffered from an overabundance of aspirations."

"There is nothing to be ashamed of in aspiring, gentlemen." Kilkenny raised his flask. "To the fools who never learn."

"Hear! Hear!" Stuart raised his can of peaches. He turned to Finnegan, who was just lighting his cigar. "Mr. Gilhooley, you made mention that you were involved with the war between the states?"

"Yes."

"Did you fight for the Yankees or the Rebels?"

"By fate, our boat landed in a northern port. I was pressed into service before I had seen beyond the waterfront."

Stuart flopped another peach into his mouth. "How old?"

"Not boy enough to avoid conscription, but not nearly man enough to heft a musket."

Stuart sneered. "Those damned eastern politicians are little better than butchers. They are lucky the people did not toss them all into the sea halfway through that war."

"They made a fair attempt at it once or twice. I recall directly after the battle at Gettysburg, we were shipped up to New York to assist in quelling a riot. The citizens where not as amenable to being drafted as I had been. I believe they were slightly better educated as to their chances of survival.

At any rate, they had quite the donnybrook, burned half the town. There were even a few navy ships bombarding the city for a moment when the mob advanced too far."

"That must have been a sight." Stuart stroked his beard.

"Oh, that was all said and done by the time Mr. Pinkerton and I arrived. I was only privy to the aftermath. They had the docks lined with bodies, both rioters and soldiers. There seemed to be nearly as many as we had left behind at Gettysburg, but, later, I would learn that was only a trick of the stacking. It may not have been as bad as all that. Still, it seemed a pity. Rather confusing, as well. I do not know if those men could be counted as casualties of war or...some other cause." Finnegan shook his head and knocked ash toward the fire. "It was one of the incidents that has forced me to postulate that there is something rather mad in the American character that cannot be remedied."

"And there is not in the Irish?" Kilkenny sipped more liquor.

"Perhaps that trait exists in all men." Stuart tossed more wood onto the fire. "I have a younger brother who served in that war. He was too young to accompany us to California, so he stayed on back east and became entangled when the conflict came along. I do not feel the experience was good for his character. Since the war he has been rather dissolute and intemperate."

Finnegan shrugged. "I cannot speak to what your brother may have experienced in the war. I can say, as many men have pointed out before me, that war often only augments or enhances what already existed in a fellow's character. If he has nursed a cruelty until the outbreak of hostilities, he will be crueler still in war. If a man is immoral, he will be more so when opportunities present themselves. A man brings nothing to war that is not already within him. I doubt

General Grant tasted his first spirits only after Fort Sumpter."

Stuart chuckled. "I doubt that, as well." He gave the gunman a hard stare. "And what was enhanced in you during the war, Mr. Gilhooley?"

Finnegan looked into the fire and gave it some thought. "As I said, only what I brought with me. The fear grew daily, along with the anger."

Kilkenny sat forward slightly. "I must say, Finnegan, I am surprised to hear you list fear among your traits."

The Pinkerton smiled. "You thought you were the only man born of woman afflicted with dread?"

"No." Kilkenny smiled back. "I have simply never noticed the affliction in you."

"Well, it is there, I assure you. I carry it, and my anger, with me today. Such things never disappear, they only wax and wane."

Reece Anderson slowly got to his feet and brought the coffee pot over to Finnegan. He filled the man's cup and retreated before asking the question he had in mind. "Mr. Gilhooley, I know it may not be my place to inquire, but do you honestly believe you can shoot every horse thief between here and the Dakotas?"

Finnegan coughed a bit, sipping his coffee. "No, sir, I should think not."

"But is that not what you were hired to do, sir?" Anderson sounded a bit disappointed to discover there would be no widespread slaughter.

"I have been employed, Mr. Anderson, to reduce the rate of horse theft as best I can, making use of whatever means are necessary and reasonable. The members of the Stock Grower's Association do not wish to be viewed as a gang of murderers and, frankly, I would prefer to avoid it, as well. Especially, if I am to become a resident of this territory."

"You may be surprised what warrants adulation in this country, Mr. Gilhooley." Stuart tossed his coffee grounds toward the fire.

"So far, this trip has held many surprises." Finnegan stood and swiped the dust from his pants before picking up the Purdey Express rifle he kept near him always. "I am certain there will be more before it is concluded. If you gentlemen will excuse me for a moment." He turned to go off toward the brush.

Kilkenny chuckled. "Feel the need for a stroll, Finnegan?"

The gunman paused. "If you must know, I go to answer the call of nature before turning in for the evening."

"With that bloody big elephant gun?" The whiskey baron grinned from ear to ear.

"There is always a chance the bears will not feel the need to turn in as early as I do, Ephraim." With that, Finnegan meandered away from the camp down a trail in the willow and cottonwoods. He had gone some hundred yards, rather enjoying the solitude away from the camp, when he came to a fair-sized tree that would be stable enough for him to lean his rifle against. He made certain the gun would not tip over and turned away from the tree. Just as he was reaching down past his gun belt in search of his fly, he looked up the trail. There, some twenty or thirty yards distant, was a massive black object. It filled the entire trail with its fur clad bulk. The breath from the beast rose in tendrils in front of its obscured face and it was thrashing at the brush on either side of it. Clearly the animal did not care for Finnegan making use of its path.

Not wishing to take his eyes off the creature for a moment, Finnegan slowly felt back behind him. Mercifully, his fingers touched the cold metal of the Purdey's barrels. He clutched them and was bringing the gun forward just as the beast before him began to charge. Hand-over-hand Finnegan brought the rifle up and planted the butt in his shoulder. When the giant was no more than ten feet in front of him, he fired. The first round slammed the animal down into the ground and the second came as fast as he could wrestle the gun back on target from recoil. Stumbling rearward, he broke the gun open, tore the two empty cases from the chambers and was fumbling two more into the gun as Stuart came running up behind him.

The pioneer had his Winchester at the ready. "What the hell have you gotten into?"

Finnegan instinctively took a few more steps back until he bumped into Stuart. "A bloody big, damn bear. Damn thing very nearly had me, sir. I could see its teeth in the damn moonlight."

"A bear? Here?"

"Here is as good as anywhere I should think." Finnegan finally got the rounds seated in the gun and he snapped the action shut. "It lies just there if you do not believe me, sir. But approach carefully; I do not know if it still lives in spite of what must have been two balls from this bloody big gun."

Stuart slipped past Finnegan and slowly made his way up the path with his Winchester pressed to his shoulder. When he came to the beast he nearly tripped over the black form. "What in hell?" He gave the body a small kick, then knelt to strike a match. "Mr. Gilhooley, you have killed a damn fine moose this night."

"A moose? I...I should think I would have seen its horns."

"It is a cow, sir."

"A cow?"

"The female of the species, Mr. Gilhooley." Stuart stood, grinning by the light of his match. "It is for the best, really. The cows are more tender. You must have excellent vision to have seen her teeth."

Chapter 8

WHITE SULPHUR SPRINGS, MONTANA TERRITORY

June 5th, 1884

"Well, what in the hell did you want me to do, Ephraim, give it a kiss?" Finnegan was becoming a touch perturbed by his friend's prodding. "It ran at me in the dark. You would have done no different."

Kilkenny shook his head dismissively. "Oh, no, Finnegan, I dare say I would not have done as well. I have never been much for quick shots." He sampled his flask. "I dare say, you may be remembered as the greatest moose killer of our time." Kilkenny began to laugh and kick around in the bed of the wagon he occupied. He finally stopped when he saw Reece Anderson emerge from the saloon the man had entered in search of one of the cowboys the party wished to pick up in the small town that had sprung up around the nearby hot springs. Kilkenny coughed and looked to Anderson. "I say, this place doesn't smell very pleasant, does it, Reece?"

"Smells like the south end of a northbound mule and always has." Reece climbed up on the wagon and shaded his eyes to gaze over the town. "Where in the hell is that boy?" He climbed down from the rig, looking disgruntled. "Checking the saloon was a waste of time, aside from taking the opportunity to wet my whistle. I doubt Teddy Blue would elect to be found in there, anyhow." Anderson leaned conspiratorially toward Kilkenny. "The man has practiced strict temperance for some time now. He knows Granville prefers that in a man and I believe Mr. Teddy Blue Abbott has some designs on Granville's daughter."

Finnegan stood in his stirrups and scanned around for the man, but realized he had no idea who he was searching for. "What does this Teddy Blue look like?"

"Thin as a reed, about as tall as you. Usually sports a mustache. At least that's what he looked like last I saw him in the fall." Anderson climbed back onto the wagon.

Finnegan scratched his chin. "Why is it we have traveled out of our way to collect this fellow?"

"He's meant to be recruiting men for us. Anybody who ain't too useful gets cut loose in the fall. Others, like Teddy, they got better situations that can be had other than sitting in a line shack freezing their backside off all winter. Teddy got a job freighting for one of the mines. He wrote Granville that he'd come down with something and had to come here to get the cure in the waters. Said he would find us some men, if there were any to be found, while he was here." Anderson paced in the wagon bed. "It ain't no small matter. The best men, the one's you can trust with a herd, they get snatched up quick, fast, and in a hurry in the spring. If you don't get good men, the roundup is a curse, and the drive to the railhead is even worse. I hope that boy found us some bucks who know their ass from a post hole."

Finnegan stood in his stirrups again. Down toward the end of the town's one and only thoroughfare, there were three men approaching, and one of them was definitely Stuart, who had gone off to check the mineral baths for the young cowpuncher they sought. The man in the middle fit the description of Teddy Blue. The third man was shorter and, even from a distance, appeared somewhat shifty to Finnegan. There was just something about the man's manner he did not care for. It might have been the fellow's dirty clothes or the Colt's revolver slung too low on one hip. "Our quarry approaches, men." Finnegan pointed down the street. "Were you hoping for more than one hired man?"

"Yeah, hoping." Anderson squinted down his eyes. "I'll be damned, that's Floppin' Bill Cantrell."

Finnegan sat back down. "Is he the type of hard worker you prefer?"

Anderson shrugged. "I can't say as I've ever seen Floppin' Bill overwork himself. On the other side of the coin, it will be nice to have one man in the bunkhouse who ain't afraid to pull a cork with me. Gets damn dreary only having teetotalers, women, and children about." Anderson looked over at Finnegan. "No offense."

"No offense taken." Finnegan removed his hat and scratched his head as the men arrived.

"Reece, put my saddle on that gelding. Teddy here can take a turn driving them damn mules for a day." Stuart turned to Finnegan and Kilkenny. "Gentlemen, these two are a couple of cowboys I employ when I got need of them. Teddy Blue Abbott and Floppin' Bill Cantrell. Don't ever get your fingers too close to Teddy's mouth, he's liable to bite down on anything if dinner's late. Other than that, he's a decent fellow. This other one, Floppin' Bill, there's nothing decent about him that I know of. His only redeeming quality is that he's too damn lazy to be a killer or a burglar." Stuart slapped the man on the back.

Floppin' Bill stepped forward and took Kilkenny's proffered hand. "Granville's talking me up always makes me blush."

Finnegan reached down to take the man's hand in turn.

"Well, as my father once told me, if you cannot be a good man, you may as well be consistent."

"An excellent way to look at it, sir." Floppin' Bill glanced between Finnegan and Kilkenny. "You'll pardon my saying so, but you two don't look much like cowboys."

"We are not." Finnegan pointed to Kilkenny. "That man is an ornithologist of some renown."

Floppin' Bill nodded. "I see. Well, ain't that something. And what might you be?"

"I am an ornithologist's assistant."

Bill nodded again. "And what might your duties be?"

Kilkenny leaned over on the side of the wagon. "Mr. Gilhooley is in charge of shooting moose and supplying me with tobacco." Kilkenny held out his hand to Finnegan. "Please see to your duty, sir."

Finnegan pulled a cigar from his pocket. "Since I see no moose about, I can only assume this is what you require."

Chapter 9

JUDITH BASIN, MONTANA TERRITORY

June 7th, 1884

"NO, SIR, YOU DO NOT SEEM TO FULLY APPRECIATE THE subtle difference in the cultures. What I am attempting to explain is that there was not simply a relaxed concept of matrimony, there was no concept of it whatsoever." Kilkenny had made something of a lounge for himself in the back of the Conestoga. After the Sulphur Springs, he had abandoned the façade of his frequently refilled flask and adopted a system where he sipped directly from the bottle. He had taken to discussing various philosophical issues with Stuart and only rarely bothered to glance at the scenery or the wildlife.

"No concept of the institution at all?" Stuart seemed highly incredulous regarding some of the tales Kilkenny had told of his travels.

"None, sir. On my honor."

"Ah, but, what of the men? It is all well and fine to say the women were blatantly adulterous, but that alone is not the issue. I have seen plenty of otherwise sensible men cut each other to ribbons over the favors of a whore whose name they could not recall in the morning."

"The men could not have cared less. After spending a month amongst them, the only cause for contention among them stemmed from the collection of a certain type of seashell that they used as currency. When it came to the women, they were no more considered the property of one man than the birds flying overhead. There was no fussing over the paternity of the children or all that foolishness. The men went about their business each day and the women theirs. That was all there was to it."

Stuart thought on it for a long moment as he bobbed up and down in the saddle. "Mr. Kilkenny, I must say I have greatly enjoyed hearing about the various localities you have visited, but I am afraid, in this instance, I must call you a liar, sir."

"I would pledge the validity of my claim on my mother's grave, sir. If she is ever to pass away, of course."

Stuart shook his head, grinning. "No, sir. It cannot be. It must be false. If you had truly found some untouched south seas paradise where the women, for some bizarre reason, are not possessed of their natural inclination toward enslaving men -- well, sir, what would ever possess you to leave such a heaven on earth?"

Kilkenny took a liberal sip from his bottle. "Ah, well, how to describe the trouble that arose? It may be difficult to believe, but after a period of time I came to rather miss...the option of defilement. If a woman knows no shame, where lies the glory in conquest?"

"Hmm?" Stuart stroked his beard. "I suppose I can understand how a man might grow to miss the...the simple enjoyment of corruption. If there is no virtue to abandon, then what is the purpose?"

"Precisely what eventually caused my departure."

"For the love of the holy mother!" Finnegan ran his hand over his face. "It seems you two have been discussing nothing other than debauchery for days. Is there truly no more enlightened subject you could prattle on about?"

Both men stared at Finnegan, but Kilkenny spoke first. "Oh, do not let his outburst sully your mood, Granville. He gets like this when he goes too long without some sort of entertainment. The man is simply incapable of appreciating the finer intellectual explorations, as we do."

"No, that is not it. I believe the young man is merely moated and shackled by his Catholic dogma." Stuart shrugged. "We give offense to your strictures, sir?"

"You give offense to my damn ears and my stomach. I would call both of you liars. If either of you had performed half of the acts you lay claim to, neither of you would have the zeal to make this trip. I should think you would both need to sleep for the remainder of your lives."

"Oh, Finnegan." Kilkenny waved one hand about. "If you no longer find enjoyment in the lively debate we are engaged in, perhaps you should find some other way to amuse yourself. Why not wander out into this wilderness a fair distance and try to locate a few specimens for me?"

Finnegan scanned around the general vicinity. "Ephraim, I have not the foggiest idea as to where on the face of the globe we currently are. If I did choose to wander out into this nothingness, how would I ever find my way back to this little caravan of ours? I haven't the faintest clue where we are going."

"Oh, hell, if you have an itch to see some other country, Mr. Gilhooley, one of these lay-abouts can serve as guide." Stuart gave his horse a small kick and moved forward to the wagon Reece Anderson was piloting. "Reece, toss a saddle on one of them swaybacks. Our Irish friend has a wish to collect some game." Stuart turned back toward Finnegan. "And I am all in favor of it. I grow weary of a steady diet of moose meat. Do you think you might find us a sage hen or a turkey, sir?"

Finnegan eyed the pioneer incredulously. "Gentlemen, of all the men on this expedition, I should think I have the least experience collecting game for the pot. How is it that I have been elected to be in charge of hunting?"

Anderson brought his wagon to a halt and hopped down. "Uh, if it's all the same to you, Mr. Gilhooley, I wouldn't mind a change of scenery for a while. Staring at the backside of a mule is no way to go through life. I can show you the likely spots to find a turkey, but you'll have to shoot 'em. I got no luck whatsoever when it comes to shooting turkey."

Finnegan brought his horse to a stop next to the man. "You are confident that you will be able to reunite us with this supply train when our hunt is over?"

Stuart wheeled his horse over. "Swing him up into the Little Belts over yonder and then cut west. We'll meet you boys at the Gap. I guess you can find the Gap all right, eh, Reece?"

"I damn well found it a few times before." Reece unhitched his horse from the rear of the Conestoga. "Anything is better than beating those mules for a spell."

Finnegan sighed. "I suppose there is something to be said for the companionship of a dead turkey; the beast will be quiet, at a minimum."

☆☆

THEY WERE some few miles from the wagons when Anderson struck up a conversation. "Would you mind my asking you a question, Mr. Gilhooley?"

"Um, well, I suppose it cannot hurt to ask." Finnegan found himself continually scanning the country for bears. The incident with the moose had done nothing to assuage his nervousness on that score.

"Sir, I was wondering how it is you came to your profession? I have never met a Pinkerton before, and I must confess I have always been curious as to how your employer selects your sort."

"The agency's hiring practices do not differ much from that of any other company I am familiar with. Many men present themselves at the offices in Chicago and make application. Some are chosen. Mr. Pinkerton has a singular ability for spotting talent in men."

"Did you make application to the agency?"

"No. My career began differently. I assisted Mr. Pinkerton during the war, when I was little more than a ragged child. In thanks for the assistance, Mr. Pinkerton took me into his service, and I have been there ever since."

Reece rubbed his face and glanced about, looking for what might be likely turkey country. "So, you have worked for the same man your whole life?"

"Since before my majority, yes." Finnegan pulled a cigar from his pocket. "How long have you worked for Stuart?"

"Well, that's hard to say. Sometimes, over the years, we been partners. Sometimes we pursued our own interests. I reckon now I am working for him. Although, it could be argued that we're both just working at not going broke and not starving. This whole damn ranching operation we've been laboring at is propped up with other men's money, other men's land; hell, I don't even own this horse I'm riding, and neither does Granville." He laughed. "We been working at getting rich since I met them Stuart boys back in California, and I think after all them years we might have finally stumbled across the venture that will make us permanent paupers." He spit down into the sage. "This one I just can't wrap my head around."

Finnegan gave the man a quizzical stare. "The cattle business does not appear overly complicated to me, Mr. Anderson. What is the cause of your consternation?"

"Oh, it's only that, of all the foolish damn endeavors me and Granville have tried our hand at over the years, this is that first where we are attempting to turn a profit, but not such a profit as to make the business appear worth possessing."

Finnegan got his cigar lit and stared over at his guide. "I am afraid I do not follow, Mr. Anderson."

"Right now, Granville and me don't actually own so much as a dollar's worth of the ranch business. I can't lay claim to a bit of it, and what Granville claims is nothing more than clever bookkeeping. His part of this venture is bought with money borrowed from Davis and Hauser. All we're really getting out of this is room and board and the honor of chasing these damned cows around."

Finnegan shook his head. "I would assume Mr. Stuart is merely looking forward several years. If the venture becomes profitable enough, he will pay down the money borrowed and own a substantial portion of a very profitable enterprise."

"Ah, yes, but there is where we find the rub, sir." Anderson grinned as if he knew some very fine secret. "Since you are new here, you may not be aware, but it is very fashionable these days for princes and potentates to own cattle ranches."

"I recently made the acquaintance of a Frenchman who could make that boast."

"Yes, well, if our enterprise becomes overly profitable our financial patrons may decide that it would be better to take the money and run, rather than continuing the hazard of owning cattle on a range that seems to always be experiencing some sort of catastrophe."

"Catastrophe?" Finnegan had heard no such talk from the esteemed members of the Stock Grower's Association.

"There is no damn end to the contention in this place, Mr. Gilhooley. When winter comes, we all collectively hold our breath, waiting to see if the blizzards have carried all the cattle away or smothered them under drifts. Now that spring has arrived, it is time to indulge in the rancor that is the roundup. All the rich men will argue over the calves until they grow weary at each other's throats. When they can no longer form speech to accuse each other, they will blame the less-than-expected increase on the Indians or rustlers. By the time that is settled, there is a chill in the air and the whole process must begin again. In truth, I sometimes long for the good old days when the men of this territory simply got drunk and murdered each other. At least there was a definite end one could count on."

"The increase in the size of the herds is not always what you hope for?"

Anderson laughed and dug a bag of chewing tobacco out of his pocket. "Give me a moment to think on how I should answer that, Mr. Gilhooley." He stuffed a wad of the tobacco into one cheek. "Let me put it this way: I have been at this ranching profession, along with Granville, for some years now. In all that time I have no damned clue how many cows we might possess. I have no reason to believe Granville might know any better. Oh, certainly, he can tell you down to the last calf what is listed in his ledgers, but, well..." Anderson motioned about the horizon before returning his bag of tobacco to one pocket. "Look this place over, sir. Can you conceive of any way to know how many of any damn thing are in it?"

"That would pose something of a difficulty." Finnegan mused for a moment. "Mr. Anderson, what would you suggest, if a man owed a certain amount of the increase on any given herd, much the same way Mr. Stuart might be owed a third of the cattle on the DHS range?"

Anderson rubbed his chin. "Uh, well, you mean if you was wanting to make sure that you didn't end up being the fellow who had to get stuck making up the difference between what's on the books and what's out there gnawing grass?"

"Precisely, yes."

"Well, if it was me on the hook, I believe I would do much as Granville does. See there ain't just discrepancies amongst the partners, there's always a bit of consternation between the ranches, as well. That's why the DHS gets out in front of every roundup. We find what should be ours, loosely speaking, of course, and leave the rest for the next fella to ponder over. I imagine there's a few small outfits down toward the bottom of the barrel that have a mighty tough time finding their stock. On the other hand, nobody ever said this world was fair." Anderson grinned with his cheek puffed out. "If it was me, I'd see to it that my cows got cut out and delivered first. That's the only way a man can end up with more than faith in his pocket in this damn country."

"I appreciate the advice, Mr. Anderson." They dropped down into a narrow ravine. Anderson fell in behind Finnegan and did not come up on his side again until they were in the bottom of the draw.

"You considering entering into the cattle business, Mr. Gilhooley?"

"Considering, yes."

"It's odd you might say that. I've always had a thought toward entering into the Pinkerton business. I don't suppose you'd be interested in switching up for a spell?" Anderson grinned again.

Finnegan chuckled. "I am sorry to have to be the one to inform you, Mr. Anderson, but I believe you mentioned you have a rather large family, and the pay for detectives is not nearly enough to support a brood such as yours."

Anderson shook his head. "No, sir, you misunderstand

me. When I spoke of switching up, I meant a switch in all aspects. You may take over my brood and I would take possession of that drunken Irishmen and guide him back to Chicago, if that is where he would wish to go."

"Ah, I see. You do not think your wife might have something to say about such an arrangement?"

Anderson waggled one finger at Finnegan. "I have already contemplated that, and have come to the conclusion that it should not matter much, to you, at any rate. She might squawk a great deal, but you wouldn't keen a word of it. My wife's an Indian, same as Granville's. Picked her up in the Deer Lodge way back when."

"In all this time she has not learned English?"

"It's more like she don't care to. I suspect she knows what she's hearing just fine, just won't lower herself to talking like a white woman."

"I'm curious, sir, what variety of Indian have you and Granville taken for wives?"

Anderson pulled his hat off and scratched his head. "The answer to that one ain't as simple as you might think. Uh, how best to explain that one?" He spit out a long stream of tobacco juice. "I would assume there's been more than one time in your life when being an Irishman gave you some trouble?"

"On occasion, yes."

"So, maybe to avoid that trouble you might have told folks you were English or American or what have you?"

"It has never been the case with me in particular, but I have known more than a few men from Cork who claimed to be Welsh or Scots to gain employment at one time or another."

"The red man is prone to the same set of fibs, when it suits them."

"I doubt anyone would believe an Indian was Welsh." Finnegan knocked ash from his cigar and smiled.

Not noticing the jest, Anderson continued. "No, they don't pretend to be Welsh, but they'll often claim to be a type of injun they ain't. Most of it depends on which type of Indian might give them the best advantage. I recall right after Custer got his hair lifted, every red man in this country was Sioux and every buck claimed to have Custer's own hair hanging back at his lodge pole. Hell, I heard ten-year-old boys claim to be the one that scalped him, all the way up to eighty-year-old crones. Didn't matter what tribe they was. For a spell there, they tried to get every white man to think they was Sioux." He laughed. "After the rest of the Army showed up, couldn't find a one that didn't claim to be Crow."

"And why was that, Mr. Anderson?"

"The Crow had thrown in with Custer, don't you know?"

Finnegan shook his head and marveled. "I am afraid I am unfamiliar with the affiliations of most Indian tribes. I had always heard that there were some Cherokee who sided with the south during the war, although I have heard of others who fought for the Union."

"Well, that's more than I can claim. I didn't fight for neither, nor would I. The way I figure, what happens in the States is none of my damn business and most injuns feel the same. Now then...oh, right, you was asking what kind of Indian my wife is. See, the complication comes into play when you take into account that her daddy was just about the orneriest old scoundrel I ever had the misfortune to trade hides with. He claimed up and down to be a Shoshone, but I always suspected they was really Flathead or Blackfoot, and he just went with Shoshone around that time to keep his backside out of trouble, what with the Blackfoot lifting so much hair right around then."

Finnegan slowly nodded and dropped his cigar butt

down into a puddle in the gully floor. "So, you suspect your father-in-law may have given you false information as to your wife's heritage?"

"Damn right I do, and it ain't as if I could hope to get a better assessment from her. Sullen wench once told me..." Anderson snapped his mouth shut as they rounded a bend in the gully. There, not fifty feet in front of them, three men were gathered around what remained of a dead cow.

Finnegan brought his horse to a stop next to Anderson and looked over the three amateur butchers. In all his days, from coal country to Missouri pig farms, he was not certain he had ever seen three more filthy fellows. They looked to be covered in several months' worth of grime, to say nothing of the fresh filth deposited on their ragged clothes from the recently chopped-up steer. Finnegan leaned over toward Anderson, grimacing at the sight of the three. "Are these men...cowboys?"

Reece Anderson swallowed a good portion of his tobacco. "Not precisely, sir. They're most likely rustlers."

Finnegan pointed to the remnants of the bovine. "How do you know the animal does not belong to them?"

"Well, I reckon if a man owns a cow, he butchers it in his own damn barn or some such, not some damn hole out in the middle of nowhere. How's that for deducing, mister detective, sir?"

Finnegan sighed. "I see. Thank you for pointing that out." The three men were standing about the butchered cow staring at Finnegan and Anderson much in the same way the two stared back at them. "Would you say, Mr. Anderson, there is a good chance that animal was formerly the property of one of the members of the Stock Grower's Association?"

"Might have belonged to U.S. Grant for all I know. What the hell difference does that make?"

"The difference being that I have not been employed to

protect the property of every homesteader or settler in this territory. The property of those men in the Association is my only concern."

From the sound of the grunt, it appeared as though Anderson had swallowed the remainder of his tobacco. "Ah, hell, you're gonna have a concern and then some here in a minute; they gone and decided."

"Those filthy tramps will decide nothing, sir."

"You just keep thinking that. There's three of them, two of us, and I can't shoot worth a damn." Anderson straightened up in the saddle as the largest and presumably toughest member of the butchers approached."

The ragged man in bloodstained coveralls held a weather-beaten shotgun in his hands and smiled up with very few teeth. "How does the day find you boys?"

Finnegan stared down. "Well enough, sir." He looked over the man and the two others. The two who stood near the dead cow had produced rifles. "Will you give us the road, sir?"

"Ain't no road. This here's a gully, our gully. I'm of a mind you ought to pay a tithe for roaming down it."

"Ah, hell." Anderson removed his hat and scratched his head once more. His rifle was tied down in a scabbard and he wore no pistol. For all intents and purposes, he had little choice but to do as the ruffian requested. He leaned toward Finnegan. "If we're real lucky, we can walk to the Gap and that'll be the extent of this."

"I am not walking anywhere in this bloody country." Finnegan smiled down at the man and swung his leg over the saddle, dismounting with the animal between him and the ruffian. Finnegan looked at the man over the saddle. "Sir, there is no need for this particular bit of foolishness." He pulled a cigar from his pocket. "I will even go so far as to acknowledge that this is your declivity and offer you three cigars as a fee for the passage."

The ruffian smirked. "You talk mighty fancy, mister. I'm afraid we charge fancy talkers a bit more than three measly smokes. I believe we're going to be needing that fancy shotgun in your scabbard," he pointed to the Purdey. "And the gun on your hip, and both your horses."

A man yelled from back by the dead cow. "You tell them dandies they ain't leaving here with them pretty clothes and boots."

Finnegan sighed again. "Sir, before we engage in the last act of this senselessness, I really must ask you a question."

The ruffian offered up what he could for a smile. "Ask away."

"We passed a perfectly fine-looking set of ponds not more than a handful of miles from here. Why not make use of them?"

"Use of 'em?"

"And therein may lie the answer." Finnegan pulled his Remington and shot the ruffian between the eyes. His horse jumped and took a step forward. One of the men further back raised a rifle and fired. The bullet struck Finnegan's horse in the rump and the poor animal fell into a sitting position. Finnegan took careful aim on the man and fired. The shot hit the fellow in the shoulder and spun him. Seeing that he had obtained some sort of hit, Finnegan moved the pistol's sight over to the remaining man who had a rifle of his own raised. The Pinkerton squeezed the trigger and saw the man hunch. One more round sent him to the ground. Without the slightest pause, Finnegan moved his gaze over to the man he had wounded. That fellow had dropped his rifle, but was fumbling to pick it up. "Leave that be, fool." In spite of the admonishment, the man knelt to get the gun. Finnegan fired and the man fell down into the alkali dust of the gully floor.

"Sweet Jesus preserve us." Anderson sat still as a statue in the saddle. His only movement during the fight had been a slight struggle to keep the horse beneath him from bolting.

Finnegan holstered his Remington and drew the Colt Frontier from its shoulder holster. He stalked forward and shot both men again for good measure. That done, he returned to his wounded horse and shot it in the head. The animal flopped into the sand and shook for a moment before quieting for good. Finnegan looked up at his guide. "It seems that every time I find a decent mount some fool comes along and maims or kills it. Poor beast."

Anderson sat and blinked toward the corpses. "You...you killed them."

"Yes." Finnegan removed three empty brass cases from the Colt and replaced them with live rounds, then carefully rotated the cylinder so that the empty chamber was under the hammer. He holstered the Colt and moved onto reloading his Remington in a similar manner. "Do you believe they may have confederates in the area?"

"Confederates? I do not know; they may have been Confederates."

"What?" Finnegan stared up at the shocked fellow. "I am asking if you think there may be any more of them, damn it."

Anderson shook his head. "I...I know as much as you do."

"Yes, well. In the event there are others, we must keep a wary eye. Dismount and help me get my saddle off this animal and select one from among theirs."

"Um, yes. Yes, of course." Anderson swung down from the saddle. "Do you...do you wish to take any of their traps?"

Finnegan gave the first ruffian's rotten old gun a kick. "You may review them if you wish. I doubt there is much of value here. I suppose we must take all the horses, whether they are glue bags or not. We cannot simply leave them out here."

"Right, yes." Anderson staggered forward while staring at the corpses.

"Oh, yes, while you are about that, see if you recognize the brand on that dead cow. Perhaps we can inform the owner as to what became of it."

"Yes, right." Anderson was a deathly shade of pale.

"Are you feeling all right, sir? You were not hit, were you?"

"No, Mr. Gilhooley, I am fine. It is just...I have never seen so many men killed so quickly."

"Then this was a new experience for both of us. I do not believe I have ever killed men so soiled. I have seen dogs that took more care in their appearance or cleanliness. They did not even bother to keep their guns clean. Something like this was bound to happen to such slovenly men eventually."

In the wide empty space of the Judith Gap, the wagons had been visible from many miles off. Almost the moment Finnegan and Reece Anderson had approached, Stuart had noticed that Finnegan was mounted on a new horse and had collected two additional animals. At that point, Anderson had rattled off the story, with only a few well-placed embellishments. Finnegan had long since grown weary of correcting such accounts, so he did not bother editing Anderson's tale.

"Well, if that don't about beat all." Stuart sat on his horse and stared over at the gunman. "You got all three without taking any lead yourself?"

Finnegan shrugged. "They did manage to kill my horse. Or mortally wound it, rather." He motioned to his new mount. "This one seems a poor replacement. It is in dire need of kindness and feed."

Stuart looked the animal over. "They must have either

been very poor horse thieves or so greedy they sold all the good ones. Don't fret, some care and grain and that mare will serve." He turned to Anderson. "What brand was on the cowhide?"

"Wells."

"Huh. Good to know we're not the only ones suffering." Stuart chuckled. "Three fewer horse thieves and cattle rustlers in the territory and we are not even home yet. You may prove to be worth your pay, Mr. Gilhooley."

"That damn well depends on which pay you are referring to, does it not, sir!" Kilkenny sat in the uncovered rear of the Conestoga with a very disgruntled look on his face. "You were supposed to be off shooting turkeys, not villains. How is it possible that you manage to shoot someone every time you leave my sight? This trip has been unbearably boring for days on end and the second you get off by yourself you find some fellows to murder. Damn you, Finnegan; I begin to suspect you are doing this on purpose."

"It was quite something to see, Mr. Kilkenny." Anderson's eyes were wide. "I ain't never seen the like. He just stood there shooting at them like they wasn't armed and trying to shoot back. I seen a man get more agitated at the dinner table." Anderson adjusted himself in the saddle. "Although, I have to say, if I had a choice in the matter, I would have happily let you accompany Mr. Gilhooley and stayed here to stare at the backside of that mule some more. The entire experience was a bit unsettling."

Stuart sneered. "You seen men get shot before. You seen men hang in Virginia City. What was different about this?"

"It was just..." He leaned away from Finnegan and toward Stuart. "He just shot 'em like he was digging a post hole or something, like it was his job."

"It is his job, you damn fool." Stuart laughed and gave his

horse a kick. "Sure as hell didn't drag him out here because I needed help with the branding."

Anderson hollered after his boss. "I guess I just got a hard time understanding how the fella can gun down three men like he's lightin' a cigar, but for some reason he damn near soils himself when he bumps into a moose."

Finnegan gave Reece a cold glare. "I did not nearly soil myself."

Chapter 10

DHS RANCH, MONTANA TERRITORY

June 9th, 1884

It might have been that Finnegan had expected more from the ranch after viewing the very fine mansions so many men had constructed in Helena. If stone was not available, Finnegan had been expecting some version of the plantation houses of the south. Instead, the DHS Ranch featured nothing but a series of low, single-story buildings constructed from what appeared to be the local timber and any sort of lumber the inhabitants could lay their hands on. There was a large main house that Stuart and his family lived in that was a sprawling set of rooms, obviously added on to as need demanded. Beyond that was a slightly smaller house, constructed from equally eclectic material, that sheltered Reece Anderson's family. The place was completed by two long, thin buildings that reminded Finnegan of barracks, but Stuart referred to them as bunkhouses.

The population of the ranch was larger than Finnegan had thought it would be, as well. It seemed that there was no end to the children who roamed around in the fields and creek bottoms. Finnegan assumed that they were all offspring of either Stuart or Anderson, but found it impossible to tell which was which as they all seemed to move between the houses at whim. In addition to the children, there were some half dozen adult women who could be seen about their daily chores. Finnegan had been introduced to Stuart's wife, Awbonnie, but the woman had never uttered a word to him. She had only nodded and returned to her washing. Finnegan could only assume the other women were relatives or adult children of...someone. The list of denizens was rounded out by the cowboys who had begun to come in to prepare for the annual roundup of the cattle.

Finnegan and Kilkenny were given their own quarters in one of the bunkhouses that the cowboys had not laid claim to yet. Since Finnegan anticipated spending most of his time in the field, either chasing specimens or chasing horse thieves, he was not overly concerned regarding the state of their lodgings, but Kilkenny found himself quite perturbed.

"Finnegan, this is rapidly becoming intolerable." The whiskey baron sat on the lower level of one of the bunkbeds built into the walls of the building.

Finnegan placed one of his bags next to another bunk. "Becoming? Ephraim, we have been here a few mere hours. It has already worn your patience thin?"

"Well, it is simply that I had not been expecting such... such rustic conditions."

"Ephraim, you have spent many, many hours recounting your trips through primordial jungles and endless deserts. Now, you would have me believe this reasonably clean and dry dwelling is unacceptable?"

"Finnegan, it is one thing to portage through the wilderness, it is quite another to live completely without a staff. Where am I to locate someone to properly handle my laundry or prepare something that can reasonably pass for food? Have you ever seen the condition of either the clothing or victuals of the American aborigines?"

"Members of that headhunter tribe you are always going on about offered finer fare and starching?"

"Well..." He shrugged. "In those situations, there were at least other attributes to the society that made life interesting and quite tolerable."

Finnegan sighed. "Ephraim, are you having a fit for no other reason than you suspect every woman in this place is either not of age or spoken for by some fellow with a gun?"

"You must admit, it does not offer much in the way of possible diversion." The whiskey baron threw himself onto his bunk. "What am I to do with my time when I am not chasing horse thieves with you?"

"Chasing horse thieves? With me?" Finnegan shook his head. "Had it crossed your mind to locate a few of your specimens? Was that not the stated purpose of this entire outing?"

"Oh, you are a nag, Finnegan. We can collect the mundane specimens I require at any time. I am in the mood for some excitement, not more gutting and scraping of hides. I grew bored just preparing your moose hide."

Finnegan rubbed the bridge of his nose. "Well, I doubt you will be able to locate any lewd women to keep company with, Ephraim. It would appear your flask will be your sole solace."

Kilkenny groaned at the prospect. "There is nothing so terrible as boredom. When is it you would like to begin chasing these horse thieves?"

Finnegan began unpacking his bag and rolling out his bedding on the bunk. "I do not know, precisely. I suppose that will depend on what sort of intelligence Stuart can provide as to their location." He paused. "Ephraim, you do understand that I cannot guarantee your safety if you accompany me in the apprehension of these scoundrels? I may have made light of their particular occupation, but that does not mean they are not dangerous. A man can be killed by all type and manner of ruffian. The fact that these men are of meager means and, likely, not overly bright, should not be taken to mean that they are not capable of viciousness. It has been my experience that, if anything, a true idiot is more dangerous."

"Oh, piffle." Kilkenny chuckled. "I am certain you will provide ample protection."

Finnegan stared hard at his friend. "I just finished explicitly telling you that I cannot."

"You are exaggerating, I am sure. It is simply in your nature to be...dull, and as such, you feel the need to keep others from enjoying themselves."

"What about chasing horse thieves do you believe you will find enjoyable?"

Kilkenny's eyes narrowed, as though he felt he had already thoroughly explained himself. "I have told you that I wish to witness a genuine American gunfight and I wish to see a man shot. Is there some aspect of my wishes I am not being clear about?"

"I am merely..." Finnegan paused to find the correct phrasing. "I am having difficulty grasping why it is that you have such an interest in such things, Ephraim. But, then again, I am hardly the fellow who should cast stones when it comes to otherwise bizarre behavior." Finnegan shrugged. "Just so it is understood: if you are maimed or injured following me after these horse thieves, I will not consider it to be due to a failure on my part. You have been warned, Mr. Kilkenny."

"Posh. You are not the first man to warn me. Now, if I were to heed the warning, that would be of note."

"Ephraim, I must say, even for a madman, you are unique."

The whiskey baron nodded. "Yes, I vividly recall, when I first considered a descent into madness, I came to the conclusion that there would be little value to the endeavor if it was not original."

"That *would* be something you would ponder before going mad." Finnegan chuckled and then turned toward the bunkhouse door where he had heard a knock. Reece Anderson stood in the doorway. "Mr. Anderson, come in, please."

Anderson entered and stood a few feet inside. "Uh, if you are all more or less settled in, Granville would like you to come and dine with his family this evening."

Kilkenny slowly raised himself from the bunk. "Ah, yes, Mr. Anderson, I believe some solid food would agree with me." He rubbed his face. "Mr. Anderson, I am told there is a fort near here?"

Anderson nodded. "Yes, Mr. Kilkenny. Fort Maginnis."

"Ah, excellent." Kilkenny turned toward Finnegan. "Perhaps we can travel there and do a bit of hiring at our earliest convenience."

Finnegan plucked his hat from the bedpost. "Hiring?"

Kilkenny nodded again. "It has been my experience that where there are soldiers, there can generally be found a reasonable supply of valets for hire. At a minimum, there are bound to be a few prostitutes."

Finnegan groaned. "Ephraim, stealing another man's prostitute seldom produces a result less fierce than stealing another man's woman."

Kilkenny's face twisted into a look of perfect offense. "Sir, I would never, never stoop so low as to steal a lewd woman from my fellow man. Most assuredly, I would never do such a thing here in this howling wilderness where a replacement would be near impossible to obtain." He stretched out his back and grew slightly calmer. "I simply meant to suggest that a prostitute, when not engaged in her normal duties, can act as a fine valet or washwoman. Oftentimes they find the diversion a pleasant one."

Finnegan groaned yet again. "Mr. Anderson, please lead the way to the evening repast."

Sitting at the Stuart family table, Finnegan was reminded of the fact that it was very hard to say who might constitute the Stuart family. That evening, the family or families had been split so that younger children and a few of the younger adults sat around a table in the kitchen, while the older people were seated in what passed for the main dining hall of the house. As Finnegan patiently waited for the food to be served, his gaze wandered down to the table itself. He noticed that it was comprised of large planks held in place with carriage bolts.

"It is designed so that it can be easily removed, sir."

Finnegan looked across the table to the source of the feminine voice. It belonged to a woman of about twenty with long black hair. She bore a striking resemblance to Stuart's wife. "I see." He smiled to the young lady. "Do you feel the need to remove the dining room table often?"

"Only when we wish to skate."

Finnegan leaned across the table a bit, thinking he had misheard. "Skate, miss?"

"Roller skating, sir." She motioned downward. "This room serves a dual purpose."

For the first time Finnegan took note of the floorboards which had been lacquered and waxed very close to a mirror finish. He looked up to notice that a railing ran around the entire room roughly four feet above the floor. "That is quite interesting, young miss."

"We grew to enjoy skating when we lived in Helena.

There was a public rink there that we frequented. When we moved here to the ranch we missed the pastime, so father had this put together for us." She gave a small nod. "My name is Katie Stuart."

Finnegan nodded in return. "Finnegan Gilhooley, ma'am."

She smiled. "You will have to excuse me, Mr. Gilhooley. I have heard a great deal about you since you arrived. I hope you do not consider it gossip mongering; it has been quite difficult not to hear most of it."

Finnegan smiled again. "I would not think there would be too much regarding myself to discuss."

The young lady rather blithely shrugged. "I am told that you killed no less than three horse thieves on your way here and intend to court the school mistress in Maiden."

"I...well, that might be one way of putting it."

"I am sorry to have heard your business secondhand, sir, but I find it terribly romantic."

"The shooting of horse thieves?"

"Your following of the school mistress this far. It is much like something out of a book with knights and ladies."

Finnegan laughed a little to keep from blushing. "It is hardly anything like that, miss. The school mistress you refer to and myself are old friends. I have not seen her in some time and wish to have a visit with her while I am in the area. I assure you, I will be slaying no dragons to win her heart." He smiled. "Miss Meagher never did have much fancy for heroics, at least not in the traditional sense. I doubt she would welcome a slayed dragon, even if one could be produced." He took a potato bowl from Kilkenny and spooned a few onto his plate. "Are you an acquaintance of Miss Meagher?"

"Oh, yes. She was one of my tutors in Helena and now we trade books a great deal. She has the mail agent from the railroad talked into bringing her many of the eastern newspapers. They are dropped in Bozeman and the freight man with the Army contract brings them to the fort."

Finnegan shook his head and passed the potatoes further along. "Molly has always been terribly fond of her papers. It does not surprise me that she has found a method to continue her subscriptions here in the territories. She is a font of information on all subjects."

"I have been quite astounded by the breadth of her knowledge on several occasions, Mr. Gilhooley." She placed a biscuit on her plate and grinned shyly. "Are you planning to visit Miss Meagher soon, sir?"

"That is my intention, yes."

"I would very much like to accompany you, sir. It has been some time since I have had occasion to visit with Miss Meagher and, of course, there are certain items that are always better procured from the mercantile by a woman. Whenever one of the hands is sent, what we receive bears little resemblance to what has been requested."

"I can see how that might be vexing." Finnegan shrugged and took a biscuit for himself. "I would assume you are the eldest daughter of Mr. Stuart?"

"Yes."

"Well, then, I would be more than happy to have you accompany me to Maiden when I go to visit Miss Meagher. That is, so long as your father voices no objection."

The young woman laughed. "Sir, I have just passed my twenty-third birthday. My father no longer holds sway over my movements."

Finnegan forked a large piece of pork onto his plate and passed the platter. Finnegan had to grin at her comment. "Young women are fond of pointing out that it is no longer proper for their fathers to scold them after a certain age. I would like to point out that it is not your being scolded that I might worry over. As I see it, a father has the right to say which gentleman escorts his daughter about, at any age. If nothing else, holding to this policy keeps me from trouble in one aspect of life."

"Given the amount of trouble you find, I can understand how you might wish to minimize such things. I will secure permission from my father before we leave."

"That would be appreciated."

Kilkenny leaned over as he passed a bowl of beans. "Miss Stuart, hello, my name is Ephraim Kilkenny. It is an absolute pleasure to make your acquaintance."

She grinned. "And you, sir. To think, this morning I had never laid eyes on an Irishman and now I am personally familiar with two. I must say, you men have lovely accents."

"I am glad you enjoy our lilt, miss." Kilkenny purloined a biscuit. "Are you knowledgeable about the town of Maiden to a great extent?"

"As much as one can be. It is not a large town, Mr. Kilkenny."

"Is there a laundry operating there?"

"One, yes. It is run by a Chinese woman, as far as I know. I have never had cause to employ her services."

"So, you have no idea what kind of wash she performs?"

"No, sir. Here we have always done our own washing."

"Ah, yes. That, young lady, is precisely what I wish to avoid."

Chapter 11

DHS RANCH, MONTANA TERRITORY

June 11th, 1884

THE MORNING OF THEIR OUTING TO MAIDEN, TEDDY Blue Abbott hitched a team of mules to one of the large Conestoga wagons. The group traveling to Maiden would include the young Mr. Abbott, Finnegan, and Kilkenny, who hoped to have some luck recruiting for the entourage he had been missing since leaving Chicago. Two of Stuart's daughters, Katie and Mary, would accompany the men. Katie had insinuated that Teddy, in the last year or so, had taken to accompanying Mary at every opportunity.

Finnegan turned out wearing what passed for his Sunday best after so much traveling. Once again, he had carefully seen to the cleaning of his guns so that they would be especially presentable. He was cinching down the saddle on his horse when Granville Stuart approached holding a coffee cup in his hand. "Good morning, Mr. Stuart." Finnegan noticed that the man did not appear to be readying for a journey. "You will not be accompanying us today, sir?"

Stuart shook his head and cast a wary eye toward Teddy and Mary, who stood jesting to one another by the wagon. "No, I will not. There are more than a few personages in

Maiden I do not get along with in perfect harmony." He sneered down into his coffee. "It is nothing of much import, but there is never a good reason to aggravate a situation more than a man must. I prefer to stay about the place today." He motioned toward his daughter and her young suitor. "I would never go so far as to ask you to act as a chaperone, Mr. Gilhooley -- something tells me you might not be well-suited to the chore -- but could you see to it that my daughters return without wedding bands or children of their own?"

Finnegan chuckled. "That should be an attainable goal, so long as they are only in my charge for the one or two days." He finished tightening the saddle and gave the horse a comforting few pats. Spending most of his life riding rented or borrowed stock had made Finnegan both kind and watchful when it came to horses. He had long since discovered that the better he treated any given beast, the less were the chances of being maimed.

"I see you have elected to carry your full complement of pistols."

"I would prefer to pass through the rest of my life without conflagration, but that is hardly my choice."

Stuart nodded. "I only mention it because I would prefer it was minimized in the vicinity of my daughters."

Finnegan grinned. "How would you suggest I keep rings from their fingers without my guns, sir?" He could see the father did not appreciate the humor. "It has been my experience that even the most drunken of fools has the decency to abstain from gunplay in the company of decent women. I do not foresee a problem."

"Yes, good." Stuart sipped his coffee. "That brings me to a small piece of advice I would like to offer you."

"Well considered advice is always welcome."

Stuart rubbed his chin. "Kilkenny made mention of the

altercation you had with some former Confederates in Coulson during your trip here."

Finnegan nodded. "Yes. The men thought I was someone I was not and...it cost them dearly. It is unfortunate how some men act without thinking."

Stuart nodded. "They were hardly the first men to let their passions carry them away, and they will not be the last. That is what I wish to discuss with you. You have mentioned you fought for the Union."

"Yes, although I do not recall being offered an alternative."

"Well, pressganged or not, you should know that a great deal of the men inhabiting this territory fought for the south." Stuart shrugged. "Several of the gold rushes occurred after their cause was lost and I suppose this seemed a fine place to begin again. At any event, there are a great deal of Confederate sympathizers about, both in Maiden and even among the men serving at the fort. For many, one army is as good as the next. What I am getting at here, Mr. Gilhooley, is that if you wish your time here to be as peaceable as possible, it may be practical to avoid mention of your service to the Union. Given the affiliation, you may also wish to avoid mentioning your pursuit of the James brothers."

Finnegan had to admit the man had a point. "Mr. Stuart, the problem I have found with reputation is not so much that it is difficult to build, but that it is near impossible to conceal once constructed. Modifying it is no small feat, either. I am seldom the fellow who mentions my history. That being said, I will do my best to keep matters dull while I am about this place. I have no intentions of ruffling anyone more than is absolutely necessary to complete my work. As I have told you, I may wish to make my home in this area someday. That would be a much more enjoyable experience if the residents do not intend to lynch me."

"That is excellent to hear, sir." Stuart rubbed down the horse's neck with his free hand. "Are you looking forward to seeing your schoolteacher?"

Finnegan took a seat on the hitching rail. "It rather reminds me of the day I heard the elder Mr. James had turned himself in to the authorities."

Stuart let out a small laugh. "The two instances have something in common?"

"Yes, of course. On the one hand, it is good for the day you have waited for to finally arrive. It is quite a fine thing to finish a task begun long ago. On the other, it does give one some anxiety to wonder what may be next. It is not always bolstering to catch what you chase."

THE ROLLING GRASSLANDS would have appeared endless if not for the rising of the Judith Mountains in the distance. While there did appear to be a physical limit to the grass where it was replaced by trees in the mountains, no one would have suggested there was an end to the possibilities for raising cattle. It would be hard to imagine that the lush, ever-expanding, knee-high grass could ever be consumed in totality. From what Finnegan could gather during the trip from the ranch to Maiden, there could be hardly any strictures on the number of cows that could thrive and multiply on such lands. As he approached the town he had traveled so far to visit, he felt quite confident little stood between him and the better life first envisioned on the train to meet Frank James in his jail cell.

The town of Maiden genuinely met the criteria to own up to the term community. It had a few streets of slimy mud, over a hundred wooden buildings, and a collection of half-buildings with wooden bases and canvas tops. It had the look of a hastily assembled mining camp, which was just what it was, but hinted at the possibility of a metropolis. The town served only to sell goods to the miners at the prosperous Spotted Horse Mine, and several other less prosperous operations in the area. The small schoolhouse, set a few hundred yards distant from the rest of the miniature city, was proof that more than single men had moved to the frontier. The merchants, ranchers, and even some of the miners had brought their wives and children along with them. The children required education, and that required a teacher.

Teddy Blue Abbott brought the Conestoga to a stop in front of the Belanger Department Store beneath the building's whitewashed sign that read CLOTHING. The large stone edifice looked very impressive next to the neighboring buildings of wood and tarpaulin. The two women appeared absolutely giddy to be close to such an institution. The young man holding the reins sighed. "Mr. Gilhooley, I fear we may be here quite some time." He pointed up the street toward the schoolhouse. "I am told you have business here with an old friend. You may wish to see to that while I linger here. As I said, it will be some time, undoubtedly."

Katie Stuart sat forward in the wagon to stare coyly around Teddy. "Mr. Gilhooley, I am sorry to be the one to tell you that the town's one and only church burned last month. If you find yourself in need of either a preacher or a justice of the peace, both men now operate out of this very store we sit in front of. Would you like me to make any arrangements for you?"

Finnegan withdrew a cigar from his pocket and stared up the street. "I do not believe that will be necessary today, young lady." He lit the cigar and took a few puffs. "I appreciate the offer, nonetheless." He pulled his watch from his pocket. "It is well after noon. What time does the school normally let out?"

Katie tittered. "If there is a set schedule, I am not aware of it, sir. I get the sense that you may have been procrastinating in this endeavor for some time, Mr. Gilhooley. Perhaps you best get to your labors, regardless of the hour."

Finnegan narrowed his eyes and turned to face the girl. "Miss Stuart, are you insinuating some form of cowardice in me?"

"Merely a hesitancy, sir. One I dare say is not in your best interest. Have a nice time at the school." Katie leapt from her seat and clambered down from the wagon. Teddy Blue watched as the two girls disappeared into the store.

The young man shrugged. "As I said, sir, you can almost assuredly find us still here when you complete your business."

"You seem quite certain." Finnegan smiled at his young associate.

"You ever escort young ladies to a large store, Mr. Gilhooley?"

"I cannot say as I have."

"Well, left to their own devices, they would never leave. You honestly could march up that hill, grab that schoolteacher, start a family, and come down the hill to buy your youngest a birthday gift, and still find the Stuart women arguing over what kind of calico to purchase. I don't know what waits for you at that school, sir, but it can't be nowhere near as trying as what I face today."

In the back of the wagon Kilkenny sat bolt upright from where he had been napping. "Good God, have we arrived?" His head swiveled around, looking over the town. "Well, this is quite a going concern, is it not? Surely there must be a tavern of some stripe where a man could procure refreshment."

Finnegan rolled his cigar from one side of his mouth to the other. "Ephraim, from what I have seen, the saloons and taverns of this country are likely places for the type of entertainment most men come to regret. If you are truly in need of a libation to refill your flask, you ought to send Mr. Abbott on the errand." Finnegan turned to the lanky cowboy. "I do hate to place an additional burden on you, sir, but do you think you might be able to keep an eye on Mr. Kilkenny while I am about my business?"

The young man shrugged from his perch on the wagon. "I have little else to occupy me. It shouldn't be a problem."

"I am obliged to you, Mr. Abbott." Finnegan turned back to Kilkenny. "Ephraim, do not draw this young man into dissipation."

Kilkenny appeared insulted. "Certainly not."

"Mr. Gilhooley?" The cowboy seemed confused. "I'm to spend my day sitting right here waiting on women. How much more dissipated can a man get?"

"Hopefully you will not find out. May God bless and keep you, young man." Finnegan gave his horse a small kick and began to meander up the hill toward the schoolhouse. In front of the building, he slowly dismounted and dropped his cigar down into the mud at his feet. Briefly, he paused to adjust his frock coat and guns. There were three steps leading to the school's front door. For some reason, Finnegan felt as though the Stuart contingent might still be watching his movements, so he climbed the steps without the least hesitation. At the door he first grabbed hold of the knob, but then paused and opted to knock instead. At the pounding the voices of several children could be heard within.

After what felt like a rather long wait, the door slowly creaked open and a girl of about nine stuck her red-haired head out. Her freckles stood out against her pale cheeks. She gazed up at Finnegan as if she had rarely seen a tall man before. "I am to ask you what you want, sir."

Finnegan cleared his throat and spoke down to the girl. "I wish to speak with your school mistress."

"What is a mistress?"

"Your teacher, young one."

"I see." The girl stepped forward a bit and stood to her full height so that Finnegan might appreciate the importance of her position. "And who should I say has come to call?"

"Finnegan Xavier Gilhooley."

"That is a great deal of name to carry around, sir."

"It has been no small labor to handle it over the course of my life. Fortunately for you, lass, you need only carry it a short distance to your teacher."

"Very well, sir." The girl curtseyed and disappeared into the building, closing the door behind her. Finnegan waited pensively for a few moments before the girl reappeared and swung the door open. "Miss Meagher says you may enter."

Finnegan gave her a smile. "Thank you, young lady." The girl held the door open, and Finnegan strolled up the center aisle between several rows of desks. At the very end of the rows stood the woman he had come so very, very far to see, Molly Meagher. Finnegan stopped some six feet from her and gave a small bow. "Miss Meagher, I hope I have not called on you at an inconvenient time. I can return later if it would better suit you."

The lady swept back her blonde hair and grinned at her old friend. "Oh, no, Mr. Gilhooley, we should have our visit now. I recall once postponing a visit with you and having you disappear for..." She held up a few fingers counting. "Quite some time, Mr. Gilhooley."

Finnegan shrugged. "I believe I mentioned in my last letter that I intended to visit when I was no longer required elsewhere for my work."

Molly nodded, smirking. "And here you stand."

"Here I stand." Finnegan took a tentative step forward. "I

am glad to find you in good health and circumstances. I..." Finnegan turned, noticing that something had taken Molly's attention behind him. A few rows back a young man of about twelve was waving one hand.

Molly shot the boy a hard look. "Yes, Timothy?"

The boy lowered his hand and glanced back and forth between the two adults, finally settling on Finnegan. "Um, sir, excuse me, but did I hear correctly that you are Finnegan Gilhooley?"

The Pinkerton sighed and pinched the bridge of his nose. "Yes, young man, that is my name."

The boy was beyond thrilled with the news. "Finnegan Gilhooley, the famous Pinkerton agent who has so diligently pursued the James brothers?"

He sighed again. "Yes, young man, the very same."

"Timothy, it is not polite to begin interrogating a man you have just met..." The boy had no time for his teacher's admonitions.

"Sir, I have often read in the *Police Gazette* that you have sworn to chase the James brothers until they are captured or killed, or you fell in the attempt to complete your quest."

"Quest?" Finnegan raised his eyebrows. "Young man, my advice to you would be to take what you read in that periodical with many grains of salt. In my entire life, I have only met a journalist from that paper once, and the man certainly did not collect the litany of quotes attributed to me and spouted off these many years."

The boy sat back in his chair a little from the rough response. "Um, sir, I only ask out of curiosity. It has been some time since I have obtained a copy of the *Gazette*. May I take it from your presence here that you have captured or killed the James brothers?"

Finnegan sighed again. "Jesse James is dead and his

brother who you would know as Frank James is in the custody of the law in Missouri."

The boy appeared elated, once again. "Oh, sir, that is very impressive. Oh, please, I would give anything to hear the tale of how you killed Jesse James."

Finnegan's lip twitched. "I did not kill Jesse James. He was shot in his own home by one of his nefarious confederates. A man named Robert Ford."

"Oh." The boy was unspeakably let down, but he brightened momentarily. "But you did capture Frank James?"

Finnegan scowled. "No. The elder Mr. James turned himself into the authorities."

The boy couldn't quite believe it. "I am sorry, sir, but that is...that is terribly disappointing."

Finnegan nodded. "I assure you, son, however much you lament what might have been, I lament it more."

"Finnegan?" Miss Meagher brought the gunman's attention back to her. "Surely you did not come all this way simply to inform Timothy Jameson as to your progress, or lack thereof."

Finnegan rubbed his chin. "I do not know this boy from Adam; why would that be my purpose here?"

"You are as blithely humorous as ever, Finnegan."

"Ah." He nodded again. "Of course, a jest. I had almost forgotten how you enjoy that sort of thing." He slowly turned to the boy again, who was waving a hand once more. "Yes, young man, what is it?"

"Sir, would you be willing to tell us something of your experiences chasing the James brothers? Even though you were unable to kill or capture them all these years, I am sure it would still be somewhat interesting."

Molly cleared her throat to get the boy's attention. "Timothy, your mother and father did not send you here today, and allow you to shirk your chores, so that you could revel in tripe and stories of trivial detective work."

The boy seemed nonplussed. "Oh, ma'am, I am sure not all of it could have been trivial."

"At any event." Finnegan paused and lessened the edge on his voice. "I would prefer not to discuss the matter this afternoon, young Timothy."

"Yes, perhaps we've discussed more than enough already." Molly clapped her hands together. "That is enough for one day children. You are dismissed."

The majority of the class needed no further permission to flee. They rose up out of their chairs and stormed to the door with the clamor of a retreating army. In bare moments, all had run amok out the front door, except for Timothy Jameson. He glanced about to make sure the other children were no longer in earshot. "Sir, now that the younger kids are no longer present?"

Finnegan shrugged. "Well, I suppose there can be no harm in..."

"Timothy, Mr. Finnegan is not here to regale you with tales you should not be hearing. Be on about your chores."

Finnegan shrugged again and leaned closer to the boy. "I will be in the area for most of the summer. Perhaps another time, young man." The boy grinned at him and leapt to the schoolhouse door in pursuit of his comrades. Finnegan turned back to the headmistress of the school. He took a moment to look the woman over. "It does my heart good to see you again, Molly. It is equally pleasing to find you in such fine feather. I take it your situation here agrees with you?"

"It does, very well." She sighed and shook her head. "It does me good to see you once more, as well." She rubbed her chin and gave him her most quizzical look. "Although, I do not recall writing you after I had made arrangements to come here to the territories. Should I assume that you were merely passing through this particular town, heard my name, and thought to drop in on your old friend?"

He laughed. "Yes, well, I am not certain how much premeditation I should admit to. It may give you a long-standing advantage I can ill afford in our affiliation."

"Ah, Finnegan, always looking for an advantage. However did you find me?"

"I am a detective, lass; finding those I search for is my stock in trade."

She shook one judgmental finger at him. "From what I read in the papers, several months old as they may be, you did not manage to find Frank or Jesse James."

"No, I did not."

She chuckled. "And now you have nothing better to do than travel about harrying schoolteachers and breaking the hearts of poor boys like Timothy Jameson?"

"Oh, if only that were all that occupied my time. As you suggested, I am not here entirely by accident, but I have not arrived in this town purely to visit old friends, either. I come here first, employed as something of a nurse to a naturalist and second, in the employ of a man I believe you know: Granville Stuart."

"Of course, you would make the acquaintance of Mr. Stuart. Who is it he wishes for you to kill?"

Finnegan held up one hand to calm the schoolteacher. "It is not that sort of employment. Mr. Stuart has commissioned me for a short time to investigate the theft of his stock and the stock of the other members of his association. It is truly not much different from what I would find myself doing if I accepted an assignment guarding a mill back in Chicago. It should prove to be quite tedious."

She nodded, not quite believing the statement. "Time will tell." She stooped and picked up a pile of books bound together with a belt. "Did you say you came here with a naturalist?"

"I did."

"And you understand the meaning of that title?"

"I do."

"So, you have come to the wilds of the Montana territory in the company of a scientist studying the behaviors of the local rodents? Upon discovering that your first pursuit did not take up enough of your time, you opted to chase horse thieves for the redoubtable Mr. Stuart?"

"In a nutshell, my dear. I should think you would be pleased to find I am being employed by a man of Mr. Stuart's standing. I am told he may one day go to Washington for the Congress."

Molly grinned. "I should think the citizens of this territory would readily send Mr. Stuart to Congress, if they were given assurances that he would not return."

"It is a fine thing to be loved by your neighbors." Finnegan extended one hand. "May I carry your books, Miss Meagher?"

"Very well, sir." She handed the bundle to him. "Did you ever read the volume of Faust I gave you?"

"Quite thoroughly."

She shook her head again. "Then I would think you would know better than to go about making deals with men such as Mr. Stuart."

"Oh, he is hardly the worst fellow I have ever shook hands with. His association has made me a rather lucrative offer in return for my services. Certainly better than I have ever been offered previously, for work so mundane as rounding up a few horse villains."

"You always had a knack for discovering lucrative arrangements, Finnegan, even if the arrangement only proved lucrative for someone else."

"We all have our cross to bear in this world, Molly." He gripped the books tight and turned toward the schoolhouse door. "If you have errands, I would be honored to escort you. I would also very much like for you to join me for dinner. Assuming, of course, that there is a respectable place to procure a meal in this town."

"I believe I might enjoy an escort, Mr. Gilhooley, and there is more than one establishment in the fair town of Maiden that offers good fare." She extended her arm, and he took it. "Did you truly come here in the company of a naturalist?"

"Oh, quite, yes. It is my duty to guard him against all manner of dangers that continually stalk men of his field. Highwaymen, renegade Indians, moose."

"I was not aware the moose of this territory were well armed."

"You are mistaken on that score, Miss Meagher. They are quite vicious and pose a very real threat, I assure you."

The group settled into a meal, Kilkenny's treat, at the Silver Dollar Café. Molly was pleased to catch up with the women, while Finnegan and Kilkenny spent the meal interrogating Teddy Blue regarding the cattle business and the possibilities for hiring help. When they were all well fed, Kilkenny announced that it was far too late for the trip back to the DHS, so he would be more than happy to provide shelter for the night at one of the local boarding houses. Molly declared there would, most likely, be room at the establishment where she boarded, as the number of transient folks in town was low when the mine was not hiring.

When the meal broke up, the two Stuart women were dropped off at the boarding house to see to the lodgings,

Abbott and Kilkenny traveled off to the northern end of town to locate a man Teddy felt might make a useful servant for Kilkenny, and Finnegan took Molly for a stroll. As the sun slowly sank behind the Judith Mountains, the two enjoyed the warm weather and the breaking of spring.

They crested a small hill and were able to turn and look back on the town. "You must be rather lost these days, Finnegan. Now that you no longer have those ridiculous James brothers to chase."

"I will confess to having some time on my hands, most days. Although, the loss of the James contingent on my dance card has allowed for this journey, so it is probably all for the best."

"It must have been an intriguing journey. I take it Mr. Kilkenny is rather well off?"

"He has the kind of wealth that can only be had in the Irish whiskey business."

She raised one eyebrow. "As for you, I am not surprised to find you are still in the employ of the Pinkerton Agency."

Finnegan gave her a confused look in return. "I have never truly been employed elsewhere." He pulled his hat off and fidgeted with the brim a bit. "All things in this world are subject to change, Molly. I assume you know that."

"Ah, and you suggest to change? Change, even though you are the way you have always been?"

"That is a possibility." Finnegan replaced his hat and took the woman's arm once again. "I believe I mentioned that I am to be rather well reimbursed for my duties here, in regard to the horse thief problem. That reimbursement, supplemented with the money I have saved, should be more than sufficient for me to begin a new venture."

She could not help but smile, rather skeptically. "And what sort of venture would that be, Finnegan?"

"I am giving serious consideration to entering the cattle business."

She laughed and felt the need to clap her hands together. "The cattle business! Oh, the things you men get into your heads."

"I am not jesting, my dear."

"I know you are not jesting. That is what makes the statement so humorous." She patted the gunman's hand. "I do not know if there is a single man in this territory who, regardless of profession or experience, does not think he can enter into the cattle business and find his fortune. A good thing it is, too. If it were not for that particular delusion, towns such as this would not have launderers, hired miners, farmers, or blacksmiths."

"You do not think I would be capable in the cattle business?"

"Well..." she patted his hand again. "I believe I know more regarding cattle than you do, and I only know enough to know I wish to avoid them when they are not being served for dinner."

Finnegan shook his head. "There does not seem to be too much to the matter. So far as I can see, all that is required is to avoid being greedy in the number of cattle turned loose on a range and some other small restraint in certain areas. I am of the opinion that, while it may be difficult to become rich engaged in such a business, it should be relatively simply to make a steady living and provide for a family."

"Mr. Gilhooley, I must say, you have quite the metamorphosis in mind for yourself. First, you presume to leave your lifelong vocation for a settled trade featuring far less excitement. Next, you intend to add a wife and children to this new existence. It should prove to be a stunning transformation. Will you be growing a beard so that your grandchildren will have something to tug at?"

He laughed at the thought. "If that is to your liking, I will surely consider it."

"To my liking?"

"Well, I certainly have no idea who else I might bother to consult."

She gave him the quizzical look once again with a bit of sorrow mixed in. "Finnegan, should I understand that you have traveled all this way and formed this rather mad plan... all with the idea of us marrying?"

"I...well...the thought had crossed my mind."

"Finnegan." She gave his hand a small kiss. "I should have known you might arrive at some farfetched conclusion such as this."

"Farfetched?" He took a step away from her. "What is that meant to mean?"

She smiled in an attempt to comfort him. "It is meant to mean that I see this for what it is, a flight of fancy of yours."

"Flight of fancy? Madam, I have traveled many a long and weary mile to stand before you here. A journey that took no small amount of planning and endeavor. And you would call it nothing more than a lark?"

"Finnegan, do not misunderstand. I...I appreciate the sentiment, I truly do, however..."

"However, what, precisely?"

"It is simply that you have not for a moment, presumably, paused to think this proposition of yours all the way through. You do understand that if you enter into the cattle business you would have to remain in the area where your ranch is located. Permanently."

"Yes, that follows."

"And, naturally, that whoever you endeavored to propagate this intended family of yours with would also be required to remain in the area?"

He squinted his eyes down, preparing to be accosted with

the eventual point she was headed towards "Yes, that follows, as well."

"Finnegan, what in heaven or on earth would ever make you believe that I would wish to remain here rearing children and cows for the rest of my days? If a life of that nature had been my wish, I dare say I could have obtained it in Minnesota with some plowboy."

Finnegan took another step back and rubbed his eyes. "Molly, as is usual, I am afraid I do not understand."

"I am telling you that I have no interest in being a cattleman's doting little wife here in a veritable wilderness."

Finnegan threw his arms in the air. "Woman, you were the pathfinder to this place. I assure you, if the choice had been mine, I would have chosen some locality much closer to a railroad and considerably less infested with bears. You are the one who always dreamed of living in Indian country and ministering to the poor red savages, not I. Now, you have finally made it all the way to your much sought-after goal, and you tell me that you wish to move on most promptly? This must be the sort of thing that drives a man to be a drunkard."

"Finnegan, I did not ask you to chase after me. Have you forgotten that?"

"No, you did not ask anything of me at all. If memory serves, you ceased correspondence with me and scampered off to God-knows-where. You did not even bother to inform your poor mother and father whether you were alive or dead for several months. I would venture a guess that, to this day, you have still not revealed your whereabouts to them."

Molly developed a very stern look and placed one hand on her hip. "You have been in contact with my father?"

"He is worried to distraction over you."

"My father, the very man who so consistently held that you were not the kind to be courting his daughter?"

"When a man's daughter disappears, I would imagine he is quite pleased to look around and discover that a detective has aspirations toward courting."

"This is...this is a conspiracy. That is what I am faced with, a conspiracy of dunces."

"A dunce? I search you out, find you in this vast nothingness, and you have the bitter nerve to call me a dunce? Well..." He straightened his frock coat and pulled down his hat. "Good evening, miss. I hope you are happy in your schoolhouse. You have no need to worry with regards to me bothering you further. A plowboy, indeed." He began walking back down the hill.

Molly sighed. "Finnegan, do not misunderstand." She called out after him, but he refused to stop or turn. "Finnegan, do not be stubborn." He continued on. "Finnegan...what does it matter that there are bears here?" She watched him go and did not call out again.

Chapter 12

JUDITH MOUNTAINS, MONTANA TERRITORY

June 12th, 1884

Finnegan had felt rather surly all morning. He had risen early so as to get his horse saddled and ready without the chance of running into Molly. That seen to, he had ridden to the limits of Maiden and waited there until Teddy Blue, the girls, and Kilkenny had come along in the wagon. Trailing behind them was a stone faced, hulking fellow whose race, color, or creed could not quite be determined simply by looking at him. Not that Finnegan cared. The man possessed the one quality he wished for, which was a quiet tongue.

For many hours and many miles Finnegan did not say a word; it was Kilkenny who finally broke the silence. He moved to the very rear of the wagon and motioned for Finnegan to come near. He sat on the very back of the conveyance and kept his voice low so that the women might not hear. "I did not notice you come into our room last night, my friend, nor discover your bed to have been slept in this morning. Might I inquire as to the events of the previous evening?" He grinned with a knowing air.

"I slept in the stable, and not much at that."

"The...the stable? Whatever for?"

"I was in a foul mood and did not feel the need for company."

"Ahh." He nodded. "So then, the reunion with the fair damsel Miss Meagher did not go as planned?"

"It did not."

"And what would seem to be the barrier between the two young lovers?" He seemed most serious in manner.

"I...she...The woman is not in her right mind."

"Well, Finnegan." The whiskey baron chuckled. "If that is a prerequisite, I fear you shall never marry."

"That will do nicely. I no longer wish to marry."

"No?"

"No." He pulled the brim of his hat down and withdrew a cigar.

"So, then, may I assume that you no longer wish to hunt horse thieves so as to gain a share of the local cattle enterprises?"

"No. I fully intend to both honor that obligation and to enter into the cattle business." He sparked the cigar. "The only substantive change will be that when I do become a successful cattleman and, I would assume, millionaire, I will be spurning the advances of any schoolteachers who may come to call at my mansion."

"I see." Kilkenny pointed to Finnegan's pocket and the Irishman complied. "Many thanks." He put the cigar between his teeth. "Finnegan, is it truly possible, that in a country where every woman's dearest wish is to ensnarl some poor man in marriage, you have traveled so long and so far only to have your proposal rebuffed?"

"That would be one way to describe it."

"You have a strange sort of luck that follows you, Mr. Gilhooley."

"You would call being refused in no uncertain terms luck?"

"Well..." Kilkenny laughed. "I suppose that would depend on your perspective. What I was specifically referring to was the way you seem to so consistently triumph, relatively unscathed, through so many violent altercations, and yet you find it impossible to sell yourself off into bondage as so many men before you have. It would seem, to you, the incredible is commonplace and the ordinary patently unachievable. It is really quite something to observe, Finnegan."

"I am thrilled that it amuses you so."

Kilkenny lit his borrowed cigar. "My friend, you take such things far too seriously. Most men take such things in stride by the time they have reached your years, but I suppose you have little experience in these matters."

"Meaning what?"

"Meaning that women are as changeable as the weather. One moment there are only storm clouds on the horizon, the next, all is serene. A firm rebuttal the previous night may be transfigured into acceptance in a fortnight."

Finnegan thoughtfully puffed his cigar. "Ephraim, you truly believe that?"

"I know it to a certainty. There is nothing more constantly malleable than the favor of a woman."

"If that is the case..." Finnegan knocked ash from his cigar. "If that is so, how can one hope to permanently cohabitate with a lady and preserve any sense of rationality?"

"Ah, now there you have stumbled across one of the great mysteries of mankind. If you discover a solution, I am sure history will record that you were, in fact, the greatest detective to ever live. Surely greater than even Allan Pinkerton."

Stuart had sent Reece Anderson over to the bunkhouse to fetch Finnegan for a meeting. It was getting on in the evening and it had been a long day traveling back to the ranch, but Finnegan had not been in much of a mood to sleep anyway. He followed Anderson over to the biggest of the houses. From the dining room that did double duty as a skating rink, Anderson brought him to the large, slightly sunken room that served as Stuart's study. The ranch manager sat behind his large, homemade desk. The frontiersman was scribbling away at some letter or another, an occupation that seemed to take up most of his time when he was not in the saddle.

A moment or two after Finnegan entered, Stuart raised his head from his correspondence. "Welcome back, Mr. Gilhooley." Stuart placed the letter he had been working on inside a ledger book and closed it. "My daughter tells me you refrained from gunplay during your mutual outing. Thank you for that."

"Contrary to what many might say, I do not necessarily shoot men wherever I go, sir."

"No, I would suppose not." Stuart turned toward Anderson. "Reece, we will not be needing you if you have other duties that need seeing to."

Anderson had moved to sit on a nearby cabinet, but halted halfway down. "Oh; um, all right, Granville." He flashed a putout grimace and walked from the room, closing the door as he left.

"Have a seat, Mr. Gilhooley. We have a few matters to discuss."

Finnegan settled into a homemade chair that proved to be unexpectedly comfortable. He shifted to allow room for his guns between the armrests. "That would probably profit us."

Stuart nodded. "These matters will require great consideration and we should be slow to reach decisions. I take it you are a man given to slow and deliberate consideration -- when circumstances allow, of course."

"I am."

"I first formed that sense about you when I heard of your interest in the schoolteacher." Stuart smiled through his beard. "A man who would chase a girl so far and so long must be a man given to the steadiest of deliberation."

"Yes, well...steady or not, it does not always profit me, but I still believe it is intelligent." Finnegan shrugged.

"Your reunion did not go as planned?" Stuart's eyes narrowed.

Finnegan found a cigar to take refuge in. "It would seem no amount of deliberation can predict the variances of the female heart."

Stuart groaned and cupped his forehead with one weathered hand. "Good grief, it is not another suitor, is it?" He pointed sternly across the desk. "Sir, if you find yourself cuckolded, I fear you will have to simply live with the injury, at a minimum, until your work for the Association has been completed. Any act you commit in the environs of this territory will reflect on the members of the association until that time."

"Mr. Stuart, I will..."

"Mr. Gilhooley, I must insist. I, of all men, can appreciate your need to gun this fellow down, and I doubt the shiftless bastard will be missed much, but..."

"There is no other suitor, Mr. Stuart." Finnegan shook his head and lit his cigar.

"Oh, I see." Stuart smoothed his beard. "Then what is at issue? You seem a decent enough sort, certainly capable of providing. Men of your profession never want for work." He smoothed his beard more fervently and contemplated the gunman. "I do not know if I would go so far as to call you handsome, but you are not ugly and possess the greater number of your teeth from what I can see. You do not indulge in liquor. What more can the daft damsel ask?"

Finnegan rubbed his eyes. "Sir, if I knew the answer to that question, I dare say I would not be pondering the rebuke I received." He puffed his cigar. "Mr. Stuart, I would submit that no two men in the history of the earth have ever found answers to these questions, so perhaps it would be more useful for us to discuss horse thieves."

"Yes, of course. Please excuse me if I strayed into an area that is not of my concern."

"Think nothing of it, Mr. Stuart." Finnegan stood and walked to a large map of the territory hung on one wall. He motioned near to the center of it. "I take it this is the general vicinity."

Granville stood and joined him. "Yes. To the west the range is largely in the hands of Conrad Kohrs and various small holders. To the east are the ranges of men like Roosevelt and that damn duke or whatever he is. Here in the center and ranging north toward the British, this is where the majority of the horse thief bands have elected to base themselves."

"I suppose that reasons." Finnegan leaned in toward the map. "There is no way that you might keep your horse herd closer to the ranch buildings?"

Stuart shook his head. "In Ohio, a man may keep his stock animals close at hand, fat and happy on corn stalks. Here, we are lucky to be able to put up enough hay to keep a few head stabled through the winter for the chores we face during the cold part of the year. It is vexing, to be sure, but there is no remedy."

"I was not asking as a suggestion for a lengthy solution. I have had some luck in the past luring villains. We have put out false intelligence regarding mail shipments and such, and it has proven effective. If we brought a larger herd of horses into this area and kept them here, might these horse thieves not come to us? It would be far less trying than chasing them all over this expanse." He swept his hand across the map.

"The very thought has occurred to me a time or two, Mr. Gilhooley, but I do not believe it would give us the opportunity we would hope for. These marauders are quite skilled at their work. They are also quite good at sensing subterfuge. I have personally encountered them on the range, and they have offered me nothing but hospitality, especially when they know they hold the advantage. They will offer a man coffee one day and rob him blind the next, all the time laboring very hard to assure the world of their complete innocence. This is no common task you face, I assure you, Mr. Gilhooley."

He nodded. "It would appear we will be in company for some time, perhaps it would be best if you called me Finnegan."

"Please call me Granville."

"Very well." Finnegan puffed and stared at the map. "You say these men often band together?"

"Frequently, yes. Though I can only venture that theory based on the number of animals they are making off with. Some of the predations would require a large outfit and a certain degree or organization."

"How many in a large band?"

"Six, perhaps ten, but that is only a guess."

"If that is their practice, the most effective method might be to locate one of these bands. I would assume they must all lay up in a place and then go out to their labors. That would allow them to obtain the horses and more readily sell them."

"Yes, that follows."

"If I can locate one of the bands, we could put together a band of our own, then place the majority of the rascals in custody. Often, even the hardest of scoundrels will surrender when confronted with superior numbers."

"And when they sense the advantage they are given to

fight. Such was the case while we were traveling here, correct?"

"Yes. Those men thought Anderson and I would make for easy prey. Fortunately, they were not very skilled at their business."

"Perhaps they were not, but some are." Stuart left the map and returned to his desk. "There is a man somewhere in this country. Some call him Jack Stringer, others, Stringer Jack. Regardless, it has long been suspected by many here, and I myself have entertained the notion, that this fellow is the lynchpin of all these horse thieves. It is said that he does a steady business with the British Army. It is said he lords over all the varied ruffians who pick at us like carrion birds."

Finnegan turned and smiled. "Ah, yes, the dark puppet master. The devious demon lurking behind the scenery pulling the strings." He shook his head and moved back toward his chair. "There is just such a tale in any location where criminals harass the populace. Fools have been spinning myths about the highwayman and pickpocket king of London for a hundred years or more. I dare say the chap must be rather aged by now. Hardly a week passes that some newspaper in Chicago does not suggest that every hooligan and street urchin in the city is held in thrall and pays a rate to an evil superintendent. They are rumors of smoke and fairy dust, Granville."

"Those instances may be pure hokum, but I have reason to believe this man Stringer may be all the tales cast him to be."

"There are often good reasons to believe such stories. Even my employer, the esteemed Allan Pinkerton has been taken in by a few over the years, but they always prove false in the end. Criminals are very common creatures, Granville. There is no need to invent some Mephistopheles flitting about to explain their actions."

Stuart shrugged. "Well, I suppose we will simply have to locate and capture a few of these bands to see who proves correct."

"That is a point we both agree on." Finnegan knocked ash into the tray Stuart kept on his desk for guests. "What is the distance to the nearest of the other ranches?"

"The closest might be twenty-five miles. There are others out about forty."

"And the cowboys in your employ interact with the cowboys from these other ranches?"

"Frequently, yes."

"So, we may be able to get news of strangers seen on the range or horses being taken?"

"That should be possible." Stuart returned to smoothing his beard. "You are thinking to get on the trail of some thieves and then..."

"Follow them back to their keep." Finnegan stubbed out his cigar. "Once located, we will sweep some of your cowboys together and bring them before whatever bar of justice there is available in this country."

Stuart leaned back in his desk chair. "Finnegan..." He drummed his fingers on the desktop. "Are you dead set on seeing these men adjudicated in the general manner?"

The gunman cracked a smile. "Granville, despite what you may have heard, even contrary to what I may have at moments of passion said myself, I make every effort to bring men, still breathing, before the bar. I consider that trait to be necessary so that I may keep separated from the men I pursue."

Stuart waved one hand. "I understand that, Finnegan, and I did not mean to insinuate otherwise. I only bring the matter up because the system of justice in place here in the territories is not as...well, refined, as the one that has been put in place in the east. Here, a man may be a highwayman one week and the constable the next. Our judges tend to be little more than saloon owners who have discovered that trials, held in the saloon, generate increased sales. Given this level of jurisprudence, I am sure you can understand how the citizens might occasionally take the sentencing of criminals upon themselves." He paused, seeming to think back. "Are you at all familiar with the vigilance committees formed in this territory during the sixties?"

Finnegan rubbed one side of his face. "I am aware they were formed. Such organizations are often formed in unsettled lands or regions far from the rest of civilization. Several like committees have been formed in San Francisco. I am also aware that it has been some time since a similar committee has been formed anywhere. Twenty years have passed, Granville. We were both recently in a fine hotel in a growing city. A railroad line brings goods and news from the east. This is not the untamed wilderness you faced in your youth."

"It is not as much changed as you might imagine."

"Even if it is not, that is no excuse for indulgence in vendettas or other rash behavior. Only a few minutes earlier you chided me for the possible consideration of rash action, as it would reflect poorly on the Association. Tell me, Granville, what stories will appear in the papers if it comes to pass that the richest men in this territory hired a man such as myself to go about and kill twenty or thirty of the poorest residents? How would that reflect on your Association?"

The pioneer nodded. "I follow your logic, Finnegan. You will have to excuse my fervor in these matters." He drummed his fingers a bit more and took a sip of coffee. "I know that horse theft and the illicit butchering of a few cattle must seem of small import to a detective of your experience, but make no mistake, it is of great importance to this territory and those with capital invested in this business. This is a crucial time for cattlemen. If we can churn off great profits now, we will have a chance when the range closes. If we can relieve ourselves of the losses caused by these thieves, profit will increase exponentially. Men with an investment, men such as you, Finnegan, will gain beyond your wildest expectations. We are on the cusp of an endeavor that can make us millions, sir. We simply need to gain and keep control of the range. If we can only manage that, we can feed a nation, and reap all the rewards that successful audacity offers."

"It is a fine picture you paint, Granville. I look forward to helping you bring it to life." He chuckled. "I also look forward to being paid."

Stuart grinned. "That is a moment we both look forward to, Finnegan. Hopefully, your being paid will coincide with my being paid."

Chapter 13

DHS RANCH, MONTANA TERRITORY

June 20th, 1884

WITH NO BETTER OPTION, FINNEGAN SETTLED INTO patrolling the area around the DHS and collecting what few specimens Kilkenny could muster enthusiasm for. Word had been put out to the surrounding ranches that information of suspected rustlers or horse thieves was to be brought to the DHS with all due haste. As always, Finnegan dearly wished he could contrive a more rapid method, but there seemed to be no better alternative to watching and waiting.

The only point of enjoyment came from Finnegan being able to finally cut his teeth doing a bit of hunting. The gunman had used Kilkenny's Marlin to collect two mule deer, a coyote, and a whitetail deer. Finnegan had intended to use the Purdey, but Kilkenny insisted that the big gun would damage the hides too badly. Some of the parts went into Kilkenny's collection, other pieces went into the DHS dinner pot. The area Finnegan had seen around the ranch was beautiful country, and certainly preferable to Chicago. Wandering the earth in untouched country was a fine thing, but Finnegan was not in the mood for recreation. He wanted to get on with his work. He wished to know if he would be able to complete his work and, thus, gain his reward.

He had frittered away a week already when he was told by Reece Anderson that he and Kilkenny had been invited to dinner at Stuart's house once again. In spite of the fact that he had little interest in socializing, he walked to the house with Kilkenny as the sun was sinking in the west.

"You made an excellent shot on that deer today, Finnegan." Kilkenny sipped from his flask in preparation for the abstention he would observe out of politeness during dinner.

"Praise from Caesar." Finnegan waited for the whiskey baron to conceal his flask and then opened the door to the house. "I must admit, there is a certain satisfaction in hunting game. It is good to get a little sport and supply the larder at the same time." They moved through what passed for the foyer and into the dining room that did double duty as a skating rink. "I can understand how you have frittered away so much time..." Finnegan stopped and gaped for a moment when he saw Molly seated at the table. He straightened. "I see we have an additional guest for supper this evening."

Katie Stuart came flitting into the room holding a large dish of potatoes. She smiled and blushed, looking between Molly and Finnegan. "Good evening, Mr. Gilhooley." She curtseyed and turned. "Mr. Kilkenny." Both men nodded. "Mr. Kilkenny, I am sure you remember Miss Meagher." Katie held out one hand toward the table.

Molly nodded. "A pleasure to see you again, sir. I have been looking forward to chatting with you again. I greatly enjoy tales from far off lands."

"And tales from your own farmstead." Finnegan straightened his coat. "I did not expect to see you here, Miss Meagher. What brings you to the cattle range?"

Katie flitted once again and took the two men by their

arms and led them to the table. "Miss Meagher is my tutor. She schools me in the finer points of both composition and elocution. I feel as though she has been very helpful in teaching me all I will need to know if it comes to pass that I leave here to attend an institution of higher learning."

Finnegan settled into the chair he had been led to. "You wish to attend university, Miss Stuart?"

"Oh, it is one of the many fancies that cross my mind." Katie blushed a bit more and took a chair across the table next to Molly.

"It is a fine mind at that." Molly patted the girl's hand.

Finnegan cleared his throat. "Well, you are well fitted to make such an assessment." He raised up, along with Kilkenny as Mrs. Stuart came to the table. They returned to their seats when she was in place. Granville entered just after her.

The pioneer found his visitors' manners amusing. "I would not have thought that the only two proper Irish gentlemen I have ever met would be a gunman and a whiskey peddler." He laughed and took a chair.

Kilkenny grinned. "I assure you, Mr. Stuart, I have never sunk to the actual labor of peddling the family poison. I prefer to limit myself to merely reaping the benefits and go no further."

"A very ethical policy, to be sure." Granville began digging into the chicken before him, skipping Grace, something he had insisted on for most of his adult life.

Since it was the practice of the house, Finnegan began spooning out potatoes. He glanced across the table several times. "Do you tutor all the children here, Miss Meagher?"

"Katie is my only student at present. I tutor her and she passes the lessons on to the younger children. It is somewhat of an apprenticeship program. It will hopefully prepare the young lady for a future profession such as I follow."

Stuart grunted out a laugh. "The girl is already too smart

to suit. She has been far more intelligent than me for years now, which I find unacceptable."

Kilkenny took up the chicken plate. "Perhaps it would be best to hand the entire operation over to the young lady. It would give you more time to pursue your hobbies."

Stuart laughed again. "Given the amount of profit the average cattle ranch produces at present, it might be better to classify what I am currently doing as a hobby. That is why I am in favor of the girl becoming a schoolteacher. I hope to live off her wages someday." The whole group laughed and began digging into their food.

Katie filled the lull in conversation. "Miss Meagher also tutors the two children who live at Fort Maginnis."

Kilkenny chewed a chicken leg. "There are children at the fort?"

"They are the children of two officers." Molly poured a bit of gravy on her potatoes. "You might think it would be a lonely life for them, but they are absolutely adored by all the men. They never want for playmates. It is not uncommon to find even the most aged and scarred soldier playing hopscotch with them."

"That would be quite a sight." Finnegan slowly took a mouthful. "So, then, you have a route you follow?"

"One of the enlisted men generally escorts me from Maiden to the fort. Mr. Abbott collects me from there and will, likely, return me to town when Katie's lesson is completed."

Finnegan nodded. "It is good to keep busy."

"And what have you been occupying yourself with, Finnegan?" The schoolteacher stared across the table. "Does the tending of Mr. Kilkenny take up all your time?"

Kilkenny fielded the question. "A score of men could not properly tend to me, Miss Meagher. Thankfully, the labors of both Finnegan and my new valet are enough to keep me alive. I am afraid that is the best that can be hoped for, given the conditions."

When the meal was completed, the entire group retired to the sitting room. Mrs. Stuart only remained for a handful of minutes before plodding off to the kitchen to see to the crockery, along with her younger children. Katie made the rounds pouring everyone coffee and they all chatted for all of about ten minutes before Katie removed Kilkenny's coffee cup from his grasp and placed it on a tray. With due diligence, she began moving about the room collecting the majority of the cups.

"Mr. Kilkenny, I know how you prefer to turn in early. Sleep well."

It took a moment for the comment to sink in. "Ah, oh, yes, quite right." He raised himself from his chair. He bowed to Molly. "I am of the belief that an abundance of sleep is the key to good health, miss. Please excuse my early departure. It was a pleasure seeing you again, miss."

"Oh, the pleasure was all mine, sir. Good evening."

As Kilkenny left the room, Finnegan pulled his watch from his pocket and checked the time. Katie moved directly to her father and purloined his coffee, as well. "I am certain you have much correspondence to see to this evening, father. You had best get to your study if you wish to complete it by a reasonable hour."

The pioneer cast a gruff look toward his daughter. "Correspondence to whom?"

"I am sure you will recall once you get to your desk." Katie winked at him.

He sighed and wrestled himself from his chair. "Pity's

sake." He stood and nodded to Molly. "Good evening, ma'am."

"Good evening, Mr. Stuart."

With her father dispatched, Katie refilled Finnegan and Molly's cups. "I must apologize to you both. I know it is terrible manners for the host to excuse herself, but I really must see to the remainder of my studies so that I can be prepared in the morning."

Finnegan shrugged. "Not to worry, miss. I had best make sure that Ephraim did not become lost on the way to the bunkhouse, at any rate." He moved to get up, but Katie shook a finger at him. "Mr. Gilhooley, it is one thing for me to excuse myself so that I may complete my work, it is quite another for you to show such rudeness and leave our guest alone."

It was Molly's turn to shrug. "I...suppose I might simply retire, Katie."

"No such thing, Miss Meagher. We share a room while you are here, and I require quiet to study. Please do not bother me for the rest of the evening." She motioned to the coffee urn. "Please help yourself to the coffee." She fairly flew from the room, leaving the two old friends alone.

Finnegan shifted in his chair. "I was not aware you visited this place regularly, Molly."

"Yes, I failed to mention that during our brief meeting."

"Yes, you did."

The schoolteacher sipped her coffee. "And now we have been rather clumsily ambushed."

"I thought it was somewhat well executed, given that it was likely the girl's first ambush." He sighed. "She would make a fine Missouri bushwhacker, with a few slight refinements."

"Finnegan, are you really so angry with me that you intended to not see me again while you are in the territories? You looked pale as a ghost when you saw me at the table."

"I was surprised. No more, no less. Neither am I angry with you. I have no reason for anger. I suggested a course of action, you expressed disfavor for the suggestion. There is nothing more to it and nothing more to discuss." He stared off into the smoldering fireplace as he spoke.

She sipped her coffee again. "Ah, well, isn't that quite succinct." She shook her head. "Finnegan, what precisely did you have in mind coming here? Did you honestly believe I had been doing nothing other than pining away for you in the wilds? I could have easily pined for you back home if that had been my intent."

Finnegan licked his lips. "Yes, well, that is not what you chose."

She sat forward. "Regardless of what choices I have made, I cannot imagine why you would think you were a part of the consideration."

"Clearly I was not."

"Finnegan, I have not seen you in...eight years. You would write, and claim to be close to another visit, but after the first dozen attempts and half-dozen years, you will have to excuse me if I began to consider your return to be a farcical promise." She gazed at him questioningly. "With nothing more than the occasional missive... how can any sane person take such an acquaintance into consideration when planning their life?"

He withdrew a cigar. "You might have been good enough to write so that I might have known where you had gone."

"You might have come by to call one of the many long days that had passed."

"I...Molly, I was otherwise engaged."

She shook her head. "Yes, engaged in serving your master, Mr. Pinkerton. Seeing to his dirty little business."

He placed the cigar between his lips and lit it. "You always did take a dim view of my work."

"I take a dim view of what your employer has done to men such as the coalminers of Pennsylvania, and countless other honest men since."

Finnegan hung his head and rubbed his eyes for a moment. "I see. You would still call me to answer for the Molly Maguires." He laughed a bit. "You have the memory of an elephant, my dear."

"Perhaps it would be easier for you to recall such things if there was not such a collection of them for you to keep track of."

"What, pray tell, do you accuse me of, woman?" He sat forward to match her. "I never put one of those coalminers in their graves. If you wish to assign blame, you had best look to the judge or the jury or the damned county attorney." He pointed to her with his cigar. "I might add that, for a woman who has never so much as shook hands with a coalminer, you seem oddly certain of their saintliness. It is a rare man who makes his way to the gallows without some stain on his soul; best to keep that in mind before casting aspersions."

"You would have me gain an acquaintance with every man Mr. Pinkerton condemns to death before drawing a conclusion as to the validity of the executions?"

Finnegan smiled. "Yes. Would that be too much to ask?"

Molly fell back in her chair. "Oh, Finnegan, I have so missed fighting with you."

"I would think you would have no shortage of combatants." He puffed his cigar.

"Most women consider it undignified and most men would simply call me hysteric."

"I have called you many things, Molly. Never hysteric." He smiled again.

"Oh, Finnegan, you are quite mad. Did you truly believe

that I would wish to take up residence here the rest of my days tripping over children and cattle by turn?"

He threw his hands up, still smiling. "I honestly have no idea what you might wish, Molly. I do not know if I ever have. If it would not be too much to ask, would you mind informing me, perhaps just this once?"

She smirked from behind her coffee cup. "How can you ask me to state my own wishes for the future, when you seem to have never had a bearing as to your own?"

"My own?" He laughed. "I am not the sort for following wishes. I strike out on the labor before me. That is how it has always been. Little has changed since the day I stepped off the ship."

"It may be that you do not enjoy change, or the prospect of it. Since I have known you, the only mention you have ever made of leaving Mr. Pinkerton's employ was the previous evening. Even then, you made it contingent on my accepting your proposal. I cannot help but feel you made that part and parcel for a reason."

Finnegan sneered. "You, of all people, would doubt my sincerity?"

"I only doubt your ability to know your own inclinations. Why, after all these years and all the blood you have been commissioned to spill, do you still cling to that man?"

He shook his head and stared into the fire. "Molly, are you aware that Mr. Pinkerton's only commission to gather intelligence of the enemy during the war came from the patronage of General McClellan?"

"I believe I have read that, yes."

"He did not have to continue his work after that man was removed from command of the army. He could have cast all of us young men in his keeping back into the ranks where we would have likely perished. He did not, Molly. He kept myself and other young men like me acting as scouts, throughout the war until its end." He stared over at her. "How do you repay a man for such an act? An act performed out of simple decency, visited upon men who would have little chance of repaying the kindness. If it were not for Mr. Pinkerton, I would not be sitting here with you today."

"Finnegan, a man doing you a good turn in your youth does not place you in servitude to him your entire life."

He laughed again. "I am not in servitude to anyone, Molly. I would submit my quite steady pay as proof of that." He shrugged. "It is not as though I have had much else to do. As you have already informed me, retirement with a family is not in the offing."

She sighed. "I do not know how to comfort you, Finnegan. Would it help to know that if I were to...to settle and marry, you would be the only man I would ever consider?"

He puffed his cigar. "That is a fine compliment, Molly. Thank you for that." He rubbed his eyes. "You still have not answered my question."

"Your question?"

"You do not wish to marry and have a family. You do not wish to remain here in the territories. You do not wish to return to Minnesota. What, dear Molly, are your wishes? You must know by now that there is nothing I would not do to assist you."

"I do know that, Finnegan, and I do truly cherish your friendship. The only trouble is that I cannot tell you what I wish for in the future any more than you can guess." She smiled and shook her head. "I came to this place...I cannot even perfectly explain it even now. I had a whimsical notion to aid the Indians, see the country, perhaps gain a pride in making my own way in the world. Considering my actions in hindsight, it seems rather foolish."

He could only stare at her. The motivations were as

foreign to Finnegan as the moon. "You are not pleased with your life here?"

"I did not say that. Quite the contrary; I am afforded great satisfaction from teaching the children, and the land is breathtaking. It is...simply not what I envisioned when I boarded the train, if I envisioned anything at all."

"I still do not understand what you want."

"I want self-same sovereignty, like any woman." She grinned at the reference, but noticed he did not understand. "It is from an old book, Finnegan."

"I see, you shall have to lend it to me sometime." He puffed his cigar once again. "So, there is nothing you would ask of me?"

"Only your continued friendship."

"That is a commodity you will always possess." He knocked some ash into the fireplace. "If, for some reason, your inclination changes regarding my previous proposal, I would appreciate your mentioning it."

"You will be the first to know, Finnegan."

"Thank you."

She took up the coffee urn and refilled her cup. "Now that you have been made aware of what passes for my wishes, do you still intend to remain here and chase after your horse thieves?"

"I am not in the habit of abandoning a chore once begun." He puffed and flicked more ash. "At any rate, it is a fine offer they have made me. Whether I intend to build a mansion and keep a fine lady or not, I can always do with added funds." He cocked his head toward Molly. "Please do not tell me that the preservation of horse thieves has become one of your pet projects now."

She could not help but grin. "No, I cannot say as I know any horse thieves, although I would venture so far as to say that the act of stealing a horse probably should not condemn a man to be gunned down."

"You may unruffle yourself on that score, Miss Molly. I do not intend to gun down anyone, unless forced. Whether Mr. Stuart likes it or not, we will be bringing these men before a constable and have them called to account by the courts."

"Well, in that case, I wish you luck."

"Thank you, my dear."

"Finnegan, if you do not mind, there is a question I have been rather aching to ask, ever since you strolled into my schoolhouse."

"Out with it, lass. It may be another eight years before we speak again, judging by our fortune so far."

"Did you speak with Frank James after he turned himself over to the law?"

"In fact, I did."

"Ah, now there is a story I should like to hear."

Finnegan sat back in his chair. "Well, now, let me think. As I am certain you read in the papers, Alexander Franklin James had grown so harried and come to fear me so dreadfully much, that in a fit of misery, he cast himself onto the protection of the law to save his loathsome carcass from the valiant Irish knight that stalked him."

"Oh, this is a fine tale."

"Just wait a moment, lass. It does nothing but improve as I proceed."

Chapter 14

DHS RANCH, MONTANA TERRITORY

June 21st, 1884

Finnegan and Kilkenny sat on the porch of the bunkhouse. Kilkenny smoked a stolen cigar and Finnegan had taken to whittling a hunk of wood into the shape of a bear, partially because he had the beasts perpetually on his mind, and partially to produce a gift for one of the younger Stuart children. He was not a very expert whittler, so the project had taken up the better part of the morning but had not produced much in the way of results.

He held the rapidly disintegrating piece of wood up for Kilkenny to inspect. "How does that strike you?"

The whiskey baron eyeballed the hunk. "It still resembles a pig."

"I narrowed the muzzle, as you suggested."

"Yes, but now it merely seems to be a long-nosed pig."

"Bloody hell." Finnegan resumed whittling, reforming one of the legs.

"That will not help much. The shape of the head and body is wherein the disproportion lies."

"I am attempting to give it cleft feet. The child will now receive a lovely wooden pig."

"Bravo, Finnegan. You have wrestled victory from the jaws of defeat."

"It is my stock in trade, my friend."

Kilkenny grinned. "And have you done the same with the lovely Miss Molly Meagher?"

Finnegan grunted and held up the newly devoted pig for another inspection. "In what respect?"

"I had begun to fear that your romance with the girl had clabbered as does the milk when it is left too close to the stove. Noticing that it took some time for you to join me back here the previous night, I cannot help but theorize you have once again found the spark to rekindle the flame."

"Soured milk, flames, sparks, women? You have crafted an accusation that is very difficult to follow, sir."

"Oh, piffle. Are you and the young lady chummy once again or not?"

"It would appear she is no longer actively engaged in despising me. Is that roughly what you are inquiring about?"

"I suppose." Kilkenny leaned back and placed his feet on the porch railing. "I apologize if my inquiry annoys, but I must confess that I am intrigued by your pursuit of this schoolteacher."

"Ephraim, I must confess that I have little to no understanding of what intrigues you. While I cannot be certain, I would suggest that during some time in any given life, every man has, to some extent, pursued a woman. There does not seem to be much to fascinate in this calculation."

"Ah, but you only scratch the surface, Finnegan. What causes my fascination is not that you would pursue. What fascinates me is that you came so close to capture and were only put off by the mercurial nature of your prey."

"Once again I do not follow." He offered the carving again. "Does that resemble the foot of a pig?"

"No. That, you have crafted close to a bear's paw. I would suggest surrender."

"Oh, what would you know of pigs." He continued to whittle. "What are you attempting to get at, Ephraim?"

"I suppose I simply cannot understand why a man such as yourself, who has led such an extraordinary life, would long to cast aside your endeavors and enter into a very ordinary existence."

"Perhaps, it is merely an extension of my previous behavior." Finnegan blew chips from the carving. "By his very nature, an adventurous fellow constantly attempts to do what he has not done before, correct?"

"Correct, I should think."

"Then it would follow that by attempting to settle into a pastoral existence, I am really doing nothing out of the ordinary whatsoever."

"By God, that is a damned fine bit of reasoning, Finnegan." Kilkenny pointed out over the grasslands before them. "Do you recognize that rider?"

Finnegan stared out. "I do not."

"He approaches rapidly."

Finnegan set his pocketknife and carving to one side. "Perhaps he is Jack Stringer, Mr. Stuart's criminal mastermind, come to turn himself in."

"I thought you said the gentleman was named John Stringer?"

"When he arrives, we can confirm his name, Ephraim." Finnegan got up out of his chair and stretched. As the man rode up to the porch, he let his hand stray down to his Remington. "Good morning, sir."

The man had a sunburned face, streaked with sweat. In appearance, he was a dead match for the majority of the cowboys on the range, about thirty and dirty enough to be suspected of hard work. "Are you Gilhooley?"

"I am."

The man's horse danced in a circle before he brought it under control. "I'm William Thompson, I ride for the Fergus outfit. We got word a piece back that you all are interested in horse thieves."

"We are."

"I seen two men that sure as hell don't look like honest gents down around McDonald Creek, headed toward the Musselshell. I can't say for certain if they're scoundrels or not, but they went hell bent for leather when I tried to ride up on 'em and they're driving seven head with 'em. I swung wide and came here to see if you want to go after 'em or at least maybe run 'em off for good."

Kilkenny jumped up out of his chair. "You have come to just the right men, sir." He beamed. "We will collect our kits and be with you presently, Mr. Thompson."

Finnegan rubbed his eyes as his friend disappeared inside the bunkhouse to make ready. He sighed. "Very well, Mr. Thompson. We will pursue. We will need you to act as a guide, of course."

"I can do that."

"Thank you." Finnegan pointed to the Stuart house. "Get something to eat and I will see about getting you a remount."

Chapter 15

JUNCTION OF THE MUSSELSHELL AND MISSOURI, MONTANA TERRITORY

June 22nd, 1884

FINNEGAN SHOOK KILKENNY'S SHOULDER TO ROUSE HIM. The gunman, the whiskey baron, and the cowboy had left the DHS with all due haste and cut the trail of the men Thompson had spotted. Kilkenny was surprisingly helpful with that portion of the chase. Many years of practice had sharpened his tracking skills and his enthusiasm kept him searching in the places where the other two men lost the trail. Over the course of a full day in the saddle, the party tracked the men north more than forty miles. By the time the sun was sinking they were nearly to the place the Musselshell hit the Missouri. The suspected horse thieves made camp and the three men following did the same, just out of sight, behind a small ridge.

They had taken turns keeping watch all through the night, wishing to approach at first light. Finnegan had the watch leading up to dawn, so it fell to him to wake the others in the grey light. He shook Kilkenny first and then Thompson. Both men sat up slowly and looked around, seeming to have a hard time recalling why they were in a small gully full of sagebrush instead of their beds.

Thompson did his best to muffle a cough with his hand. "Are they still yonder?"

Finnegan nodded in the dim morning that seemed much like the night it was slowly replacing. "I can still see a slight glow from the fire." Finnegan moved back from the two other men and began looking over his horse.

Thompson stood and stretched. "You want to rush 'em?"

Finnegan shook his head. "We will approach slowly, on foot. We will surprise them in their bedrolls and interrogate them as to their purposes. It will not do to simply rush up on them and fire. There is no way to know if they are horse thieves with bad intentions or merely travelers, as yet."

"The way they're scooting across this damn prairie they sure seem like they're running from something or to something a hell of a lot better than what they got. I ain't too worried about discovering they're a couple of church deacons when we roll them out."

"I would tend to agree, Mr. Thompson, but our suspicions are not enough to go about shooting men in their sleep." Finnegan motioned to the horses that were tied to a toppled cottonwood. "Mr. Thompson and I will approach, and you will bring the horses up behind us, Ephraim."

The whiskey baron rubbed his eyes and got to his feet. "Finnegan, I would prefer to approach with you. I have yet to see anything interesting of this sort in this country."

Finnegan rolled his eyes. "As I have just finished explaining, Ephraim, there will not be anything of interest for you to observe. We are going to wake these men and speak with them. After that, there will likely be nothing much other than binding their hands and many weary miles to transport them to some sort of court or constable."

Thompson sneered in the dim light. "I got to kind of agree with this here drunkard, Gilhooley -- this don't offer much in the way of entertainment."

"You will be more than welcome to find some entertainment when we bring these men to a town for adjudication. If you prefer, Mr. Thompson, you may bring the horses instead of Ephraim, but I would prefer to have you on hand from the beginning in case there is a possibility of you identifying these men so that we may know their motives for being here. If they are only cowboys from another ranch moving quickly for want of whiskey, it would be a pity to have Ephraim shoot one for sport." He smiled and withdrew the Marlin from Kilkenny's scabbard. "I will borrow this for a moment."

"Very well." Ephraim appeared a bit put out. "Oh, and I am no drunkard, Mr. Thompson. I simply exist in an Irishman's natural state. Mr. Gilhooley is the aberration here, not I."

Thompson stared at the whiskey baron for a moment. "Uh, well, my apologies, then."

"Think nothing of it. You are not the first man to make such a mistake."

Finnegan and Thompson very slowly crept over toward the other camp. It was not the easiest chore to keep quiet while avoiding sagebrush and other hazards along the way. In spite of the difficulties, the two men made it up near to the camp without rousing either of their quarry from sleep. As Finnegan stood over the two men who slept with their heads close to their campfire, neither fellow seemed less than tranquil. Finnegan nodded to Thompson, who drew his Colt from the holster. The Pinkerton gave the closest man a small kick on one foot. "Wake and hold steady."

The man slowly let his eyes peel open. He squinted in the early morning gloom. "What? Who the hell do you think you are coming into another man's camp?" The second man woke and sat bolt upright. He opened his mouth to speak, but snapped it shut when he saw the muzzle of Thompson's Colt glowering down at him.

Finnegan kept the Marlin leveled on the man. "Do not concern yourself with who we might be, what is of issue here is who you are. Or, more to the point, what your profession might be."

The first man shook his head to clear out the cobwebs. "And who the hell are you to go around inquiring as to other men's business?" His arms stirred under his blanket.

Finnegan flipped back the hammer on the Marlin. "Do not attempt anything desperate, sir. I assure you, it will not end well for you. Mr. Thompson, remove whatever weapons these men might have concealed in their bedding, if you please."

"Sure." Thompson holstered his pistol and pulled the blankets from the men. Underneath there were two Navy Colts wrapped in their gun belts. "Guess you boys was planning on shootin' a rabbit for breakfast, huh?"

"You don't sleep with your pistol, Will Thompson?"

"I do, just not near so soundly." Thompson held up the guns and tossed them back into the sagebrush.

"You know these men, Mr. Thompson?" Looking the fugitives over, it seemed to Finnegan as if the men should know each other. They were certainly dressed similarly, and all appeared to follow the cattle profession in some manner. The only difference between them was Thompson's sunburn and close-trimmed hair. The men on the ground were of dark complexion with long, dark hair.

"Yeah, I know 'em." Thompson pointed to the chatty fellow. "He's Narcisse Lavadure. That other one's Joe Vardner. Couple of half-breed horse thieves if there ever was two."

"That remains to be seen, Mr. Thompson. Tie their hands and we will look over the brands of these horses."

Thompson pulled a couple of short lengths of rope from his coat pocket. "I wouldn't believe for a minute them horses are stolen. I'm sure as sunrise these two bought 'em with what they earned working real hard, or with the inheritance from their sainted grandma." He cinched the rope lengths down around the men's wrists. "Probably the first time you boys been up early in a while, huh? Ain't no roundup boss to wake you for stealin'."

"Please check the brands on the horses, Mr. Thompson. I will watch them." Finnegan let Thompson move off to the horses. "Where are you men coming from?" They stared at him silently. "Where is your destination?" They remained silent. "You men will find our time together more tolerable if you speak when questioned."

Lavadure chuckled. "Ah, so now there is a more tolerable way to perish? I, for one, do not see much difference in the end. Will you find a softer rope to hang us with if I answer your questions?"

"No one is going to be hung today, sir." Finnegan glanced over to check on Thompson's progress. "You men in this territory speak too lightly of hanging for my taste."

"I cannot say it is to my taste, either, sir, but I doubt your damned Association will inquire as to my likes before fitting me for a final collar."

Thompson strolled back to the fire. "Yup, them's Wells stock and if these two paid for 'em, I was born in a damned manger."

Lavadure spit down into the dirt next to the smoldering fire. "Wherever you send me, Will Thompson, we'll be seeing each other again, I can damned well assure you of that."

Thompson winked at the man. "You'll be arriving well in advance of me, Narcisse. You go ahead and feel the place out for me, huh?"

"Fool. I have already told you, the only place you are headed is to a constable." Finnegan turned to Thompson. "Where would you recommend we take these men?"

"The nearest tree." Thompson grinned.

Finnegan cleared his throat. "Sir, I have never leveled judgement on a man far enough to hang him, but I assure you, I have shot men for far less than being glib when I am not in humor for it."

Thompson shifted around uneasily. "We can take 'em to a fort, but the man who acts as judge on occasion in Lewistown and Fort Benton, he lives over by Rocky Point. It ain't far, closer than Lewistown, anyhow."

"Then that is where we will take our prisoners." From the corner of his eye Finnegan could see Kilkenny coming with the horses.

The whiskey baron brought the animals into the camp. He seemed rather disappointed that Finnegan's plan had panned out. Kilkenny sat on his mount, staring down. "So, these are the villains we pursued so long?"

"It was a day and a night, Ephraim, hardly the quest for the holy grail." Finnegan handed the Marlin up. "Thank you for the loan."

"You do not appear to have used it, so I cannot say as much appreciation is required."

Finnegan hung his head for a moment. "Ephraim, I dare say you seem disappointed. Is it really so terrible that I should want one out of every ten or so of my plans to come to fruition?"

"No, you have that right, I suppose. Even if it does tend to make events tedious."

Since the prisoners did not enjoy his company, and he was the man best suited to the job, Thompson was given the duty of herding the stolen horses. As the animals were the only real evidence of the prisoners' crime, Finnegan had insisted that they be brought to the house of the judge.

Thompson informed Finnegan that there was no need to insist, since the Wells ranch was beyond Rocky Point, and no one had appointed Thompson to return every damned stolen horse in the Montana Territory, anyway.

Thompson kept the horses moving along a few hundred yards in front of the two Irishmen and the two prisoners. The cowboy had sworn that somewhere out in the undulating prairie an old judge's house could be found, but Finnegan certainly could not see it yet.

The Pinkerton and the whiskey baron bracketed the two horse thieves as they rode. Finnegan had the more talkative fellow, Lavadure, nearest to him. There seemed to be nothing wrong with making some conversation, and Finnegan had found over the years that it often helped to ease a prisoner's nerves. "Where do you hail from, Mr. Lavadure?"

The horse thief shrugged as he bounced in the saddle. "I cannot claim any one place for my birth. It must have been somewhere between here and the British. Somewhere in these parts my father ran across my mother and, well...I suppose that is the lot of a half-breed."

"I have been told that it can be difficult for a man with your lineage to find a place of welcome in the territories, currently."

Lavadure nodded. "I am not welcome on the Reservation, and I am not welcome elsewhere." He smiled at Finnegan. "Although I have been told your people suffer much the same trouble, and I cannot help but think it must be true. If a man would come so far as you have to hang a horse thief, you must be truly doomed to roam all your days."

"The world is not so big, if traveled in small increments."

"Perhaps so." Lavadure gave his capturer a quizzical look. "Where the hell is Ireland, anyway?"

"Oh, a few thousand miles across land that way."

Finnegan pointed east. "Then, there is an ocean to cross, which I believe is a few thousand more."

"That would explain why I have never stumbled across it."

"It surely would, sir."

Lavadure motioned to his compatriot. "Of course, if I got it bad, I reckon Vardner here has always had it worse. My momma was a squaw, but Varder's daddy was a redskin. Crow won't have a damn thing to do with him on account of him having weak blood. I guess I don't need to explain why the white folks don't want him at their dinner table."

Kilkenny brought his horse up close to Varder. "Are you truly the son of an aboriginal, Mr. Varder?"

The quiet horse thief turned toward Kilkenny and finally spoke. "None of your damn business." In a movement so quick that it could be thought he had done it before, Vardner reached down and pulled Kilkenny's Marlin from the scabbard with his bound hands. Fast as a snake, the horse thief brought the butt of the rifle up against Kilkenny's chin. The whiskey baron's eyes crossed, and he fell from the saddle while Vardner kicked his spurs and began to tear off across the prairie with the rifle awkwardly clutched in his hands.

Finnegan pulled his Remington and took careful aim on the fleeing man. The first shot tried missed the mark, but he thumbed back the hammer and made another attempt. That bullet thudded into Vardner's shoulder, and he fell from the saddle some fifty yards from where his ride had begun. Finnegan brought the Remington to bear on Lavadure. "Do you wish to make an attempt?"

Lavadure slowly looked from Finnegan to Kilkenny and then to Vardner where he lay in the dirt. After a thorough review, he offered an answer. "I would rather not."

"Very well, then. Inquire to see if Mr. Kilkenny still lives." Finnegan turned and saw Thompson approaching at a gallop. He was headed straight for Vardner, who was actively engaged in picking himself up out of sagebrush. The horse thief still held the rifle, but due to bound hands was incapable of operating it. Thompson rode to within ten feet of Vardner, drew his gun and fired. Finnegan hung his head. "Bloody hell."

Kilkenny heaved himself up off the ground and stood with blood dripping from his chin. "Holy mother of Mary, what the hell has happened?"

Finnegan returned his Remington to the holster and sighed. "You were the victim of an assault and the man who perpetrated the act lays dead."

Kilkenny scanned the prairie. "Damn you, did you shoot that man while I was out of my wits?"

"That is your greatest concern at this moment?" Finnegan rubbed the bridge of his nose.

"Finnegan, you are orchestrating these episodes to my disadvantage intentionally."

"You had best see to your chin, Ephraim. Without some cleaning that is bound to scar." Finnegan looked to the remaining horse thief. "Mr. Lavadure, aid Mr. Kilkenny. I can only assume that witnessing what has just transpired has convinced you of the futility of attempted escape."

"Most assuredly."

"Good. Dismount and help him with his wound. Mr. Thompson and I will retrieve the missing animals."

Lavadure spit down into the dust. "You gonna have Thompson shoot me too?"

"If I wished you shot, I would have seen to it myself where I found you. Be about your business, sir." Finnegan trotted over to where Thompson stood, assessing the dead man.

Thompson glanced up, smiling. "You really must be some kind of professional shootist like in them nickel books. I ain't never seen nobody hit nothing with a pistol that far off, and running too. Hell of a thing, Mr. Gilhooley."

"Mr. Thompson, you should not have shot this man. You were damn well informed that I wished to deliver him to the magistrate alive."

Thompson rubbed his chin and holstered his Colt. "Uh, well, I reckon you did mention that. I suppose I thought you'd surely changed your mind, though, when you took to shootin' at him."

"I did not kill him when I shot at him, Mr. Thompson."

"Uh, Mr. Gilhooley, I complimented you on the shot, and it was damned impressive, but can you truly claim to have been aimin' fer his shoulder?"

"Of course not, it was only luck that I hit him at all."

"So, you was trying to kill him?"

"Yes."

Thompson rubbed his chin again. "So, when you try to kill him and don't, it's good. When I try to kill him and kill him, it's bad?"

"Yes."

"Mr. Gilhooley, you'll have to excuse me, but that don't make no damned sense."

Finnegan rubbed his eyes. "Oh, to hell with it. See to collecting the horses."

There was not much to speak of wealth at the ranch Thompson led the group to. It appeared as though some attempts had been made at farming, or perhaps only gardening. There were a few head of cattle lounging about and one old nag of a horse stood in a corral pawing at the dirt. The only impressive structure on the whole place was a strange barn, roughly half the size of an eastern barn, that had been constructed out of actual cut lumber, possibly when times had been better.

As they approached, a man who looked to be in his sixties came limping out of one of the small cabins littered about near the barn. He had long white hair and a long white beard that whipped around in the prairie wind. Finnegan rode up with Thompson by his side. The old man nodded to the cowboy and cast a suspicious glance at Finnegan.

"Will Thompson, it's been some time. Is this fella in the frock coat a preacher? You know I shot the last man who brought a preacher to my door."

"He ain't no preacher, Mr. Langford. He's...well, I reckon he's one of them stock detectives old man Stuart keeps yappin' about every time we see him." Thompson shrugged. "I picked him up at the DHS and we run down some horse thieves. We got one left and this detective fella right insisted on bringing him here." Thompson leaned forward, looking serious. "He's got some strange notions regarding who ought to get killed and how and such." He glanced over his shoulder at Finnegan. "Well, I guess I'll let him explain it himself."

Finnegan nodded and walked his horse forward a step or two. "Mr. Langford, my name is Finnegan Gilhooley, and I have been commissioned by the Stock Growers Association to arrest anyone suspected of theft and deliver them to the proper authority. Mr. Thompson has informed me that you sit as judge in this area."

The old man chuckled. "I suppose you could say that. The last tavern I held court in was many leagues from here, sir." He motioned all around him. "As you can plainly see, it will be difficult to empanel a jury, if you wish for this man to be tried today."

Finnegan nodded, looking glum. "Yes, that would seem to be the case, sir."

Thompson sat up in the saddle and snapped his fingers.

"You know, Mr. Langford, the other boys from the Fergus outfit will be making a swing right through here in two days' time. I guess it wouldn't be too much trouble to snag you and this here horse thief when we pass through. We could all head to Lewistown and have another one of them trials in the saloon there. I got to say, I enjoyed the last one."

Langford nodded, grinning. "Well, so long as you enjoy yourself, Will Thompson, that's the important thing." He shook his white head and combed back unkempt hair. "One of the stalls in the barn should serve as a proper cell for the fellow, so long as he remains bound." Langford looked at the sky and then back down to Lavadure. "Not much chance of freezing in the night this time of year. You picked a fine time to be arrested, young man."

Lavadure smiled. "I recall thinking to myself back in March that just as soon as the snow was gone I really ought to see to getting myself arrested."

Langford walked over and patted the man's leg. "That's the sort of lighthearted demeanor that gets a man fed regular while he is in custody." The judge turned to Finnegan. "Go ahead and deposit him in one of the stalls, stock detective. Then, you can come in the house and see to some food. I got some liniment for that fella's chin too, if you want it."

Kilkenny nodded. "That would be much appreciated, sir."

Finnegan dismounted and motioned for Lavadure to do the same. The prisoner complied and both men walked to the barn. Finnegan fumbled the crudely built door open and they went inside. The interior of the building was rather dim, but it looked clean enough, and would not have been considered untenable for a man to spend some time in. Finnegan had seen many a jail that was much worse. "Ah, this is not so bad, Mr. Lavadure. You will be out of the sun and out of the rain. That old coot Langford seems amiable enough, and I believe he will feed you." Finnegan opened the door to the nearest horse stall. "One of us will stay near to keep you company. After we depart you will have to be more thoroughly bound; I am sure you understand."

"I do, yes." Lavadure looked about the place. "You are right, as barns go, this is not so bad. It is unfortunate, what happened to Vardner."

Finnegan nodded and took two cigars from his pocket. He offered one and the prisoner accepted. "Yes, a pity. Having been there, Mr. Lavadure, you realize I had no choice but to shoot. It is unfortunate that Mr. Thompson chose to finish your friend. It was not what I would have preferred. Sadly, Mr. Thompson is inexperienced in this sort of thing. I believe he acted more out of excitement than malice."

Lavadure stuck the cigar between his teeth and leaned forward while Finnegan struck a match for him. "I would agree, sir. Will Thompson never did have a kind word for Vardner, that I can recall, but he never did him a lick of harm before he shot him down. I suppose that is the risk a man runs in such a profession as ours. Although, I cannot blame poor simple Vardner for trying to run. He had his chance to avoid the rope and he took it. My chances appear to have all passed me by, so I will resign myself to it."

Finnegan laughed and shook his head. "You men here in the territories do so dearly love to spin yarns about hanging. If I may make an observation without too much offense, sir, I would point out that you are a ne'er-do-well horse thief. You will be transported to some village, perhaps this Lewistown they keep speaking of. Once there, they will convene a trial. I am sure there will be talk of hanging you bandied about, but it always amounts to nothing more than talk in the case of crimes such as yours. They will package you off to the territorial prison for some paltry term as five years or the like. Well short of a year the warden will grow tired of feeding you and either allow you to scamper away in the night or simply throw the door open one day without any sense of shame."

"Ah, that would be a fine way to wriggle out of this one, Mr. Gilhooley." Lavadure puffed his cigar. "This is a fine smoke, sir. I thank you."

"Think nothing of it."

"I must say, it would be agreeable to me to think they will give me a trial and a trip to Deer Lodge to help on the farm, but I cannot say I can convince myself of it." He motioned up. "If I was given to gambling, I would wager all I've got that I will hang from one of them beams up there after you and that other Irishman are on your way."

Finnegan shook his head again. "It is one thing to threaten and quite another to act, Mr. Lavadure. Even more so after passions have had a chance to cool. I doubt that old man will be so bold as to come out here and hang you himself, at any rate."

"That is likely correct. I cannot say I am so sure about them other boys riding for the Fergus brand, though. Time will tell, I suppose." Lavadure shrugged. "Although that's more or less the risk we all run, ain't it? Fella might get hung. He might get thrown from his horse. Some bastard might come along and shoot you just for the hell of it."

"A man may be eaten by a bear."

Lavadure gave the Pinkerton a perplexed stare from behind his cigar. "Um, well, yes. I suppose that is a possibility."

"Sir?" Finnegan tapped ash down and carefully stepped on it so as not to light the barn ablaze. "You are the first man of your profession I have had much discourse with; would you mind me asking you a professional question?"

"Oh, I suppose. Just so you don't go trying to make out like I confessed to anything in particular at this fancy imaginary trial I'm to be having."

"I would never dream of it, Mr. Lavadure. Your defense is your own business, as far as I am concerned. I would simply like to know if you have ever made the acquaintance of a man named Jack Stringer, or John Stringer?"

Lavadure laughed wholeheartedly. "Oh, if only I had! From the tales I've heard there is a man who will never hang, certainly wouldn't be caught napping like me and poor Vardner." Lavadure chuckled. "No, Mr. Gilhooley, I'm sorry to tell you that Jack Stringer is an old wives' tale, no more real than Jesse James. A story made up by newspaper men."

Finnegan gave the fellow a sideways stare. "Mr. Lavadure, Jesse James was quite real, I assure you. Flesh and blood -- until the day he died, of course. What on earth made you think the man was not real?"

"Well..." Lavadure shrugged. "Way I heard it, he was some great outlaw, robbed scores of banks and trains and outran the law every time."

"That would be one way to assess the man, yes."

"Well, if the fella was smart enough to do all that, why the hell didn't he take the money from the first five banks, deposit it in a sixth bank and live off the damn interest? Nobody ever accused me of greatness, but even I know robbing five banks and getting away with it is a hell of a lot better than robbing forty and being dead."

Chapter 16

DHS RANCH, MONTANA TERRITORY

July 2nd, 1884

"Mr. Stuart, I am afraid I must agree with my countryman in this instance. I fail to see the proper significance. It seems a very odd choice for a national holiday."

Granville threw his hands in the air. "What in hells bells can be so difficult to understand? It is the Fourth of July. The date commemorates our Continental Congress formally signifying our Declaration of Independence to the British Crown."

"That much is understood, Mr. Stuart." Kilkenny grinned and shook his head. "I believe what Finnegan and I fail to appreciate is the selection of that particular date."

"What is there to be confused about?"

Finnegan laughed. "It confuses because it, in actual practice, commemorates nothing more than some grey old men signing a sheet of paper. After it was signed, there were still many years of war to be fought. It seems silly to celebrate a gathering of despondent farmers signing a letter to a king they had never met. I have never understood the practice and I would point out that the 4th has ceased to be celebrated in the southern states since the end of the war, at least from what I have seen."

Stuart shook his head. "Well, what would you gentlemen suggest we celebrate instead?"

"Something more tangible." Kilkenny took a sip from his flask. "Those who disfavor the current government in England are quite fond of the 5th of November, which is when a rather bold fellow made a somewhat sorry attempt at blowing up the Parliament. Now, that is a fine way to thumb one's nose." He put the flask back into hiding. "Or, better still, commemorate a battle. The Mexicans have their 5th of May."

"The French have Bastille Day," Finnegan interjected. "Was there some date during your revolution where the geezers accomplished something more substantial than signing and posting a letter?"

Stuart drained his coffee cup and sneered. "I believe it is merely that you Irishmen are incapable of understanding the customs of free men in a free nation. Perhaps someday your tiny little island will cast off the yoke forced on it by that other tiny little island and you both will have an Independence Day of your own."

Now it was Finnegan's turn to throw his hands in the air in exasperation. "When that day comes, Granville, I can only hope we will have the good sense to set the date on the day of the final battle, or at least when the last Englishman in the country is run down and shot, or some such date of significance. You Americans place far too much importance on documents, if you ask me. I recall the great fuss that was made during the war when Lincoln issued his Emancipation Proclamation."

"Yes, that struck me as rather silly, also." Kilkenny nodded.

Stuart leaned back, eyes wide with amazement. "You fail to grasp the importance of Lincoln freeing the slaves?"

Finnegan shook his head. "What I fail to grasp is why a man of Lincoln's practicality would bother issuing proclamations to a nation that was no longer in his custody." Finnegan turned to his fellow Irishmen. "All the negroes were well out of Mr. Lincoln's reach, but he persisted in issuing legislation in regard to them. It was quite trivial, and any fool would consider it such, but the American papers and even the soldiers in the ranks did no end of blathering on about it."

Kilkenny placed his feet on the porch railing and stretched. "Rather smacks of sour grapes, wouldn't you say? Attempting dictates to those who had already left the club."

"I certainly always thought so. A proper statesman really ought to save that sort of business for a time after the war has been won. Until a fellow can claim victory, he should avoid proclaiming much of anything."

Stuart sighed and hung his head. "Perhaps it is simply beyond the comprehension of foreigners."

Finnegan shook a finger at his employer. "I would be careful who I classified as a foreigner if I were you, sir. I know full well I have lived more of my life in the states than you have."

"That is a good observation, Finnegan," Stuart grinned. "If not for a battle here or a treaty there, I might be Spanish or, God forbid, British."

"Now there would be a tragedy." Kilkenny stood and stretched. "I assure you, Mr. Stuart, you would make a very poor Brit." Kilkenny pointed to the door of the bunkhouse where his new valet loomed. "Oman is letting me know that it is time for my shave and bath."

Stuart craned his neck around to view the valet. "He is mute?"

"I believe so. Finnegan, have you heard the man speak?"

"I have not." Finnegan tipped his hat to the giant.

"Do you know anything of the man's history, Mr. Kilkenny?"

"I was told he previously served a general, of some sort, in some capacity."

Finnegan moved around in his chair uncomfortably. "Is he truly going to give you a bloody bath, Ephraim?"

The whiskey baron laughed. "He will draw me a warm bath after boiling the water and preparing the mixture of soaps and oils I prefer. He does not scrub me, if that is what you are wondering. I am not a baby."

"No, not at all, certainly." Finnegan stood and adjusted his guns. "If it is all the same to you gentlemen, I believe I will make myself scarce for the next few hours. I do not think I will be required for bath time." He motioned to some low-lying hills in the distance. "Your man Teddy said he was going over there in search of the wolf that prowls about, correct?"

"He did." Granville nodded.

"Then I will attempt to assist him. I assume you would welcome a wolf pelt for your collection, Ephraim?"

"Very much." Kilkenny pointed to his silent assistant. "Oman gives an excellent shave, you really should avail yourself of his expertise."

"Thank you, but I believe I will continue to shave myself, at least for the time being."

While Finnegan could not claim to be looking forward to the management of cattle (he had seen enough of the cowboys' day-to-day activities to know that was not the profession for him), he did enjoy the freedom of the cattle range. It was easy for him to understand how a man like Stuart would want to live in such a place and keep his family there. The hunting made for a fine distraction and the wild country was certainly preferable to Chicago or even Helena.

Finnegan was in a fine mood, mounted on the horse he had acquired from the three cattle rustlers near the Judith Gap. The day was sunny, he was making progress in his work, and he had come to believe that Molly's temperament might someday swing back to his favor. He had intended to search over the small gullies and stands of trees in the hope of locating a wolf for Ephraim's collection, but Teddy Blue came galloping up before he had the chance. The cowboy's horse was lathered and the man himself was out of breath.

"My goodness, Mr. Abbott, what has you in such a dither." Finnegan glanced around and his hand stole over to the Purdey by his side in a scabbard. "Did you chance upon a bear?"

"A bear?" Teddy stared blank-faced for a moment. "Uh, no, no, I chanced upon Sam MacKenzie, though, sure enough."

Finnegan slowly pulled his hand back from the rifle. "Is that of note, Mr. Abbott?"

"Granville, uh, Mr. Stuart, he's been telling us all to keep an eye out for the rascal, on account of him being known to have made off with some of Conrad Kohrs' stock already. I'd say he's here looking to make off with some of ours, but he might just be following up on them wolves I spotted the other day." The cowboy paused in his tale to rub his chin. "You know, for a worthless drunk and a horse thief, he's a hell of a wolfer."

Finnegan grinned. "I enjoy the way you always point out the best aspects of a man, Mr. Abbott."

"Well, I figure every man's due a compliment now and then." He motioned over his shoulder. "MacKenzie's got a cold camp right over there where that wooded draw passes to the creek."

"You're certain it is the fellow Mr. Stuart asked you to look out for?"

"I've seen him plenty, and he's the only man I know that travels with a fiddle."

"A fiddle?"

"Yeah, carries it with him and plays all the dances." Teddy frowned. "Ah, damn it, if you shoot him, I don't know who'll provide the music around here."

"I am not in the habit of shooting fiddle players. I doubt today will change that."

"I sure would appreciate that, Mr. Gilhooley. It'll get gloomy around here right quick without a little fiddle playing now and then. Although, if you don't shoot him, I guess he'll be getting' hung or freighted to Deer Lodge. I will miss dancing with Mary."

"Perhaps the territorial prison would trade this fellow MacKenzie for a piano player?"

Teddy scratched his head. "They do that?"

"It cannot hurt to inquire." Finnegan motioned to the area Teddy had indicated. "Guide me close and I will approach the camp myself."

"I can go with you if you need assistance, sir. I've never been in a shooting scrap, and I cannot say I'd care to be, but I'm not yellow, neither."

"You have done your job, now I will do mine, Mr. Abbott. I promise to do my best to avoid damage to Mr. MacKenzie or his fiddle."

"Oh, that would be good, Mr. Gilhooley. If you could save the fiddle, maybe one of the other boys could learn to play it."

"That is a well thought out solution, Mr. Abbott."

The two men slowly made their way down toward the creek bottom. When they reached a stand of pines, Teddy motioned forward, and Finnegan dismounted. He left his horse with Teddy and crept through the trees, his Remington at the ready. After about two hundred yards he came to a small clearing. There, amongst a small cluster of poplars, a rather bedraggled looking fellow lay napping with his head on a saddle and a well-used mare hobbled not far off. Being careful to avoid various sticks littered about, Finnegan slipped up next to the napping man and removed the Henry rifle that leaned on a sapling by his head.

Holding the rifle in one hand and the Remington in the other, Finnegan kicked the man's leg. "Rouse yourself slowly, Mr. MacKenzie. Do not move your hands, sir."

Without so much as twitching any other parts of his body, the sleeping man opened his eyes. "What the hell kind of talk is that? You one of the British?"

"I am Irish. You have never met an Irishman before?"

"Not nearly so soon after my nap." The man raised his eyebrows. "Ah, you must be that stock detective old Granville hired."

"And you would be Sam MacKenzie?"

"No good sense in denying it. Most of the DHS boys know me. I played at many a dance for them and sold them many a wolf pelt."

"I see." Finnegan took a step back. "Stand up, sir." The man lifted himself up from the leaves. "You are aware that Mr. Stuart has employed a man to hunt horse thieves for him?"

"Not sure if there's a man in the territory who ain't."

"If that is the case, Mr. MacKenzie, why are you here, in the neighborhood of the DHS?"

The prisoner shrugged. "I more or less reckoned that you'd be out hunting horse thieves. Never imagined you'd be sitting here on your ass waiting for one to come to you."

"I suppose that was a fair enough assumption, sir." Finnegan pointed to MacKenzie's traps. "Collect your fiddle and come with me carefully. I have made assurances that it will not be damaged."

THAT EVENING, Finnegan sat in the bunkhouse with a well satisfied look on his face. MacKenzie was bowing out a rather mournful old Irish tune and seemed to be enjoying himself, as well. Kilkenny was enjoying the performance to no end, while Reece Anderson and Teddy Blue sat smiling. Even Stuart had stopped by to get a look at the freshly captured horse thief, but had promptly rushed off to compose a letter to Conrad Kohrs to brag.

Leaning back in his chair, Finnegan puffed his cigar, feeling as though he had finally worked out a proper method for arresting horse thieves. He patted Kilkenny on the shoulder. "You see, Ephraim, this is how the arrest of a petty criminal is meant to transpire. No shooting at the outset, no shooting while the prisoner is transported. If one is lucky, as I was today, the detective can locate a rogue with a knack for music and then all parties are pleased."

MacKenzie ceased playing and took a sip of the whiskey Kilkenny had been decent enough to provide for the musician. "I must say, it is always unsettling to be arrested, but it will be much nicer to spend the night indoors. There were storm clouds gathering as you were packing me off, Mr. Gilhooley."

Finnegan sipped his coffee. "Yes, well, it is best to be appreciative of the small blessings."

"I would feel a bit better, though, if I knew what, precisely you intend to do with me." He sipped the whiskey again. "I have heard that Stuart is damned fond of hanging men when the notion strikes him."

Finnegan waved the smoke away from his face and shook

his head. "Sorry, Mr. MacKenzie, but you will not be swinging this evening. Mr. Stuart's reputation has been greatly exaggerated in that regard. Lacking a proper authority to turn you over to, you will be taken to Fort Maginnis in the morning. The soldiers at that establishment will see to it that you are transported to whatever town you stand accused in." Finnegan turned to Reece Anderson. "Where does this Conrad Kohrs reside?"

"Deer Lodge." Anderson helped himself to a nip of whiskey.

"Very well, then. Mr. Kohrs has accused you. As such, you will go to Deer Lodge."

MacKenzie laughed. "Conrad Kohrs claims I stole his horses, eh?"

Finnegan shrugged. "That is what I have been told."

"Well, how the hell would old Conrad know how many he had when he started? I doubt that man's been able to keep count of his horses for twenty years. Rather miserly of him to begrudge me one or two. I believe I'll bring that deficiency in his character up during my trial."

Finnegan smiled and sipped his coffee. "That is your right as an American, Mr. MacKenzie."

"Sir, if you would not mind too much..." Kilkenny poured the fiddle player a fresh glass of whiskey. "I would very much like to discuss your wolf hunting practices. You say you have killed more than two hundred of the beasts?"

"Probably many more." MacKenzie raised his glass and smiled. "Since I was pulling on my momma's apron strings, I been making my living off wolf hides. Oh, and fiddling, of course."

"And stealing horses." Anderson stared at the musician over his whiskey glass.

"I suppose you ain't never filched a biscuit and ain't never forgot to pay for a drink in all your born days, Reece?" MacKenzie picked up his fiddle once again.

"I don't know about that, but I ain't never stole a horse. That I know for sure."

MacKenzie shrugged. "Well, if you do take up the habit, don't steal one from Conrad Kohrs. Old sot's too grumpy to find it humorous."

Anderson sneered. "If I was a flat busted, half-breed wolfer, headed for the penitentiary, I don't think I would be casting aspersions on a man like Conrad Kohrs."

MacKenzie let out a chuckle and had to lower his fiddle. "Well, now, Reece, I was unaware you was such good friends with old Mr. Kohrs. I had no idea you two was so close. I must admit, I did not know he held my being a half-breed against me, either. Does he hold it against your children, Reece?"

"Why, you lousy little son of a bitch." Anderson stood and made a lunge toward the fiddle player. Finnegan lunged at the same time and shoved Anderson to the floor. Anderson stared up with an angry scowl. "You taking that damn horse thief's side?"

"There are no sides to choose in a matter this absurd, Mr. Anderson." Finnegan glared down at the man. "You have had too much whiskey, sir. I believe you should turn in for the evening." Finnegan reached down, grabbed one arm, and pulled Anderson to his feet.

Anderson was a bit surprised to find himself standing again so quickly. "I, uh, well, yes, perhaps. I sometimes overindulge. I meant no offense."

Kilkenny slapped Anderson on the back. "No offense taken, Reece. I dare say an evening is not a proper adventure if no two men attempt a donnybrook. Sleep well."

"I will." Anderson nodded to the assemblage and left the bunkhouse.

After a few awkward moments of silence, Teddy Blue spoke. "Hey, you're a quick one, Mr. Gilhooley. I ain't never seen somebody knock Reece down so fast."

Finnegan returned to his seat and resumed smoking. "Every man has a talent of some sort. Personally, I rather envy you cowboys having such ability with those ropes. I believe it would take me many years and much frustration to learn to throw one of those loops around a cow's head."

"I bet that ain't near so tough as playing the fiddle." Teddy pointed to MacKenzie. "I don't suppose you'd be willing to give me a bit of instruction in that device? I know a young lady who's terrible fond of fiddle music and I can't say as knowing how would hurt my chances."

MacKenzie mused on it for a moment. "Well, I got no objection to trying to teach you a song or two. Although, I got to tell you, in my experience, women prefer money to fiddle playing, and I made far more money stealing horses than I ever did playing fiddle. Maybe it would be better if I taught you the art of horse theft instead."

Teddy shook his head, grinning. "I don't believe that would be a good idea this evening." He leaned forward conspiratorially. "I might take you up on it sometime later, after Mr. Gilhooley has moved on."

Just as the sun was rising, Finnegan checked on MacKenzie to make sure he was still firmly bound to the bunk he had been placed in at the end of the previous evening's entertainment. With the prisoner seen to, the Pinkerton walked the short distance to the Stuart house and passed through the back door into the kitchen. Inside, he found Awbonnie Stuart silently going about her morning chores. Finnegan tipped his hat to her, and she poured him a cup of coffee.

He sipped it and smiled at the lady. "Ah, that is fine Arbuckle, ma'am." The lady smiled back, so far, the most emotion Finnegan had witnessed from her, before returning to her cooking. Knowing that eggs and possibly some bacon would soon follow, Finnegan took a seat at the table.

Granville came in from the other portion of the house and sat down across from Finnegan. "Good morning, Finnegan."

"Good morning, Granville. Did you sleep well knowing there is one less horse thief about?"

"I did, but not near so well as I will sleep tonight if we can catch a couple more."

"More?"

"Conrad Kohrs told me last winter that MacKenzie was working with at least two others. By my reckoning, if MacKenzie was lazing around here, there's a good chance he was doing it while waiting for his friends to show up. Does that seem reasonable to you, detective?"

Finnegan nodded and sipped his coffee. "It does." He sat back, smiling, as Awbonnie set his breakfast in front of him. "I will make a wide circle and survey the country on my way back from the fort, after I deposit Mr. MacKenzie with the authorities there."

"Eh, let Reece take that vagabond over and drop him with whatever rebel general they're calling captain there currently. He's meant to go and collect the mail and the schoolteacher today anyhow."

"Miss Meagher is returning?"

"As per her rounds." Granville could not hide his grin beneath his beard. "Thought you might be glad to hear that."

"I am. I have always enjoyed the young lady's company."

"Well, she should be here by the time we return from our rounds investigating the location of MacKenzie's friends."

"You wish to join the expedition?" Finnegan began exterminating his eggs.

"I could do with some distraction. I grow weary of balancing books and placating my business partners."

"It should be a fine outing, sir." Finnegan sipped his coffee. "Oh, drat. It may not be a good idea to let Mr. Anderson transport MacKenzie to the fort. The two of them had a bit of a row last night. Some rather harsh words were exchanged."

Granville sneered. "They were drinking?"

"Naturally. I have found that a few glasses of whiskey is useful for keeping a prisoner sedate. Mr. Anderson was invited to join in by Mr. Kilkenny."

"Yes, well, where one fool ventures another is likely to follow. I wouldn't worry over it much. There is barely a man in this territory who has not felt the need to thump Reece Anderson when he is in his cups. I have done it once or twice myself. He is always quick to forgive and never one to hold a grudge." Granville chuckled. "What is it you think old Reece might do to the fellow, anyway?"

Finnegan shrugged and finished his eggs. "It is only that I prefer my prisoners be delivered without undo injury."

Granville sat back while his wife placed his food in front of him. "I have known Reece a long time. To tell you the truth, he probably doesn't recall the argument or what prompted it. He will do your prisoner no harm. Teddy Blue or one of the other men will go with him, at any rate. If I sent Reece out with MacKenzie alone, there's a good chance the two of them would become overly chummy during the ride and end up in a saloon instead of at the stockade."

"That would rather defeat the purpose of arresting the man in the first place." Finnegan drained down the remainder of his coffee and popped his one and only slice of bacon into his mouth. "Have you heard any news regarding the man I left with that ghostly, old alleged judge?"

Granville shook his head. "No, but that is hardly unusual. It may be a month yet before we hear anything. The next time one of the boys is headed for Lewistown, I will have the fellow make an inquiry. I can only hope that old scoundrel Langford did not release the man in exchange for the stolen property he was found with." Granville scowled. "It is hard to trust men in this country to act correctly, Finnegan. When men find themselves apart from civilization, they often begin to shirk the responsibilities of it."

"Well, a man must make use of that which is available, Granville. I had little choice but to leave the prisoner there."

Stuart nodded and began to collect his eggs with his fork. "Yes, but it would be terribly aggravating to discover that all our efforts were unraveled the moment we are out of sight."

"That is the hazard any man runs."

"We did not risk it in Virginia City."

"Things change, my friend." Finnegan smiled. "About what time do you expect Miss Meagher?"

Chapter 17

DHS RANCH, MONTANA TERRITORY

July 6th, 1884

"THERE YOU ARE, LASS." FINNEGAN DOUBLE-CHECKED the cinch on Molly's horse, and she climbed back into the saddle. "That should be enough to ensure that he does not make it to the fort without you." Finnegan remounted his horse. "I must say, of all the 4th of July celebrations I have ever been privy to, yesterday's was surely the oddest."

Molly gave her horse a kick to make it resume plodding down the rough-hewn road between the DHS Ranch and Fort Maginnis. "How so?"

"It was odd, in that, the 4th of July is an American holiday, but there were so very few Americans in attendance."

The schoolteacher laughed. "You still do not consider yourself to be an American, Finnegan?"

"The time for patriotism is before a man is conscripted, Miss Meagher. A man is rarely in the mood for such things afterward." He brought his horse up close beside her. "Kilkenny is certainly not an American. I dare say neither Stuart, Anderson, nor their respective families could be called Americans, either. The people of these territories are not allowed the franchise in elections; they are not likely to consider themselves proper citizens unless they were born in the states. I doubt Mrs. Stuart would lay claim to American citizenship if it were offered."

"Nitpicking fine points is hardly the purpose of a celebration, Finnegan. The purpose is to enjoy the day, eat a bit of pie, and forget the worries of the world for one day. Did you manage that?"

The Pinkerton nodded. "I did, in fact. I found the whole affair rather relaxing. You may have noticed that I did not wear my guns when we danced."

"I did notice. You waltzed quite well. Have you had occasion to practice since I taught you all those years ago?"

"I cannot say as I have."

"You always did prefer to stay busy. It was kind of Mr. Stuart to let that gentleman Mr. MacKenzie stay another day so that he could play the fiddle for us during the celebration. He seemed an amiable enough fellow; is he truly a horse thief?"

"He is, and had no shame in admitting it. Although, if he is wise, he will cease doing that during his trial. He had no stolen property with him when I detained him. As matters stand, he should be turned loose after his first hearing. The army will ship him over to some place called Deer Lodge where they will place him in front of some sort of judge."

"You do not feel he will be convicted?"

"Even a system of justice as capricious as the one you Americans practice does call for some sort of proof for determining guilt, dear."

"Well, perhaps that is for the best." Molly shrugged. "He will be inconvenienced by the journey to Deer Lodge and that will serve as a suitable fine for his transgressions."

"Indeed." Finnegan pulled his hat down as the wind

gusted. "Most importantly, the gentleman will spend the remainder of the summer being freighted about and will bother Mr. Stuart no further." He smiled at Molly. "Over the years I have found that the number of criminals removed from the field is not nearly so important for a detective as the contentment of clients."

The schoolteacher laughed. "You have always been a very honest man, Finnegan. I suppose you would readily admit that if it had not been for Jesse James there would have been little need for all those railroad agents Mr. Pinkerton provided?"

"All men need a counterpart, Miss Meagher. Saints need sinners to make them feel saintly. What good is the priest if there is no one to come to confession? Without bad men, how could I be heroic in the eyes of young ladies such as yourself?" He grinned. "If you are asking me if Mr. Pinkerton played on the fears of the railroads or possibly made the reputation of Jesse James greater so as to accrue more contracts? Well, as I said, even you Americans require proof to determine guilt." He laughed. "I will say that if Jesse had been killed during his first robbery attempt, I am sure Mr. Pinkerton would have found a suitable replacement for him in short order. My employer is nothing if not practical."

Molly narrowed her eyes and gave her old friend a close inspection. "Would you truly make this place your home if Mr. Stuart and the Association were to make good on their promises to you?"

He shrugged. "One place is as good as another, in some respects." He rubbed his chin. "What would make you question the Association making good on our contract?"

She offered a crooked smile. "The businessmen of this territory are not known for their honesty, Finnegan. At best, they are all speculators, running from one botched venture to another. Some eventually hit upon a manageable scheme and become respectable. The rest...well, they do have a habit of overextending themselves."

"All ventures represent a risk, lass." He sat up a bit straighter in the saddle. "It does not much matter, either way. You have already informed me that you do not intend to remain here. Obviously, I will follow. I cannot build a ranch here if I am to be traipsing after you down to South America, or perhaps Australia will be more to your liking? I have heard the seasons are reversed there; it should be interesting."

"You would follow me, Finnegan?"

"It is my sole form of entertainment, lass."

They rounded a corner in the road and had climbed to the top of a small rise. At the crest a massive fir tree towered up into the azure sky. "Finnegan, if you were to stay..." She jerked back on the reins of her horse and brought the animal to a stop. Her eyes were set on the fir tree in front of them.

Finnegan chuckled. "Is there a ghost in that tree, lass?" He let his horse stroll forward a few steps. Closer, he could see the pair of stocking feet that hung amongst the limbs. Following the feet higher, the rest of Sam MacKenzie could be seen. There was a note, scribbled on yellowed parchment, pinned to his chest. It read *THIEF*, and nothing more. "Bloody hell." Finnegan brought his horse up on the side of Molly and slowly began moving her and the animal around the tree and farther down the road. "Do not look on it, Molly. I am sorry you have seen such a thing."

When they were well beyond the tree, she raised her head and gazed at Finnegan with tears in her eyes. "That was the man from the 4th of July dance, was it not?"

"It was, lass."

"You told me no harm would come to him. You told me he would be sent to Deer Lodge. You promised, Finnegan. You swore and now there he hangs just as those poor Molly Maguires did."

Finnegan grabbed her reins and brought both their horses to a halt. "Woman, you damn well know I had nothing to do with that man's fate."

"You arrested him, you handed him over to whoever is responsible for his death. How can you say you had nothing to do with it?"

"There is a great distance between arresting a man for horse theft and hanging him from a tree. Even you must know that."

"Just take me to the fort. I cannot argue like this while that poor man dangles from a tree limb." She hurriedly glanced back and forth from the road to the tree. "No, I misspoke; we must bury the poor man. He deserves better. He deserves a Christian burial."

"I am not taking you to the fort. The daft bastards who killed that man likely reside there. I cannot return you to the ranch, either. We will ride straight through to Maiden. If a man is capable of such an act as what was done to Mr. MacKenzie, he may be capable of anything. You will be safest at Maiden. I will procure some tools and see to the man's interment, I promise."

She stared down at her saddle. "I am sorry, Finnegan. I should not have accused you of...of having knowledge of an act like this."

"It is jarring to see such a thing, Molly. Do not think on it again. I will not." He looked over the country before them. "We should get moving. We have a long way to go, and I have much to do. I assure you, Molly, I will not let this pass without discovering who is responsible."

Night had fallen by the time Finnegan could return to the fir tree. He had purchased a spade and a lantern in

Maiden, knowing he would have need of both. It took some doing to first ascend the fir tree and then cut the man down. MacKenzie's body fell to the ground and the tree shook, nearly making Finnegan lose his footing on the branch he stood on. On the ground, Finnegan saw that MacKenzie had been hung with a length of heavy rope best used for wagon rigging and not a lariat. He briefly inspected the note to see if it offered any clues as to the man's killers.

The ground in the neighborhood of the tree proved far too rocky for digging. Finnegan was forced to drag MacKenzie down into a hollow where the earth was sandier and loose. After hacking out a respectable hole, Finnegan deposited the body and rolled several of the larger rocks he could find on top of the disturbed patch. He could not be certain that wolves or coyotes would not dig the man up, but it was the best he could do under the circumstances. The Pinkerton stood over the grave for a few moments, contemplating the issuance of a benediction, but nothing seemed proper. Perhaps some family to MacKenzie could be located and they could see to whatever they thought best.

With his undertaking seen to, Finnegan rode to the DHS Ranch. When he arrived, he saw that a light still burned in Stuart's office. He let himself into the house and quietly stalked into the study. Stuart looked up just as Finnegan was closing the door. "Good evening, Finnegan. You are getting in late. I hope everything went all right transporting Miss Meagher."

"Not as well as I would have hoped."

Stuart looked the man up and down. "You are rather dirty, Finnegan. Were you thrown from your horse?"

"I have been digging a grave, sir. Such things are rough on a man's wardrobe." Finnegan moved forward and set the note formerly pinned to MacKenzie's chest on the desk in front of Stuart. "You will explain this."

The pioneer glanced from the note to the Pinkerton and back again. "Explain what, precisely?"

"A murdered man. You placed MacKenzie in the care of Anderson and Abbott. Did they perpetrate this act, or did you have men from the fort see to it?"

"Perpetrate what?"

"Do not play coy with me, Granville."

"I play at nothing. You are the one running a game here. Speak plainly. What the hell is going on?"

"MacKenzie has been hung. Molly and I found him twisting in the wind while we were on the way to Maginnis."

"MacKenzie? Are you certain?"

"I got a damn fine look at him as I labored to dig his grave. Yes, it was MacKenzie, and there will damn well be repercussions for this."

"I..." Stuart stood up from his desk. "Finnegan, truly, I had no knowledge of this. I told Reece and Teddy to take the man to the fort." He threw his arms up for a moment. "Reece, perhaps, could be capable of such a thing. But Teddy? No, that young man would not have done this or would have told me of it, at the least. No, if that man is hung it is those damned blue bellies at that sham fort who did this."

Finnegan eyeballed his employer suspiciously. "You would have me believe the soldiers of a government fort would lynch a man?"

Stuart guffawed. "I doubt the enlisted men would have the initiative for it. My guess would be the commander or one of the officers is responsible."

"Granville, I have spent more than a little time around Union officers. I have known plenty who would commit the most unthinkable acts upon the enemy. I have known many to abuse their own men terribly. But I have never known one who would bother with the murder of a horse thief. What would possibly motivate them?"

"Oh, who the hell knows." Stuart got up from his desk and began to pace. "I have never seen the eastern army you speak of, Finnegan, so I cannot say for certain, but the specimens I have observed in the territories are not nearly as well ordered as what you describe. Hell, most of the men billeted at these frontier forts were formerly Confederates. If the man currently commanding at Maginnis does not have a southern accent, I will eat my hat. They have no interest in the reputation of the army. They have no hope of advancement. They have nothing to occupy their time. They do not even have the opportunities a chance Indian massacre once afforded them." He shook his head. "Why not hang a horse thief, if there is nothing better to occupy your time some afternoon? We may come to learn that MacKenzie's vocation had nothing to do with the matter."

"How so?"

"He may have simply cheated the fort's captain at cards. They may have quarreled over a squaw in the past. Who can say what gets a man hung?"

"Cheated the captain at cards? What the hell kind of place is this, sir?" Finnegan was having a hard time believing what he was hearing.

Stuart chuckled. "Well, it is not as if General Sherman will be along anytime soon to chide the man for his behavior. Forts such as Maginnis are meant to afford protection to operations such as the DHS. In practice, they are nothing but a damned nuisance. For three seasons now they have been claiming that I cannot take in hay from the bottom land below the fort." He threw his hands in the air. "As if the damned army owns the land or could possibly lay claim to the grass on it. An absurdity if I have ever heard of one."

Finnegan pinched the bridge of his nose. "Granville, I do not give a damn about your hay."

"Oh, well, no, I suppose you would not." He sat back

down in his desk chair and briskly scratched the back of his head. "Now that you mention it, I am more than a bit confused as to why you care so much about MacKenzie's unfortunate conclusion. I will grant you, he was an amiable enough fellow, but I think we can both admit he was headed for a bad end. The method by which it was meted out does not much matter."

Finnegan scowled. "You yourself have stated that this sort of thing places a black mark on the reputation of the Stock Growers Association."

Stuart raised one finger. "I said news of this sort of thing could hurt our reputation. I doubt anyone at the fort will speak of the incident and you have, as you said, already buried the body. It would have been preferable to have the man seen to as we planned, but every eventuality cannot be planned for. What has you in such a dither?"

"Miss Meagher saw the man hanging."

"Ah." Stuart leaned back in his chair. "Yes, I suppose that must have been rather upsetting for her."

"To say the least, sir."

"Yes, indeed." Stuart set his elbows on his chair arms and folded his fingers. "So, you are more...vexed by the effect the incident had on Miss Meagher than by any miscarriage of justice perpetrated against Mr. MacKenzie?"

Finnegan sighed. "Shall we say that it matters little which point vexes me more. The duty imposed on me is the same."

"Duty?"

"Granville, someone, somewhere, in some way, must be made to suffer the consequences of that man being lynched."

Stuart laughed. "Simply because the object of your affections will not let you hear the end of it if it is not?"

"And because if it is not handled properly, in a manner that suits Miss Meagher's sense of greater morality, she will rant to every periodical in the territory and most of the better-known ones in the east. If there is a way to make that woman hold her tongue, Granville, I have not found it."

"I imagine the backside of my hand might do for a start."

"Any such action and you will quickly find yourself placed in the vicinity of Mr. MacKenzie, Granville."

The pioneer cleared his throat. "You are damned prickly about that schoolteacher." He sat forward slowly. "Of course, I was only jesting." He shook his head. "All right, very well then. Something must be done to placate the woman. What would you suggest? If you propose to shoot down the captain of the fort, that will only increase our troubles, I should think."

"Before I decide on a course of action it will be necessary to discover who is responsible." Finnegan shrugged. "My burden would be lessened if we find Mr. Anderson was the guilty party."

Stuart grew pensive. "Oh, Finnegan, I will agree that the hanging of a man without real cause is a low act, but MacKenzie was a low man. Would you really insist on killing poor, dumb Reece? I have known him longer than I can recall. He is really all I have left that would pass for family."

"That may be, Granville, but it does not mean he can go about hanging who he pleases."

The older man sighed. "I can agree with that, but does this transgression, if in fact it was his transgression, truly warrant killing him? Would not a good drubbing placate the schoolteacher?"

"Well, now, how the hell could I know a thing like that?"

Stuart contemplated the problem further. "On the other hand, Reece and his expansive progeny are a great drain on my resources. Now that I mull it a bit, you removing Reece from my ledger might save enough that I could abide a fair number of horse thieves."

Finnegan leaned against one of the upright posts that

supported the study roof. The conversation was wearing on him. "Sir, I try to be as...limber as possible when attempting to please an employer, but I cannot assign guilt in this matter based solely on your double-entry bookkeeping system."

Stuart rubbed his eyes. "Yes, a good point. That is probably not the proper tool for reaching a conclusion."

Chapter 18

FORT MAGINNIS, MONTANA TERRITORY

July 7th, 1884

THE FORT HAD OBVIOUSLY NOT BEEN BUILT WITH AN EYE toward defense. There was no outer wall, not even a demarcated line for pickets. Finnegan thought it far more closely resembled an eastern barracks placed in a town and designed to blend in. Approaching the place, it would be hard to tell that it was not a trading post or simply another collection of ranch buildings thrown down in the prairie with little planning for future developments. There were a few low log constructions that served for blacksmithing and the boarding of animals. The more impressive buildings were two stories with brick and stone bases and upper levels built with milled lumber.

By Finnegan's count, there were roughly forty men billeted in the fort, which, by his standards, was a very small complement of men. Small wonder that Stuart was not impressed by the protection they offered, especially given the way they all seemed to be lounging about with no officers seen to be directing them in any particular way. Riding up, Finnegan had not seen a single man doing more than reclining on a porch or lazing about. It appeared as if the fort served little purpose and the soldiers stationed there were not overly interested in discovering one.

Stuart led the way and rode straight to the officers' barracks. The upper level of the building had been set aside to serve as a sort of office and meeting area for the fort captain. Finnegan, having been in the army, felt as though some sort of adjutant or at least a sober corporal should be located prior to bothering the commanding officer, but Stuart suffered from no such difficulties. He had dismounted and climbed the stairs, then entered the building without even knocking.

Inside the gloomy room, they found a bleary-eyed man in a blue uniform who did not seem much bothered by the breach in etiquette. The fellow's belly was about to overflow from his ill-fit and near worn out coat and showed considerably when he rolled back in his desk chair. "Uh, Stuart." He let his eyes bob around in his head for a moment. "It has been some time since you have called." He motioned to a girl who stood in the corner of the room. She could not have been more than thirteen or fourteen years of age. "Belle, get us a proper drink, my dear. I am sure these men must be thirsty."

Stuart paused a few feet inside the doorway. "You know I do not imbibe, Captain Hatcher."

The officer waved one meaty paw. "Then this other fellow, perhaps?"

"Mr. Gilhooley does not partake, either." Stuart sneered and looked to the girl. "Be on your way, young lady." He pointed to the door and the girl scurried from the room. Finnegan closed the door behind her when she was gone. Stuart walked forward into the captain's office and stood in front of the man's desk. "Captain, I know you have not dwelled in this country as long as some of us, so I will pass on a small bit of advice. The purloining of a girl such as that may seem a fine diversion when first considered, but can end quite badly."

The officer chuckled. "You fear she will break my poor heart?"

"You should fear that her father will creep in here some night and lift your hair while your soldiers drunkenly nap."

"Oh, balderdash, Stuart. The tales you spin." He laughed again. "I have met that girl's father and compensated the old coot rather well. I imagine he obtained the girl's mother in much the same way." He grinned. "She has a sister, if you are in need of some fresh entertainment." He looked to Finnegan. "Or you, sir."

Finnegan smiled at the man. "Captain, I notice you have a lovely southern accent to your speech. Dare I venture a guess and say Virginia?"

"Born and bred, sir. You have an excellent ear."

"You are not the first captain from Virginia I have had dealings with." There was a sharp edge to the statement that the captain did not notice, but Stuart did.

"Easy on, Mr. Gilhooley." He patted the gunman on the shoulder. "Captain, we are here to inquire as to an incident that has occurred."

"Incident?" He scratched one floppy jowl.

Stuart swallowed and removed his hat. "I sent a man here the other day, a man arrested for horse theft. Reece Anderson and another of my men were to turn him over to you so that you might transport him to Deer Lodge when it suited you."

"Hmm." The captain slopped forward, butting up against the desk. "Ah, yes, I do recall your man Anderson. What of it?"

Stuart stiffened. "The arrested man, MacKenzie, what did you do with him?"

"Do with him?"

"Yes, damn you. Is that a difficult question?" The pioneer had more than a little edge in his voice.

"No need to get impassioned, sir." The captain stroked his jowls again. "Uh, as I recall, I turned him over to my lieutenant and ordered a court martial."

"A court martial?" Finnegan was somewhat astounded. "He was not a soldier."

Captain Hatcher's muddy eyes settled on Finnegan. "Of course, Lieutenant Bowden is a soldier. What the hell else would the man be doing around here?"

"MacKenzie, you sot." Finnegan turned to Stuart. "I am satisfied, Granville. This man is responsible for the incident. Shall I see to his punishment now?"

Stuart slowly turned to the Irishman. "While nothing would please me more, I am afraid it will not do." He turned back to the captain. "You tried the man?"

"Uh, well, after a fashion. I am sure the lieutenant did as he thought was best. I had no reason to inquire further and have not, as yet, discussed the matter with him. What is at issue here, Stuart? You sent the man here to...for someone to see to his adjudication. What is the difference if it was the lieutenant or some law booking imp who saw to it?" Hatcher began to search a desk drawer for the bottle he knew lurked somewhere inside. "What was the final disposition of the man's case?"

"Your lieutenant thought best to hang the man from a tree." Finnegan rested his hand on the butt of his Remington.

"Well, from the look of the fellow, he was either a half-breed or an outright Indian. The tree was likely the best place for him." Hatcher withdrew a whiskey bottle. "Ah, victory. Would you men care to join me?"

Finnegan withdrew his pistol. "Granville, I am going to shoot this drunken buffoon. He has worn on my last nerve, and I will suffer him no longer."

"Finnegan." Stuart grabbed the gunman by the arm. "You cannot shoot the commander of a fort in his damned office. Even here, such things are not tolerated."

Finnegan considered drawing his Colt with his left hand, but thought better of it. "Very well. I shall return and shoot the bastard when he is out of his office, and you are not involved."

Hatcher lolled around in his chair. "Did you say you meant to shoot me?"

"Hush, you ass." Stuart reset his hat. "We should go. We will get no satisfaction here and you have discovered what you wished to learn. This fool and his lieutenant are to blame. Tell that to your schoolteacher. Even she could not conceive of blaming me or the Association for the actions of this pathetic hulk."

The captain hiccupped. "Did you have your sidearm drawn, sir?"

Finnegan ignored the question. "Yes, I suppose this explanation will deflect Miss Meagher's indignation. Although this may lead to many a weary hour of trailing her around so that she may harass this man's superiors. Is there a territorial governor to be found in this place?"

Stuart shrugged. "We are always burdened with one. Whether or not he resides in the territory is anyone's guess."

Hatcher stood and leaned over his desk with shaky arms holding him up. "I believe you did, in fact, threaten me, Mr. Fill-fooly, or whatever your name is."

Finnegan reached out, took hold of the mop of hair Hatcher sported, and slammed his flabby head down onto the top of the desk. The captain collapsed and slowly slid from the desk down to the floor. The Irishman looked to Stuart, who wore a very judgmental look on his face. "Oh, come now, Granville. The man was being a pest. He is fortunate I did not do worse."

Stuart sighed deeply. "Regardless of the degree to which he deserved a drubbing, we should be on our way. Perhaps he will not recall the cause of his headache when he rises."

"Very well." Finnegan straightened his coat. "Let us find the girl and be on our way."

Stuart stopped with his hand on the door. "The girl? What girl?"

"That young Indian girl who was in attendance when we arrived."

"The girl in attendance." Stuart stared, only able to blink for a moment. "Find her to what damn purpose?"

"We will take her with us. We certainly cannot leave her here with...that wretched thing." Finnegan spoke as though it were the most obvious course of action.

"Take her with us? Take her where?"

"We will return her to her family."

"Family...by Christ, I can barely recall, but I believe this is what it was like to be drunk." Stuart shook his head. "Finnegan, her family sold her to that man. The only question was which party could negotiate a better trade. I may have jested about her father returning for Hatcher's hair, but it is likely the old bugger cannot even recall where he left her or what he traded for."

"She is leaving here with us, Granville. When she is away, she can make up her own mind where to proceed."

"Her own mind? You Irish have some damn queer notions." He motioned over toward the inert mass of the captain. "That little squaw is that man's property. To take her from this fort is no more or less than stealing the man's watch or taking some other bobble."

"I meant to take his life for a moment there. As I said, he should consider himself lucky. Now, let us be about finding the girl. I will not leave here without her."

"Oh, damn it all, then." Stuart opened the door to the outside. "This is going to be a rather trying summer."

Chapter 19

DHS RANCH, MONTANA TERRITORY

July 10th, 1884

Katie waved to both the young Indian girl and Kilkenny's valet as they began their trip in the light wagon Stuart kept around for shuttling visitors and such. Miss Stuart walked over to the bunkhouse porch where Kilkenny and Finnegan sat in their respective rocking chairs. The young lady had a desperately proud smile on her sweet face as she approached.

"You seem quite pleased to have stolen my valet, Miss Stuart." Kilkenny watched the massive butler disappear into the rolling prairie. "The man was an absolute wonder at starching my collars. I do not know how I will go on without him."

Finnegan investigated the visage of the whiskey baron, but could not determine if he was being earnest. "Ephraim, Katie has told you that your man will only be gone a handful of days. I would hope you can find some method for survival, even lacking a base necessity such as a starched collar, for a few paltry days."

Kilkenny sighed deeply. "Time will tell."

"A far greater curiosity I would like unraveled would be

to know how Miss Stuart managed to sort the Indian girl out at all."

Katie blushed. "It was all quite simple, Mr. Gilhooley. I could not understand the girl, nor could my mother. Naturally, we inquired of Mr. Oman and discovered that he could speak her particular tongue fairly well."

"Inquired of him?" Finnegan sat back in his chair. "I have never heard the man utter a single word. I thought for certain he was a mute."

"Oh, no, nothing of the sort." Katie continued looking a bit shy. "It is only that, well, I am not sure how I should explain it so as not to give offense."

Kilkenny sat forward. "Offense, how intriguing. Please go on, young miss."

"Well, Mr. Kilkenny, it is only that...Mr. Oman comes from a very respectable lineage and he... well, he simply will not speak to...those he believes to be beneath him in some way."

Finnegan rubbed his chin. "Beneath him?" He grinned. "That would explain why he refuses to speak to Mr. Kilkenny, but why would he not make conversation with me?" He laughed, looking to the whiskey baron to judge his reaction.

Kilkenny ignored the jest "Lineage? What...what on earth is he referring to?"

Katie shrugged. "He claims descent from an African king, a Hebrew prophet, and no less than an Incan emperor."

Finnegan chuckled. "Where, pray tell, is the country of Inca?"

"They were a tribe in South America conquered by the Spanish." Kilkenny fell back into his chair. "How marvelous."

Finnegan produced a cigar. "Very well, Miss Stuart, it would seem that Mr. Oman is of a far higher grade than either Mr. Kilkenny or myself, but that hardly explains why he will converse with you or the Indian lass. Does he believe you to be a descendant of the English Stuarts?"

"Oh, no, Mr. Gilhooley. I do not believe he would speak with my father even if that were the case. He dislikes white men, or, rather, would consider speaking with a white man to be below his station."

Finnegan laughed again, he simply had to. "Are you telling me that man is willing to be in Ephraim's employ and dress him like a little girl's doll every morning, but he refuses to utter a word to the man?"

"Um, yes, precisely, sir."

"That is a bit of bloody cheek." Kilkenny reached out to take Finnegan's cigar without a pause. "I would terminate the fellow's employment immediately if I was not so fascinated to hear the man's reasons." He lit the stolen cigar and took a puff. "I may be forced to bring that hoity scoundrel home with me. It would make me the envy of the entire club when they learned I had Incan royalty for a valet."

"You would truly keep a man employed who believes himself to be too good to speak a word to you?" Seeing he had been outdone, Finnegan found a second cigar.

Kilkenny waved his cigar about. "Oh, to tell you truly, I rather enjoy the man's silence. The constant yapping of the average valet becomes quite vexing after a while."

"Of all the beasts we have encountered on this journey, Ephraim, you are surely the strangest." Finnegan turned to the young lady. "And why do you continue to wear such a sly grin, lass? This cannot be the most amusing oddity you have seen Mr. Kilkenny indulge in."

She blushed. "Oh, well, no, I suppose not. I smile because I am so very pleased with your actions, Mr. Gilhooley, and my father's actions, as well."

"Our actions?"

"Rescuing that girl from the clutches of that awful

captain at the fort. It is most similar to a fanciful tale of a maiden being rescued by a knight."

Finnegan chuckled again. "As I recall, that is how you described my visit to Miss Meagher. As a trained detective, I might say that it is less likely I am a knight and more likely you have read too many romances."

"I have already written to Miss Meagher to make her aware of your actions." Katie blushed even more deeply.

"Oh, lass, I do not know if I would have had you do that." Finnegan rubbed his beard grizzle. "I have always had difficulty determining what strikes Miss Meagher's fancy and what does not."

"Surely this will." She thought on it for a moment. "Even if it does not, it is the truth, and I believe it is always best to let the truth be known."

"The fine points of that particular theory are something else I could elaborate on, as a trained detective, but you are far too young to hear of them, for now."

With nothing in particular to occupy their time, Finnegan and Kilkenny spent the better part of the morning sitting in their chairs and discussing the various theories they could concoct regarding the origins of Mr. Oman. They had just about exhausted their supply of preposterous notions when a large group of riders appeared in the distance. Kilkenny noticed them first, but Finnegan was the only one of the two who stood and truly took notice.

"Oh, this may develop into a bit of a row."

Ephraim stood and joined Finnegan at the edge of the porch. "A row? You do not even know who those men are as yet, old boy."

"I know they are coming from the direction of the fort,

and I cannot think of another dozen men who would have cause to come here. I might also mention, I believe I can just barely make out blue jackets."

Kilkenny removed his flask and took a quick nip. "No, that cannot be. I am aware that the American Army is notoriously uncivilized, but, honestly, Finnegan, you cannot believe the captain of that fort has really sent a patrol out to collect his stolen prostitute."

"Or to collect the men who drubbed him in his office."

"Ah, you failed to mention that." He took up the flask again. "If that is the case, then, yes, there may be a bit of row. Will you turn yourself over if they are indeed here to collect you?"

Finnegan turned to his friend with his eyebrows up as far as they would go. "Ephraim, I am not in habit of going quietly...anywhere. I doubt Mr. Stuart will feel any differently."

"Ah, well, perhaps I will finally witness a shooting."

"You will take your Marlin and your Purdey and retire to the main house. You did not hire me to involve you in a gunfight with the Army."

Kilkenny raised a hand. "Um, Finnegan, if that is the case, why will I be carrying an arsenal up to the Stuart house?"

"To kill those soldiers if they attempt to enter. I will not allow trash, such as those soldiers are, near the women or children of this place. If they enter, fire into them and do not cease until they are all dead." Finnegan turned and went into the bunkhouse. He began strapping on his Frontier Model Colt and Cloverleaf Colt to supplement his Remington. "If you must shoot one, you must shoot them all, Ephraim. The dearly departed tell no tales. If you wish to avoid hanging, I would suggest you be thorough."

"Finnegan, I have never gunned down a man in my life and now you wish for me to dispatch an entire platoon."

"Hopefully not." Finnegan leaned his Marlin just inside of the bunkhouse door and leaned his Purdey on the other. "With a bit of bluster, perhaps I can see my way clear to no man being shot. I simply wish for you to understand that there can be no half measures here. Either all soldiers live, or all soldiers die. Is that clear?"

"Yes...I understand."

"Good. Be about your business and get up to the big house." Finnegan handed him the second Marlin rifle. "Get the other Purdey and go." Finnegan watched as the whiskey baron grabbed the extra English double gun and ran for the Stuart home. He rubbed his face with both hands. "Bloody hell, this may be an ugly business." He took in a deep breath and stepped back out onto the porch. Some quarter-mile off, he could clearly see the U.S. cavalry approaching. Many times, in his distant past, he had greatly welcomed the sight of mounted troops clad in blue. That day, the sight was not comforting. As they grew near, Finnegan could see that the troop was not being led by the oversized form of Captain Hatcher. Although, that should have been expected. A man such as Hatcher was not likely to place himself in the forefront of any action.

Finnegan leaned against one of the posts that supported the porch roof as the troop rode up in front of the bunkhouse. A young man in a very jaunty blue cap and a rather immaculate uniform pointed one gloved finger at the Irishman. "You are not a cowboy, and you do not possess Mr. Stuart's fine beard. You must be Gilhooley, the Pinkerton."

Finnegan smiled. "And you would be Lieutenant Bowden, if I am not mistaken."

"You are not mistaken." He sat up a bit straighter in the saddle, clearly pleased that his reputation had preceded him.

"I had heard that old Granville had hired a gunman to see to his dirtier labors." The lieutenant's eyes rolled over Finnegan. "You are certainly well armed enough."

"I have been told there are a great number of bears about, Lieutenant. A man cannot be too careful."

"Bears? Yes, well, I wouldn't know about that."

"And what would you know about, sir? What brings you and your...men here today."

Bowden grinned at the Irishman's impertinence. "My purpose here is threefold, Mr. Gilhooley. First, Corporal Burke of the signal corps has brought the telegrams received for the various people who dwell here. I believe there is even one for you, sir."

"Ah, most excellent. I do so enjoy receiving telegrams." Finnegan nodded to the red-haired young corporal. "Is this cattle range really so perilous that the Corporal must travel with such a large escort?"

The lieutenant seemed to be enjoying the outing a great deal. "Oh, these other fellows are to assist me with my chores. Corporal Burke is quite capable of seeing to his duties without aid."

Behind the lieutenant the young Corporal began to dig in a saddle bag. "I believe your note is right here handy, Mr. Gilhooley."

All heads turned to the corporal, but only Bowden educated the boy. "Not now, Burke. Your business will wait."

Finnegan chuckled. "Yes, and what is your business, Lieutenant?"

The officer turned and settled his gaze on the gunman. "Ah, yes. My captain, who I believe you have met, has sent me here to collect his...let us call her an aide-de-camp, shall we?"

"That might be the most cultivated way to call it." Finnegan looked over the faces of the other soldiers. The lieutenant was enjoying himself, but the rest only looked scared or a bit ashamed of their errand. None of them seemed remotely interested in pushing their duties to the last measure. "And what are your orders, sir, if your initial commission cannot be accomplished?"

"In that instance, I am to collect you and Mr. Stuart, so that you may explain yourselves to Captain Hatcher."

"I see." Finnegan offered what he hoped was a kind smile. "Well, Lieutenant, I must report that the lass you seek has already departed and is not likely to return. I know that must be disappointing for you to hear. While I was in uniform, I always felt disappointed when I was not able to fulfill my orders."

"Perhaps my default orders will be fulfilled, and the day can yet be saved?"

Finnegan hung his head for a moment. "Ah, I may have some unwelcome news for you on that score, as well."

Bowden rubbed one side of his face. "You truly believe it is your choice to make, sir?"

"A man always has a choice in such matters, Lieutenant. The choices proffered may not be to his liking, but there is always a choice." Finnegan looked over the soldiers one more time. "One does hate to see pleasant fellows like these become embroiled in unpleasantness." Finnegan left his leaning position and stood up straight. "Lieutenant, are you familiar with the Confederate general James Longstreet?"

The young officer licked his lips. "I have heard his name."

"He is credited with first saying that an officer cannot lead from the rear." Finnegan smiled. "I will make you an offer, sir. If you will take the initiative and come up on this porch to disarm me, I will go with you quietly. Will you take the initiative?"

The lieutenant sighed. "You are a bit of a strange one, Mr. Gilhooley." He swung down from the saddle and straightened his uniform. "I must confess, when I first heard you had stolen the captain's squaw, I knew you must possess some strange ideas." He began to approach the porch. "Now I hear you prattling on with this foolishness." He stepped up onto the porch. "What does it matter which of us disarms you, Mr. Gilhooley? Does this honestly make you feel as though your honor will remain intact, having chosen not to fight?"

"Perhaps." Finnegan continued to smile.

"A famous gunman asking terms, I cannot believe what I am hearing."

"Perhaps you hear too much." As the lieutenant stepped to within arm's reach, Finnegan drew his Remington and set the cylinder next to the man's ear before firing. The bullet from the gun flew harmlessly up into the overhanging porch roof, but the lieutenant fell to the floor, nonetheless. A powder burn covered the side of his head and his eyes lolled around in his skull. "Surely impressive what the report of a gun can do, eh, Lieutenant?" The man stared up from his knees. "Yes, well." Finnegan holstered his pistol and turned to the closest cavalryman. "Sergeant, I suggest you collect your officer and be on your way."

The man pulled down on his small-billed cap. "Uh, I...I guess I don't rightly know what I ought to do. Did you...you didn't really shoot my Lieutenant in the head just now, did you?"

"Hardly." Finnegan reached out and shoved the lieutenant over so he lay on his side. "As you can plainly see, the vessel remains intact. Take him back to your fort, as per your orders."

"Our orders was to get the squaw or get you. What you're suggesting ain't either."

"This officer's orders were to get the Indian girl or obtain my arrest. Your orders were to assist him." Finnegan gave the lieutenant a small kick. "I would say he is in desperate need of assistance." Finnegan placed his hand on the butt of the Remington. "Unless you prefer to press the issue and see how many of us can be killed or maimed over some squabble resulting from your fool captain and this asinine lieutenant. You will have to excuse me, Sergeant, but I do not see how any of it is our business."

The sergeant spit out a stream of tobacco juice. "When you put it that way..." He pointed to one of the privates near him. "Callowly, place Lieutenant Bowden on his horse and stay close. He does not appear steady."

Finnegan watched as the private collected his officer and slung him up in the saddle with the assistance of a few others. When their work was completed, the private mounted and held one of the lieutenant's shoulders to keep him from falling. Finnegan waved to the corporal. "Young Mr. Burke, you mentioned a telegram?"

"Oh, uh, yes, sir. I suppose I did." He rode forward and handed the missive to Finnegan on the porch.

"Thank you." Finnegan placed it in his vest pocket. "Corporal Burke, as a member of the signal corps the duty of passing messages rightly falls to you, is that correct?"

"It is, sir."

"Excellent. Would you mind telling your captain, when next you see him, that I intend to stop by and pay him a visit before my time in the territory comes to an end? Since the man was kind enough to send this lieutenant to visit me, it would only be polite to return the favor. Can you tell him that?"

"Um, yes, sir. Word for word, sir. I may need to write it down if you wish for me to relate it just so."

Finnegan waved one hand about. "Oh, as long as he understands the basic idea, I believe it will suffice. Have a lovely day, Corporal."

The young man tipped his cap. "And a good day to you, sir."

Stuart sat behind his desk reading and rereading the telegram. Finally, he raised his eyes and locked them on Finnegan. "Mr. Gilhooley, I must point out that most of the turmoil we are experiencing is the direct result of your... strange notions."

"My strange notions?" Finnegan moved around in his chair a bit. "Granville, you cannot possibly hold that foolishness with the soldiers against me."

"An armed troop of men rode up to my door, Finnegan. Rode up while my wife and children resided within. They came here to set you straight and regain that captain's property. Now who in the hell *should* I hold responsible?"

"I am not the man who placed two lecherous jackasses in charge of an army outpost."

"Finnegan, who else is ever placed in charge of a fort? I never should have let you talk me into taking that girl." He hung his head, but he came up grinning. "Did you really blow the man's ear out?"

"It seemed the sensible response." Finnegan shrugged. "It has been my experience with officers that embarrassing them is far more effective than killing them. Surely it is less trouble." He pointed to the telegram Stuart held. "That, on the other hand, may bring no end of damn trouble."

"This?" Stuart tossed the message to one side of his desk. "That can nearly be construed as good news. True, it is sad how far I have fallen to take it as such, but any bright spot gladdens my mood, currently."

"Good news?" Finnegan rubbed his eyes. "Lavadure was hung, Granville. That grey-haired old fake judge hung the man in that barn just as Lavadure predicted he would." He shook his head. "What is worse, the crazy old bastard has sent me a telegram bragging of the exploit. Who can say how many others know of it already?"

"The more, the better." Stuart stood and moved to the map on his wall. He swept one hand across it. "Hopefully that lunatic Langford has told every fool in the territory."

"Granville, I thought we agreed that this sort of thing was to be avoided so as not to sully the good name of the Association?"

"We have." He shoved his hands into his pockets and shrugged. "So far, things are going brilliantly. MacKenzie was hung by the army, which has nothing to do with us and Langford is not a member of the Association. I can imagine no better outcome. The horse thieves are hung, and it cannot be construed to be our fault. Hell, you did not even personally kill that one fellow you arrested along with Lavadure. This could not be going better if I had planned it." He shook one finger at Finnegan. "Although, I could have done without the damned lieutenant. The day may come when I do not find the humor in that."

"Oh, posh. Needs be I will move the next bullet slightly to the left and he will cease to be a problem." Finnegan stood. "I suppose if you are not overly upset regarding Lavadure, there is not much left for me to inquire about, other than what we should attempt next."

Stuart turned and tapped the map with one knuckle. "Somewhere, out here, between us and Roosevelt and that damned duke or whatever he is, there is a large contingent of those villains gathering. This is their season, and it must be your season as well, Finnegan. The news of Lavadure and MacKenzie will do us some good, but we must make an example of one of the larger gangs if we are to make any real progress."

"What would you suggest?"

He gazed at the map once more. "More than a third of the summer is passed. At the first puff of cold weather these men we seek will let out for warmer climates or hide themselves in legitimate trades. If we can only place two heads on the wall, your presence here will have been a waste." He took a deep breath. "The best course of action may to be go out in search of them, in force."

"In force?"

"You and I and the ten most steady men in my employ."

Finnegan rubbed his brow. "Granville, a large troop is surely the best method to assure bringing your villains in alive, but without some knowledge of their whereabouts..." He motioned to the map. "We could easily roam about the country endlessly. I would also point out that you can hardly put ten men in the field when there is much work to be done about this place involving the cattle." Finnegan crossed the room and patted his friend on the shoulder. "Give it a bit more time. We will get word of some scoundrels again. There is more time left than gone. Our luck will kick in."

"I should certainly hope so, Finnegan. If it does not..." The pioneer paused, hearing a knock on the study door. "Yes, what is it?"

Teddy Blue stuck his head through the door. "Um, Mr. Stuart, Mr. Gilhooley, I'm sorry to bother you, but a fella's just come in to join the crew and he's got a missive he brought with him for Mr. Gilhooley."

Finnegan gave the young man a quizzical look. "A missive?"

"Well, um, yes. The fella, he comes by way of Maiden and Miss Meagher sent the note, sir." The cowboy held out an envelope. "I figured you'd want it before morning, so I come here."

"Yes, of course." Finnegan walked to the door and took the envelope. "Many thanks, Mr. Abbott."

"It was no trouble, sir." Teddy nodded and slipped out the door.

Stuart sighed. "Wonderful to know Miss Meagher feels the need to communicate so often. I can only assume she writes to ask if we could emancipate the cattle and turn them loose, in the name of freedom and liberty and such."

Finnegan chuckled. "She is not as bad as all that, Granville." He tore open the envelope and gave the letter within a quick read. "Well, that is...she writes to ask if I have any news regarding Mr. MacKenzie, of course."

"In the name of all that is decent, please inform her the damned Army hung the man so that we can be done with it."

"I surely will, at my earliest convenience." He held up the letter. "She also wishes to know if I am available to escort her to Lewistown to attend something called a rodeo." He gave Stuart a confused glance. "What the devil do you imagine that is?"

THAT NIGHT it took quite some time for Finnegan to fall off to sleep. It did not help that Kilkenny felt the need to endlessly lament the loss of his valet after they had turned out the light. The man had prattled on for what felt like forever regarding the gross injustice of Mr. Oman's being pressganged into service for something as silly as returning a young girl to her family. Kilkenny even took the time to suggest that it would have been better for her to remain at the ranch so that she could act as a laundress in his service. After that, Finnegan had more or less begged him to shut the hell up.

Even after Kilkenny had been silenced, Finnegan had

trouble nodding off. He spent an odd amount of time, for him anyway, replaying the day's events and wondering if there might not have been a better way to handle the upstart lieutenant. In the end, he reminded himself that such second guessing did little good in the long run. After that, his thoughts turned to Molly, and he was able to drift off wondering what new adventure might await them in the city of Lewistown.

It was well after midnight when the sound of the door being pushed open caused him to wake. It was only a very small, very soft sound to begin with, but it was followed by the unmistakable sound of the door being forced. The small block of wood that served to hold the door shut was rent asunder and rattled to the floor just before a large shape, black as night, trudged into the bunkhouse. The sound of its massive feet sweeping across the wooden floor chilled the very blood of those who resided within. The great beast moved past the doorjamb and into the space between the bunks. It paused directly between Kilkenny and Finnegan.

Slowly, ever so slowly, Finnegan took hold of the Purdey he kept leaned against his bunk. "Ephraim?" He hissed out the word as a low whisper. "Do you sleep?"

"Who in Christ's dear name could sleep through that?" The whiskey baron answered in an equally low whisper. "Do you have a rifle?"

"I do. What manner of beast is it?"

"It's a bloody giant bear, you daft bastard." Kilkenny took hold of himself after letting his voice rise too far. "Do not shoot just yet. Let it move a bit so you do not kill me."

Finnegan seated the butt of the double gun in his arm and moved just slightly to make certain he would not shoot one of his feet off, firing from a lying position as he was. "Give the word." He pushed the safety forward on the rifle.

"Hold...hold." The great beast took a slouching step forward. "Fire now! Now!"

Finnegan let fly with the first barrel, wrenched the gun down out of recoil and fired in what he hoped was the same spot the first barrel had been aimed. Instantly, he leapt out of bed and broke the gun open. He found the spent shells and tore them from the breech before feeling around on the bunk above for two fresh rounds. When he located them, he reloaded and snapped the Purdey shut once more. There was little to no light, but he could just make out the enormous mass of animal, a black monolith, that was collapsed on the bunkhouse floor. "I...I believe it is finished, Ephraim. Thank the Lord."

"Yes, yes, quite." The whiskey baron pulled himself up on shaky legs and found the lantern. "You truly saved my arse that time, old boy. I dare say, hiring a Pinkerton is money well spent." He found a match and lit the lantern. As he turned down the flame, he drew near to the animal and held the lantern up to one end of the mass. "Oh, dear. Um, I say, this might prove to be a bit embarrassing. Possibly for the both of us, Finnegan."

"Embarrassing?" Finnegan approached his most recent kill.

"Yes, well, as you can see, now that we have the lantern going." He reached down and grabbed one horn. "This specimen is clearly not a bear. I believe this is one of Stuart's better bulls, if I am not mistaken."

"Bloody hell." Finnegan lowered the Purdey. "Well, damn it, man. The moose I take full responsibility for, but this poor beast's demise is clearly your fault, Ephraim."

"My fault? You fired on the animal, not I."

"You told me to fire. You told me it was a bear. You told me it was a bloody giant bear."

"Well, how the hell should I know what is or is not a bear?"

"You are a damn naturalist, are you not?"

"I mean that it was dark, Finnegan. You thought it was a bear, as well, damn it." He held the lantern up to the bull's bloody muzzle. "Oh, this will not please, Stuart. I seem to recall he felt this bull was an exceptional animal. He took the time to point it out to me." Kilkenny scowled.

"Yes, it will be troubling to him. I am lucky to be accompanying Miss Meagher to her rodeo."

"Yes, well, I have no idea what a rodeo might be, but I believe I should definitely accompany you as a chaperone. There will be hell to pay when this is revealed." Kilkenny ran the lantern's light over the entirety of the bull. "Might we claim the beast attacked us? I have heard that bulls can be quite vicious when the mood strikes them."

Finnegan sat down on his bunk and set the Purdey to one side. "I suppose you may spin whatever yarn you think is best, Ephraim. I can do little but agree. You are, after all, a naturalist."

Chapter 20

LEWISTOWN, MONTANA TERRITORY

July 13th, 1884

"This is a fascinating bit of provincialism, Finnegan." Kilkenny found Lewistown to be an intriguing outpost. He was most thrilled to discover that the citizens of Lewistown were not as abstentious as the majority of the residents of the DHS Ranch. The beer and whiskey ran freely during the town's rodeo and Kilkenny was truly in his element. Finnegan did not care for it greatly, but Molly seemed to be enjoying herself, so he could live with the bedlam for a while. It appeared as though half the population of the territory had stumbled into the rather small town for the shindig, and everyone from the grubbiest cowboy to the most well-bred looking women were enjoying themselves in the lovely summer sun.

"I am glad you find it amusing, Ephraim." Finnegan motioned around at the revelries. "It is a puzzlement why they felt the need to give this festival such a strange name. In the rest of the country this would be referred to as a horse race and nothing more." He nodded to Molly, who was in conversation with some other ladies not far off. "I expect Miss Meagher is quite pleased to be in a place where things are named so strangely, and she has the opportunity to pepper her letters with odd terms."

"Such is the hazard when you court a schoolmistress, Finnegan." Kilkenny sipped the beer he had purchased to supplement his flask. "Oh, my goodness, that is... not what I had previously thought to be the taste of beer."

"It is likely well past its prime, Ephraim." Finnegan chuckled and offered his friend a cigar. "It has been some time since I have noticed a brewery. I imagine it must be freighted many a mile to bring it to this town."

"Yes, well, it is still preferable to water." Kilkenny set his drink on the wagon deck and took up the cigar. "Rodeo is a Spanish word, Finnegan. I believe it is used to describe something like what Mr. Stuart calls a roundup, but I cannot recall just now."

"Spanish?"

"Yes."

"I chased the James brothers across half of Texas and never heard the term. It must not be much used. I cannot see what makes this different from a horse race with a bit of a cotillion thrown in."

Kilkenny pointed with his cigar to a corral that held a selection of rather perturbed looking horses. "I believe the departure from an eastern horse race lies with those animals over there. They are untrained stock, you see, and a goodly number of the men around here intend to ride them for sport."

"Sport?"

"Yes, they will ride them in turn and the man who can remain mounted the longest wins a prize."

"The cowboys at the DHS have done little other than that for weeks now. I cannot say as it looks very entertaining, and I certainly would not suggest it as sport. Some of them will surely lose a limb or some such maiming before it is over.

I would not think a sane man would do such a thing without the guarantee of pay."

"An odd statement from a man who so frequently engages in activity no sane man should attempt." Kilkenny pointed across the racetrack. "Now, would you look at that fellow? What do you imagine he is supposed to be?" A man was strolling around in a long-tailed coat with pinstripes of red, white, and blue, with an oversized top hat colored to match.

"Ah, now, this I can explain." Finnegan found a cigar of his own. "That is a character by the name of Uncle Sam. He is rather like John Bull, only meant for Americans, of course."

"I see." Kilkenny lit his cigar. "And was he a real fellow or a simply a fiction?"

"A fiction, as far as I know. The outfit never changes, but the subject matter does from time to time with Uncle Sam. They normally trot him out to brew up patriotism for some bit of foolishness. He's mostly a northern contrivance. I must say I am surprised to see a fellow larking about dressed in that manner with so many blatant former confederates here. The north rather took custody of the fellow during the war as I recall."

"Ah, there you are. Someone has decided to take offense, as you predicted." The two Irishmen watched as the flag-bedecked Uncle Sam was approached by a couple of rough-looking cowboys who promptly shoved him to the ground and began taunting him with small kicks and flicks of muddy earth. "Well, there you have it. No mascot is safe once the club splits, I suppose."

"Yes, it was not a well thought out entertainment." Finnegan chuckled, but cut the laugh short as he looked off to his left and saw Molly standing at the side of the wagon.

"Do you two mean to simply sit here and observe that man being assaulted?" She wore a very stern look.

Finnegan glanced back to the woebegone caricature who was currently being shoved down into the mud once again. "Well, Molly, I am not a resident of this place and I have no idea what might have caused the quarrel. For all I know, those men may have reason, and if they do not, that fellow should have his own friends or kin to come to his aid."

"He does not." She pointed across the track. "His name is Bob Jackson. He has no family that I know of and was invited to dress as Uncle Sam for the opening parade. Those ruffians are picking on him for no reason, and if you were any kind of men at all you would put a stop to it immediately."

Finnegan merely stared at her for a moment. "Put a stop to it?"

"Yes."

"You wish for me to stop two men I do not know from harassing a third man I do not know?"

"Yes."

"Molly, I have never done such a thing in my life. What in the name of Saint Peter would possess a man to do such a thing? Are you unaware that sticking your nose into stranger's business can only lead to trouble?"

"He is not a stranger; I know him."

Finnegan rubbed the side of his head. "You know him and wish for me to intervene in his being teased a bit?"

"Yes. What baffles you about this? Go help that man or I will not let you soon forget it, Mr. Gilhooley."

Finnegan sighed and hopped down from the wagon. "Very well. I would only request that you recall this was your prerogative, not mine."

Kilkenny hopped down. "Shall I accompany you, Finnegan?"

"Oh, goodness no. If you would do me the favor of pulling Miss Meagher under the wagon when this all goes quite wrong, I would appreciate it."

"Wrong? What do you anticipate?"

Finnegan smiled at Molly. "Mayhem and perdition, my normal companions. Try not to get the lady's dress dirty when you pull her down, Ephraim."

Molly stuck out her tongue. "I believe you are exaggerating what hangs in the balance, sir."

"I forget on occasion that you are mostly only familiar with me from our time in your father's parlor." He tipped his hat to her and began walking across the currently unused horse track toward the men who continued to sling mud at Uncle Sam. As he approached, he did his best to appear amiable. When he was some ten feet from the men, he stopped and cleared his throat to get their attention. The two cowboys turned away from Uncle Sam and looked over the stranger. They were both armed. One lanky fellow with long hair sported a pair of Colt revolvers. The other, a short man with a bit of a gut growing under his shirt had a Smith & Wesson hung low on his hip. Both appeared quite drunk and foul tempered. Finnegan offered a smile. "Gentlemen, might I have a moment of your time?"

They both stared, obviously somewhat confused. The tall one spoke first. "Gentlemen? Ain't been called that in a spell." He looked Finnegan up and down from his frock coat to his relatively unmarred slouch hat. "And what are you, eh? The new preacher, come to save our souls?"

"No, friend, I am not a preacher. I am only a visitor passing through."

The short one chuckled. "Then you best get to passing then, eh?" They both laughed, finding the comment quite funny for some reason.

Finnegan continued to smile. "Yes, well, very jolly, yes." He walked past them to where Uncle Same lay in the mud. Finnegan extended his hand and helped the young man to his feet. "I know you fellows are only enjoying a spot of fun, but some of the ladies have complained." He gave Uncle Sam a stern look. "On your way, then." The young man nodded and began trudging off away from the racetrack.

The tall one took a step toward Finnegan. "Hey, maybe you don't understand so good. You talk funny, so I assume you ain't a proper American. You don't seem to ken why we might be aggravated by a damn half-breed dressing up like Uncle Sam."

Finnegan squeezed the bridge of his nose. "What is your name, sir?"

"Rattlesnake Jake." The tall man hooked his thumbs into his gun belt, rather beaming with pride at his moniker.

"Yes, well, Mr. Jake, in all earnestness, would you mind answering a question for me that has been nagging me for some time?"

Rattlesnake puffed out his chest a bit. "I imagine there's all sorts of things I could explain to you."

"Grand. Would you mind explaining why it is that, while every person in this place seems to be a half-breed, as you say, or the father of a half-breed, or the mother of a half-breed, or the associate of a half-breed, you all get into such a dither when one of these men comes out into public? Every white man in this territory seems interested in little else but brewing these half-breeds, I find it terribly odd that they should have such a difficult time walking about town."

The short one sneered. "What the hell you suggesting, Mister?"

"My name is Gilhooley, Finnegan Gilhooley, and I cannot say as I am suggesting anything whatsoever. What is your name, sir?"

"Charlie Owen, and I ain't got no damn half-breeds in my family, if that's what you're insinuating."

Finnegan nodded to the stumpy fellow. "Certainly not." He adjusted his frock coat. "Well, it has been very pleasant visiting with you both. Unfortunately, I must see to my other social obligations. I am sure you can both understand. Good day." He took a step back, meaning to back away from them until he was a reasonable distance away. His new acquaintances did not look like the kind of men he wanted to turn his back to. As it worked out, he was right.

Jake spoke up. "You think you can just wander over here, take that half-breed when we ain't done with him, and then wander back to whatever whore we was offending that got you browbeat over here to begin with? I ain't one to stand for that sort of thing."

Finnegan sighed. "You are clearly a man of principle."

Owen scoffed. "You got a damn sharp tongue. Talk like you're better than us."

The gunman was growing weary of the cowboys. "I apologize, Mr. Owen. I suppose I have let my manners slip somewhat in this rusticated setting. Of course, how could I know that I would have the luck to meet not one, but two, of Queen Vic's bastards who would require such greatly enhanced etiquette."

"Did you dare call me a bastard?" Jake seemed more befuddled than angry.

"I bloody well did." Finnegan leapt forward as Jake was reaching for one of his guns. With well-practiced deftness, the gunman drew his Remington and planted the trigger guard of the weapon between Jake's eyes. The ruffian stumbled one step back and fell to the ground. Finnegan turned to Owen, who wore a very shocked expression. "And what of you, you damned dwarf?" Finnegan held the Remington on him. "Do you wish to make further trouble?"

Owen held up his hands. "Uh, well, no, I can't say as I would care to." His look of shock turned to something closer to worry. He was staring past Finnegan. "Although, I dare say they might." He pointed behind Finnegan.

Long ago, Finnegan had learned that it was not wise to look behind you when an adversary pointed that way, but he decided it might be the proper course of action when a bullet thudded into the corral post near his head. Whirling around, with his Remington at the ready, he saw Uncle Sam and another man approaching. They both carried rifles. "Hells bells." Uncle Sam raised a Winchester. "Do not fire at me, you dizzy bugger." Uncle Sam fired and the bullet hit the mud at Owen's feet.

"To hell with this." Owen began running for the town's main street.

"You stop that damn foolishness, Sam, or Jackson, or whatever the hell your name is." Finnegan glanced to his side and saw that Rattlesnake Jake had regained his feet. He had one of his pistols out and was aiming at his attackers. "Jake, do not aggravate this..." Jake fired off a round that went wide of Uncle Sam and Sam's friend fired back.

Jake's pistol was torn from his hand and the ruffian stumbled once again. He held up his hand for Finnegan to see. "Piss and perdition, they shot my damn finger off."

Finnegan stared and confirmed that the man was, in fact, missing the middle digit of his right hand. Another bullet from the fellow Finnegan had saved slammed into a corral post. "Bugger this. You are on your own, Rattlesnake Jake." Finnegan hopped the rail fence nearby and took off in the same direction Owen had fled. Behind him, he could hear more gunfire and assumed that Jake had remembered that he still possessed another hand and a pistol to go with it. As Finnegan traversed the corral, the number of people shooting seemed to have increased considerably. It appeared as if the greater portion of the citizenry had a dislike for both Rattlesnake Jake and Charlie Owen and were taking the opportunity to throw some lead in their direction.

As Finnegan neared the wagon where he had been sitting

only moments earlier, he could see Kilkenny and Molly shoe-horned in under the conveyance. Kilkenny's eyes were wide as he bobbed his head up and down, trying to get a look at the opposite side of the corrals. "Who is shooting, Finnegan?"

"Everyone! Keep your empty head down, damn it!" Finnegan dropped to roll under the last crossbeams of the corral and ran in a crouch to the wagon. Once there, he crawled underneath and pressed Molly closer to the ground. "Somehow I knew this would end in a damn row."

Molly pushed Finnegan up and he bumped his head on the underside of the wagon bed. "Stop trampling me, I cannot see what is happening."

"Trampling? He pushed her back down. "You wish to have a better view of the bullet that kills you, woman?"

"I want to see what has happened to poor Bob Jackson."

"To hell with Bob Jackson, he very nearly shot me in his stupidity." Finnegan got as low as he could, but he was a might tall to really gain cover from the wagon, especially with two friends cowering beside him.

"Is Bob Jackson the man dressed in that ridiculous striped suit?" Kilkenny could not hide his excitement at finally being privy to a gunfight, even if it wasn't amounting to much in terms of dead men.

"Yes, the fool in the striped suit is the reason I was very nearly shot down at a damn picnic. Apparently, he is one of the great men of this territory. Well worth my being sacrificed so that he may continue wandering about and shooting at those who are most helpful to him."

Molly smacked an elbow into Finnegan. "Don't be churlish."

Kilkenny pointed down the town's main street. "I only inquire because that chap dressed like...what did you call him?"

"Uncle Sam." Finnegan sighed.

"Yes, well, he's running down the street here and I believe that fellow who ran off when the shooting began is lying in wait for him."

"Good riddance." Finnegan received another elbow for the comment.

Molly began shoving her protector toward one side of the wagon. "Of all the cold-hearted...oh, go save him."

"Save him?" Finnegan put one boot against a wagon wheel to remain concealed during the shoving. "From what I have seen, your innocent friend has instigated this donnybrook. If he wished to be saved, perhaps he should not have taken up his rifle and begun this."

"He's a poor, unfortunate orphan..."

"And a half-breed and an attempted murderer, and God-knows-what-else. I am far too familiar with his history." Finnegan was losing his sense of humor as more bullets hit the wagon in search of Rattlesnake Jake on the other side of the corral. The citizens of Lewistown were proving to be very poor marksmen.

"Finnegan, you go save that poor boy or I swear I shall never speak to you again." She ceased shoving and sat back against one wheel with her arms crossed.

"The last time you spoke to me I was very nearly shot. I should think it might be great boon to me if you would begin holding your tongue." Finnegan shrugged as best he could in his crouched position.

Kilkenny gave Finnegan a small kick. "Finnegan..." He hissed. "You cannot expect a woman's wishes to always be in line with yours."

"Not in line? Have you gone off your bleeding head?" He glanced between the whiskey baron and the schoolteacher. "Upon further consideration, I might prefer the fusillade to my current position." He offered a sardonic smile to Molly. "If that fool kills me, I will not let you forget it in the next world." He slid out from underneath the wagon and began running down Lewistown's main throughfare.

As Finnegan rushed in the direction Uncle Sam had scampered off, it truly did seem that most every grown man in Lewistown, and a few not yet grown, had taken it upon themselves to try and kill the two ruffians. It reminded Finnegan of a skirmish during the war. The only difference was that no one possessed a uniform. As he rounded the corner of a livery stable, he came upon Uncle Sam, who was raising his Winchester to fire on Owen. Owen had located a horse and was mounted. The short-statured ruffian held a pistol in one hand and the reins of the highly agitated beast in the other. Finnegan shoved Bob Jackson to the ground just as Owen fired a round in their direction. The bullet passed where Jackson's head might have been and tore the shoulder from Finnegan's coat, taking a small portion of meat with it.

Jackson looked up from the ground, appearing quite angry. "What the hell did you do that for?"

"Oh, do shut the hell up." Another bullet zipped past. Finnegan drew his Remington and fired at Owen. The ruffian took the bullet somewhere in his gut, but managed another round that thudded into Jackson's leg. Finnegan emptied the revolver, hitting both Owen and his unfortunate horse. The wounded animal took off down a small alleyway with its badly wounded rider slopping in the saddle.

Jackson was clutching his leg as blood began to cover his brightly striped pants. "I've been shot! Oh, good God, it hurts! Fetch me a doctor and some whiskey, damn you."

"Limp off and find him yourself, worthless cur." Finnegan reached down and snatched up the Winchester the patriotic impersonator had dropped in the dirt. "Intolerable jackass." Finnegan left the fool to his own business and stalked down the short alleyway the horse had disappeared into. The poor beast was standing in the street with blood trickling down one flank. Taking careful aim at the animal's head, Finnegan squeezed the trigger and the horse fell to the ground with Owen still perched on its back. Levering the action Finnegan took aim on the wounded man's head and fired again.

His work done, Finnegan walked back to the wagon where he had left Molly and Kilkenny. They had emerged from their hiding place. Kilkenny wore a visage that was a mixture of fear and irritation. "Ah, Finnegan, good. I had begun to think one of these provincials had put you under." His eyes grew wide seeing the gunman's crimson coat sleeve. "Bloody hell, have you been shot?"

Finnegan sighed. "As it happens, I have, and I must say its rather painful."

Molly rushed over and began fussing with the wound. "My God, is it serious?"

"It is a trifle, I suppose." He grimaced as she tore his coat sleeve.

"Is Mr. Jackson all right?" She continued to rend his clothing.

"Oh, yes, Mr. Jackson. He has a slightly larger hole in his leg, but I fear he will live. May Christ forgive me for preserving him. Who can say what mischief he may yet be responsible for?"

"You have done the right thing, Finnegan. You should be proud of yourself." She smiled and pulled his sleeve from him.

"I have never before in my life paused to consider whether or not I have done right action, I have no idea why I should bother myself with it now." Finnegan scowled. "Do we really need to destroy my coat over this? I somehow doubt I can locate another in this outpost."

"Do not be contrary." Molly probed his wound.

"Damn it, woman!" He pulled his shoulder away and she

drew it back. Giving up, he turned his attention to Kilkenny. "And what has your goat?"

The whiskey baron took out his flask and shrugged. "Oh, it is only...I suppose this conflagration was a bit of a disappointment. I did not see that man killed over by the corrals. I have no idea where that other man got off to, but since the shooting has ceased, I can only assume he was killed out of my view, as well. This American gunfighting does not offer much for the spectator, I must say."

"Perhaps if you pass through Washington on the way home you could complain to President Arthur. He will surely be livid to hear you were not properly entertained."

Kilkenny waved one hand dismissively. "I doubt that very much. That is the trouble with the elected officials this country makes use of: they have no real sense of national pride." He took a long drink and wiped his mouth with his sleeve. "Oh, I see you have procured a new rifle. Is that considered something of a prize for remaining standing through a thing like this?"

"Ephraim, of all the oddities I have witnessed today, you are surely the oddest." Finnegan glanced down at the Winchester he still held. "Although, now that I take the time to notice, it does have rather nice wood, does it not?"

Chapter 21

DHS RANCH, MONTANA TERRITORY

July 16th, 1884

STUART SAT BEHIND HIS RATHER LARGE DESK, attempting to appear stern but mostly coming off as frustrated. Finnegan and Kilkenny had taken their liberty from the ranch after explaining the situation involving the bull to Teddy Blue. They had felt it would be best to let some time pass after the incident so that Stuart might have the opportunity to appreciate the lack of intent regarding the bull's death. It did not seem the plan had been very effective.

"I just cannot understand why you chose to kill the creature. Could you not have simply shooed it out again?"

Finnegan licked his lips. "I and Mr. Kilkenny were under the impression it was a bear, Granville. In the dark, under duress, it was a mistake any man might have made. If it comforts you any, I can tell you the beast did not suffer."

"Suffer! Who gives a damn about its suffering? Do you have any idea how much that bull was worth? It was the finest breeding bull on this range and would have given excellent service for many years if you had not taken it upon yourself to gun it down in cold blood."

"Granville, Mr. Kilkenny is more than willing to compensate the ranch for the loss of the animal, given the fact that he played a prominent role in its demise."

"I cannot fathom how two grown men, one a naturalist and the other a professional shootist can accidentally kill my best bull."

Finnegan withdrew a cigar from the frock coat he had purchased in Lewistown. From what he could see it was the only garment remotely in his size in the entire settlement. He winced as he moved his arm. "Bugger, that might have been located in a more convenient spot."

"Ah, yes, and now you have been wounded in a fight that was not any of your concern. No doubt the men you shot will turn out to be some of the city fathers and I will not be allowed in the confines of Lewistown once it is discovered you are in the employ of the Association."

"Try not to exaggerate quite so flagrantly, Granville. I assure you the one and only man I shot was not a pillar of the community and I would point out that I only shot him after many others already had at him." Finnegan lit his cigar and sighed. "The citizenry seemed quite happy to be rid of both men who were killed, and I heard no complaints." He shook his head. "It is not as if I planned the damn thing, Granville. I was attempting to placate Miss Meagher and the situation rather left my control."

"That schoolteacher of yours is proving to be a damned nuisance."

"Granville, might I remind you, I am not the one who brought her here." He smiled but his mirth was not contagious.

"Sweet mercy, do not remind me." The pioneer hung his head and brought it back up looking a bit hopeless. "You realize none of this puts us one jot closer to eliminating the damn horse thieves and none of this does one damn bit of good for my ledger books."

Finnegan nodded. "I understand that, Granville. Do not forget that I have as much of a financial interest in improving your lot here as any man."

"Then perhaps you should stop shooting my bulls and start finding the damn thieves who are stealing my horses."

Finnegan stood up from his chair, feeling weary. "I assure you, I intend to cease one and see to the other."

"For both our sakes, I sure as hell hope you do."

Chapter 22

DHS RANCH, MONTANA TERRITORY

July 17th, 1884

Finnegan and Kilkenny occupied their usual seats on the porch of the bunkhouse. They were staring out at the countryside and were both becoming a bit bored. Nothing of interest had occurred at the ranch since their return. No cowboys had come in with news. There had been no visitors from the fort. Even the ranch employees were a dull bunch. They did little other than locate bogged down cows and break horses in preparation for the round-up that should occur in August. The summer was slipping by, and the lack of progress was beginning to grate on Finnegan's nerves. The lack of entertainment was beginning to grate on Kilkenny's.

Finnegan placed his feet up on the porch railing. "I believe Stuart is being a bit overly dramatic regarding the loss of the bull."

"Yes, he has been in a snit since that occurred." Kilkenny was flipping through an ornithology tome he had brought with him.

"I can see no reason one bull should not be as good as the next. It is not as if one is apt to try and breed these cattle so they are more attractive before they are chopped up into steaks."

"It is difficult to say what motivates a man like Stuart." Kilkenny held the book open so Finnegan could view one of the illustrations. "Have you seen one of these about?"

"No." Finnegan resumed staring out. "Miss Meagher will be by again in a week's time."

"Ah, yes, very good. How did you leave things with her when we returned her to Maiden?"

"Leave things?"

"Yes. Was she pleased that you performed so heroically and saved that idiot from himself during the gun battle?"

"I believe she was. Although, with Molly it is always difficult to say what her being pleased truly profits a fellow. It is also difficult to say if what pleases her one day might not perturb her the next."

"Well, that is the difficulty in dealing with women the world over." He held up the book again. "Have you seen one of these?"

"No." In the far distance, a small speck was moving along the road that led to the ranch. "Someone approaches."

"Good Lord, it is not those damned soldiers again, is it?"

"No, it is only a single wagon."

"Ah, very good." Kilkenny flipped the page and held up the book. "This one?"

"No."

"Well, damn it, have you seen any birds in this wretched country?"

"Very few." Finnegan pointed out toward the road. "I may be mistaken, but that may be your valet approaching, Ephraim."

Kilkenny snapped his book shut and set it down. "Well, praise Christ, I am delivered. Do you really think it's him?"

"He left in a wagon; it would reason that he should return in one."

"I certainly hope so. I have not had a tolerable shave since that man departed."

Finnegan eyed his friend and shook his head. "Mr. Oman supposedly despises you to the point he will not speak to you, but you allow him near your neck with a razor?"

"Posh. It is not that he despises me personally, Finnegan. It is only that, as a descendant of an emperor he looks down on all plebians such as us."

"Ah, well, so long as it is only that and nothing personal." Once he was certain only a single wagon and nothing more was enroute to the ranch, Finnegan sat back in his chair and pulled his slouch hat down over his eyes. Mr. Oman did not appear to still have a passenger on the buckboard with him, and that was all that concerned the gunman. He had drifted off and did not hear Kilkenny leave the porch to greet his long-absent valet. The gunman was having a perfectly lovely dream involving Miss Meagher when he felt something tugging on his foot. Panicked that it might be a bear come to haul him off the porch, he flopped backwards in his chair and would have fallen, if Mr. Oman had not caught the back of the chair and stopped his descent. Finnegan opened his eyes to stare up at the bulk of the strangely stoic butler. "Ah, Mr. Oman. I am obliged, of course." The valet blinked and gave a small nod as he held Finnegan near horizontally. "Um, would you mind terribly righting me?" He gave another small nod and heaved the gunman back into a sitting position. Finnegan looked about and saw that Katie Stuart had joined them on the porch. "Hello, Miss Stuart."

"Hello, Mr. Gilhooley. Did you have a nightmare?"

"Oh, no trouble." He glanced around from the valet to Kilkenny and back to Katie again. "What brings you to our humble barracks, lass?"

"Mr. Oman has brought news of something that may interest you, Mr. Gilhooley."

Finnegan turned to the valet. "Ah, wonderful to hear. What news?"

The valet stood mute, so Katie took the initiative. "While he was escorting the young lady from the fort back to her home, Mr. Oman has come upon a rather large collection of horses in the possession of some men that Mr. Oman knows to be of low character and not in funds enough to purchase stock. He did not approach close enough to check the brands of the horses in the corral, but he feels near certain they must have been obtained through nefarious methods."

"Ah, yes, that is of interest. Where, precisely, did Mr. Oman discover this den of thieves?"

"Just north of the junction of Crooked Creek and the Musselshell, Mr. Gilhooley. It is a sort of trading post, the way Mr. Oman describes it." Katie smiled. "I am glad to be of assistance. Do you believe this news will cheer my father?"

"I certainly hope it does." Finnegan stood and stretched out his back. "A goodly number of horse thieves brought to task is just what his disposition needs." Finnegan looked to Oman, considered making a comment regarding his prejudices, but thought better of it. If the man was willing to supply news regarding horse thieves, through whatever channels, he was welcome to choose his own company. Finnegan smiled at the valet. "Many thanks, Mr. Oman."

"Oh, yes, I know the place well enough." Stuart tapped a spot on his wall map with one finger. He had been out assisting the cowboys, or nagging them, depending on one's perspective, all day. He and the men had returned for their evening meal, and it was the first chance Finnegan had to inform the ranch foreman of the good news Mr. Oman had brought. Stuart was quite pleased, just as his daughter had hoped he would be. "That colossus in Kilkenny's employ is not mistaken; it is a trading post of sorts, owned by a man named William Downes. The man is a first-rate scoundrel. If he is in possession of stock, in any numbers, you can be assured it will show the brands of this ranch and many others. Without a single bill of sale, I would wager."

"What sort of chap is Downes?" Finnegan sat in his usual chair, smoking his usual cigar.

"Oh, formerly a buffalo hunter. I do not think he has yet reached fifty. He does a steady business trading with whoever might happen up or down the Musselshell and sells much whiskey to Indians. He does well with the steamboats, of course, but he'll take most anything off of whatever villain darkens his door. I would not doubt for a moment that you may find Jack Stringer himself sitting at the man's table when you get there."

"Yes, well, we shall see. Do you mean to say you are not to accompany me?"

Stuart rubbed his tired eyes. "I would like nothing better, but I cannot. This place is in a damnable condition. Reece Anderson has not been keeping those rotten cowboys in order. I cannot claim to know where half the cows or half the cowboys might be at any given moment." He snapped his fingers and pointed to the map again. "Here's a thought: take Reece and a few of the hands with you. I assume you will need some assistance. You have no way of knowing what may await you at Downes' place."

"I will certainly need assistance, especially if I hope to bring any of them back alive, but are you certain Anderson is the man to commission? As I recall, he once told me he is not much of a marksman, and prefers to avoid such things."

"Is that not preferable?" Stuart shrugged. "You plan to

more bluff than fight these men into manacles, do you not? Reece does prefer to avoid donnybrooks. He will keep the other men in line and make certain none of them oversteps. Your taking him will also allow me to get the remainder of the cowboys working again. I fear, left to his own inclinations, he draws them into dissipation rather quickly."

"And if he becomes dissolute while we are chasing horse thieves?"

"Plant your boot in his backside and remind him of the pecking order."

"Would it not be better to leave Anderson here, where you could boot him into line of march?"

"Reece may be rather difficult to suffer sometimes, but all the men know he is my representative, and his word will keep them in line while you are in pursuit of these villains. Put Reece under your thumb and the rest will follow his lead. Without some chain of command, they are nothing but a useless rabble of idiots. With Reece, you can at least count on them being a browbeaten rabble that will move in a uniform direction behind you."

"Granville, you make me wonder if it might not be best to go alone. Perhaps I will pass a tavern along the way and will be able to recruit some drunks and loafers to assist."

The pioneer returned to his desk and took up his coffee cup. "From what I am told, the dustup in Lewistown was quite a confused scene. Much shooting and chaos."

"To say the least, yes."

"Well, my cowboys are drawn from the spring, Finnegan. If you require professional men, who can be counted on to show restraint, I suggest you harken back to Chicago and collect a few of your fellow Pinkerton men."

Finnegan chuckled. "Pinkerton agents can be counted on to be more accurate with their fire; I do not know if I would credit them with restraint." He gave his cigar a few puffs and came to a conclusion. "I will take Reece and four of your cowboys. With Kilkenny, that will make six of us altogether. That should be a large enough party, if well-armed, to properly intimidate any number of thieves we may encounter. It should push them into flight, at least."

Stuart arched one eyebrow. "You intend to take your whiskey baron with you?"

"I cannot imagine what would keep him from it."

Stuart scratched his head. "Were you not originally employed with the intention of keeping him from danger just like this?"

"I suppose that was the initial intention."

"Will he wish to bring that...odd valet he employs?"

"Oh, yes, Oman. I had not considered that."

"Yes, well, one does often forget what an important role a valet can play in hunting horse thieves."

Chapter 23

CROOKED CREEK, MONTANA TERRITORY

July 19th, 1884

FINNEGAN EYED THE SMALL CABIN AND COMPLEX OF corrals with Kilkenny's binoculars. The sun was just coming over the mountains in the east and the grey light had twisted the color palette to be seen through the glass. There was no way to tell how many men lingered inside the crudely constructed domicile, but two fellows could already be seen out in the corrals, saddling horses and getting ready for whatever kind of work they engaged in during the day. Finnegan lowered the glasses and turned to Kilkenny. "That is a poor piece of luck."

The whiskey baron squinted. "How so? There should be enough of them piled in there to satisfy Stuart. From the sound of the chivaree they had last night, there might have been a hundred of them jammed in there."

"Yes, but it would be better if they all still slumbered. These two being early risers may queer our approach."

"Even if they alert the others, can the men in the cabin do much to ready themselves before we are on top of them?" Kilkenny was taking particular enjoyment in being allowed to help plan the raid on the small trading post.

"That is not the main problem. They will more likely run when we approach." Finnegan looked back over his shoulder at Reece Anderson, Floppin' Bill Cantrell, and the three cowboys Stuart had selected to round out the posse. The three were apparently on loan from other ranches in some respect, and Stuart had chosen them more for the fact that they were not chummy with each other and that he did not feel they would be missed working on the range than their ability to deal with ruffians. "If we send some of them out to collect the stragglers, I fear we may never see them again. Aside from Anderson, they do not appear to know where we are or where we are going."

"Then we shall chase them down."

"And leave them to handle the rest?"

"Finnegan, we shall be on them in the blink of an eye. All Anderson and the rest must accomplish is to order them to put their pants on and march them outside. It should be no great chore to collect those two if they choose to flee. We will return in a jiffy, certainly before these fellows have opportunity to get into trouble."

Finnegan considered it for a moment. "Perhaps I should give chase alone."

"If they flee very far you will have difficulty finding your way back. You know you have a poor sense of direction."

"I do not have a poor sense of direction." Finnegan looked around the prairie. "I merely have difficulty with this particular landscape."

"Which is why you and I should collect the stray horse thieves, if they do, in fact, flee." Kilkenny offered a shy smile. "I have never had opportunity to ride down an escaping villain, Finnegan. I would very much like the chance."

"Oh, well, far be it from me to cheat you out of amusement." He handed the binoculars to Kilkenny. "Very well. We will explain to the others and see to our work." They slid backwards out of the sagebrush they had hidden in and made their way down to the bottom of the ravine the rest of the posse was concealed in. Anderson and Cantrell were busily jesting back and forth while the rest sat awkwardly silent in the saddle. "All right, gentlemen." Finnegan swung up onto his horse. "Our villains are all there, but two have risen early. We will ride down on them briskly. If the two in the corrals depart, Mr. Kilkenny and I will give chase. You men will secure those who still slumber in the cabin." He looked over the faces of the cowboys before him. "Are there any questions?"

Reece Anderson shook his head. "We will secure them, Mr. Gilhooley."

Finnegan pulled down his hat. "The rest of you understand, as well? Surround the cabin, allow Mr. Anderson and Mr. Cantrell to burst inside and secure the men within. They will be taken completely by surprise. They will likely offer no fight." The assemblage all nodded slowly. Their rather blank faces offered little comfort. "Oh, to hell with it. This is what I get for taking a position outside the agency." He gave his horse a small kick. "Let us be off."

They rode up out of the ravine and galloped toward the trading post, closing the quarter mile in hardly any time. It was, however, more than ample time for the two men in the corrals to notice the coming posse and begin their flight.

"Ha! Those foxes are offering fine sport, Finnegan. We should have brought a trumpeter." Kilkenny urged his horse forward and Finnegan followed, waving the others toward the cabin as he and Kilkenny swung wide to get around the corrals and give chase to the fugitives. The two Irishmen charged up out of the creek bottom and onto the plains above. It appeared as though the two absconding horse thieves had chosen excellent mounts. They were pulling away from Finnegan and Kilkenny quite steadily. Not to be deterred,

Kilkenny pressed his horse on, and Finnegan's kept pace as well as it could.

Few things can make men lose track of distance or time the way a rapid chase can. Before either Finnegan or Kilkenny realized it, they had passed more than five miles in pursuit. Finally, the thieves' horses began to tire, and the distance began to close. Before they were completely upon their quarry, Finnegan saw the men pass into a coulee filled with stunted pine trees. Kilkenny spurred his mount on even more, feeling an end to the hunt was close at hand. Finnegan called out to his friend. "Damn it, slow down, Ephraim." But the whiskey baron plunged into the coulee, heedless of the warning.

Once in the trees, it was impossible to see more than a few yards ahead. Kilkenny crashed into the undergrowth well ahead of Finnegan. A bullet whizzed through the branches. "Bloody hell." Kilkenny reined up his horse and drew the Colt revolver he had borrowed from Stuart. Another bullet crashed by near at hand. Kilkenny cocked the revolver and aimed at the brush in front of him. Something moved to the side of him, and he swung the gun at the motion. As he fired, he barely noticed the shape of his horse's head pass in front of the muzzle. The beast collapsed to the ground with Kilkenny still firmly set in the saddle. To an onlooker, the equine might have appeared to have gone to sleep.

Finnegan came to Kilkenny's side. "What in hell is this?"

Kilkenny looked from the revolver to the dead animal and back again. "I...well, I dare say I am not certain. I believe I may be responsible."

"You shot your own horse?"

"Perhaps."

"Well, this is not the place to discuss it. Swing up." Finnegan extended a hand and Kilkenny pulled his feet from his own stirrups. He swung on behind Finnegan. The two were about to begin moving when another bullet came through the undergrowth. A spray of blood came across Finnegan's face and his horse began to stumble. It made a few faltering steps to one side and then fell to earth, tossing the two men from it. "Damn these bastards." Finnegan thrashed in the brush for a moment and got to his feet. "Are you struck, Ephraim?"

The whiskey baron patted a few of his parts and shook his head. "I do not think so."

"Damn them." Finnegan pulled the Marlin from the scabbard of Kilkenny's horse. He glanced into the trees and could see movement. Levering a round into the chamber he brought the gun up on an opening in the trees. When the rider passed into it, he fired and saw the man torn from the saddle. The horse fled through the undergrowth. Another horse could be seen moving through the trees in the direction they had all entered the coulee from. Finnegan broke into a run up the side of the coulee and came out in the open just in time to see the second rider racing out onto the prairie. Levering the action again, he rested the rifle on the nearest sapling and took careful measure to lead the fugitive just a bit and kept the muzzle swinging as he squeezed the trigger. In the distance, the fugitive fell from the saddle and the horse continued on at a dead gallop. "Serves you right, you damned bushwhacker."

Kilkenny came walking up behind Finnegan rather slowly. He shrugged when Finnegan turned to see him. "Well, that was a rather exciting fracas, was it not?"

"Indeed." Finnegan wiped sweat and horse blood from his face and leaned the rifle against the sapling. "Were you paying attention? Did you finally view a man being shot?"

Kilkenny nodded. "Yes. Even at a distance, it was a...a novel experience. I must say, I thought being in the thick of it would be more...remarkable, but the whole affair ends as quickly as it begins, does it not?"

"With any luck it does." Finnegan motioned to the coulee. "I take it both our mounts are dead?"

"You are correct in that thinking."

"Well, that places us in a bit of a pickle."

"Yes, well." Kilkenny shrugged again. "Accidents will happen."

"Yes, they will." Finnegan pointed back the way they had come. "How far to the trading post do you suppose?"

"A good distance, certainly."

"Of course, you do not comprehend the real danger we face, Ephraim."

"I do not?"

"Most of my cigars are on that pack mule Anderson drags behind him. We may perish in this wilderness."

It was a long walk back to the trading post. They left the tack and saddles attached to the dead horses and only carried what they felt was essential. Finnegan had pulled the Purdey from his scabbard and Kilkenny had regained his Marlin. Both men took their saddlebags and canteens and Finnegan counted out their meager supply of cigars. Neither man was much pleased with the way the day was working out. They marched back toward Crooked Creek silently for a mile or two. Every now and then Kilkenny would glance sullenly down at the Colt that still hung on his hip. Finnegan noticed his rather morose mood.

"It is not such a rare occurrence, Ephraim." Finnegan felt the need to offer up some commiseration as they trudged through the prairie. "I saw many a cavalryman shoot down his own mount during the war."

The whiskey baron looked over at his friend as they weaved through the sagebrush. "Truly?"

"Oh, yes. They, of course, always blamed the dead animal on the rebels. Cavalrymen love to brag about how many horses the Confederates shot out from under them, but I always thought about half were the product of a misplaced pistol ball from the horse's rider."

Kilkenny stumbled and looked to the Colt again. "I must confess, I have little experience with this sort of weapon, and the foreshortened barrel creates a rather dangerous situation in some instances. Have you ever accidentally shot anything with your pistols?"

"Oh, I have let the hammer slip on them once or twice, which is ruinous to the occasional floorboard. I must say, the proprietors and fellow travelers at boarding houses do not appreciate that sort of thing."

Kilkenny laughed. "No, I would imagine not."

"I suffered the full range of accidents one might expect when I carried the old cap and ball models of the Colt and other revolvers. I had one rather come apart in my hand once. That was unnerving. They were also prone to having more than one chamber fire from time to time. That aspect of them was hard on the nerves and knuckles."

"I suppose it would be."

"There are more than a few men shot every day in this country, I would imagine, simply because they allow the hammer of their revolver to rest on a live cartridge. I have heard that the Smith and Wesson revolver is not subject to that danger, but I have yet to confirm it, and I doubt I would trust it to a certainty, at any rate."

"It would not be worth betting a limb on until it was properly vetted." Kilkenny paused in his trudging and held one hand up to shade his eyes. Below them, Crooked Creek was spread out with the trading post not more than a half mile distant. "Ah, salvation. It is sad how quickly a man becomes unfitted for rambling about on foot. Rail travel and riding has made me soft, Finnegan."

The gunman squinted at the cabin and corrals in the distance. "Ephraim, are your binoculars in your kit there?"

"Somewhere, I should think." He pulled the saddlebag from his shoulder and dug the binoculars out of it. He handed them to Finnegan. "Something seems amiss?"

Finnegan fussed with the glasses and observed the trading post. "It is strange. I can see the other fellows down there, but I do not see our villains. They should be gathered outside. I did instruct them to remove the men from the cabin, did I not?"

Kilkenny took the opportunity to grab a quick drink from his flask. "You did, but you must remember, Finnegan, these men are not the professionals you are accustomed to working with. I think we should count ourselves lucky that they have not wandered off and left the villains to their own devices."

"Perhaps you are right." Finnegan passed the binoculars back and the two men resumed their trudging. In ten minutes' time, they arrived at the trading post and were leaning their gear against the corral while Reece Anderson and Floppin' Bill Cantrell approached. Finnegan wiped the sweat from his brow and took a long swig off his canteen. "Hello, gentlemen. Our apologies for being so tardy in our arrival. We suffered several unforeseen difficulties."

Anderson pulled his hat from his head and scratched his brow. "Where are your horses?"

Finnegan took another drink and wiped his lips. "Dead, both of them. Killed in the ambush the two fugitives laid for us." Finnegan looked to Kilkenny, who felt no need to elaborate on the statement.

"What became of them two that let out of here?" Floppin'

Bill seemed overly excited for a man who had been only standing about for several hours.

Finnegan took out one of his cigars. "They are dead, as well. Sadly, it was unavoidable." Finnegan looked over the trading post and the attached corrals. "How many men were within?"

"Uh, six, all told." Anderson continued to scratch his head rather obsessively.

Finnegan lit his cigar and passed one to Kilkenny. "Six, well, they were living in tight quarters, were they not?" Finnegan smiled, pleased to hear of a large catch. "You are keeping them inside? I assume you have thought to search and remove all possible weaponry from the cabin there?"

"Well, we removed some things, yeah." Floppin' Bill stared down at his boots.

"Excellent." Finnegan puffed and grinned. "It will make for quite the parade when we march them into Lewistown, eh?"

"Mr. Gilhooley..." There was an audible click as Anderson swallowed. "Them inside there, they ain't going to be marching nowhere. They're...they've all passed over."

Finnegan took the cigar from his lips. "Passed over?"

"They're dead, sir. Been shot." Anderson stared blankly.

Finnegan slowly put the cigar back between his teeth and walked to the cabin. As he crossed the corrals the other three cowboys avoided his gaze. At the cabin, he pushed the door inward. Inside, still in various bunks with limbs hanging akimbo, were the six dead men. Most of them were still covered by their bedding. None of them had their boots on. The man closest to the door had a revolver lying on the dirt floor near him. The rest of the guns, both revolvers and rifles, were either still in holsters or leaned in corners seemingly out of reach. Finnegan let his eyes roll over the scene and then pulled the door shut. He walked back to Anderson and Floppin' Bill. He ran one hand over his face and stared into the distance for a moment before settling his eyes on Anderson. "What happened?"

"Um, well..." Anderson moved his eyes between Finnegan and Floppin' Bill. "Like you told us to, we surrounded the cabin there. I went to the door with Bill and them others, they went to the windows there on each side. We opened the door up and, the one fella, he got to fussing with that pistol. You can ask Floppin' Bill, he'll tell you the same damn thing. Gospel truth."

Finnegan turned to the other cowboy and the man spit out supporting evidence. "He ain't lying one bit, sir. That fella by the door, he went for that gun, sure as daylight. He grabbed it up by the barrel by accident and was fussing with it. He was in a bit of stupor from just waking up, I guess. That's the only reason we was even able to get the drop on him and defend ourselves like we did."

Finnegan rubbed his face. "It was necessary to kill all six?" Finnegan drew his lips back into a scowl. "Most of those men were not armed and could not have reached their guns if they had wished to."

Anderson threw his hands in the air. "Well, it ain't like we do this sorta thing every Saturday. That fella got to fussing and I reckon I shot, or Bill shot, and then...well hell, then we was all shootin' and we emptied our guns. We couldn't tell what was done and what wasn't with all the smoke. I don't know...damn it. This ain't my damn fault, Mr. Gilhooley."

Finnegan grabbed the man by his coat lapels and threw him down to the ground. "You killed those men for no damn reason, when you damn well knew I wanted them alive."

Floppin' Bill stuck his chest out. "Well, what a man wants ain't always what he gets in this world."

Finnegan swung hard and hit the cowboy in the jaw,

knocking him down. "Damn you. I ought to shoot you both for disobeying my very simple orders."

Anderson stared up from the ground. "You shot them two you went after."

Finnegan's hand went to his Remington. "Damn you..."

Kilkenny came out of the small cabin and surveyed the scene before him. "Finnegan. Stop this." He leaned against a corral post, looking pale from what he had seen within the cabin. "Killing two more fools will not undo what has been done today." He hung his head. "Nothing can undo a thing like this."

Finnegan let his hand fall away from his gun. "You are right." He ran his hand over his face once more. "Anderson, Cantrell, haul yourselves up and find a shovel. There is certain to be one around here someplace."

"A shovel?" Anderson slowly made his way to his feet, keeping a wary eye on Finnegan.

"You killed them, you will bury them." Finnegan pointed to the other three cowboys. "Find two suitable mounts in that collection of horseflesh there. Mr. Kilkenny and I require new horses." He looked to Cantrell and Anderson, who were fully erect once more. "There will be hell to pay for a thing like this, gentlemen. Hell to pay."

Stuart was even more haggard than usual as he sat on the edge of his desk draining a coffee cup. The posse had not returned to the ranch until late after dark, but the news of their trip would not keep until morning. Finnegan had sent Anderson to rouse Stuart and the three had gathered in the foreman's office. Stuart smoothed his beard and squinted through bloodshot eyes in need of sleep.

"All dead?" He set the coffee cup carefully on the desk.

Finnegan nodded slowly. He stood, staring malevolently at Anderson. "Shot down in their bedclothes. The other two who fled attempted to ambush Mr. Kilkenny and I. Our hand was forced." He sneered at Anderson. "The other killings were the result of...foolhardiness."

Anderson spit out a stream of tobacco onto the plank floor. "Damn it, they was armed and..."

"Shut up, Reece." Stuart rubbed his eyes. "And quit spitting on the damn floor. You'd think we were still in that tent in California the way you behave." He sighed. "All dead?"

Anderson swallowed his next mouthful of saliva and grimaced. "Yeah, all dead."

"And you buried them?" Stuart looked to Finnegan.

"Well, yes." The gunman shrugged. "It seemed like the proper course of action."

"Then it may not make a tinker's damn bit of difference." Stuart licked his lips, looking pensive. "They were scoundrels, not likely to be missed, and you have put them under, so..."

Finnegan laughed. "Bloody hell, Granville, that is a fairy tale if I have ever heard one. Even in a place as empty as this, eight graves in close proximity to the trading post that was formerly populated will not go unnoticed. I must also point out that I have yet to meet the scoundrel so low that his own mother does not show some concern when the man stops writing. Even the James brothers had a mother, and she was a formidable old hag when it came to penning newspaper editorials." Finnegan pressed the bridge of his nose and motioned to Anderson. "During our return trip, Mr. Anderson made mention of the fact that the now deceased Mr. Downes has family in Fort Benton, I believe you said?"

Anderson cleared his throat. "Uh, yes. A sister, a brother, perhaps a cousin or two."

"All of whom are apt to visit the trading post at some time

and may be puzzled to discover the graves and the absence of Mr. Downes."

"Ah, hell and perdition." Stuart pounded one fist on the desk. He looked truly at a loss for a moment, but then latched onto the first idea that struck. "Well, then, we must attempt to staunch the damage. If the bodies are discovered..."

"When they are discovered, Granville." Finnegan leaned against a bookcase and found a cigar.

"Yes, well, I suppose they must be, at some point. When they are discovered, there is nothing in particular to link them to us, is there?"

Finnegan stared at his employer for a long moment. "Granville, every grown man in this territory is aware that you are attempting to rid this country of horse thieves and that you have hired me to facilitate it. Who in Christ's name would have a reason to shoot eight horse thieves other than us?"

"I don't..." Stuart pounded the desk again. "That is not proof, damn it. It is not as if you carved your names into their grave markers."

"The newspapers will not need proof to print their stories." Finnegan lit his cigar looking resigned to his fate.

"If pressed we can blame it on a pack of Indians. It is a well-known fact that Downes trafficked with them regularly. We can suggest he pushed his luck too far and the savages had at him."

Finnegan sighed. "Granville, when is the last time a group of Indians perpetrated such an act in this vicinity?"

"It has been some time."

"Then it is not likely anyone will believe that tale if you choose to tell it." The gunman shrugged. "All together, there may be little purpose in attempting to weave a fiction here, Granville. In matters such as these I have found that the truth makes for an excellent foundation to build a story that fits the requirements after the incident has gone awry."

Anderson nodded vigorously. "You believe a rather apocryphal version of events is required?" Finnegan and Stuart both stared at the tobacco-stained cowboy for a moment. "I've heard Miss Katie use the word, it means, like you said, Mr. Gilhooley, you sorta bend the tale so as to end up where you want to be."

Finnegan slowly nodded. "Yes, thank you, Mr. Anderson." He turned back to the astonished Stuart. "It will ultimately profit us most to admit involvement and make the details somewhat apocryphal, as Mr. Anderson suggests. There will be no way to keep this secret for long, at any rate. Those three men you chose to accompany us will scatter to the four winds in no time and spread the tale wherever they go. Young men such as them cannot be expected to conceal such a story. I would imagine that cur Cantrell is entertaining the others in the bunkhouse with it as we speak."

Stuart rubbed his eyes yet again. "Very well. If there is no concealing it, as you say, we shall attempt to cast it in the best light possible. Men in the employ of this ranch did shoot those men, but it was in defense of their life and limb and all the deceased were men known to be of low character, prone to viciousness when they were alive."

Finnegan nodded. "That should do nicely. You may wish to add that Mr. Downes was well-known to engage in the selling of whiskey to Indians, thus corrupting their souls, and so on and so forth. Those members of the public such as Miss Meagher will appreciate minor details such as that."

"Ah, yes." Stuart smiled. "We are not greedy cattlemen killing poor horse thieves, we are servants of the greater good, attempting to purge the territory of those who would take advantage of the defenseless or ignorant."

"Allan Pinkerton himself could not have said it better,

sir." Finnegan gave his cigar a few thoughtful puffs. "It will be important to keep the story somewhat consistent." He turned to Anderson. "Inform Mr. Cantrell as to what is expected of him and make him aware that if he becomes troublesome, he may yet join Mr. Downes."

Anderson grimaced and nodded. "I will, Mr. Gilhooley. You may count on me, as well, sir."

"I had better be able to. I know of one sure way to be certain a man will keep a secret, Mr. Anderson. Do not force me to employ it. I did not wish for those six men to perish in that cabin, but that does not mean I wish the same for you." He knocked ash from his cigar. "Go now, and inform Mr. Cantrell what is required of him."

"And do it in a manner he damn well understands, Reece. Apocalyptic had better not pass your lips."

Anderson raised his eyebrows. "Apocryphal, Granville."

"A pox on the bunch of you, be gone, damn it." Stuart watched the man leave the office and turned back to his hired gunman. "Do you believe this will give us trouble, give the association trouble?"

Finnegan sneered and shook his head. "In truth, it seems as though the general attitude in this territory is that most of these scoundrels are better shot than roaming about causing mischief."

"That is the majority opinion. There are only a few citizens, your friend the schoolteacher comes to mind, who will raise a fuss regarding any endeavor which shows some sense."

"I will admit that her inclinations are unpredictable. Miss Meagher does not worry me near so much as the possibility of some newspaper in the area taking umbrage. They are all but joined now thanks to the telegraph. What is news here is news in New York in a few days' time and is always enlarged out of proportion. If they begin yapping of these shootings the dead will multiply a hundred-fold and this will become some sort of war in short order. Any man in Washington who can tell fact from fiction is rapidly run out of town. If they declare some sort of martial law, it could have effects on land ownership and the current condition of this cattle range. Both those items are of concern to us both presently."

Stuart leaned back on the desk. "You do not think it could go so far as all that, do you?"

"You have heard of what the Union did during the time referred to as Reconstruction in the south, have you not? Half of this nation was placed under martial law, and half the land changed hands. When it was over the rebels woke to discover their former nation had been stolen or lent as collateral, to be presently seized. The greed of men knows no bounds, Granville. This area is not a state but a territory. It would be much easier to do here than it was in Georgia or Virginia."

"We will have to tread more carefully in the future, Finnegan."

"Lest we lose the ability to tread at all."

Chapter 24

DHS RANCH, MONTANA TERRITORY

July 24th, 1884

Molly dismounted the wagon looking quite stern. Finnegan was pleased to see her, but had been somewhat dreading the arrival at the same time. From the look on the schoolteacher's face, he could see that news of the most recent raid had reached her. The only question was what form the news had taken and to what degree she would choose to hold Finnegan and Stuart responsible.

"Hello, Molly. Pleasant journey, I assume?" He smiled and smoothed his frock coat.

"It was. Mr. Abbott's company is always to my liking." Her eyes moved over the other men who had assembled for her arrival. "Mr. Kilkenny, it is good to see you again. How is the collection of your specimens progressing?"

"Slowly. I am afraid a man such as myself is constantly faced with distraction." He smiled as though he did not have a care in the world.

"I am sure you are." She turned to Stuart. "And the work about the ranch proceeds, Mr. Stuart?"

"It does, Miss Meagher. As always, the cattle are easily

herded; it is only the tending of the cowboys that poses a difficulty."

"I can see how it might." She turned her tightlipped gaze to Finnegan. "Mr. Gilhooley, I am rather stiff after the long ride in the wagon. Would you mind escorting me for a stroll so that I might loosen up?"

Finnegan cleared his throat and extended one arm to the lady. "It would be my pleasure, Miss Meagher." The other men tipped their hats, and the couple began their walk out into the grasslands that surrounded the ranch. After a few hundred yards, far enough to be out of earshot of the ranch buildings, Finnegan broke the silence. "How is it at the schoolhouse?"

"It goes well, although this time of year I am rarely troubled with students. Most families choose to keep the children home to get some work out of them."

"Chores are helpful for building character."

"Yes, they are. How are your chores progressing?"

Finnegan cleared his throat again. "Some better than others. We captured some form of ferret the other day that Ephraim is quite pleased with. He has it in his head that it may prove to be a new species. He formerly discovered and named a vulture somewhere in some abominable jungle, but for varied reasons is not fully satisfied with the outcome. I believe he would very much like a second opportunity to name an animal, now that he has some experience to draw from."

"Many men wish for second chances with many things." She straightened her bonnet with one hand. "There have been a few strange incidents in Maiden."

"Have there?"

"Two men, one supposedly from the Fergus Ranch, the other from William Burnett's place, came into town and were heard to boast of shooting down an entire gang of horse thieves by the Musselshell."

"An entire gang, no less?"

"So they claimed. Later, a woman by the name of Mrs. Flannery, Downes as a maiden lady, came to town inquiring at the department store and schoolhouse to see if her brother had been seen to pass through. I had never met the man, but have been told that he ran a trading post in the vicinity of Crooked Creek. Mrs. Flannery's son passed by the place and found it abandoned and no one can say what has become of the owner."

Finnegan sighed. "For a howling wilderness this territory certainly has a busy social scene. I wish to God it were not so."

Molly stopped in her tracks and turned to him, wearing a scowl. "So, you have knowledge of this?"

"Molly..." He rubbed one side of his face, wishing she did not know him as well as she did. "Very well, I have never lied to you previously; there is no cause to begin now. Yes, I know the fate of William Downes. He was killed in his bed a little less than a week ago and buried in the soft earth of the creek bottom. He lies with seven of his former associates."

"Seven! My God, Finnegan."

"Molly." He held up a hand. "I shot two of the men and had no choice. They were in flight the moment they saw us and attempted to murder both Ephraim and myself from ambush. The others...the others were killed while Ephraim and I were away, but their deaths were the result of stupidity more than any malice. The men we were forced to make use of were inexperienced and panicked while seizing the scoundrels."

"I...I do not doubt that whatever you did was warranted, Finnegan. You possess too fine a character for me to believe otherwise, but eight men lie dead and..." She glanced about, not knowing quite how to continue. "Eight men dead and you have not even made the authorities aware?"

"Authorities?" Finnegan let a small chuckle slip before catching himself. "Molly, the last so-called authority I have met in this place was a supposedly reformed cannibal whose word on the matter did not seem trustworthy. There are no sheriffs, no policemen, no constables. The last judge I made the mistake of trusting hung a man in his own barn. Probably, the moment I departed."

"You should, at least, make the commanding officer at the fort aware..."

Finnegan gaped at her. "The commanding officer at the fort is capable of little other than debauching himself. Not a month ago I gave him a richly deserved drubbing and removed an Indian girl from his keeping. The cur did not even possess the courage to come and attempt to reclaim her himself. He sent his lieutenant and some enlisted men in his stead."

Molly eyed the gunman closely. "Finnegan, please tell me a cavalry troop does not lie nearby?"

"No, although that damned captain may yet, when I have the time. The Indian girl was little more than a child. It is very undignified behavior for an officer." He took a deep breath and calmed himself. "At any rate, informing the captain of our skirmish would prove nothing." He thought on it for a moment. "Although, it might be enjoyable to watch the bugger squirm at the news."

Molly hung her head for a moment, but brought it up looking more sympathetic. "Oh, Finnegan, you do find your way into such difficulties." She sighed. "If it brings you any comfort, I have it on good account that Mr. Downes was known to do a steady trade of whiskey with the local Indians and was formerly held responsible for several of the smaller incidents that have occurred involving the tribes. The consensus in Maiden is that if the man has been done away with, the territory is better for it. Although, naturally, his sister feels differently."

"Even the worst of men have someone who will miss them."

"We must make that poor woman aware of what has become of her brother, Finnegan."

The gunman nodded, slowly. "We shall. Even I am not so coldhearted as to leave a woman in perpetual worry regarding her own brother. You may write to the woman and tell her what I have told you, but I must insist that you wait."

"Wait? Why? As you say, you had cause and the news that the woman's brother met a hard end will probably not come as a shock. Certainly, her calling her brother a trader is only a façade she puts on. She surely knows his true character and will take it into account."

"It is not the reaction of a single bereaved sister that concerns me, Molly. If you will only allow for the passing of a month or perhaps two? Allot me that time so that I may finish what work needs to be done here without a public crucifixion hanging over the Association that employs me. I do not trust the men of the Association to pay me what is owed if they can find the slightest provocation. If they do not make good on this contract, all of this will have been for nothing."

Now it was Molly's turn to chuckle. "I find it hard to believe that even a man such as Sam Hauser would dare to not render payment owed to you." She arched one eyebrow. "Certainly, he was aware of your reputation when you were hired."

Finnegan smiled. "I would assume he would pay. What I am chasing here is more than my fair wages, Molly. If this is done properly, my work here can be the beginning of a new life in a place where I am welcomed."

"Finnegan, I have already told you..."

"I know what you have told me, and I have taken it into consideration. That being said, I know your heart and your inclinations to be rather mercurial on occasion. You may yet change your mind." He smiled again. "And if you do not, I will still welcome the income I have been promised. Will you give me the time to finish my work, Molly?"

"I will." She turned and they resumed walking. "Was the captain truly keeping a girl as a...concubine? Katie sent a note regarding the incident, but I could hardly credit it."

"He was."

"Then you should have shot the scoundrel."

"I may, yet. I have quite the list of scoundrels to see to."

She turned and eyed him quizzically. "Finnegan, are you the reason Lieutenant Bowden has that odd burn on the side of his head?"

"I am. How are the children at the fort?"

"Very well. They play tricks on Bowden and find it very funny that he can only hear on one side now."

"He is a vexing man. Someday it will cost him more than an ear."

"Finnegan, if all goes well, and you receive your just and proper payment, do you believe you truly could settle into a peaceful life here?"

He looked down at her as she walked beside him. "It does not appear to be an overly complicated proposition."

"I only ask because, as you yourself have told me, you began this journey with the intention of collecting birds and beasts with Mr. Kilkenny and resuming our friendship. Now, you find yourself shooting horse thieves and soldiers regularly."

"I did not shoot the lieutenant."

"Either way, this is not the peaceful outing you intended. What makes you think your life here would be any more peaceful?"

"Whether it is or not, it is worth the attempt. Do you not agree?"

"I suppose one must try for peace, no matter how elusive." She grinned. "I have received a letter from Bob Jackson."

"Bob Jackson?"

"The oddly dressed fellow you saved in Lewistown. Surely you cannot have forgotten."

"I recall. I had simply not thought of the matter recently. How is the young man?"

"Now that he has had the chance to sober, he is eternally grateful to you, and wishes to thank you ardently."

"I ardently wish that he had chosen to bunk down with William Downes the other morning. I do not believe I will ever be able to form a friendship with that particular young man."

"Are there many you can be friendly with?"

Finnegan rubbed his eyes. "Would it shock you to learn that I truly do make the attempt in most instances?"

She shrugged. "You do have a terrible habit of attempting the impossible."

Chapter 25

DHS RANCH, MONTANA TERRITORY

July 31st, 1884

KILKENNY TAPPED THE TOP CARD IN THE DECK. "I WILL venture it is the ace of spades."

Finnegan sighed. "The ten of diamonds."

Kilkenny flipped the card over to reveal it was, in fact, the nine of hearts. "Damn." He tapped the next card. "Very well, I wager this to be the ace of spades, then."

Finnegan rubbed his chin. "Has the ace of spades not already been shown?"

"Has it?" Kilkenny swept up the discard pile and began sorting through it. He held up the ace of spades when he found it. "I will be damned. How long have I been guessing the ace of spades will come up?"

Finnegan shrugged and puffed his cigar. "Oh, half the damn night, I believe." In the rear of the bunkhouse the stoic Mr. Oman emitted a low moan and hung his head. "By God, Ephraim, this is a new low. We have become so tiresome that even Mr. Oman feels the need to comment."

"That is quite something, is it not?" Kilkenny hung his head. "Finnegan, perhaps Mr. Oman is not the only man at the end of his tether. I have enjoyed our diversions here as much as you, but perhaps...I found the incident in Lewistown quite exhilarating. It fit quite well with my expectations, but those men in that cabin, Finnegan -- that was not as I had hoped it would be."

The gunman slowly nodded. "It is often the case that such incidents occur in this type of work, Ephraim. Men lose sight of their commission. They begin to behave as badly or worse than the men they have been charged to capture. It is the reason wars always end so very badly. Even the agency's pursuit of the James gang took a similar turn once. Although, I was not present to witness it." He shrugged. "It is unfortunate, but those men chose their path. They know full well what the consequences of such behavior can be long before they steal their first horse. Men like Stuart remind them of it every chance they get. Still, they persist, and that is the sum of it."

The whiskey baron nodded, not entirely liking the explanation. "It is hard to imagine that those young men in that shack came so far and passed through so much, only to die in their beds. Pigs are given more warning."

Finnegan sighed. "I suppose they did travel far to meet such an ignoble end." He puffed his cigar again. "Having seen many a man meet his end, I feel compelled to mention that it may be preferable to simply be snuffed out like a candle without warning. You may reach the same conclusion when your time comes, Ephraim."

"Perhaps so." The baron found his flask and was about to take a sip when he was stopped short by a soft knock at the door. "Good Lord, you don't believe that might be my end, do you?"

Finnegan stood and walked to the door. "The knock would seem to reside somewhere between fair warning and none at all." He swung the door open. "Oh, Miss Katie, how lovely to see you."

The girl gave a small curtsy on the other side of the door jamb. "Gentlemen, I come with news, if I may enter."

"Of course." Finnegan stepped aside and motioned to the interior. "If you can grit your teeth and bear such crude company. You bring us news?"

She gave another curtsy to Kilkenny, and he stood as she entered. "Mr. Kilkenny, Mr. Oman." She turned, grinning, to Finnegan. "Mr. Gilhooley, my father tells me that he has gained knowledge of the location of one Jack Stringer."

Finnegan rubbed his chin and tried not to appear placating. "Your father has searched for that fellow some time now." Finnegan grinned. "It is well that you found him. I must say, for a woman of your years you have a very well-developed web of spies and informants. Perhaps you should consider returning with me to Chicago so that you may join the employ of Mr. Pinkerton."

She laughed a bit and blushed. "It is not I who provided the information. It comes by way of Mr. Cantrell."

Kilkenny gave a start. "Floppin' Bill somehow knows the whereabouts of your father's nemesis? I say, that fellow has more depth to him than I might have credited."

Katie shrugged. "I do not know the particulars. Father merely sent me to inform Mr. Gilhooley of the good news and to ask him if he might come up to father's office so they may discuss the matter. He is in much better humor than he has been. I believe he has almost entirely forgotten about the bull." She looked around the bunkhouse. "Oh, it has cleaned up quite well in here, has it not? You would think such an incident would leave a longer lasting..." She looked to the two men who were clearly not pleased to be reminded of their transgression. "Well, it was lovely to see both of you." She smiled at Finnegan. "Did you and Miss Meagher have a nice visit?"

"Your spy ring need know nothing of the local romance." He smiled. "I will be with your father presently."

FINNEGAN DID NOT HAVE to travel far into the main house to find Stuart. The foreman had abandoned his office for the kitchen. He stood, digging in the pie safe. When he emerged and saw Finnegan, a wide grin was spread across the aging man's face. "Ah, my stock detective. It is good you are here, since there is some stock that requires detecting." He motioned to the table. "Take a seat."

Finnegan swung in behind one of the benches and Stuart set an apple pie opposite him. "Very well shaped pastry, sir."

"It is indeed." Stuart produced two plates and slid one across. "Awbonnie has always excelled with pie. She has made them that pretty and perfect since I first settled us into a place with a proper oven. I have no inkling of where she might have learned. Her mother certainly did not train her in the art. That woman would not have known an oven from a boulder." Stuart dug a large hunk of pie out of the pan with a butcher knife and flopped it onto his plate. "Would you care for a similar cut?"

Finnegan nodded. "I would not be opposed to it." Stuart served it up with the knife and slid a fork to the gunman. "Many thanks." Finnegan tried the pie and found it quite pleasing. "Ah, that is fine."

Stuart settled in behind his own chunk. "The woman makes a fine pie. I wish she did not produce children so frequently, but her skills with pastry are beyond reproach."

"We all have our areas of excellence, I suppose." Finnegan swallowed down a bit and looked across at Stuart.

"Miss Katie has informed me that Mr. Cantrell either excels in holding his tongue or spinning yarns; which do you believe it may be?"

"First one and then the other, perhaps." Stuart stuffed his mouth and smiled. "Of course, he has had his reasons for both." He snatched up a cloth and wiped his whiskers. "I do not suppose anyone around here has informed you that Cantrell's father served with a fellow by the name of Quantrill in Missouri during the war?"

Finnegan sliced off another bite of pie. "I cannot imagine why anyone would take the time to mention such a thing. Who a man's father served with is not of much note, even if it was with a scoundrel such as Quantrill, and I did not travel to Missouri until the war was long ended."

Stuart shrugged. "As far as I know, Cantrell is the only man who has ever made a fuss about it. At any rate, since you served for the Union and Cantrell's father was presumably next in line to the throne from Jefferson Davis, the silly bastard had it in his head that we were going to hand him over to the law to be held accountable for the men shot during the last raid."

Finnegan raised an eyebrow. "Not a bad notion. Although I doubt it will become necessary." He returned to his pie. "Fear of standing on the scaffold alone has motivated him to speak? It motivates most men to run."

"I believe he is too lazy for the second option." Stuart got up and retrieved the coffee pot from the stove. He grabbed two cups on his way to the table. "The blackguard has come and told me quite a tale. It would seem that he was unavailable for the roundup two years ago due to his being employed by Jack Stringer. He claims to have spent the whole summer stealing horses, sipping whiskey, and frequenting a British whorehouse with very reasonable prices."

"That is a unique tale. It is always interesting to see what one man adds and another disavows from a story." Finnegan set his coffee cup forward and Stuart filled it. "Naturally, he recalls the location of Mr. Stringer's secret lair?"

"He claims to know that very thing."

"Is the hideout located near the North Pole, or perhaps in the vicinity of that Incan kingdom Mr. Oman was reared in?"

"Incan?" Stuart stared quizzically, but decided to move on. "He claims it is where Fourchette Creek hits the Musselshell. It is a woodlot. A revolving band of miscreants is known to frequent the spot, alternately cutting wood for the steamboats to make ends meet and stealing whatever is not nailed down. White men, half-breeds, Indians -- it is hard to say what we may find there. I once encountered an actual Jew at the place, if you can believe that."

Finnegan popped a piece of crust into his mouth. "It is my understanding there are a fair number of them wandering the earth, Granville." He chewed the crust and sipped coffee. "I will grant you, it sounds to be a likely place to find a few horse thieves. Knowing what you do of the place, you could have guessed that long before Mr. Cantrell told you his tale."

"Yes, but knowing a place is frequented by villains is one thing. Having Floppin' Bill testify to the fact that Jack Stringer can almost to a certainty be found there is another."

Finnegan sighed. "Granville, my guess would be that Floppin' Bill takes the term testify rather loosely, when he takes it at all."

Stuart shrugged again and tried his coffee. "That may be, Finnegan. It may be that he has only told me this yarn so that I will not hand him over to some constable when it serves my purposes. It may be a pure fiction." He gobbled more pie. "What is not a fiction is that you, and I, and Floppin' Bill are going to that woodlot. We are going to investigate which villains truly reside there and which do not. If it comes to pass that we discover a large horde of stolen horses and the thieves to punish, I will give Bill the first pat on the back. If we arrive there and find only a few old men struggling to cut wood, I will leave Bill hanging from one of the cottonwoods, and be none the worse off than when I began."

"That seems a reasonable plan, Granville."

Chapter 26

MUSSELSHELL RIVER, MONTANA TERRITORY

August 3rd, 1884

STUART CLEARLY HAD NO INTENTIONS OF REPEATING ANY of the mistakes that had occurred during the first raid, at least not any that could be avoided by the application of additional manpower. Fifteen men were camped on the bank of the Musselshell drying their clothes and other traps after swimming the river. The crossing had been necessary if the party wished to have the element of surprise when they fell upon the woodlot the following morning.

Stuart had seen to it that all men were well armed and provisioned. The stock they had brought was the best that the DHS had to offer. The party had even stopped at a few neighboring ranches on the journey over to borrow better rifles or revolvers for some of the men. Stuart had given cash money, collateral, or notes to obtain the additional firearms. If he had inquired to Finnegan regarding the need for the extra guns, the Pinkerton would have said they were not truly necessary, but Stuart felt differently. He seemed to believe that if only he had the proper equipment, he could force luck to get into line with his inclinations. Finnegan had seen that sort of thinking in the past, and might have explained the futility of it to Stuart, but there was little purpose in telling a man what he might learn for himself in short order.

After crossing the Musselshell, Finnegan and Stuart had gone ahead to survey the woodlot for themselves. As the sun was sinking, they lay on a ridge above the place looking down with a spyglass and Kilkenny's binoculars. They had left the rest of the group some four miles behind them and risked letting the posse approach no further lest the smoke from the fires be seen.

Stuart shivered from the water that still clung to his clothes. Montana rivers are cold and even the summer heat was not keeping the chill off him. "Just once I would like to cross that river without nearly drowning. It is a sad sort of river; I cannot say why it troubles me so consistently."

"Perhaps it dislikes you personally." Finnegan steadied the binoculars on some sagebrush.

"I do not believe such a thing is possible." The pioneer grinned. "A man cannot step into the same river twice, Mr. Gilhooley." Finnegan only stared back as a response. "Heraclitus?" The stare continued. "It is a silly bit of Greek philosophy, Finnegan. Not really worth knowing."

Finnegan groaned and returned to the binoculars. "I am pleased that you are willing to say that, Granville. Miss Meagher is constantly at me to read on subjects I find to have rather questionable use. If you were to hoist another on to me, I am not certain I would have the time to devote or the ability to keep any more of it straight." He fussed with the focal knob. "I must say, much of it seems quite ridiculous. Take the fellow you just mentioned, I assume he is considered a man of tremendous learning?"

"One of the great thinkers of history."

"And the bloody buzzard was too daft to understand that a man can cross a river and then turn around and cross it again without a jot of trouble? One of the great thinkers of history was too stupid to know that he could turn around and go back where he came from?"

"Well, that was not what was meant to be..."

"Oh, it never is. If there is one thing I have learned about great thinkers, it is that they can never say anything that makes any damn sense." Finnegan pointed down the hill, wishing to change the subject. "This is quite the settlement you have brought us to, Granville. There are many men down there."

The pioneer nodded and resumed his spyglass. "That is what we were hoping for, is it not?"

Finnegan chuckled. "A man hopes for just the proper number of villains in a situation such as this. Obviously, we require enough bad men to make the trip worthwhile. At the same time, I would certainly never wish for such an overabundance that they might possibly triumph and win the day." Finnegan smiled at his employer. "It will not matter much how we planned or how we connived if the horse thieves are the only men left to tell the tale."

"You have a very grim sense of humor, my Irish friend. My father would say it is bad luck to jest in such a manner."

"I have been expecting to die nearly every day since before I had chin whiskers. I suppose it has made me strange in some respects. How many men do you believe linger down there?"

"I have counted as many as a dozen at one time. I would assume there were others concealed out of view at that moment. Would it be going too far to say we are evenly matched?"

Finnegan nodded and lowered his binoculars. "If more come during the night, we may find they outnumber us by morning. Men often drift into such places quite late." He rubbed his chin. "Hopefully, they will not continue to drift in until the break of day. It would be a pity to have a repetition of the last raid."

"I am here. If you must give chase, that sort of work is what you have been hired for. I will be with the men to make certain no one loses their composure."

"Very well." Finnegan slithered back a bit from the ridgeline and stood. He brushed the dirt from his clothes and found a cigar. Stuart joined him. "There are certainly enough of them down there to make for the triumph you have been wanting, Granville. If they are all brought over to the law, or St. Peter, it will surely do wonders for the horse thieving in these parts."

"That is all I wish to achieve this summer."

"I suppose it is good for a man to get what he wishes for... some of the time."

Chapter 27

FOURCHETTE CREEK, MONTANA TERRITORY

August 4th, 1884

Twelve men stalked forward on foot as the grey light of day crept upon the country. Three of the posse, those who wished not to have a part in the fray, stayed well behind with the horses. Mr. Oman, as everyone had assumed he would, stayed back. Kilkenny rather surprised the group by volunteering to do the same. Last, Stuart had somewhat surprised everyone by ordering Teddy Blue to remain in the rear. He had given no particular reason, only that he would feel better if the young man was in charge of the stock. So it happened that a cowboy, a whiskey baron, and a valet were commissioned to make certain of the animals while Finnegan, Stuart, and a motley collection of saddle tramps approached the outlaw camp.

Finnegan might have been pensive about the endeavor if he had not engaged in so many similar actions over the course of his career. Many times, Finnegan had stealthily approached the stronghold of various bad men, in the company of men barely more reliable or respectable than the villains being fallen upon. Finnegan had Stuart with him, who seemed a capable man, and that was more than he would normally have on hand for such a raid. Finnegan knew there were some unfortunate occurrences that might prove to be unavoidable near in the offing. He would need to avoid being shot by his own men while avoiding the fire of any ruffians who wished to put up a fight. He would need to see a clear path through the chaos that might erupt. He would need to see to it that things did not get too far out of control. Finnegan had seen soldier's work degenerate into grotesque cruelty in the war. There were lines that even gunmen were not meant to cross, and they must be observed. As they approached the camp nestled in the creek bottom Finnegan knew he had much to do, but he moved forward as always. He had come to accept such duties and, as always, he would do his best.

They came to a fallen log some hundred yards from the edge of the camp. By some miracle, the twelve men had managed to close the distance through the cottonwood bottom without making enough of a clatter to alert anyone in the camp. Stuart crouched by the log and peered forward through the gloom. "Damn me, there may be something to that talk of Irish luck."

Finnegan leaned close to whisper back. "The whiskey from the night before is the likely confederate in our success. They sounded as if they were having quite a time."

Stuart nodded and glanced over at the rifle Finnegan held. "Where did you acquire that Winchester? I have not seen you with it before."

"Oh, yes, it is nice, is it not? I picked it up in Lewistown. Got it from the fellow dressed so strangely that I told you about. I am especially fond of the sight on the tang."

"What cartridge is it chambered for?"

"It is a 45-75. They had no shortage of the stuff for sale in Lewistown. It is much easier to obtain than my old Spencer ammunition, I will tell you that."

"I had considered it, but wished for the heavier ball." Stuart held up his 50-95 Winchester Model 1876 that was one of his most prized possessions. "I have heard the 45 is a more accurate cartridge."

"This particular rifle shoots very well. I was trying it with Ephraim the other day and..."

Floppin' Bill stuck his head between the two men. He looked white as a sheet in the early morning light and the sweat stood out on his forehead. "Are we to remain here discussing your rifles or do we have other business this morning?" Stuart had insisted that the informer accompany the posse on the raid and Cantrell had not been pleased since hearing the news. Now, on the edge of the precipice, he was becoming somewhat puffed up, hoping to get through the next few hours on pure bravado, if possible.

Stuart eyed the man in the low light. "Bill, if we are not moving along quickly enough to suit you, I freely give you permission to rush forward and capture those rascals yourself. Mr. Gilhooley and I will remain here cursing ourselves as cowards while you charge."

"I'm here, ain't I?" Cantrell pulled the collar of his coat close and held his pistol with one shaky hand.

Stuart smiled. "Yes, failing to find an alternative, you have done the right thing, Bill. Now..." he motioned forward. "How do you wish to approach, Finnegan? I would assume you have some thought on the matter."

The gunman nodded and pointed to the left. "You take about five of them and spread out moving forward. Put yourself close to the bank of the river. If they break out, you will find them easily potted in the water. I will take the other side. If they wish to flee up that steep bank to the plain, we will have fine action on them. If they attempt flight down the flat of the river, we can drive them quite well and collect them when they are forced to either the water or the bank again."

Stuart eyed the collection of small cabins. "And if they do not flee?"

"We can easily surround the buildings."

"They may be well-armed, and they will have cover in those lodges."

"Yes, but they cannot come out. In a day's time thirst can do the work of a hundred bullets, Granville. If we show perseverance, we are bound to be rewarded."

Stuart let a small chuckle out. "A very neat plan, Finnegan. I suppose it was wise to hire a man such as yourself. I would have suggested burning them out at the first sign of trouble."

Finnegan shrugged. "If boredom sets in quickly, I will consider it." He smiled. "Pick your five and let us be about our labors."

Stuart, Finnegan, and Cantrell all moved back to the main group of men. Stuart picked five of them to accompany his side of the operation. Noticeably, he left Cantrell to form up on Finnegan's side of the party. Stuart saw that the gunman was puzzled and leaned in close so that the others could not hear. "I have a pang of regret, having forced him to be here. If he falls, I would prefer it was out of my sight."

Finnegan grinned. It was not the first time he had witnessed such antics. "Keeping him out of sight is probably best then." He eased down the lever of the Winchester to make certain the chamber was loaded and then eased the lever closed again. "Let us be to it. If we wait much longer, they will have had breakfast and moved along of their own accord."

They began moving forward, slowly, once more. Stuart and Finnegan led their respective portions of the party. As they proceeded, both sides first moved around the compound of small cabins and then circled them toward the front of the place. When Finnegan and Stuart were both set to very nearly meet up again, having left men behind at intervals, the door of what appeared to be the main sleeping cabin creaked open and a man in his long johns came stumbling out into the dim light. Finnegan stopped dead in his tracks, caught in full view of the early riser. There was nothing for the gunman to do other than freeze as he watched the fellow first stretch, then rub his eyes, then proceed across the small space between the cabin and the privies which Finnegan stood in front of. The early riser walked with a determined stride and kept his eyes glued to the ground directly in front of him as he made for the outhouse. He walked closer and closer until he bumped right into Finnegan at a trot. Having hit the gunman, the early riser took a single step back and stared at this stranger who was keeping him from his morning ablutions. The fellow might have opened his mouth to inquire as to Finnegan's business there in the yard, but Finnegan brought the butt of his Winchester across the man's chin and knocked the early riser cold to the ground.

Cantrell took a few steps out from behind the outhouse and joined Finnegan. "Uh, well done, I suppose." Floppin' Bill stared down at the disabled man.

"Grab one of his arms. We must get him out of sight so that the others do not..."

Finnegan's thought was cut off by a man inside the main cabin hollering out. "Ah, who goes there. What are you about with Bald Mike?"

Finnegan grabbed an arm and quickly dragged his prey back behind the corner of one outhouse. Looking at the fellow's head, it appeared as if he could easily be referred to as Bald Mike. "Damn it." Finnegan dropped the fellow and craned around the privy to see if Stuart had closed the gaps around the buildings. It looked as if the place had been surrounded, at least from what Finnegan could view. There seemed to be nothing to be lost with a bit of palaver. He turned to Cantrell first. "Tie this lout."

"Tie him?"

"Yes. You are a cowboy, tie him as you would one of those steers you are always fussing with. Head and feet, if you please."

"Tie him with what?"

"Some rope, fool."

"I ain't got no rope with me. You said to bring this here gun." Cantrell held up his Colt, pointing the muzzle toward Finnegan. The gunman swept the gun away and scowled. "Anyhow, I got this gun and no rope. If you wanted me to bring rope you shoulda said something, damn it."

"Use this, damn you." Finnegan produced a few small rope lengths from his coat pocket. As he held the strands out to Cantrell, the man on the ground below them moaned and moved to sit up. Finnegan gave him a swift boot in the head and the early riser slept once more. "Get to it, before I must kill him, and you for the trouble, as well." Finnegan left the cowboy to his work and moved to the corner of the privy. "You, in the cabin, can you hear me?"

"You're damn right I can hear. What the hell you done with Bald Mike and what the hell you doing down here? You ain't got no damn business here."

The idea of concealing the raid's purpose seemed a bit ridiculous by that point, so Finnegan decided to try the truth on for size. "We have it on good account that you are in possession of a goodly number of stolen horses, sir."

"What we are or ain't in possession of is none of your goddamn business! Send Bald Mike back over here."

"The horses are indeed our business, sir. We represent the stock owners they formerly belonged to. I can clearly see the corrals have many horses. When I check the brands on them, we will know if there is perfidy afoot here. I do not hear you denying it."

The man inside the cabin sounded a bit confused. "Did you say something about persnickety feet?"

Finnegan sighed. "Sir, you may surrender now, surrender later, or make the very stupid decision to attempt a fight. Please elect to be intelligent. We have you surrounded on all sides, and you are outnumbered."

"Damn it, we ain't done nothing to you. Get the hell out of here."

"We will not do that, sir."

"Damn you." There was a fairly long pause while the man inside the cabin presumably reviewed his options. "You send Bald Mike back over here, you bastard."

Finnegan considered the request and came to the conclusion that it could not hurt to see what the man might be amenable to. "Very well. He may as well reside with you until this is over. He is injured and cannot walk. Send two unarmed men over here to collect him. Sir, if those men are armed, I will not hesitate."

"You'll give 'em back?"

"You have my word. Send your men."

There was a lapse of some five minutes. Rapid discussion and more than a little outright yelling could be heard inside the cabin. Finally, the door opened a small crack and two men, fully dressed and looking quite terrified, slid from the opening. They walked nervously across the small yard and approached the privies on shaky legs. They moved around to the rear of the outhouses and stood in front of Finnegan. They took turns looking from the gunman to their compatriot tied up on the grassy ground.

Both men stood rigidly with their eyes bugged out in their unshaven faces. Neither man appeared portly, but the huskier of the pair spoke. "Well, give us Bald Mike, huh?"

Finnegan shook his head and drew his Remington. "No. Get down on your knees and allow Mr. Cantrell here to tie you. Resist and I will kill you." He thumbed back the hammer on the revolver.

The skinnier of the two looked over to Cantrell. "Bill, would this bastard shoot us after he promised safe passage?"

Cantrell swallowed with an audible click. "This one'll shoot a man for near anything."

"Very good, so there you have it." Finnegan moved the muzzle of the Remington between the two men. "Or will it be necessary for me to kill one of you so that the other will appreciate my earnestness?"

"Naw, that ain't needed." The huskier fellow got down on his knees and the skinny one followed suit.

Cantrell slowly moved behind the two and began tying them. "Sorry, about this, Frank, Cooney."

The husky one stared up at Finnegan. "He gonna hang us, Bill?"

Cantrell cleared his throat and began tying the second man. "Ain't nobody getting' hung. We ain't hung nobody."

"The hell you ain't." The skinny man glanced between Finnegan and Cantrell. "You hanging folks is the news of this whole damn territory."

Finnegan sighed, yet again. "Sir, unless your intention is to argue for your own execution, I would suggest you remain quiet. I intend to let you live through this capture, but you can surely change my mind given the correct amount of annoyance." The man snapped his mouth shut and looked down at the ground. "Excellent."

The negotiator's voice could be heard from the cabin once again. "Hey, Cooney, Frank, don't be dawdling, damn it. Get back over here with Bald Mike."

Finnegan chuckled and stepped close to the corner of the

privy. "They have become injured, sir. Send two more to help them back."

"What?"

"Send two more men to assist the last two."

"You...you're a damn liar. There ain't nothing wrong with them. You grabbed 'em same as Bald Mike. Damn you for a liar, sir."

Finnegan shook his head. He had heard a good number of similar speeches in the past. "Yes, very well. We have established that I lied to you. You are very clever to have figured it out. Now, you have already lost three men. We outnumber you and have the advantage over you. Cease your stupidity and come out into the open with your hands empty and raised. Even you must be able to understand that there is no hope for you in this."

"To hell with you."

"Come out peaceably and none of you will be hurt."

"You're a damn liar. You tell that pack of lies to William Downes before you slew him in his damn bed?" A collection of muffled yells came from the cabin. "You that damn Irishman they hired to kill innocent homesteaders around here? Goddamn devil Pinkerton."

"I am employed to capture horse thieves. The condition you are captured in depends on you, sir. Will you surrender?"

"Go to hell."

Finnegan leaned against the privy and withdrew a cigar. "You may come to regret your truculence, sir. It will be very warm soon. I assume you have only liquor in that shack of yours and no water." He lit the cigar and smiled at the three bound men. "Out here we will take our leisure at the creek and possibly cook up a few of these hogs you keep for our dinner. Have you any food in there?"

"We got a damn fine pile of ammunition." The man had

wished for the statement to sound more resolute, but it fell short.

"Excellent. Please inform me as to how well it cures your thirst or fills your belly." Finnegan lit his cigar. "I have plenty of tobacco and, if I am not mistaken, I can hear a chicken clucking about in this vicinity. Perhaps I will have some eggs for my breakfast."

"Damn you, Pinkerton."

"You seem to know me. What might your name be, sir?"

"Jack Stringer, and you'd better damn well remember it. I'm about to be the man that killed you, Pinkerton."

"Finnegan, Finnegan!" Stuart was calling out from the other side of the yard. "Did you hear that, Finnegan?"

The gunman rubbed his eyes. "Yes, damn it, I heard."

"Jack Stringer, you have seen your last morning, you lousy son of a bitch. I always knew this day would come." Stuart was half-laughing with elation by the end of the statement.

"Who...who is that out there?" The voice in the cabin sounded to have lost some of its confidence.

"Granville Stuart, Stringer, and I am about to be the man that killed you."

Finnegan groaned and took a puff on his cigar. He looked up at the sky. "For the love of St. Michael, Lord, deliver me from these fools." He took a deep breath and hollered around the corner of the privy. "No one is killing anyone. Stringer, come out of there with your hands raised and no harm will come to you."

"Now, I damn well know that's a lie, and I don't have to send fools out to prove it, neither. Granville Stuart would just as soon hang a man as look at him, and the son of a bitch been hanging men all summer. I don't need to ask these other boys if they'd rather fight or walk out of here into a noose, neither. To hell with you, Pinkerton; we'll fight."

Finnegan set the back of his head against the privy wall. "I am not offering you a fight, Stringer. You can sit in there and starve or you may surrender."

"You ain't gonna be the one to choose that, Pinkerton." Glass began breaking on the two sides of the cabin that were adorned with windows. On the other two sides the chinking was shoved from between the cottonwood logs.

"Damn these cowboys. Why must everything be so absurdly difficult with them?" Finnegan moved away from the corner of the privy and put an extra wall between him and the cabin. "Make sure you have cover, men. These fools mean to..." Gunfire began flashing from the cabin. Around the outbuildings and the small barn, the fire was returned. Finnegan hung his head. "Hold your fire, jackasses. It is a waste of ammunition to fire at them inside that..." A scream coming from the general area of the barn cut off Finnegan's comment.

"Oh, Jesus. Lord have mercy boys, I been hit. For God's good sake, somebody come and help me." The voice coming from the small barn sounded as plaintive as could be imagined.

Finnegan squeezed the bridge of his nose and looked to the men bound in the grass at his feet. "Why is it that vexatious men such as that can never be killed cleanly?"

The husky horse thief shrugged from his supine position. "Perhaps it is so you may know who is vexatious and who is not. If the man had not been wounded, then you would never have known his tendencies."

Finnegan arched one eyebrow. "Perhaps I should send you off to discuss Greeks and rivers with Mr. Stuart. He is a great contemplator of the kind of inanity you take interest in."

The man shrugged again. "I have little else to consider, currently. Although, even in in this condition, I cannot say as

I would care to spend much time with Mr. Stuart. I have heard that his only use for horse thieves is to place them as a weight at the end of a rope, and I have no reason to doubt the rumors."

"I do not know if housewives or horse thieves are the worse gossip mongers. If you might..." There was a crashing noise and fresh gunfire blotted out the sounds of the man in the barn. "Bloody hell." Finnegan peeked around the side of the privy and a bullet collided with the wood just as he was looking. Chips blew back into his face. He withdrew, but fired off two rounds from his Remington around the corner for good measure. "Ah, hell and perdition." He wiped the splinters and blood from his face. Blinking, he made certain his sight was still in order. Peering around the corner once more did not improve his mood. The men, formerly in the cabin, were running, in a mass, toward the barn.

Stuart's voice came from the other side of the small compound. "What should we do, Gilhooley?"

"Shoot them, damn you!" In most circumstances, Finnegan waited until his hand was forced by an adversary, but having his own blood drawn always ruined his charitable disposition. He holstered the Remington and snatched up the '76 Winchester. The front sight of the rifle fell on a horse thief's back as he approached the barn. Finnegan thumbed back the hammer and touched the trigger. The horse thief fell to the hay strewn ground and barely even twitched. The gunman worked the action on the rifle and fired another round. That bullet hit a man low somewhere just before the last fellow disappeared into the barn. "Damn it to hell."

"They made it to that damn barn, Finnegan." Stuart sounded a bit disappointed.

"I have seen, Granville. Thank you."

"I believe that's Jim O'Hara they got in there as a hostage, now."

"I see." Finnegan kneeled and got a rest on the edge of the privy. If he saw movement through one of the barn windows he could try a shot. "I am afraid I do not know Jim O'Hara."

"I only mention it, since we probably ought not fire the barn to get them out."

Finnegan sighed and hung his head once more. He yelled out to his compatriot on the other side of the corrals. "Granville, normally the strategy of a siege such as this is better discussed in private."

"Oh, right, sorry."

"Pinkerton, you out there?" It sounded like Jack Stringer.

"I am."

"I reckon I damn near got you."

Finnegan stiffened up and did his best to keep his anger at bay. "Yes, you nearly did. Unfortunately, you came up just a bit short. Your friend in front of the barn was not so lucky."

"Barely knew the man, Pinkerton."

Finnegan turned to the husky horse thief. "I dare say this man does not take much of an interest in the safety of his hired help."

The husky fellow sneered. "It ain't much of a job, really. Kind of every man for himself in most of these outfits."

"I see. I will have to keep that in mind if I consider becoming a horse thief." Finnegan turned back toward the barn. "Your position has changed Mr. Stringer, but not your condition. You are still surrounded, and we will still remain here until you see reason."

"I got your man, Pinkerton."

Finnegan scoffed. "You shot the idiot, you deal with him, Stringer."

"I'll kill him, sure as sunrise."

"You have already tried to kill him and fouled up the job. Why should your next attempt go any better?" Finnegan grinned at his small joke, but neither Cantrell nor the hogtied horse thieves grinned back. "You territorial people are a sullen bunch."

"Finnegan, Finnegan, can you hear me?" Stuart's head could be seen poking around a corral post.

"Yes."

"Meet me behind their cabin. We need to discuss this development."

Finnegan glanced over to Cantrell. "Development? That is one word for it." He sighed. "Can I count on you to keep an eye on these fellows?" Cantrell nodded. "Very well."

Cantrell motioned to the side of his head. "You're bleeding out that ear there, Mr. Gilhooley."

Finnegan felt around and pulled an exceptionally large splinter out of his earlobe. "Bloody hell. Shot once and scarred by outhouse wood. I did not bleed so much during the whole damnable war as I have bled in Montana."

"Men tend to bleed here, sir."

Finnegan nodded and turned back to Stuart. "I will move around to the back on my side. Do the same." He nodded to Cantrell once more and left around the rear of the privy. There was only a small gap between the buildings he needed to traverse to get to the rear of the cabin and no one inside the barn managed a shot at him while he crossed it. As he came around the back of the cabin, he nearly tripped over the large pile of whiskey bottles that had been deposited there. He looked up to see Stuart come around the opposite corner. "It is apparent what these fellows spend their ill-gotten gains on. I am amazed any of them is sober enough to shoot straight."

Stuart shrugged. The pioneer was gripping his Winchester tightly and had sweat standing out on his forehead. "Straight shooting is not required to hit a man like O'Hara; the man has always suffered from terrible luck. He lost an eye breaking horses, and most of his teeth when he irritated his wife."

"And now he has been shot. I dare say, that is poor luck."

Stuart took a second take at Finnegan's face. "Have you been shot?"

"Only nearly. They are splinter wounds from a near miss." Finnegan wiped more blood. "What is it you wish to discuss, Granville?"

"This is degenerating badly, Finnegan."

The gunman cocked his head to one side to facilitate splinter plucking. "Oh, it is not going so poorly as all that. We have three of them captured and we have bounced them out of this cabin and into the barn. We know how many of them there are now."

"We do?"

"Six, still at large. Did you not count them as they ran?"

"Well..." Stuart rubbed his eyes. "I made an attempt, but was busy shooting."

"That will happen, Granville." He found a particularly jagged fragment and pulled it free. "Damnation." He threw down the small hunk of wood. "Granville, how we view the situation does not much matter. What precisely would you suggest as a course of action?"

"I am not entirely certain how we should proceed, but we must free Jim O'Hara or make an attempt to free him."

Finnegan ceased plucking for a moment. "Must? Whatever for?"

"We cannot allow the other members of the posse to believe we would leave a man to die with these ruffians." Stuart spoke the words as if they were part of a well-prepared speech to a constituency.

"Granville, who gives a tinker's damn what this troop of deadbeats holds as true? I would say they are hardly worth their feed. Every one of them had a fine chance to shoot at those men while they moved from this cabin to that barn, and I see only one dead ruffian. They are here as mere window dressing. I am not certain we are safe so long as they are armed."

"Well, at any rate, I would prefer it did not get around that I left one of my own to perish." Stuart wiped the sweat from his forehead.

"I...I had not paused to consider how Mr. O'Hara's position might affect your reputation, Granville. Although, I must confess, learning that you wish for his return has not caused me to conjure a method for his safe extraction."

"Yes, well." Stuart shrugged again. "I had rather hoped that you could think of something."

"Such as? Truly, Granville, I have collected many a thief in my day, but these added strictures are quite new to me."

"We could offer to trade one of Stringer's men back to him."

"That sort of dealing is how I got the last two bound behind an outhouse."

"Ah." Stuart smoothed his beard. "Yes, Stringer may have caught onto that sort of thing."

"Stringer will be very loath to part with O'Hara. I would be. O'Hara very nearly guarantees that we will not lay proper siege to that barn and light it aflame."

Stuart glanced furtively over toward the barn. "We could...the others have no way of knowing whether O'Hara is alive or dead. We could announce that the bastards killed him and then fire the barn."

Finnegan removed what he hoped was his final splinter. "If that suits your fancy, Granville. I must say, I do not even recall being introduced to O'Hara, and I do not much care what becomes of him. Although, even this lot may question how you came to know the man had been killed." He cleaned the blood from his fingers as best he could on his pants leg.

"Now, how would you prefer to proceed? You are, after all, my employer. Do you wish to..." There was a crashing sound and gunfire erupted once more. "What fresh hell is this?" Finnegan pivoted and saw what looked to be all six men from the barn, mounted and fleeing the compound. "Daft bastards." He brought up his Winchester. His first shot went wide, the second hit a horse in the rump, the third slammed into a fugitive's legs. "They are in flight, Granville." He levered the gun once more, took careful aim, fired, and got nothing for his trouble but the sight of the last rider disappearing over the bank out into the plains beyond. Finnegan lowered his rifle to see that Stuart stood beside him. The pioneer had not fired a shot. "Bloody hell."

Stuart looked from the barn to the place the men had disappeared, and back again. "They made off quite briskly."

Finnegan pursed his lips to hold in another curse. "Yes, Granville, it was a neat escape. I take it there were horses in that barn."

"It would certainly appear so."

"Yes, yes it would." Finnegan removed his hat, wiped his brow and returned the garment to his head. "Well, I believe, now that the siege is at an end, I will find Mr. Kilkenny, procure a mount, and give chase."

Stuart nodded, still looking a bit puzzled that his horde of horse thieves had slipped from his grasp so quickly. "Yes, most certainly, we must give chase."

Finnegan motioned toward the barn. "Do you not think it would be best if you first inquired as to the condition of Mr. O'Hara?"

"Oh, yes, of course." Stuart turned to go, but stopped. "Finnegan, do not pursue those men without me. I will have it out with Jack Stringer, come hell or high water."

Finnegan took a seat on a hitching post. "Granville, those men are the only men we have seen in the last two days.

They are currently leaving the only horse tracks to be found in this vast nothingness. I see no reason to hurry. I know I injured one man and one horse. Perhaps, through some fluke of luck, your men injured others. It is best to let villains bleed at times like this. The longer we wait, the easier they will be to deal with."

"Ah, very well thought out, Finnegan."

"Hopefully it will prove a correct notion." Finnegan stood and turned to go find Kilkenny and the horses.

"I will let the men know we will be leaving in pursuit."

Finnegan turned back to Stuart. "Oh, no, Granville. I have had quite enough of that damn posse. Those fools may take what we have caught to Lewistown. You may come, but for mercy's sake, let the rest go home or shoot them, I do not much care which."

FINNEGAN REINED up his horse and drew his Remington. Something was moving in the sagebrush in front of them, but he could not say what it was precisely. Kilkenny came to his side. "Do you see it, Ephraim?"

The whiskey baron swallowed and pulled back to keep his horse steady. "Yes, I see. If it is a man, I would think they would have fired on us by now."

"Yes, in all likelihood."

"From the way these horses are acting, I might venture a guess that it is the horse you shot. You said you were certain you hit one, correct?"

"Yes." Finnegan frowned at the memory. He disliked to shoot anything without good reason. "Keep back and I will see what it is." He dismounted and handed his reins to Kilkenny. Some fifty yards back, he could see Stuart, Teddy Blue, and Mr. Oman lingering. He waved for them to come forward, then turned to walk ahead. Inside of a few paces he could see that the shape in the sage was none other than the bay horse he had shot earlier in the day. It lay on the soft, sandy earth, still possessed of only enough life to give a small kick now and then. Finnegan sighed. "My apologies, horse. You deserved a better end." He placed the muzzle of the Remington a scant inch from the horse's head and fired. The beast gave one small kick and was still.

"Many thanks, listening to her go was wearing on my nerves."

Finnegan almost jumped out of his skin at the sound of the voice. He spun around with his pistol leveled. Off in a small declivity, some ten yards away, a man lay. Dried blood covered most of his visible parts and alkali dust covered the rest. "Damnation." He approached the pale figure. "You appear to be in rather poor health."

"Ah, that would be one way of sayin' it." The man tried a laugh, but could not quite manage.

Stuart came up and stood in his stirrups to get a better look at the man. "Does he live, Finnegan?"

The Pinkerton looked the man over but could not see a weapon in his vicinity, so he holstered his gun and moved up next to the fellow. "He is not departed as yet, but is well on the way." Finnegan knelt down. "I would assume you are aware of that, sir."

"I began to suspect it when Carl Duffy pushed me from the saddle with no more trouble than you'd have knocking over a calf." He sneered. "Always liked Duffy, pity we had to end on poor terms. One of you shot his horse, you see, the animal you just put down. One of you shot me, as well. When the horse went down, Duffy got to thinking and decided that since I was as shot up as the horse, we might as well stay together. Sort of a matched pair." The man coughed and grimaced.

Finnegan motioned to Stuart. "Your canteen, if you please, Granville."

The pioneer pulled his canteen from his saddle horn and tossed it down to Finnegan. "It's more than the rascal deserves. Both of those horses he has so glibly discussed are probably mine."

"Well, he will bother you no further, soon enough." Finnegan uncapped the canteen and gave the man a small sip.

"That you can damn well bank on." He coughed again and smiled, looking at Finnegan. "Is he Granville Stuart, from the DHS?" Finnegan nodded. "You that Pinkerton Stringer's so apoplectic about?"

"I am." Finnegan leaned closer. "That man, the one I spoke with, is he truly Jack Stringer?"

From the look on his face, the man clearly thought it was a silly question. "That is what he has called himself since I've known him. Who can say what his Christian name might be? If I was him, I wouldn't tell nobody, neither." Finnegan nodded again. "Hey, Pinkerton man, how'd you like to ask him?" The fellow had a small coughing fit, but continued with what looked to be dire determination. "I don't much care for the way I been treated. They took my horse, took my guns, took every damn thing but my boots and left me here without even a drink of water. I ask, what kind of way is that to treat a man who ain't never done nothing to you?"

"I can understand you feeling put out regarding their behavior." Finnegan offered the canteen again. "Where are they going to, sir?"

"I wouldn't mind a bit if you was to shoot them, or Stuart over there was to hang 'em."

"We will do our best, sir. Where are they headed?"

"They mean to take the money for them blue bellies at

Fort Maginnis. Leave them to shift for themselves for a month, Jack says."

"They intend to steal an Army payroll?" Finnegan turned to Stuart. "Can five ragged men hope to accomplish such a thing?"

Stuart nodded slowly, looking almost impressed by the plan. "The pay for Maginnis is not brought by soldiers. It comes in the mail shipment. Hell, I was even asked to transport it from Maiden to the fort once. Those fools should have no trouble relieving whatever other fool is tasked with freighting it this month."

Finnegan, given to taking an interest in such matters, queried the first question that came to his mind. "What does the fort payroll amount to, monthly?"

Stuart chuckled. "Oh, it cannot be much more than five hundred. They pay those soldiers what they are worth. My cowboys are far better compensated. Those blackguards would be better off trying to steal the DHS payroll at the end of the roundup. Of course, our men are better armed and show more interest in their pay." Stuart spit down into the brush. "Still, I am a bit surprised that Stringer would attempt such an audacious scheme. It will damn well pay better than picking off my horses one at a time." Stuart leaned forward in the saddle and pointed to the mortally wounded man. "You may turn out to be the lucky one among your friends. When a man begins to steal payrolls, he quickly finds himself hunted by more than irritated ranchers and such."

The man coughed and gripped his bloody leg as best he could. "I will feel lucky when the Pinkerton puts an end to this." He turned his alkali caked face toward Finnegan. "I have told you all I can." He coughed. "Uh, I nearly forgot, there is another wounded man, goes by Burr; he was hit in the belly but will not admit it. You may find him in your travels, as well." He smiled. "That is all I know about Jack

Stringer and his companions. I ain't done nothing to make you have any malice toward me, Pinkerton man. If you would put me out of this, I would be much obliged." He turned his head toward Stuart. "Just so you know, a man would rather be shot than hung." At the last word, Finnegan stood, drew, and shot the man in the head. The chore seen to, he holstered his gun and handed Stuart his canteen back.

Stuart had a rather blank look on his face. "Just like that?"

"He seemed to be in a hurry, and we are, as well."

Mr. Oman was forming some sort of dinner that smelled wonderful in the small Dutch oven he rather expertly kept lashed to the back of his horse. The thing did not even flop or make noise during transit. The newly comprised posse had been pushing their horses since just after sunup, and now that the sun had set it was time to let them have at least a short rest. They could not continue to track the fugitives in the dark, at any rate.

Finnegan reclined on a fallen log while Teddy Blue saw to the horses and Kilkenny sipped from his flask. Stuart's first inclination had been to dig out his coffee pot and had just returned from the creek with water. Feeling inclined himself, Finnegan walked to the fire and pulled a small stick free to light a cigar. He returned the stick and nodded to Oman. "The aroma promises a fine meal, sir." Mr. Oman nodded, stone faced, and went back to his cooking.

Stuart set his coffee pot near the flames and grinned to Finnegan. "Despite the difficulties, we are making fine progress out here."

"Indeed." Finnegan puffed his cigar. "These men we have been dealing with today most certainly must be the largest gang in the general area. If there were more horse thieves than them about, we would all be afoot."

Stuart smiled contentedly. "Yes, aggravating, but a fine day. Would you care for me to look over your face by the fire?"

Finnegan resumed his seat on the log. "It is not bothersome for the moment. I would appreciate a review in the morning. That fellow today, he seemed quite pleased to needle you about hangings."

Stuart fussed with his coffee pot. "Most folks know I was amongst the vigilantes in Virginia City, not that most honest citizens of the town were not. I suppose I am one of the few that still remain." Stuart stood and stretched out his back. "I suppose I have never been one to deny it and I have never been shy about mentioning it. I have no more regrets about what we did back then than I do regarding what transpired this morning. Men of low character, men who would take another man's property by force. Men who would kill for the price of a cheap watch. They come to places such as this because they believe they will be able to do as they please here. They believe there is no one in places such as this to level consequences upon them. They are wrong in their thinking."

Finnegan tapped the ash from his cigar. "It would certainly appear we have proved that much over the course of this summer." Kilkenny laughed and wandered toward Finnegan. The gunman took another cigar from his vest and handed it to his friend. "You do not agree that we have made good progress these few months, Ephraim?"

"Oh, I would agree you have made progress." The whiskey baron held up the cigar. "Many thanks." He moved toward the fire. "What amuses me, what causes my mirth, is merely the observation that men, at their base, truly are all the same, regardless of race, color, creed, or birthplace. We all hold with the same ridiculous notions."

Stuart eyed him. "And what notions might those be, Mr. Kilkenny?"

"The comment you made regarding your reasons for searching out these horse thieves, their lack of a moral center, it rather reminded me of something a chief once told me in the Solomons."

Finnegan sat forward, interested to hear a tale regarding his favorite of Kilkenny's many old haunts. "One of those headhunter chaps you were telling me about?"

Kilkenny nodded. "The very same. The old fellow resided in a shack that was positively overflowing with heads and was quite well thought of in his community. He may have killed more men than even you, Finnegan, and bear in mind: that fellow never would have used an implement more complicated than a rock tied to a stick to do his business."

Finnegan nodded. "It is always impressive to meet a man who clings to tradition at his own hazard."

"Oh, he was impressive, I will say that for him." Kilkenny knelt and lit his cigar. "I asked the old boy, once, why it was that his village raided the neighboring village. He told me that they raided to avenge what the neighbors had done during their last raid. I asked why the neighbors had raided. He told me it was to revenge the last raid perpetrated on them." He chuckled and smiled at Stuart. "It was a sad sort of unending waltz."

Stuart shook his head and stared down into the fire. "I would think you, of all men, Ephraim, would know the difference between the enforcement of some order, some law, and the practices of a race of savages living in huts in the jungle. My dislike for horse thieves has nothing to do with revenge, only a wish to live without parasites plaguing me."

Kilkenny shook his cigar at the pioneer. "Mr. Stuart, you

misunderstand me. I do not accuse you of vengeance. I do not believe, if pressed, that old chief would have attributed his actions to vengeance, either. No, I would say the trait you share with that ancient savage was not vengeance, but rather hypocrisy."

"Hypocrisy?" Stuart raised his eyebrows. "I have been called many a vile slur over the years, Ephraim, but that is novel, I must say." He grinned. "I might be insulted if it was not so unexpected. In what manner am I a hypocrite in your eyes?"

"You claim you are pursuing these men because they stand outside the strictures of society, yet your behavior is outside of the laws of this country, as well." Kilkenny sat down next to Finnegan. "You call these horse thieves immoral, claim they would kill a man for the price of a watch." Kilkenny produced his pocket watch and held it in the fire light. "You have killed, or hired killed, many a man this summer over the price of a horse. This watch would fetch the price of a score of these glue factory rejects in London. I cannot help but ask you, Mr. Stuart, who is the savage and who is not in this territory?"

Stuart sneered a bit and tossed wood on the fire. "These buzzards would eat away at the decent people of this territory until their children starved and their fields lay fallow. They would do that for the chance to frequent a brothel and buy more of your family's rotgut. I ask you, Mr. Kilkenny: if these bastards were breaking up your whiskey barrels, would you do any differently? Who among us can claim the higher ground, morally, when his livelihood and very existence is being threatened?"

Finnegan stood and had a good laugh for himself as he approached the now percolating coffee pot. He knelt and filled one of the nearby cups. "I would agree with both of you on several points, gentlemen. First, Ephraim is correct. Men, the world over, are exactly alike. I have heard this very conversation before, over many campfires, in a variety of accents, during the war. Second, Granville is surely correct in stating that all men move to defend what is theirs, and inevitably claim it to be their right. Third, Ephraim is correct in calling you a hypocrite, Granville. All men are hypocrites to one degree or another. Finally..." He sipped his coffee. "I would submit that if some moral obligation, the price of a horse, or the price of a watch, does not motivate a man to kill his fellow man, some other motivation will soon be discovered. What has occurred here this summer has been occurring somewhere, for some reason, since Cain slew Able, and just such a thing will occur when winter arrives, assuming it is not too cold for one man to slew another in this godforsaken place." He drained his coffee cup. "Mr. Oman, how are you coming with those victuals?"

Chapter 28

FORT MAGINNIS, MONTANA TERRITORY

August 5th, 1884

KILKENNY SAT RATHER UNEASILY IN THE SADDLE, looking up to the second story balcony where the Army private had disappeared when asked to find the captain. He glanced around at the lolling but still rather intimidating soldiers. They were clearly not the cream of the crop, but they were still armed men under orders. "Finnegan, do you truly believe this to be a wise decision?"

The gunman adjusted himself in the saddle. "We seek men intent on stealing the pay from these soldiers. Is it not reasonable to inquire as to whether or not their payroll has arrived?"

"I only broach the subject because you have had dealings with this Captain Hatcher before and they did not end well." Kilkenny glanced around once more. "I would assume that one-eared lieutenant is somewhere around here, as well."

"Lieutenant Bowden." Stuart said, eyeing the balcony more than the soldiers. "You are rather baiting a lion in its den here."

Finnegan shrugged. "If I am to remain in this country after these horse thieves are collected, I will need to settle accounts with these men eventually. Today is as good as another. Besides, I doubt even these fools would be hotheaded enough to attempt shooting me down in front of so many esteemed witnesses."

Kilkenny was still pensive. "Unless they choose to shoot us, as well."

"Ah, I assure you, Ephraim, the disappearance of an Irish whiskey baron and one of the founding fathers of the territory would face much more scrutiny than the disappearance of a mere Pinkerton detective. We disappear all the time, and our own associates rarely take the time to investigate." He was forced to pause in his comforting of Kilkenny. Captain Hatcher came limping to the railing of the balcony above. Next to him stood Lieutenant Bowden. The junior officer still wore a bandage around his head. "Good afternoon, gentlemen." Finnegan smiled up at them. "We come to inquire as to your financial condition."

The captain only looked confused while Bowden appeared quite angry. He fielded the question. "You lousy bastard. I ought to take you to a tree and give you your due and proper."

Finnegan retained his smile. "Of course, you are welcome to attempt it, Lieutenant, but I hardly understand your malice. I would think, of all men, you could appreciate the great distance that lies between the side of your head and the center of it. To all other men it is a bare inch or two; from your perspective, the two points are a world apart."

The notion seemed to quiet the man's rage a bit. "What the hell is your business here, Gilhooley?"

"We come to inquire as to whether or not you have received your payroll yet."

"Our pay? What interest is that to you?" Bowden looked to his commander, but turned away when he saw the same dull visage that always presented itself. "Corporal Burke has been sent to Maiden to collect it, along with the mail. What of it?"

Stuart interjected. "Jack Stringer intends to relieve you of it, Lieutenant. Perhaps rightfully so, if you are so callous as to send only one red-haired young boy to guard your money."

Bowden sneered. "As usual, Stuart, you have your nose in what is not your affair. How can anyone rob a fellow when they have no way of knowing he is on the road? Only Burke and the officers of this fort know when the payrolls arrive."

Stuart laughed. "Then I would wager one of the officers stands to double his pay this month, assuming Stringer is successful."

"Oh, tell your delusional tales somewhere else, Stuart. You have been pestering me about this Stringer you have invented since I have been posted here. Are you not lonely, being the sole fellow who has knowledge of this phantom?"

Stuart grinned at the young officer. "Stringer is a phantom no more, Bowden." Stuart motioned to the men around him. "All these fellows have seen him, in the flesh. We pursue none other than him, and I will rather cherish bringing his corpse here for you to view. If it is convenient to me to do so."

Oddly enough, Bowden turned to Finnegan for confirmation. "You pursue Jack Stringer?"

Finnegan cleared his throat and glanced between Stuart and Bowden. "We pursue a man who calls himself Stringer, yes." He felt it best to change the subject. "When do you expect Corporal Burke to return?"

"Either this evening or tomorrow. This is not Philadelphia, Mr. Gilhooley. Here, the mail arrives when it arrives and not a moment sooner." Bowden chuckled. "You cannot possibly think I will dispatch any of my men to aid in this foolishness. I have heard many a tale of a willow-the-wisp such as Jack Stringer, but I have yet to hear of one stealing an Army payroll."

Stuart stood in his stirrups and pointed to Bowden. "Be assured, Lieutenant, I would only ask for the assistance of this trash you call soldiers if the last Indian and the last drunkard in this territory were no longer available to choose from. We came here for information, and you have given it. Jack Stringer is our affair; no need to rouse any of these reprobates to foul things up."

Finnegan smiled at his employer and tipped his hat to the officers above. "Good day, gentlemen."

"Gilhooley?" Bowden stared down.

"Yes, Lieutenant?"

"I am told that you may have an interest in remaining in this area, engaging in the cattle business?"

"I am considering it, yes."

"If that is the case, we may yet finish the conversation we began on the porch of your bunkhouse."

Finnegan sighed. "Lieutenant, I am not one to tell another man his business, but if you are truly of a mind to hand out someone's due and proper, I would suggest the degenerate by your side as more deserving than I. It was not I that placed you on that porch, Lieutenant." He tipped his hat again. "Only a notion, one soldier to another -- do with it what you may."

THE MEN HAD DISMOUNTED and were slowly walking up the rutted wagon road that led between the fort and Maiden. Their horses had nothing left to give, and should have been rested long ago, but both Finnegan and Stuart had been in favor of pressing on. They knew that the horses under Stringer and his men could not be in any better condition.

Victory in the contest would likely go to the group that pushed harder or proved luckier in terms of horse flesh.

Kilkenny walked near the edge of the wagon road, peering down into the grass on occasion. He paused, sighed, and motioned to Finnegan. "Here is another place where someone or several men departed the road. I cannot say if it is our villains."

"Damn this." Stuart spit down into the road mud and glared at his horse with obvious disappointment. "To be so close and not know if the rascals are within a mile, now. Damn this, it is vexing."

"These are the trials one faces chasing scoundrels, Granville." Finnegan rubbed his face and motioned up the road. "Are we nearing the outpost you mentioned?"

Stuart rubbed his eyes. "Yes. A mile, perhaps? Chamberlain normally keeps some stock corralled there for his outriders. I hope to hell there is something there today." He looked up the road and then down in the other direction. "This is maddening. We do not know if they came by this road. We do not know if they took another route. We do not know if they lie in wait near the fort or near Maiden. For all we know, they have already relieved the boy of the payroll and are dead drunk in Lewistown."

Finnegan resumed trudging up the road, more dragging his horse than leading him. "There will always be things that cannot be known in an endeavor such as this, Granville. That is why attempting a thing such as this is considered so bold. Take comfort in the fact that you have tried while your fellow ranchers remain at home by the fire."

Stuart grunted a sour laugh. "They remain at home considering more prosperous opportunities. I am not here from boldness, Finnegan. I am here from necessity." He hung his head. "I must confess, I do not look forward to telling Reece Anderson the particulars of this trip. When he discovers that we failed to shoot horse thieves in their beds, while he succeeded and was chided for the success...well, I will never hear the end of it."

Finnegan did not bother to look back at the pioneer as he addressed him. "We were not trying to kill them in their beds, Granville. We were attempting to capture them alive."

"Oh, to hell with that. I would have happily shot them in their nightshirts." The frustration of the chase was clearly making Stuart a bit mean. "I swear, this Montana Territory does grind a man down. There was a time when I had the choice of turning north or south. To go south would have required me turning Mormon, or convincing those damned Saints that I had turned Mormon. At the time, it seemed a terrible chore and rather disingenuous. Now and then, I damn well regret it, I do not mind telling you boys." He sighed. "On the other hand, hanging Mr. Jack Stringer from the schoolyard flagpole in Maiden will go a great distance in showing folks I am not to be trifled with. To say nothing of the crow that will be forced upon them who always contended the man was a myth. I would include you among them, Finnegan."

"Yes, I suppose you might." The gunman continued to trudge, mostly because he had nothing better to do. "I think you might have made a fair Mormon, Granville. They are a very abstentious people, from what I am told."

Stuart nodded. "I have been told the same. Do not misunderstand me: it is not that I do not respect their tenets; I simply could not imagine the tortuous conditions a man would have to suffer if he was constantly surrounded not only by God-bothering bible thumpers, but thumpers so zealous they felt the need to write their own damn bible. No, I could not have found a way to abide it. If I must march like this the rest of my days, it would be preferable to that sad fate." He stopped in the middle of the road. "Ah, there lies Chamberlain's outpost and, if my eyes do not deceive me, there are horses in the corral."

Finnegan wiped sweat from his brow. "Ah, well, there you have it. We have been delivered by the grace of God, regardless of how you view the matter, Granville." He smiled at the pioneer.

Stuart shook his head. "Unfortunately, as a man currently dabbling with agnosticism, I can only go so far as to say you have been saved by your God and I was an unwitting bystander."

Finnegan resumed trudging. "Somehow, I doubt it was my reputation that brought about God's mercy."

Kilkenny trudged past both men, finding new energy with the sight of the clapboard outpost. "This is obviously my doing, Gentlemen. As both an Irishman and a drunk, God delivers me on a daily basis. Let us pick up the pace a bit; my flask is empty and if I know anything of these territorial cowboys, there is bound to be a bottle in that shed."

Finnegan laughed. "Yes, assuredly, but will it be up to your standard?"

"Right now, my standard is somewhere below champagne and above lamp oil. Anything in between will do nicely."

Chapter 29

MAIDEN, MONTANA TERRITORY

August 6th, 1884

THEY HAD SPENT A RESTLESS NIGHT AT THE RANCH outpost and resumed their pursuit an hour before full light. Only Finnegan, Stuart, and Teddy Blue had left the outpost in darkness. Kilkenny had discovered a bottle of questionable origins under a cot, and had consumed the contents in short order the night before. The whiskey baron was still out cold and drooling on a ticked mattress when the time for departure arrived. Mr. Oman had remained behind to keep an eye on his employer, while the rest of the party continued.

The three men threaded their way down the wagon road and soon enough were nearing Maiden. Teddy had been quiet most of the morning, but came up next to Stuart as they were approaching the town. "Mr. Stuart, do you think it was wise to pause at the station through the night? How can we know that Burke didn't pass us while we were in that shack?"

Stuart, who had not had much sleep leaning against a plank wall through the night, gave Teddy a cold look. "You might be willing to ride this road in the dark to get somewhere, but that child corporal sure as hell never would. We did not find him at the fort, and we did not meet him on the road. He would not have left this town nearing night. That boy is still in this town. I would bet my last dollar."

Finnegan reined his horse up before entering the town proper. There were no people stirring who could be seen. He rubbed his face and gave one cheek a small slap. He had not slept well, either, and there had been no coffee to be had. "We will have to work delicately here, men. It may be best to locate the Corporal's horse before searching out the Corporal."

"His horse?" Stuart scowled. "What do you want with his horse?"

"I do not want anything with his horse, I only wish to determine what the Corporal's condition is."

"Condition? What the hell kind of condition can a pup corporal be in?" Stuart was definitely not in the mood for intrigue.

"Granville, as you pointed out to the Lieutenant, if Stringer and his band intend to steal this payroll, someone must have informed them of the date it would be available for theft. Only Burke and a select few had knowledge of this payroll. Burke may, very likely, be the man who informed Stringer. They may be in collaboration together. I am even more inclined to think it is so, since the young man remains in Maiden. He may only be lingering here because Stringer's bunch has not yet arrived. Burke would not be the first man to work with an assailant in the commission of a robbery. Certainly, there are more than a few mail clerks robbed by cousins every year."

Stuart rubbed his eyes again. "What do you propose, Finnegan?"

"One of us can approach, and determine if the young man's horse is in the livery. If the animal is there, we will observe from a distance and follow the Corporal, without his knowledge, when he leaves town. Somewhere, whether the

Corporal is a confederate of Stringer's or not, we are certain to meet up with our villains."

Stuart groaned. "More waiting?"

"For a man who was once a professional hunter, you seem to loath waiting, Granville."

The pioneer sighed. "I was young, then. Truth be told, I ran down most of those deer with the vitality of youth. I never really had the temperament for waiting."

"Well, it is never too late to try and develop it." Finnegan pointed to the third member of their party. "Mr. Abbott, if you would not mind? You would probably draw the least amount of attention. Please, look into the livery and see if an Army pony resides there. Use all due caution."

"Yes, sir."

Finnegan motioned up at a small hill. "Meet us there, by the cemetery, back in the aspens."

"Yes, sir." Teddy gave his horse a small kick and cantered into the town of Maiden.

From their vantage point, Finnegan and Stuart could look down on the livery. The sun was slowly rising, and their view improved every minute. Stuart was restive. "Do you honestly believe that boy-soldier could be in cahoots with the likes of Stringer?"

"No." Finnegan took out a cigar. He did not think anyone in the town below would notice if he enjoyed a smoke. "But what I believe does not always prove to be in keeping with actual events. If I had to name a likely suspect as Stringer's accomplice, I would name the local mail clerk. Although, as a Pinkerton, I am naturally fond of suspecting mail clerks of all manner of terrible deeds. Still, a payroll being transported by a boy of Burke's years would be tempting for those who knew of it." Finnegan lit his cigar.

"Mr. Kilkenny seems to have lost his stomach for this business."

Finnegan puffed his cigar and watched Teddy slip into the livery. "As it is not his chosen business, I suppose it is his right to withdraw when he pleases."

"It is his right. I only find it strange, since he was so enthusiastic when we began -- so much so that he abandoned the search for his specimens in favor of it. Odd that a man should change his inclinations so quickly."

"Men try new endeavors; some develop a taste for them, and others do not. The rapidity of the developments matters little." Finnegan saw Teddy slip back out of the livery and mount his horse. "That went smoothly." He pointed to the town. "At least one damn thing during this pursuit has been executed properly. I only wish I could claim responsibility for it."

"You are not the only man among us who would like to lay claim to a single right action of late. I am losing my taste for this, as well, Finnegan."

"Then it is fortunate we are nearing the end." Finnegan watched as Teddy ascended the hill at a trot. Teddy brought his horse into the aspens next to Finnegan. "What did you find, Mr. Abbott?"

"Sure enough, sir, there's a regular Army pony in the livery. Just the one, too. So, it must be Corporal Burke's horse."

"Very well, then." Finnegan smiled and nodded with his cigar clamped between his teeth. "All we need do now is wait and watch. Mr. Burke will not leave town without our noticing. When he does, we will accompany him." Finnegan turned to Stuart. "One way or another, if Mr. Stringer wishes to have that payroll, he will have to contend with us to get it."

Stuart sighed. "They will have to contend with the two of us, Finnegan. Young Mr. Abbott is to return to the DHS now."

Abbott's brow furrowed. "Mr. Stuart, the last thing I am is yellow. I got no problem facing them rascals that have been taking our horses."

Stuart nodded and gave the young man a pat on the shoulder. "No man can call you coward, Teddy." He smiled at the boy. "I want you to return to the DHS and inform the men there of what is going on and what has already happened. I would also like for you to check and make certain that half-wit Cantrell has brought our catches to Lewistown or the ranch. I would be appreciative if you would let my children know I am doing well and close to finishing up."

"Sir, I can..."

"Yes, you can, but you can also be of use elsewhere. Now, you had best get to it." Stuart gave him another pat on the shoulder.

Finnegan cleared his throat. "Uh, Mr. Abbott, if it would not trouble you too much, could you please look in on Mr. Kilkenny and Mr. Oman during your return trip and make sure they recall the way back to the DHS."

Stuart laughed. "Yes, Teddy, please see to that. It would not do to misplace a man of Mr. Kilkenny's stature to something as mundane as them losing their way."

Teddy Blue pulled his hat down tighter. "Well, I guess I'll see you gentlemen back at the DHS."

"Be careful on the road, Mr. Abbott." Finnegan waved to the young man as he turned and rode away. Finnegan thoughtfully puffed his cigar. "There are four men with Stringer as far as we know."

Stuart shrugged. "All the more reason to leave that boy

out of it. Victorious or not, my daughter would never forgive me if I wagered him."

"Liquor and love have reduced our numbers a great deal on this trip."

"Oh, I do not lament it all that much." Stuart rubbed his face and smoothed his whitening beard. He looked to have aged a great deal since the woodyard. "We should be content that none of our men have been killed yet. Even that fool O'Hara should survive if Cantrell does not manage to kill him transporting him back. It is best that you and I see to this last bit of business ourselves. We are the only two men with a truly vested interest."

Finnegan nodded. "That is true." He knocked the ash from his cigar. "It is good you sent the boy on his way. He is a fine young fellow, and it would be a pity for him to get shot over something as trivial as stolen horses, or, God forbid, an Army payroll."

Stuart groaned. "Do not tell me you have come to agree with that damned whiskey peddler. There are matters of more importance at work here than the mere theft of horses."

"There are." Finnegan knocked more ash. "You will have to excuse Ephraim. He is new to this sort of thing and a man often finds himself conflicted when participating in something of this nature for the first time. He is in a fit of melancholy now, but in six months' time he will be raising a glass in some Chicago tavern extolling the thrilling tale of how he rode the trail with...Stuart's Stranglers is undoubtedly what the papers will go with."

"Oh, bosh!" The pioneer exclaimed it loud enough that his horse twitched beneath him. "That is a terrible concoction. We have not hung a single man."

"No, but some have been hung and the world does so love alliteration."

Stuart slowly turned to the Pinkerton. "Alliteration?"

"You are unfamiliar with the term?"

"Yes."

"Ah, allow me to inform you as to its meaning. Mr. Pinkerton explained the nature of alliteration to me some years ago and, I must say, I have found every aspect of his theory involving the matter to be both correct and practical."

As LIGHT slowly gathered in the eastern sky, the citizens of Maiden began their daily routines. As Finnegan explained the finer points of alliteration to Stuart, people could be seen lighting lamps and moving about. When it was nearly full light, Finnegan pointed down into the town while fumbling to get Kilkenny's field glasses out. "Granville, if I am not mistaken, is that not young Corporal Burke exiting the boarding house and walking to the café?"

Stuart squinted. "Well, I do not know who the hell else it would be in a uniform."

Finnegan stopped searching out the binoculars. "Ah, yes, excellent point."

Stuart pointed off to the west of town. "Finnegan, have I gone mad, or does that appear to be five men approaching on the road?"

Finnegan chuckled. "I...well, yes, it does appear to be." He leaned back and finally pulled the glasses free. He peered through them at the gang of men. "I cannot claim to know any of them by sight, but I do not imagine it could be a coincidence. They...do you imagine they trotted past both Mr. Abbott and Mr. Kilkenny on the way here?"

Stuart laughed. "I would damn well wager it is a possibility." He fidgeted in the saddle and the sullen sleepiness left his eyes. "Mr. Gilhooley, those men can in no way expect we have beaten them here. It is likely they are ignorant that we have even followed."

Finnegan nodded. "We should continue to follow. We will circle them and approach them from behind. If we can crowd them in somewhere, the corner behind the livery or along the one declivity there, we can reduce their number and make surrender an attractive option for those survivors who remain."

"A fine plan, Finnegan. Anything is preferable to waiting."

With little trouble, Finnegan and Stuart descended from the aspen grove and rode around the rear of the small hill that loomed over Maiden. When they emerged from the trees, the two hunters were roughly two hundred yards behind their prey. Finnegan could hardly credit his good luck. After nearly a hundred miles of travel he had managed to come up directly behind the men he had been chasing and would now be able to take them at a disadvantage. True, it was the first piece of real luck he had experienced since assaulting the woodlot, but he would take it and count it as a blessing, nonetheless. He leaned over to whisper to Stuart beside him. "We will hang back and close the distance when we see where they intend to go." Stuart nodded and they rode on, slowly.

When the small gang entered the city limits of Maiden, a line defined by the placement of a ramshackle blacksmith shop, they brought their horses to a stop, had a brief conference, and then continued down the street, straight to the café where Corporal Burke was leisurely having his breakfast. Stuart leaned toward Finnegan. "They are making straight for Burke. Do you suppose he is meant to meet them there?"

"Or the knob simply has breakfast in the same café every visit and they mean to relieve him of the payroll." Finnegan smiled. "They likely will be disappointed to discover the young man does not carry the payroll satchel with him to get his morning coffee." They were still some seventy-five yards behind the men who had now taken the bold step of tying their horses off directly in front of the café. "Perhaps they merely want breakfast before robbing a payroll. Regardless of their profession, all men must eat."

"It has been a long trip. I would not turn down an egg and a cup of coffee my own self." Stuart watched, somewhat amazed, as the long-traveling horse thieves strolled into the café. "I will be damned."

"I have seen no one else enter that café, Granville. How many others should be inside?"

"There is the old man who runs the place. Dewey, I believe his name is. I once saw a young man injured in the mine who waited the tables some, but he would not be there this early."

Finnegan swung his horse over to a hitching post by the department store and Stuart followed suit. "So, there is one old man, Burke, and our gang of villains in that small café?" He swung down from the saddle.

"Indeed, sir." Stuart lowered himself to the ground and tied off his horse. "I am sure old Dewey will know how to handle himself, or he should by his age." Stuart smiled. "Young Corporal Burke was made aware of the danger of his profession when he put on his uniform."

Finnegan pulled his Winchester from the scabbard on one side of his horse. "We all run the hazard in this life." The two men, rifles in hand, crossed the street and approached the café on the boardwalk. "How many tables in the place? I do not recall."

"Three, perhaps four."

"Good." Finnegan reached down and undid the thong on his hip holster, then reached up and undid the catch on his shoulder holster. "I will start things off when we enter. I believe after this much chasing we no longer owe these men warning."

"Fine by me." Stuart assessed the café. "You go through the door, and I will fire through that window out front. I will be more than happy to reimburse Mr. Dewey for the glass when we are finished."

"You will make a fine politician someday, Granville." Finnegan passed the aforementioned window and leaned his Winchester to one side before opening the door and drawing his Remington. Inside the small café, every man present raised his head to see who the new arrival might be. Finnegan leveled the front sight of the Remington between the eyes of the closest horse thief and fired. The man flopped back in his chair and then slipped to the floor. Finnegan had more or less assumed that the first round he fired would bring about fire from both the miscreants and Stuart, but inside the café all men froze. Outside, Stuart stood with his Winchester aimed, but did not fire. The Pinkerton's eyes moved over the remaining foes sitting at their tables. They all appeared quite shocked. Finnegan cocked the Remington. "You men are all under arrest for the crime of horse theft..." The accusation did not sound as though it warranted his recent actions, so he decided to add a few more charges. "Attempted assault or murder of men commissioned to restrain you, and the attempted theft of government property." He moved the muzzle of the Remington over the remaining men. They looked to be satisfied with the list of crimes.

"Mr. Gilhooley?" Burke's voice drifted over the horse thieves. He was seated at the rear of the café and had a spoonful of what appeared to be oatmeal halfway to his lips.

"Good morning, Corporal Burke."

"I have a telegram for you, sir."

"Thank you, Corporal. I will get that from you a little later."

The man Finnegan could only assume was the fellow calling himself Jack Stringer was twisted around in his chair to stare at the gunman who had just shot another member of the dwindling gang. He craned his neck to look back and forth between the corpse and Finnegan. "You followed us all the way from the river, you bastard."

Finnegan nodded. "We did, sir."

Stringer's lips pulled back into an evil sneer. "Goddamn you, Pinkerton." He began raising up out of his chair, but a bullet from Stuart spun him and he stumbled to the floor. The remaining horse thieves, three in number, were all of different minds when it came to the proper course of action. One man wished to fight. He leapt from his chair and drew his Colt as another of the horse thieves made a run for the back door of the café. Finnegan fired three rounds into the aggressive horse thief. Through the smoke, Finnegan saw the aggressive fellow fall backwards and accidently fire his thus-far-unused Colt toward the fleeing villain. The bullet struck the more discretionary man in the lower back. He screamed out in pain and crashed against the rear door, causing it to burst open. Finnegan fired once more into the aggressive man and drew his Colt Frontier with his left hand just as he saw a shape pass through the smoke and out the backdoor.

The Pinkerton moved to follow, but stopped, noticing one man still remained seated. This fellow, seemingly lacking in initiative, had not moved an inch since the shooting began and appeared rather unconcerned about it in general. He wore no gun belt, although the Colt formerly belonging to his aggressive compatriot was nearby. Finnegan brought his revolver to bear on the young man, somewhat dumbfounded. "Uh, you wish to surrender?"

The teenage bandit swallowed and grimaced. "I do not believe I have much choice in what will happen shortly." He turned to the window. “Good morning, Uncle Granville. Nice to see you again and to see you are in good health.”

“Dixie.” Stuart hung his head for a moment and then looked up at the boy. “I thought it might be you. We met a man on the road here who said a fellow named Burr was with them.” Stuart appeared more than a bit flustered. “Finnegan, this is Dixie Burr, my wife’s nephew.”

Finnegan nodded and holstered his empty Remington. “I see.” He approached the young cowboy. “I take it there is a wound under that rag you hold on your stomach?”

Burr peeled the wet rag away from his abdomen to reveal a shirt and pants that were covered in blood. “I have not felt well for some time now.”

Finnegan gave the bullet wound a brief inspection. He frowned, seeing the location. “Oh, son, I am sorry, but I do not believe you are long for this world.” He glanced around the café. “Damn it, that fool who calls himself Stringer has escaped out the back of the building.” Finnegan moved to the front door, but paused again, seeing the café’s proprietor. The old man stood stock still and white as a sheet. “Our apologies, sir. We intend to reimburse you for all damages.”

The old man’s lower lip quivered. “And who the hell is gonna give me back the ten years you just scared off my damn life?”

“You will have to inquire to Mr. Stuart about that matter.” Finnegan stepped to the front door, holstered his Frontier and snatched up his Winchester. “I will find Stringer.”

“Mr. Gilhooley?” Burke was peering around what was left of an overturned table. He had some of his breakfast oatmeal in his hair. “Your telegram, sir?”

“Ah, good to see you alive, Burke, but truly, I must be off. Give it to Mr. Stuart.”

Stuart nodded somberly. "Go see about Stringer. I will see to matters here...between myself and my nephew."

Finnegan nodded back and began running down the boardwalk, checking between the buildings as he went. He knew the horse thief kingpin could not have gone overly far. A bullet from Stuart's big rifle had struck the man somewhere, and there were not many places to hide within the confines of one block in Maiden. Just as Finnegan was considering moving to the rear of the buildings to search, he spied a man running away from the town. The gimping figure had decided to leave civilization behind and try his luck at hiding in the trees on the outskirts of town. Stringer was moving at a slow pace, his wound troubling him, and was roughly halfway to the schoolhouse. Finnegan rested the Winchester on a post from the awning of a saloon, thumbed back the hammer, and fired. The round went wide and low. "Damn it." He worked the lever, took a deep breath, adjusted aim on the fleeing cripple, and fired. Stringer fell, but fought up to his feet once more. Finnegan levered the action, took a slightly higher hold, and fired. The horse thief fell to the ground, rolled over to face the sky, and did not move again.

As Finnegan walked to the recently deceased Jack Stringer, the door to the schoolhouse burst open and a single, small figure ran from the door with yells and even a few curses from Molly following him. Finnegan quickened his pace, but the boy beat Finnegan to the corpse, nonetheless. When Finnegan made it to the body, the boy looked up with wide eyes. "Oh, Mr. Gilhooley, I saw you fire from the window of the schoolhouse. A wonderful shot. A quarter mile, at least."

Finnegan shook his head. "Timothy Jameson, you are a bold one."

"Was this man a James gang confederate, sir? Did he

attempt to assassinate you in vengeance, even though you did not capture the James brothers?"

Finnegan sighed. "This man was a common horse thief and only notable for the number of miles I was forced to track him." The Pinkerton looked back to the post by the saloon he had fired from. "Do not bandy about that quarter mile nonsense. If that is an inch over two hundred yards, I will eat my hat."

A dull thud could be heard from the town and Stuart emerged from the café to lean against the outside of the building. The boy squinted in the morning sun. "Is that Mr. Stuart?"

"It is." Finnegan pulled off his hat and wiped the sweat from his forehead. "Well then, I can only assume that is the end of our horse thieves." He turned back toward the school where Molly stood in the doorway. "Oh, hell. I may come to regret some of my choices this morning, young Mr. Jameson." He leaned over toward the boy. "Would you please run and tell your teacher that this dirty business is at an end so she will not worry over the children?"

Timothy ceased giving the corpse a series of small pokes with his shoe. "You do not wish to tell her yourself, sir?"

"No. For the moment, I wish to make myself scarce."

Timothy nodded with a sympathetic look on his face. "That might be best, sir. She does not appreciate such things as this and is terribly difficult to be around when she is in a temper."

Finnegan took a seat on the small bench Stuart occupied. It was composed of a plank supported by two large firewood rounds someone had not found a use for one winter. Both men sat with their rifles between their legs. Stuart smoothed his beard with one hand and looked over at his sole remaining accomplice. "So, I take it you found him?"

"I did."

"He lies yonder by the schoolhouse?"

"He does."

"That is well, at least."

Finnegan sighed and began to search for a cigar. "Mr. Burr?"

"He has passed." Stuart turned to Finnegan. The pioneer's face had turned a shade of grey. "He had lost much blood and...well, such are your fortunes when you turn outlaw."

"Yes, I suppose so."

With one tired hand Stuart pointed to Finnegan's rifle. "Where did you say you obtained that?"

"In Lewistown. It was in the possession of a young man who would have only found himself in more trouble if he had retained it. Why do you ask?"

"With the longer stock it resembles those issued the British. Your young friend most likely stole it from a mounted policeman."

Finnegan contemplated the gun once more. "Now I am even more fond of it." He leaned the rifle against the café wall and lit his cigar. "Anything purloined from the British is welcome with me. Do you believe your wife will mourn her nephew? Were they close?"

Stuart shrugged. "He did seem to be one of her favorites, when he came around." He appeared to think on the issue for a long moment. "She will understand, and if she does not, she will not make a row of it. I will say that for Indians; they rarely make a row when silence has the same effect. A row will not bring the young man back, so why make a bother?"

"A wise policy."

Stuart reached into his pocket and produced a yellow

envelope. "Mr. Burke wished to return to his boardinghouse room and see to his hair." Stuart extended the missive and Finnegan took it.

The gunman tore his mail open with the stick from the match he had just used and withdrew the telegram rather absentmindedly. He let his eyes roll over the words. "Bloody hell."

Stuart raised one bushy eyebrow. "Bad news?"

"Uh..." Finnegan pulled the cigar from his lips and lowered the telegram to his lap. "Allan Pinkerton is dead. His son, Robert, sent this." He slowly drew in a breath, unsure how exactly to proceed. "He asked that I return with all due haste."

"Huh..." Stuart grunted. "That may be a wise choice. It is best to be on your way after a thing like this."

Finnegan stayed seated on the bench for what felt like a long time. Stuart wandered off to stand on the edge of the town. Several times he mounted his horse, only to climb down a minute later and resume staring off at the mountains. Finnegan watched various townsfolk come and go and intermittently reread his telegram. Allan Pinkerton had been a mentor, a father, an employer, and a guiding star in many respects. Now that he was gone, the world felt oddly tilted and difficult to take in.

Finnegan had just finished reading and folding the telegram once more when a familiar voice broke in on him. It appeared most everyone in Maiden had been too afraid to approach him as he sat staring at his piece of paper. Of course, there was one person who never feared him and never would. "You look as if that missive carries bad news, Finnegan."

He brought his head up to see Molly. "It does, indeed."

She glanced into the café and looked away quickly. "Can it be worse than what has already transpired here?"

Finnegan swallowed and heard a click. "Mr. Pinkerton, Allan Pinkerton that is, has died."

"Oh, Finnegan..." She sat next to him. "I am sorry. I know I have said many an unkind word about the man over the years but...I know you loved him." She took one of his hands.

Finnegan cleared his throat. "I knew him a long time." He let out a small laugh. "Longer than I knew my own father, now that I think on it. He was good to me, Molly. I will miss him."

"Come, now, Finnegan. You should rest. Come and lie down in my room at the boarding house."

He shook his head. "I should see to matters here."

She stood and pulled him up from the bench by one arm. "Come along. You have seen to enough here."

When Finnegan awoke, it was dark outside the window of Molly's rented room. It appeared as though he had slept the majority of the day away and felt quite better for having done it. He sat up on the squeaking bed and swung his legs off. His boots sat by the side of the bed. His guns and coat were in a chair in one corner. Molly was nowhere to be seen.

He dressed and walked down to the dining room of the boarding house. Through the window, he could see Molly sitting on the front porch. He walked out to join her and slowly lowered himself into the porch swing she occupied. She looked over at him and wiped an errant tear from her cheek. The telegram Finnegan had received earlier was in her hand. She offered a sad smile. "You may not recall, you gave this to me before you slept." She handed the paper to him.

"Yes, well..." He shrugged. "I suppose after you have read a thing like this there is little point to keeping it." He folded the telegram and slipped it into his vest pocket, despite the admission. "It is a lovely evening."

"It is." She looked one way up the street and then the other. "Things have quieted down. It is strange. People here seem to have only been concerned to see if the men -- the men in the café -- were local to this area. When they discovered they were not, there was only a small fuss. Mr. Stuart has made arrangements to pay for the damage to the café and..." She shrugged. "That would appear to be the end of it."

"Is that the end of it for you, Molly?"

She gave him a small smile. "As I grow older, I question whether I should continue to agitate over events others give little worry to. If such things do not bother the townspeople, and they certainly do not seem bothered, then I am not going to waste my time agitating over it." She took his hand. "I know what you did was required. What you do is always required. The day I cannot say that with certainty is the day our...association must end."

"Then I shall have to be sure to never give you cause to question it."

"Thank you." She glanced at him. "You will return to Chicago, as Robert Pinkerton requests?"

He nodded. "For a time, yes."

"Even from the grave the man beckons you."

"His son and the realities of business beckon me, Molly." He surveyed the town. "It may be favorable to my prospects here to absent myself for a time, at any rate. These people may claim indifference, but some may change their minds if I am around to give them cause to." He looked back to Molly. "Perhaps when I return you may have reconsidered your position on certain matters, as well?"

She squeezed his hand. "It seems as though we have done this before, Finnegan. I recall a night much like this. We were on father's porch swing. You were called back by Mr. Pinkerton that night, too."

"As I recall, Mr. Pinkerton was not the only one who thought my convalescence should come to an end. Your father made mention of it frequently."

Molly nodded and grinned. "Yes, he did. I believe you mentioned that he has since formed a better opinion of you."

"I do not know if I would go so far as to say that. I would say that lost daughters often make for strange alliances. Do you intend to remain here, Molly?"

She let out a small laugh. "Well, after today I would certainly never need worry about anyone being rude or offensive to me. I could merely inform everyone I am engaged to Fearless Finnegan of local café fame and do as I please, for all time."

Finnegan laughed. "Feel free to suggest whatever you like."

"I do not know if I will remain here, Finnegan. I may go to the Orient or the Andes. Although, from what you have told me, a journey home to Minnesota may be timely."

Finnegan grinned. "Please, inform your father that I convinced you to visit." He adjusted his frock coat. "It may prove useful to me in the future to have him somewhat in my debt."

"I will laud you copiously, Mr. Gilhooley."

Finnegan sighed. "So, then, here we are. After all these years and a great distance traveled, we find ourselves in the same place we began, or ended. I suppose I am not sure which."

"Oh, Finnegan." She leaned over and placed her head on his shoulder. "Let us think of this as our second beginning. Hopefully, we may yet have a third and a fourth. I would prefer to do without endings."

Chapter 30

DHS RANCH, MONTANA TERRITORY

August 7th, 1884

Finnegan traveled from Maiden back to the ranch alone. Stuart had departed the day before while the Pinkerton slept. The Pioneer had made all applicable arrangements concerning the townspeople and then had been on his way. Finnegan did not mind his employer leaving without him. He had spent too much time in the company of others recently and enjoyed the ride back to the ranch. It gave him an opportunity for contemplation.

His chance for quiet introspection abruptly ended when he came into the ranch compound. Katie Stuart came running up to him before he even had a chance to dismount his horse. The girl had a frightened look in her eyes. "Mr. Gilhooley, please, you need to help."

Finnegan stared down at the scared young lady. "What is it, Miss Stuart?"

"Mr. Gilhooley, father and some of the other men have taken Floppin' Bill back behind the barn. Sir, I believe they intend to hang him."

Finnegan raised one eyebrow. "Hang him?"

"Yes, sir. Please, you have to stop them. You cannot allow them to do such a thing. I know father is angry, but, please, you must stop him."

Finnegan looked over the ranch house and the nearby implements. Aside from the harried young woman, everything appeared quite pastoral and correct. "Miss Stuart, I am sure your father does not intend to hang anyone in his own backyard." He reached down and gave the girl a pat on the head. "Calm yourself." He smiled. "I will look into the matter. I assure you, no one is to be hung, lass." Finnegan gave his horse a nudge with one boot and guided the animal to the barn and around to the rear of the building. There, bound and standing on a chair, he found Floppin' Bill Cantrell. The cowboy had a prominent noose around his neck with the other end attached to the boom arm for loading hay into the loft. Stuart and several of the other men from the ranch were gathered around. Finnegan groaned and hung his head for a moment before dismounting. "Granville, this is a novel sort of entertainment."

Stuart rubbed his chin. "Damn well warranted."

Finnegan looked over to Kilkenny, who was leaning against the barn wall with his flask in one hand. The whiskey baron appeared barely able to stand, but deeply interested in the festivities. "Ephraim, would you care to explain this?"

"Ah, yes." Kilkenny wiped his mouth with one sleeve. "Mr. Stuart is upset due to the fact that Mr. Cantrell took it upon himself to hang the three men you took as prisoners the other day. Some questioning has taken place, but Mr. Stuart has been unable to determine if Mr. Cantrell hung the men out of simple spite or because they intended to inform against Mr. Cantrell to Mr. Stuart, in some manner or other. In response, Mr. Stuart has decided to hang Mr. Cantrell. It is all terribly poetic, Finnegan."

The Pinkerton sighed. "Yes, Ephraim, that is the aspect of it that a fellow finds most striking." He turned to Stuart. "This man hanged our prisoners?"

Stuart nodded. "He did indeed."

Finnegan looked over the man on the chair and walked to within a few feet of him. The cowboy was shivering in spite of the hot Montana sun. "Did you hang our prisoners, Bill?" He took a step forward and put one boot on the rather rickety chair. "Tell me truly, now."

The cowboy's Adam's apple bobbed under the noose. "Mr. Gilhooley, I did hang them men, but it weren't all my doing. Them men were no-count scum if ever there was some and the others..."

"You were left in charge, Mr. Cantrell. That carries a burden that cannot be displaced." Finnegan gave the chair a small push. "Why did you hang those men, Bill?"

He moved his eyes down as far as the tightened noose would allow to view both Finnegan and the chair. "I...I thought it would please Mr. Stuart. He's always telling us about how he hung them boys in Virginia City, and..."

"It will not please me to see vigilante stories in the newspaper, Mr. Cantrell." Stuart smoothed his beard. "You must have had a damn good reason to want them men dead to risk this." Stuart motioned to Finnegan. "You should congratulate Mr. Gilhooley, by the way, Bill. He shot down your friend Jack Stringer in front of the schoolhouse in Maiden."

"That man weren't no friend of mine, Mr. Stuart." Cantrell moved gingerly on the chair to look at his employer. "That man wasn't really Jack Stringer, neither, sir. That's just some damn name they pass around. Fella calling himself Jack Stringer, when I knew that bunch, he was about ten years older than that damn charlatan and about a foot taller. Fella I saw leading that bunch at the river, he used to call himself Fisk, before he was Stringer."

The color drained out of Stuart's face. "Finnegan, hang the son of a bitch."

Finnegan smiled up at Cantrell. "I am bound by contract to comply with the wishes of my employer." He gave the chair a hard kick and it collapsed beneath the cowboy. Cantrell fell to the ground and the rope spooled down around him. The cowboy writhed in the dirt for a long moment, then slowly opened his eyes to stare up at Finnegan. "It is either by the grace of St. Peter or the fact that Mr. Stuart tied a slipknot above you that you still live, fool. May you make better use of this chance at life than you did the last one." Finnegan shook his head. "Get up and be off with you."

"Not until we are finished with him." Stuart pointed to Teddy Blue. "Apply the tar and feathers, then set him on one of the horses from that bunch we shot. Hopefully, it will carry him to meet his friends." Stuart turned and walked off in the direction of his house.

Finnegan watched as the other cowboys collected Cantrell and hauled him off to get befeathered. The Pinkerton leaned against the barn wall next to his friend. "How does the day find you, Ephraim?"

"Disappointed, Finnegan. These Americans never seem to kill the right men. Have you noticed that? I, myself, would have happily hung the gentleman on the chair. He seems a vile sort, but he has been given a reprieve while the men he killed were shown no such mercy." The whiskey baron slid sideways on the wall, but Finnegan caught him by the shoulder and righted him. "Ah, thank you. How did things work out for you? Stuart mentioned that you have dispatched your quarry." He hiccupped. "I do hope that is the last man you intend to kill on this trip. I would rather like to go home now."

Finnegan clapped him on the shoulder. "We will be returning to Chicago, Ephraim. I have been called back."

"Very good. Capital." He took a long drink from the flask and slid on the wall toward Finnegan. "I believe our next trip should be to the Solomon chain. They are not such a bloody bunch of savages in the Solomons. It is a pity we never found a bear."

A Look at: Scorn to be Guilty (Finnegan Gilhooley 3)

The outlaws are gone. The real war is just beginning.

Finnegan Gilhooley has spent his life chasing bad men for the Pinkerton Agency. But with Allan Pinkerton dead and his sons running the show, Finnegan's old-school methods—and his gun—are no longer welcome. The new bosses prefer strikebreaking to justice, and there's no room for men like Finnegan. Until a bomb explodes in Chicago.

When a deadly attack rocks an anarchist rally at Haymarket Square, Finnegan is pulled back into action to pursue a new kind of threat. From the plains of Montana to the deserts of Mexico, he assembles a rough-edged crew for a pursuit that may be more political than personal—and far deadlier than he ever expected.

As the country changes, so does the enemy.

AVAILABLE FEBRUARY 2026

About the Author

R.F. Ryan lives in Montana with his beautiful wife and comparatively ugly gun collection. When he is not writing, he can usually be found out in the woods hunting. He's currently retired from a variety of odd jobs that have interfered with his free time, including (but not limited to): ranch hand, green chain operator, bounty hunter, private investigator, and process server. Robert has written over twenty books in multiple genres, both fiction and non-fiction, and has penned hundreds of outdoors-focused articles for websites and print magazines.

About the Author

[illegible]